A Summer With Persephone

Jayelle Dee

Barn Owl Books

This is a work of fiction. Names, characters, organizations, places, events, and incidents are either products of the author's imagination or are used fictitiously.

ISBN 979-8-9881054-6-6

ISBN 979-8-9881054-7-3

Published By Barn Owl Books

Cover by Jennifire

For all the souls dealing with grief...
...and for those who are the lights in the darkness.

Contents

Preface

An excerpt from the work of Mr. Thomas Buckhorn. Hades and Persephone: Grief Transformed by Love.

"Death is inevitable. So is the gloom that follows. We must wallow and mourn as long as is necessary to fully appreciate our pain. But the tricky thing about pain is it never truly goes away. We can't run from it, and no amount of sulking or celebrating will release it. It plants and grows like an endless tuber from a weed. And no matter how we try to pluck it out, so long as some small piece of it remains, it will regrow.

"Lord Hades ruled this region of life. A lord of grief was he. But he didn't concern himself with the tears of the mortal world. He focused on the life after death. He embraced the inevitability that the mortal shell must be cast away for something greater. A new life, everlasting.

"It is in this way that I respect him. Hades took power over death by focusing on what happens after and accepting the pure tragedy of it with the grace of a king. We must, ourselves, take power over our grief. Rule it. Show it where it belongs in our lives. If we must have a moment to cry, then cry we must. But there is always an "after that."

"Persephone understood that it is only from our own darkest places that we can heal. Only from the warm, shadowed feelings of our deepest love

can all transformation begin. She knew that, like a seed buried down in the earth, we must take the first chance to grow as soon as we sense the light of the sun or the moisture of possibility. The soil may be dense, and our struggle difficult as our tiny green tendrils reach through heavy dirt. But reach we must. Indeed, Persephone taught Hades that it is only from the deep, dark places of our soul, of our earth, that all life can spring."

Chapter 1
Homecoming

Holly's heart plummeted at the sight of the eviction notice taped to the outside of her apartment door. She stared at the note and shifted her weight, trying to keep her purse on her shoulder while holding the box of items she'd cleared from her desk at work.

The weight of disappointment crouched imposingly on her as she realized she could no longer fight the shrinking spaces of her life.

Great. Isn't that just perfect timing? She thought to herself. *Why not?* As if getting fired wasn't enough for one day. Her general frustration had spit on her bland disregard for her job and created a paste of failure that glued itself to her.

She freed a hand to rip the notice from her door and stuffed it in the box. The hallway's stale smell added to her annoyance. *I hate the stink of this place, anyway.* Wriggling her keys free, she opened the door to her studio apartment. The box thudded on her dining table as she dropped it with her keys and purse. Taking a deep breath, she rubbed her eyes, trying to dislodge some of the negativity of the day. Finding another job and another apartment in Dayton shouldn't be too hard—right?

She didn't like that job, anyway. Besides, this was another chance for a new beginning. And beginnings were always the best part of something.

She numbly stepped into her kitchenette in search of a strong drink. Surely there was something left? She already knew the refrigerator was empty. No use looking in there. Then she remembered the half-empty bottle of whiskey under her sink. She pulled it out. *To glass? Or not to glass? What difference did it make?* Holly unscrewed the cap and took a long pull from the bottle. Her phone chimed from her purse. By the ringtone, it was her best friend.

"Hey Janet," she answered.

"So? How did that little talk with your boss go?" Janet's cheery voice and West London accent accosted Holly's sour mood.

"Oh... He fired me." Holly's voice stayed calm, as if she didn't care. Getting fired was always humiliating. At least it was something interesting. Life had been dull lately, with one day blurring into the next.

"He what? Tosser! I'm so sorry, sweetie!" There was a pause. "What about, you know, your rent? Will your last paycheck cover it?"

"Nope. I'll be just short. Again. But it doesn't matter. Got the notice on my door when I got home. Thirty days to GTFO."

"Oh, no! But you can find something in thirty days. You've done it before."

"Probably. But I won't get paid fast enough to keep this dump. Guess I'll be living in my car for a few weeks."

"Absolutely not! I won't hear of it. You'll stay in my spare room."

Holly opened her mouth to protest.

"And don't bother arguing with me. I know you're proud. But damn it, I won't have you homeless. That is not an option. Alright?"

Holly's shoulders slouched. Living with Janet was one thing. Living with Janet's corny husband and their six and three-year-old children was another. But there was no arguing with Janet once she made her mind up about something. Despite the guilt from needing help, Holly's heart swelled with gratitude that she wouldn't have to sleep in her car. She and Janet always had each other's backs.

"Alright. Thank you." An impish tone entered her voice. "Besides, dealing with Wesley and the brood will be good motivation for me to find another job and a new apartment."

Janet's musical laughter jingled out. "Good. Take a few days, recover, rest and pack. We can move you and clean that place at the end of the month."

"I can clean it, Janet. There's not much to it."

"I know you can. But wouldn't you like the company?"

Holly smirked. "It wouldn't be bad. But I feel like I did this to myself. I should deal with this myself."

Janet clicked her tongue. "Tsk-tsk. Rubbish! Your boss was a jerk. It's not your fault."

"It kind of is, though. I wasn't paying attention and missed an entire data field."

"Mistakes happen."

Holly chewed her lip. "I missed many data fields on many reports. It was frequent."

Janet sighed. "Okay, so attention to detail isn't your forte. My darling, have you considered an alternate field of occupation?"

"I could sell my body."

Bolting laughter sounded. "No! You wicked thing. Perhaps data entry isn't for you."

"Or data compilation, or reports, or spreadsheets. Jesus, why did I even go to college?"

"Sweetheart, I think it's time you tried something else."

"I know. But I can't for the life of me think of what that could be. I've tried waitressing, front desk admin, transcription, data entry for three different companies and insurance claims processing. Every time, I could feel the life force draining out of me. I honestly don't know what to try next."

"You've just never explored a job that can use your real talents."

Holly was silent.

Janet continued, "You know what I'd suggest, but you won't listen to me."

Holly cast a glance at her Roland keyboard which sat against the small wall of her living room area. "I've never tried fast food."

Janet huffed. "Be serious, Holly."

"I'll find something. I'm an optimist, remember? There's always a way. I can be an office grunt. Just need to find the right boat to row for.

So far, not so good. But I'll figure it out. You know me. Ms. Bounces Back! It'll be okay."

There was a pause on the line. "Holly, you are literally one of the smartest people I know. Why you waste yourself in meaningless office jobs makes absolutely no sense to me. You're almost thirty-three! You should be climbing the ladder in some big company by now."

"Now, you sound like my mother."

"Fine, then. At least that makes two people in this world who believe in you."

Holly smiled and swigged from her whiskey bottle again. "Thanks, Janet. Guess I just never figured out what I wanted to be when I grew up."

"Oh, you knew. You just gave up on it."

Holly fell quiet and cast another disdainful glance at her keyboard. Eighty-eight weighted, touch sensitive keys sat silently. It was her favorite and most hated thing. A reminder of what could have been. "I don't want to talk about it."

"Okay. I didn't mean to poke a wound. Just—promise you'll call me when you sober up."

Holly smirked. "What gave it away?"

"I can hear the bottle swishing."

Holly giggled. "I deserve a decent hangover."

"No argument from me, sweetheart. Talk to you soon. And remember, there's always light from somewhere. Always."

"Yep. Coming out of your sunshiny ass!"

The two giggled and hung up.

Holly headed to her bedroom to change out of her clothes from a day filled with disappointment. She despised office jobs. Of course, she could perform them, but they all seemed so uninteresting and devoid of energy. Lifeless workplaces filled with lifeless people all gossiping or chatting about meaningless garbage. Eventually, she'd get bored and careless, then fired. One of the offices she'd worked for had a book club, which she actually enjoyed. But then her boss had made a pass at her, and that was the end of that.

Her true passion, and the path which she thought her life was on had come to a crashing end. Literally. Trying to find a replacement for the one thing that filled her soul was impossible. So, she let lame excuses frame her point of view and gave up easily now. Her optimism about finding an alternate future was failing.

I can't give up. But what kind of life is worth fighting for? I can't keep reinventing myself like this. The dreary cycle of trying to start over again and again was wearing her thin. What life could be better than a life filled with music?

Something had to snap, and she was afraid it might be her.

Holly stepped out of Janet's car after she parked in her long, curving driveway. Janet's house was a two-story colonial with white siding and black shutters. Typical for Dayton's upper class. Complete with two grand pillars holding up a pointless outcropping of roof.

The week before, the pair had packed and cleaned Holly's dingy studio apartment. Everything fit into a small, 400 square foot storage space. Holly regarded her furniture and boxes before closing the door on the space. Her entire life, stacked into something smaller than half of a one-car garage.

She'd imagined her life being much grander by the time she'd reached thirty-two. She'd had dreams of playing in a symphony and giving her own solo concerts by now. But that dream had long since faded. No sense in wallowing or crying about it now. She closed the door and turned her back on it, hoping to find a solution soon. No use in dragging out heartache. Besides, she had Janet's comforting force. At least that was something nice.

She made her way to the back of Janet's Lexus SUV and began hauling suitcases into the house. Janet insisted that Holly pack her clothing into suitcases and had brought her family's entire luggage set to do it.

Janet's husband, Wesley, emerged. "Fine day for a move!" he called out cheerfully. "Light cloud coverage with no chance of rain and a high of seventy-four." Wesley was a meteorologist for a local news station. He was a walking, talking weather report.

"Hi, Wesley. Thanks for taking pity on me," said Holly.

"Oh, it's no trouble! A friend in need is like a tornado. They're coming, and you'd better just get ready for it and hope for the best." His large grin and blue eyes sparkled at her.

Holly smiled but couldn't tell if that was an insult or a compliment. The three of them moved suitcases into the spare room together until the car was empty. Holly stared at the seven plaid Samsonite cases around the bedroom. All of her stuff. Seven suitcases and one small storage space. Janet came into the room and put an arm around her.

"I haven't seen you this distraught since finals week during our senior year. And you were brilliant! You were superb at finals week." She squeezed Holly's shoulder. "And you'll be superb at starting over."

Holly's head sagged. She placed a hand on Janet's shoulder. "God, I'm such a fucking failure."

At the first sign of a sob, Janet swooped Holly into her arms. "Oh no, my darling. You're not a failure. You're just... on a quest for success."

"I'm so sorry. I really don't want to burden you."

Janet held her firmer. "Holly, now listen to me. I understand you'll need some time to feel sorry for yourself. I've seen it before. Many times."

"Okay, okay."

"So, here's what I want you to do." Janet pushed Holly's drooping form to right her. "I want you to unpack, have a shower and when you're ready, come say hello to your niece and nephew. Then enjoy some wine with me, and we'll have dinner. That's all you have to do for today. Tomorrow is the first day you face your challenges. But not today. Today is for transition. Understand?"

Holly's red, tearing eyes examined her friend. "Thank you. Thank you for being so good to me."

Janet's own eyes began to water. She pulled Holly's face towards her own to study affectionately. "I am only a reflection of you. You were there for me when I was at my lowest of lows. Of course, I'm going to hold you up now."

She brought Holly into her comforting embrace. "I will never, ever, let you completely fail. You practically finished my junior year of college for me, and I promised you I'd always be there for you."

Holly thought back to that year in college and the fear in Janet's eyes as she stared at the double lines on her pregnancy test. Driving Janet to the clinic and helping her hide everything from her family had felt like the least Holly could do to support her friend at the time. Janet's family were affluent, and this would have been a scandal in the circles in which they floated. Holly never left Janet's side. Even doing her finals reports and homework for her while she had a breakdown over it all, and nobody was the wiser.

Holly finally brought her arms around Janet and sobbed into her shoulder. When she'd helped Janet out all those years ago, she did so because she loved her and because it simply needed to be done, and never with the expectation of any emotional compensation. Janet was suffering, and Holly wasn't about to let her fail. And now here she was, grateful for her friend's generosity even through the sting of her own humiliation.

Janet said, "Take all the time you need. Find yourself. Get grounded. And when you're ready, I just hope the world is ready for you."

Chapter 2

Prelude

Thomas woke. Another gray day. It was sunny outside, but it all seemed bleak to him. He rolled over and gently smoothed his hand over Evelyn's side of the bed. It was almost a year now. He could still smell the rotten cancer in the air. Its distinctive scent was not easily forgotten. She'd wanted to die at home and not in a hospital room. And she did. He'd kissed her and went to get her medication and some tea. She was gone when he came back.

He slowly sat up and sighed. What was on the roster for today? Best to keep the mind busy. First, some coffee. Then toast. A shower and a shave. Then, his splendid books. His beautiful, dusty, delightfully old, worn pages. He could read and take notes today. A project had been sparking his mind, for which he was most grateful. And, of course, the internet. He could dive into its pit of infinite knowledge, like the ancient blue Mayan pools of Xibalba.

Thomas relieved himself of his blankets and went to his bathroom for a pee. Then coffee, then toast. Evelyn always made him scrambled eggs, but he couldn't bear the task. He'd no wish to replace her methods or motions and simply desired dry things.

He showered and shaved. He glanced at his bed. Evelyn's side was flawless. Untouched and perfectly tucked. His own side was thrown. He ignored it. So long as Evelyn's side was neat, that's all that mattered. He dressed and went down to his study. His desk faced a series of windows overlooking the backyard. The three remaining walls were covered by bookcases from floor to ceiling. Dark cherry-wood cases filled with delicious-smelling tomes that held the knowledge of mankind's myths and legacies. It satisfied him to be among them. Old and comforting friends who would steady him with their consistent presence.

He turned on his monitor, and while it warmed and blipped to life, he regarded his yellow notepad. The last note read:

Persephone, Daughter of Zeus and Demeter. Wooed by her uncle Hades. Never eat anything in the underworld.

Thomas huffed, realizing he hadn't brought his coffee with him. Back to the kitchen he went for his mug, and hastily returned to his books of Greek mythology, his notes on love, and the trickery of hell with its layered metaphors. With a click, click, click of his mouse, the document opened before him. After reading a few lines to remember his place, he typed:

Indeed, the idea of nourishing oneself in the darkest, most unsavory and tortuous of places may seem off-putting at first. But the Greeks remind us of our human condition. We must eat. Persephone, wanting nothing more than to return to the arms of her mother, Demeter, succumbs to the most basic of human needs. Hunger.

His phone rang. Thomas' eyes flicked at it with irritation.

His sister. He answered.

"Why is it that every time I sit down, and settle into a pace with my work, you seem to call?" he addressed her stolidly with a fringe of warmth.

"Thomas, I wondered if I might pop by this afternoon. Just to check on you."

Another agonizing sigh. "Oh... I suppose. But don't expect sandwiches. I haven't made anything."

"I'd be happy with a glass of water. That is, if your water is even still running."

He smiled. "Tea is at four. See you then. And bring sandwiches." He heard his sister's delightful tinkling laughter, and they hung up.

Janet held a container of sandwiches and opened the door to her brother's house. The stale air of defeat blew upon her. She cursed herself inwardly for neglecting to check on him for so long. The anniversary of Evelyn's demise was only four months away, and she hadn't checked on her brother in several weeks. Unfortunately, the interruption of her children into his sterile world had proven unsuccessful at best. Their novice curiosity and incessant need for entertainment strained him.

She knew he loved his niece and nephew, but his emotional state was far from a place of resilience. Janet had no intention of stressing him with youthful exuberance or prying little fingers. So, she waited. Now, with Holly at her house to babysit, she had an opening at last to visit with him peacefully.

"Thomas?" she called.

"In here!" His voice came from his study. She went towards the back of the house, observing dishevelment everywhere. The kitchen was dreadful. Dishes stacked, glasses spreading along the counters. No pots or pans.

"Have you been eating out a lot?"

"Yes."

Janet nodded, noticing a heaping trash bin at the edge of the kitchen and a tied trash bag by the buffet that needed taking out. Her eyes wandered down the hallway across from the kitchen and fell upon the disaster area that should have been his dining room. It was layered in papers and books. Wine glasses, brandy snifters and all sorts of stemware were strewn throughout the domicile on nearly every surface. Surely, every plate, bowl, cup, and glass was dirty.

She walked through the living room. The floor-to-ceiling windows at the back of the house looked out at the backyard. But every curtain was pulled closed, containing the gloom. Making her way to the doorway at the back corner, she found Thomas slouched over a book in his study, one hand on its pages and another hand holding a pen on a notepad. Typed words filled his glowing computer screen.

"Is there tea? I brought sandwiches."

Thomas kept his eyes in the book. "Yes, it's in the cupboard. The teapot is... in the kitchen."

Janet sighed and kissed him on the top of his head.

"I'll get it together." She went to the kitchen and hunted for his teapot. It was buried behind plates, glasses, and takeout boxes in one corner of his countertop. Janet cleared a space on the stove, filled the pot with water, and put it on the stove to boil. Tea boxes were in the pantry, which was alarmingly low on supplies. "When was the last time you went shopping?" she called.

"The what? Look in the fridge!"

Janet shook her head and forced a patient smile. It was tough watching her brother struggle, but she had to give him time. Thomas had watched his wife wither and die for nearly three years. They were only married for ten years when she passed. College sweethearts and the light around which each of their worlds revolved. It was the happiest day when they married. And the most dark, horrid day when she passed.

Evelyn was an effervescent intellectual. Charming and well composed. Witty and affectionate. Even when her diagnosis came in, she never soured. She had a special smile for everyone. Her passing was a great loss for the Buckhorn family. Janet thought about her as she dunked teabags into the pot. Evelyn would have surely pommeled Thomas for the state to which he'd let the house get.

She washed a dish on which to place her perfectly trimmed tuna salad sandwiches and cleared an area on the coffee table in the living room. She also washed two cups and brought the tea to the table. Then Janet quietly entered his study.

"Your tea is ready, sir."

"Mmm," he acknowledged.

Janet watched him typing.

"Thomas. Find a place to stop, please."

"Yes."

"Thomas!"

He jolted up. "What?"

"Tea is ready, and I've brought your favorite tuna salad sandwiches. Now, please unplug and sit with me." She kept her eyes soft, but her voice let him know he had no room in the matter.

"Of course." He looked around as if confused and finally pushed his chair back. "Is it four o'clock already?"

"It is, Thomas."

"I see." He followed her out to the living room. "It was only eleven this morning a moment ago."

Janet pulled the curtains aside and opened a sliding glass door. Fresh, April spring air and radiant sunshine filled the room. "Just look at that." She viewed the backyard and garden. "Isn't it lovely?"

"Hmph. It's all gone to weeds," he said, pouring tea into their cups.

"Not the garden. The air! The sun! It's a beautiful spring day, and you're in here cooped up like a sauerkraut."

"The finest aging of things takes place in dark, dank places, Janet."

She sent him a sharply raised brow. "Surely, at only thirty-five, you don't think that you're an old, aged thing."

He smirked at her, making his first eye contact since she'd arrived. "Did you say tuna salad sandwiches?"

"Yes." Janet had cut them diagonally, knowing that Thomas adored diagonally cut sandwiches. Without the crust. Perhaps it reminded him of their very British childhood.

After being brought up in the higher echelons of West London, their father had taken an opportunity to buy a country club in Dayton, Ohio. The move to America had strained their family, especially Thomas, who had no desire to leave his homeland. Janet was just sixteen and met new people easily, and it hadn't been long before she'd met her best friend, Holly.

But Thomas had been nearly nineteen and feeling his blood. After two years at a local college, Thomas went back home to England and studied at Cambridge. He fancied himself an English gentleman and only regretfully returned to America when their father became ill.

Evelyn had followed him back to America. She was a true English lady of refinement and tradition. Settling in Ohio, to be near his family while his father ailed, was not what he'd wanted. But Evelyn thought it quite exotic and adored everything. He contented himself in American minutia as long as she was by his side.

While Janet's English accent had softened over the years, and she'd adopted a more American demeanor, Thomas never let England leave his soul. That stiff upper lip of his never seemed to relax.

Janet and Thomas sat quietly, sipping tea. Also, a tradition he refused to abandon. Evelyn was accustomed to teatime, and Thomas was only too pleased to observe it. When she could, Janet would take tea with her brother. Though, sometimes she wondered if she wasn't filling in some delusion for him. But she didn't have the unkind heart to say anything. She was good at indulging people. Not contradicting them.

But something needed to be said about the state of the house. She sipped her tea to help her swallow a bit of sandwich. "Thomas, I don't mean to butt into your style or the uh..." she glanced around the room. "Or the way in which you've become accustomed to living your life. But honestly, I don't understand how you can function in this mess?"

Thomas stuffed the last tuna salad sandwich into his mouth, chewing happily and staring out the large windows. "You know, it really *is* a nice day out there."

Janet raised her eyebrow. "Don't change the subject. Your house is a pit."

Thomas swung his head towards her. "It is not a pit."

"Really? When was the last time you actually *looked* at the state of things here? I can't even imagine your laundry."

"My— Oh dear. I think I did a load of washing, um..."

"At Christmas?"

"Don't be daft! Of course, I've done laundry since Christmas!"

"Have you? How many days have you worn that shirt?"

Suddenly self-aware, he scanned his chest. "This shirt?"

"That shirt. How many days?"

"Couldn't be more than two or three. Maybe four."

She sat, aghast. "Thomas, that is it! I've hit my limit. I'm far too concerned now."

"Janet, please don't make a fuss. I don't care for fuss."

"Too bad!" Janet nearly slammed her teacup onto the coffee table. "My darling, I have stood by you with everything and all things. But I absolutely cannot watch you rot."

"I'm perfectly fine! I'm working and giving lectures! I'm nearly finished with my book about Persephone and temptations."

Sarcasm drenched Janet's voice. "Well, isn't that fantastic? Do you even notice how you smell?" She slapped her legs for emphasis.

"I don't smell. I shower every morning."

"But you don't wash your clothes. You're rank."

A look of horror overtook his eyes. "Dear Lord, am I?"

His sister offered him an enthusiastic nod.

"Damn it."

"Look, I know you're deeply involved in your research, your writing, and your lectures. But I think you might need a housekeeper. This house is gross."

He sipped his tea. "It isn't as bad as all that."

His sister's narrowed eyes explained that she disagreed.

"So, uh, a housekeeper. To cook and clean?"

"And also, a gardener."

"To mow and weed?"

"It's a jungle out there."

"That's odd. I haven't heard any monkeys."

Janet giggled at hearing her brother's humor. It was a very long time since he'd cracked a joke. He used to have such a wicked sense of humor. In fact, she hadn't heard him laugh in two or three years. A thought sprang from her mind, and she gasped.

"Oh, Thomas! I've just had the best idea!"

"Oh dear. I hope it isn't one of the better of your best ideas. You're a source of trouble when you get to scheming."

"Leave off! I'm not scheming. I think we can solve two people's problems with one solution."

"Sounds revolutionary. Let me know when you've got it sorted and where to sign. I'm going back to my work."

Janet's heart bubbled with joy. She began collecting the teacups and the sandwich plate. "Yes. This is perfect!"

"You want me to what?" exclaimed Holly. "Janet! I am *not* a housekeeper! You've seen my apartment." Holly's eyes quickly rounded Janet's pristine living room as they sat on the couch.

Janet sighed. "Fine, you're not the tidiest, but you've always kept your home clean."

Holly picked up Samantha, who was poking her ridiculously strong three-year-old fingers into her side. Samantha held a stuffed animal, sucking on it and making a growling, gurgling sound.

"Janet, I couldn't do that! I mean—for a job?"

"Ana Hollee play," begged Samantha, pulling on Holly's light-brown locks.

"In a minute, baby."

"Play."

"Samantha," came Janet's stern mom-voice. "Auntie Holly will play when she and I are done talking."

Samantha's wide eyes stared at her mother. She lowered her head. "Kay. Poo me dow."

Holly set her back on the ground, and she toddled off to bother her brother, who was attempting to build the world's tallest Lego tower on a nearby rug.

Janet's sweet blue eyes played on Holly's resolve. "I do wish you'd at least consider it. It really is the perfect situation. You need a job and a home. He can provide both."

Holly played with her fingers in her lap. "I'm not sure I want to be a maid, though."

"Oh, you wouldn't be a maid! You'd clean, yes. But you wouldn't be at his beck and call like a servant. And there's also laundry and gardening—"

"What joy."

Janet ignored her. "And you'd have plenty of free time after to do whatever you like."

Holly shrugged. "He doesn't like me."

Janet sighed and watched her daughter trying to destroy her son's Lego tower. He was yelling and tackling her. "He doesn't like anybody right now. His light went out when Evelyn died. He's impossible." She put a hand on Holly's. "But at least I'd have the comfort of knowing that my very best friend would be there looking out for him," she pleaded.

Holly continued wincing.

"Dammit, Holly, you have to try something! I love having you as a babysitter, and your help here has been wonderful. But you've got to try something! It's been weeks, and you're still wallowing. I can't keep your mood up and his and deal with the children! I need you to try. I need you both to just sodding try."

Holly cringed. "Are you using your mom-voice on me?"

Janet landed her face into her hands with a huff. She poked an eye through her fingers. "Is it working?"

Holly let out a defeated sigh and offered a weak smile. "Shit. It's not like I have anything else going on. Babysit children or babysit a thirty-five-year-old man. Not much difference, I guess." She watched her friend's hopeful face. "What is it that you say? Sod it? I'll do it. I can always look for another job while I tend to your sweet Thomas."

Janet balled up with an inhaled squeal. "Oooh! Brilliant! I'm so happy!" She burst forth and swept Holly up in a hug.

Holly had the distinct feeling she'd just signed her life away to a strange arrangement that was out of her control. Honestly, what did she have control of at the moment?

"You know what I love the most about this besides giving you a home and an income?"

"What?" Holly smiled.

"Thomas is familiar with you. We practically grew up together. Who knows? You may even open him up a bit. Maybe he'll come back to us."

Holly pulled away. "Oh, Janet. Please don't put that responsibility on me. I'd die if I disappointed you."

Janet's blue eyes kept their sweet light. "I know. And I don't expect miracles. I just—I suppose I'm hopeful that a familiar and friendly face might pull him out of his abyss. But if it doesn't, I won't hold it against you."

"Promise?"

"I promise. I'll just be glad he isn't wearing the same rank clothing every day or eating off of soiled plates. For God's sakes. It's terrible."

"Janet?"

"Yes?"

"Do I have to cook?"

Chapter 3

The House of Dust and Sorrow

Holly sat rigidly in the passenger seat of Janet's Lexus SUV, annoyed by her friend's continuous smile. Like Janet knew something she didn't.

"Will you quit it?" Holly scolded.

"Quit what?"

"That constant jester's grin. You're freaking me out."

"Am I? I'm sorry. I'm just so excited! I can't help it."

"You look like a fucking Cheshire cat."

"Oh, that's another thing. The swearing. You might want to reign that in."

Holly's brows fell flatly. "I am not going to edit myself for the sake of the tender delicacies of your poor Thomas. Not going to happen."

"Swearing makes him cringe."

"I don't give a fuck! Let him cringe. I'm a grown woman who can use her mouth as she wants. Wasn't it you who suggested that it would be comforting for him to have someone he knew around? If he knows me at all, he knows I swear like a fucking pirate."

"Fine, fine. I'll let you two sort it out."

"I'm a swearing swearer who swears."

Janet chuckled. "Thomas would say, 'a mouth most foul.'"

"That's me."

"Splendid."

"Quite."

Both of them pursed their lips and broke out cackling. The truth was, Janet's mouth used to be equally brash. But she stuffed most of her foul vocabulary the moment Jake was born.

They arrived at the two-story, dark, vine-covered, brick Tudor-style home of Thomas Buckhorn. Even the charming dormers looked as though they sagged with the sorrow of the place. The white trim had yellowed. The shrubs were wild. Weeds ran mockingly throughout the grass, and Evelyn's prized rose bushes had bolted every which way. Holly gaped.

"This is impossible," she whispered to herself.

Janet heard her. "You haven't seen the inside yet."

"Oh, God." Holly braced herself.

She and Janet started carting in the seven suitcases. The reek of old food and rotting trash heavy in the dank air walloped Holly in the face.

"Ah... fuck me."

"Thomas!" Janet called cheerfully. "Thomas, we're here!" No response. Janet jerked her head to the stairs off the foyer, indicating for them to climb. "Your room is up there. Well, all the bedrooms are up there."

"I know," Holly said. "I've been here before, remember? Years ago, but I remember where things are." She followed Janet up the curving, tight, creaking staircase.

At the top, a short, open room with a window and a chess table greeted them. Thomas' master suite sat to the right.

Janet headed across the small room to a narrow hallway that led to the other two rooms and a bath. "Here at the end. You'll be right next to the bathroom." She sat down a case and opened the door. "You're on the back corner of the house, and I think you'll adore all the windows. They line the entirety of two walls!"

Holly followed her. Upon entering, she was certain she'd never seen a more sterile room. Hospitals had nothing on it. It had the semblance of a room that hadn't seen a human in decades. Stuffy and uncomfortably placid. They dropped the luggage they carried and went back for more. Once the room filled with suitcases, Janet went to the white curtains covering all the windows on the two walls that made the outer corner of the room and pulled them back. She opened several windows. Bird song fluttered in with the breeze.

"Isn't that lovely?"

Holly stared at the room and at her sweet friend by the windows. "I like the birdsong. I hate this room."

"Why? There are tons of windows!"

"I think I may want to grab my own comforter and a chair out of my storage. Maybe a rug and some other things. This place is so..."

"Beige?"

Holly nodded. "It's dreary. I need color." Holly surveyed the bland room, feeling as if she'd stepped into a mud puddle. "I hope this was the right decision."

"Oh, don't worry. You're going to be magnificent." Janet stepped away from the window, navigating through the suitcases to her friend. "Besides, you love projects." She grabbed Holly's hands. "You're great at organizing things."

"Tell him not to yell at me."

"He won't yell. He'll grouse. But he won't yell. Just be yourself. You're very sweet when you want to be. And he needs sweetness. Besides, if you need anything, I'm only a phone call away."

Holly nodded.

Janet shook Holly's hands, jiggling her arms. "Remember, we've all been friends for years."

"But we're missing Evelyn. She always made him nicer than he really was."

Janet tilted her head. "It's true. She brought out the best in him. We all miss her. But my brother is very sweet on his own. You'll see. He was always nice when we were growing up, remember? I was the mean one."

Janet's sharp smile pinched her cheeks. "Thomas is a love. He's just... down right now. I'm completely sure he'll warm up to you. Then you'll see how adorable he can be."

Holly shot Janet a skeptical sideways glance. "Adorable? Thomas is adorable?"

"Very. You'll see."

The two of them went back down the stairs. The kitchen accosted Holly's eyes. She gasped.

"Dear Christ."

"I told you it was, um, pretty bad."

"Pretty bad? This needs gasoline and a match!" She let Janet lead her through the living room, which was piled with old mail, more dishes and glasses, and takeout boxes. Holly glanced down at the floor. The dark hardwood was gray with dust, and the large rugs were fuzzy with lint.

Holly said, "When was the last time he vacuumed? Or swept?"

"Who knows? Honestly, I'm not sure it's been done at all since Evelyn last cleaned."

Holly gritted her teeth. "God, Janet, what have you gotten me into?"

Janet flashed a quick apologetic look and brought Holly to Thomas' study. "Thomas?" She peered in at him.

He was typing away furiously. There was a pen behind his ear and another in his mouth.

Janet cleared her throat. "Thomas!"

He startled. "Huh?" Thomas turned to them. He pulled his pen from his mouth. "Ah. Holly. You're here. Good." He looked her up and down awkwardly and returned to his computer. Holly shrank.

Janet took Holly's hand and led her back to the living room. "You know where I'd start?"

"Dynamite?"

"Grocery shopping."

"That's not nearly as fun."

"Come on, I'll help you with some meal planning. Then I'll grab his bank card so you can go to the store. There's no food here."

"No food? What is he eating?"

"Can't you tell by all the takeout cartons?" Janet adopted a very serious expression. Her brows knit together, and her blue eyes began their plea. "Holly, please. I'm so worried about him. I haven't talked much about it, but he's not well. I'm worried he'll work himself sick or worse. He needs human contact. Human interaction. He needs to come back to us. Can you bring him back?"

Holly gaped at her. "Fuck's sake, Janet. I'm not Mother Teresa."

"I know. But you're robust and defiant. You've got so much sass and spirit in you. I'm hoping you'll piss him off just enough so that he'll want to live again."

Holly chuckled. "Well, you're probably right about one thing. I'm definitely going to piss him off."

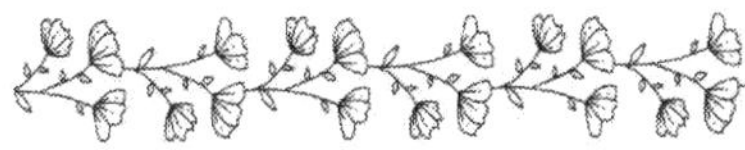

Holly carted bags from her car into the hall. There wasn't any place to put bags on the counter tops or tables. Everything was covered with garbage. Once unloaded, she put away the groceries. Then she took a stroll through the stuffy house. She went from room to room, picking up as many dirty cups and glasses as she could and made her way to the kitchen.

The kitchen had a buffet overlooking the living room and a cozy nook in which sat the hulking form of a piano, which was covered with a white sheet. Holly's fingers twitched from looking at it. It had been a few years since she last played a real piano. She'd attended the Academy of Music on a scholarship with dreams of becoming a concert pianist and performing with a symphony. Her eyes glided longingly along the sloping curves of the instrument under the sheet.

It was laughing at her.

Deciding to ignore it, she set herself upon the kitchen. The kitchen was always her favorite place to begin whenever she cleaned her own home. It was like the heart of the home. If the heart was clean, the rest would follow.

After loading the dishwasher, she filled the sink with hot soapy water, and filled a trash bag with old food and takeout containers. Walking through the house, she found more glasses, mugs, and Styrofoam boxes. Two more trash bags were filled with muck and takeout containers, which she carted to the outdoor trash cans. A few plates and glasses were stuck to the counter so badly, she had to work at soaking them off. *Jesus, how long had it been this way?*

Once all the dishes were cleaned, rinsed, and dried, she tried to figure out where everything went. Thomas didn't seem much of a kitchen connoisseur, so she figured it wouldn't matter where she put things as long as she knew where they were.

The sun began dipping lower into the horizon. Holly had better figure out dinner. She wasn't a great cook, but she knew how to turn out a few really great dishes. And there was always YouTube.

She reached for some ground beef. Meatloaf was easy and always a good starter. Eggs, onions, garlic, tomato paste, basil, a dash of Worcestershire sauce with salt and pepper, and some breadcrumbs. She formed the loaf on a pan and plunked it in the oven, covered for at least thirty minutes, then uncovered for fifteen. Broccoli and some pan-fried potatoes would go nicely with a mushroom gravy. She went to work. Music played from her phone as she drank red wine, chopped, sauteed, and stirred.

Thomas crawled out of his study to investigate the noises and smells. He stood in the living room, on the other side of the buffet, watching her dance to Snow Patrol, and stir a pot. The kitchen was white. *How long had the kitchen been white? Was it always white?* He stared, nearly in shock. Holly sipped a glass of wine, swinging her hips to the music and humming along. He hadn't noticed her all day, but now his fears were becoming realized. She was an intrusion. A literal attack on his serenity.

"I beg your pardon," he interrupted.

Holly spun around. "Oh, hey! You're alive. How nice. I've got meatloaf in the oven, and I'm working on some pan-fried taters with mushroom gravy and broccoli." She smiled brightly at him.

He stood stiffly, not sure what to say or even make of the situation. "Is this to be your habit every night?"

"What do you mean?" Holly stopped dancing.

"This—this ruckus?"

She dropped her head and widened her eyes at him through her surprised brows. "Ruckus?"

"Yes. Music, movement. This is far too—too boisterous."

Holly righted her posture and cocked her head at him. "Oh, I'm sorry, Tom."

Incredulously, he blurted, "Turn off that noise!"

Her eyes widened. "I'll turn it *down* if it bothers you."

"It bothers me quite a bit!" he snapped. "Off. Turn it off!"

Holly's breath quickened as though she'd been smacked. "Jesus, Tom. It's only a little music."

"I don't enjoy it. I'm going to watch the news. Notify me when dinner is ready." He strode to the TV room at the front of the house.

Holly stood in shock, heart pounding. "Notify you?" The spatula in her hand quivered. A sharp inhale of air found its way to her brain, and she slammed the spatula on the countertop.

"Nope. Uh-uh. That is not how we're starting this." She strode to where he was sitting in the TV room. Her fist nearly denting her hip as she shoved it into her side. "Thomas."

"Yes?" He didn't look at her but continued staring at the TV, brandy in hand.

"Excuse me, but I've just spent over two hours shopping for your groceries, three hours cleaning your disgusting kitchen and picking up every glass and dish stuck to every surface I could find. Not to mention filling nearly three garbage bags with the trash that was literally everywhere, and now I'm cooking your dinner."

"Yes. Well done. It's exactly what I'm paying you to do."

"And I can't have a little music and enjoy myself?"

"Drinking my wine, aren't you?"

"Dude."

"Don't 'dude' me. Keep your music down. If I can hear it, it's too loud."

Holly made fists and bit her lip. Message received. He'd established that they weren't friends. Not even acquaintances. He was her boss. She'd envisioned this as a roommates-helping-one-another type of situation. That was out the window.

During her furious storming back to the kitchen, she huffed under her breath, "Fucking prick." Then sadness filled her. He really had become completely miserable. And now she was stuck living with him. Well, not for long. She'd be back on the job hunt tomorrow. That was definite.

Janet said this was a good idea; that Thomas needed human interaction. Since Holly was homeless at the moment, it seemed a reasonable solution. But she didn't want to be a housekeeper. And Thomas was barely a human anymore. She began questioning her life choices all over again.

Holly woke in the darkness to a bump downstairs. The clock said 1:30 am. She rolled over. Another bump. She sat straight up. After slowly getting out of bed, hyper-aware, she pulled a robe around her. Holly had been sleeping naked for years. It was comfortable and freeing, and she loved it. But here, in the house of Thomas, she had to be more careful.

She opened her door to look down the hallway. Holly tiptoed toward Thomas's bedroom. The door was wide open. One side of the bed was perfectly made, and the other was pulled apart. But no Thomas.

Holly crept to the top of the tight, winding stairs. She heard a sigh and a sob. Her instinct was to run towards it. Thomas might be in trouble. Then a moan sounded. *What on earth was he doing? Maybe I don't want to know.* A round of sobs hit her ears.

She daintily toed down each step, alert and watching for movement. Halfway down, she saw him sitting on the floor, slumped over the coffee table in the TV room. She stopped and watched. A short glass of golden liquid in his hand. His head buried in his elbow and shoulders shaking. His free hand raking his hair as he sobbed and moaned. A mostly empty bottle sat near him.

Holly crouched, observing. His head lifted, and he wiped his face. Thomas and Janet shared many of the same features. Dark brown hair with blue eyes. Large-boned noses and cheeks with strong, sloping jaw lines. Well-formed and quite attractive. They were both very like their father.

Thomas gripped his mouth. As he shook, tears poured from his eyes. He gulped down the liquor and poured the last of the bottle into his glass. There were quite a few bottles in the trash Holly had taken out earlier. It hadn't occurred to her that he might be drinking one every night. Dousing his pain to numbness.

Her heart filled with sorrow. He was suffering. Suffering and shaking in unquenchable pain before her. She watched him drink until his tears stopped. If she let her presence be known or went to comfort him, she knew she'd shatter this moment of quiet, personal emotional release. She kept her distance out of respect. And she wouldn't mention this to him later. But she couldn't leave him either. So, she stayed with him from a distance on the stairs.

Eventually, he stood, wobbly on his legs, grabbed the empty bottle, and brought the glass to the kitchen. He went from her sight, but she heard him drop the bottle into the trash and rinse the glass. Holly fled up the stairs to the hall and leaned against the wall in the darkness. He shuffled clumsily up the stairs to his room and shut the door.

Holly's breaths were quick from her haste. When he shut his door, she went back to her room and crawled into her bed. This may be darker than she suspected. What on earth could she do? Was there even anything she *should* do? Janet was right. He wasn't well. Thoughts of immediately looking for another job left her. Thomas may be an ass. But he shouldn't be alone.

Holly would wait and see if this was a regular thing for him. Perhaps it was his way of dealing with Evelyn's passing. She had no right to interfere.

Grief was the most difficult emotion of them all.

Chapter 4

Intro

Holly had been wrong to think Thomas was just an ass, she decided. He was in pain. And also, he was an ass. She'd gone about their first day together all wrong. In her mind, they were old friends. But upon analyzing things, she realized that she and Thomas had never been friends. He was the brother of her best friend. A familiar person, but certainly not a friend.

She hadn't even been friends with Evelyn. Though she'd adored Evelyn. Shit, everybody adored Evelyn. She was charming, beautiful and fucking English.

After catching Thomas in his moment of grief and drunken vulnerability, Holly decided a gentler touch would be a better approach. He'd been mostly shut up in this house for nine months. He wasn't usually good with people on one of his finer days, much less after months of solitude and grieving.

Holly woke, dressed, and went to the kitchen to make coffee while pulling her light brown waves into a ponytail. Today, she would begin to dust; pull things off of surfaces to oil and polish. Then, she would wipe the chotchkies and whatnots, dusting books and whatever else was on shelves and surfaces. Dusting day.

She sat at the buffet and scrolled through Facebook on her phone. Halfway through her first cup of coffee, she jumped when Thomas lumbered down. She rose from the buffet stool. "Coffee?" she asked.

His eyes wearily landed on her. "Please. I like it black."

"Alright." She poured a cup and handed it to him. "Is there anything I can fix you for breakfast?"

He squinted at her. "Why are you being so nice?"

She blinked. "Thomas, I'm surprised at you. We're old friends! And I'm here to do your bidding." She curtsied ever-so-slightly.

His brows furrowed in annoyance. "Listen, I'm sorry I put you in your place last night. I'm not used to having other people about. Just uh... Let's stay out of each other's way, and we'll do fine."

"And keep my music down."

"I'd be most grateful." He took his T-shirt-clad, pajama-bottomed self to the buffet, landing on a stool heavily.

Holly guessed he was suffering from the remains of whatever was in that bottle he'd finished off last night.

She asked, "Do you like to have breakfast? Or are you more of a brunch guy? I personally can't eat first thing in the morning."

His eyes remained heavy, not looking at her while he indulged in his black coffee.

"I'm not trying to be a pain in your ass or anything. I just need to know what's expected of me in the mornings. We never talked about meals, or even if there's shit you like or don't like. You need to tell me stuff."

Thomas heaved a long, slow sigh. "Holly, I appreciate your communication. I require at least one and a half cups of coffee before I can interact with other humans. Ask me again then."

"Okay." She turned and refilled her cup. Holly hated mornings, too, but for some reason, she was feeling particularly present and alert this morning. Very out of character for her. She took her cup and returned to the stool next to him, continuing her Facebook perusal. When Thomas went for his second cup, he approached her and stood next to her.

"I like English muffins," he said.

Holly's wide brown eyes regarded him.

He stared at her. "One English muffin, halved and toasted with butter and a side of strawberry preserves."

"I'll have to go and get that. Will toast do for today?" she asked.

He blinked and stared into his coffee mug. "Yes." He stood, unmoving in a moment of hesitation. "I also like—well, Evelyn," he took a quick inhale, "used to make me scrambled eggs."

Holly tilted her head gently. "I can definitely scramble you some eggs. How many?"

"Two. With cheese. I like them with cheese."

She smiled. "Who doesn't?"

Thomas' dour expression almost lightened. Almost. He turned and walked to his study.

"I'll take them in half an hour, please."

A grin began its journey across Holly's face. She nodded.

Thirty minutes later, she had two slices of golden toast with butter alongside two scrambled eggs with a generous sprinkle of cheese and brought the plate into his study. Although there were no preserves, she planned to grab some before starting her dusting day. She presented it to him. He barely acknowledged her. She left, thinking it was preferable for him to say nothing rather than uttering something grumpy or stuffy. Moments later, as she was enjoying her own toast and eggs, she heard him raising his voice in protest.

"No, no, no! This is all wrong!" He came stomping from his study. "This isn't how Evelyn did it at all!"

Holly cocked her head at him, eyes flaring.

"There's too much salt, not enough black pepper. There's a complete absence of onion powder, and the eggs are not well blended. I can still tell the whites from the yellows." He dropped the plate next to her on the buffet.

Holly stared at him. "Sweetheart, I've never had Evelyn's perfect scrambled eggs, and I have no idea how she made them. But I can always change it up. You just have to tell me—"

"Ugh!" he exclaimed. "What an utter disaster." He turned and started for the stairs. "I'm going for a jog. And don't call me Sweetheart."

Holly stiffened. "You don't have to be such a jerk, ya know!" she yelled at the stairs. "No one will ever do things exactly the way Evelyn did!"

Thomas suddenly appeared, leaning over the railing. He growled, "Don't you think I know that!" and he disappeared back upstairs.

"Jesus, shit." Holly regarded her plate. "Well, I thought the eggs were good." She stuffed another load of scrambled eggs into her mouth. She reminded herself, *he's in pain, he's lashing out because he's in pain. Calm the fuck down and do better tomorrow. Blend the eggs better, add onion powder, and less salt. Was that everything? Shit.*

Thomas' stomping feet boomed down the winding stairs, and he slammed the door as he left.

When she finished eating, Holly cleaned up the breakfast dishes. Thomas had returned by the time she emerged from her room. She heard him showering as she was dressing to go out for English muffins and strawberry preserves. Before she left, she poked her head into his study.

"Anything else I can get for dinner so I can ruin it for you?"

He scowled and thought a moment. "Roast chicken would be good, thank you," he mumbled stiffly.

"No worries," she breezed, "just make sure to give me a list of herbs. Wouldn't want you throwing a fit because I've left out the Rosemary."

When she returned, she finally tackled dusting day. The house was in such a state of neglect, it would be simpler for her to break things down, day by day, into categories. Dusting day. Then sweeping day. Then wiping and mopping day. Then vacuuming day. That should cap her week. Next week would be a deep clean of the bathrooms, stairs and halls. The windows would need a once over, and the curtains should be pulled and laundered. Once the house was reasonable and able to be more easily maintained, she could have a look at the yard and garden.

At the end of dusting day, Holly had a long, hot shower. She threw on a maxi dress and went to make dinner. But before she lay finger one on the chicken, she thought she'd better check with his Lordship about it. If she bothered to make this meal and he had a fit, saying it wasn't the way Evelyn did it, she'd be ready to shove the dinner up his ass.

"She always stuffed butter under the skin," he told her. "I remember that. A compound butter. So, the herbs would soak in, and the skin was perfectly crisp."

Holly nodded and worked on it. She watched a video about how to make the best roasted chicken. One that mentioned compound butter. She stuffed the cavity with salted onions and lemons with a sprig of thyme. The compound butter had sage, salt, garlic, onion and marjoram.

Then she massaged the bird with olive oil and a dash more of salt and stuck it in the oven. Roasted new-red potatoes with chalets and asparagus would complete the sides, along with a robust chicken stock gravy. She drank red wine and wiped up the countertops.

While out shopping for the strawberry preserves and English muffins, she'd stopped into a Walmart for some Bluetooth earbuds. That way, she could listen to her music without bothering his Lordship.

Holly swayed to the bluesy rhythm of Hozier in her ears as she held her wine glass. Her long, brown hair was still drying from her shower. At first, she was unaware of the pair of eyes staring at her from the study. Then she caught him watching her from the corner of her eye. She ignored him as he stepped towards the kitchen. He stopped, watched her move a moment longer, and then she saw him shuffling off to the TV room for the news and a brandy.

Holly resumed cooking, deciding to ignore his odd behavior. She scrubbed red potatoes and chopped off the ends of the asparagus.

When dinner was ready, she turned off her phone and pulled out her earbuds. She set the table in the dining room and lay out the food. She placed a fully carved, perfectly roasted chicken in the center of the table. A video helped her learn how to carve it. Some of it got a bit messy, but she was mostly happy with it. She walked to the TV room and cleared her throat.

"Ahem."

He glanced at her.

"Dinner is served, your Lordship."

"Five more minutes. The news will be over then."

He'd brushed her off. Again. Did he treat Evelyn this way? Was he this obtuse with her? Holly's memories of him with her were always so loving. She couldn't imagine him being this short with his wife. But perhaps no one would ever know.

Holly tried to tell herself it didn't matter. And who knows, maybe Evelyn thought it was charming? Whatever. Holly went to the cleared, dusted, oiled dining table and made her plate.

Exactly five minutes later, Thomas stood in the doorway of the dining room, aghast.

"What?" Holly asked with her mouthful of amazing roasted chicken. Thomas couldn't move. His palms brushed his pant legs as he gathered himself.

"Forgive me. I just haven't seen this room be a—a dining room in so long."

"All your things are neatly stacked in your office. I don't think you even noticed me going in and out."

He took his place, sitting across from her. "I did not."

She watched him nervously as he piled chicken and sides onto his plate. Right before he took his first bite of chicken, she interrupted him.

"Um, Thomas. It may not be Evelyn's roasted chicken. But it is my roasted chicken. Please be kind. Or at least don't spit it out."

He raised a brow at her. "I'm sure it's acceptable. The bird is massacred and hardly carved correctly, but I'm sure the flavor will be fine."

"God, I'd be happy with fine. Please let it be fine," she said under her breath. She watched him put the chicken in his mouth. His expression didn't change. They continued eating, and he cleaned his plate. That surely was a good sign. Holly rose and cleared the table. Thomas brought the plate of leftover chicken into the kitchen.

"Holly," he set the chicken on the counter and went for the aluminum foil to cover it up, "it was good."

She glowed with relief. "Thank God."

"It was really good. I think you should continue asking me for tips about how Evelyn did things. She was wonderful in the kitchen. It could be a great help to you."

Holly sank. Of course, Evelyn got the credit. She sighed. "I'm glad you enjoyed it, Thomas."

They put away the remaining leftovers, and Thomas disappeared into his study, closing the door. Holly rinsed the dishes and looked for his brandy bottle. She poured herself some and opened the sliding glass door in the living room before walking outside onto a flagstone patio. Loungers sat covered in dirt. Another thing to clean. There was a fire pit and a lawn that spread out until it met the tree line. The lawn was full of weeds, of course.

But Holly did her absolute best at tuning out more potential chores. For now, just for this moment, she wanted to enjoy the scent of Spring.

Springtime in Ohio was laden with the fragrance of fresh greens and new flowers. Thick, slightly humid loveliness wrapped around her. It was April. The lighting bugs would appear near June. Evelyn died in August.

"Shit." Holly wondered how Thomas would be if she managed to stick around until then. He'd be unbearable. Inconsolable. While she'd decided to stay and be a comforting human presence, she was no therapist or councilor. Might be best for her to move on by that time. She could be warm and helpful, even comforting. But Holly knew Thomas wouldn't accept anything from her. So, why bother trying? She decided that once the house was settled, she'd look for a new job. In the meantime, she could save up enough money for a new apartment. Maybe get to repairing her shit credit.

"What are you doing?" came Thomas' voice from behind her.

Holly spun in his direction. "I'm enjoying the evening air."

"There's a chill."

"There's not a chill. Come here."

He tentatively scanned at the patio. "I need another brandy."

"Oh, good. You can refill mine." She held out her glass to him.

He grimaced and took her glass. When he returned, his feet were halting upon the flagstone. He handed her the glass.

"I love spring. It's dreamy." Holly sipped her brandy. "So full of life and expectation. Like it's promising you something."

Thomas stood stiffly next to her. "There are no promises. Or dreams."

She cast her shocked face his way. "That's horrible. Of course, there are promises. And dreams." She took a cleansing breath. "You can smell it in the air. A welcoming. A dewy goodness that wants to help you grow. Just like the earth grows."

He raised an eyebrow at her. "How many of these have you had?"

"Just one more besides this. Same as you." Her eyes fell bashfully down. "Sorry. I think I get poetic in the spring. I can't help it. It's my favorite time of year."

"You do seem somewhat... altered."

"I guess I'm relaxed. I'm happy with my work on the house. And with my cooking. You haven't spat anything out in a whole twelve hours."

Thomas sipped his brandy. "Yes. I've been peevish, it's true. I'm not used to talking to others. I suppose I come off as somewhat abrasive."

Holly guffawed. "Somewhat?" She sipped from her glass, took one more lungful of the lovely air, and turned to go back inside. "I'm going to bed. Tomorrow is sweeping day. Lots to do."

"Sweeping day?"

"Yeah. Your house is awful. Like, I honestly wanted to burn it to the ground."

"It isn't that bad."

"You really didn't think it was bad?" She gaped at him.

He blinked and glanced around defensively. "Well, no. I mean... no."

Holly sighed. "Thomas, when was the last time you actually looked at anything in here?"

He fidgeted. "I'm not sure I understand what you mean."

She blinked sarcastically at him, her light brown eyes assuming a patronizing glint. She sipped her brandy. "Dude. There are trails in the dust on your floor from where you walk. There are cobwebs on your books. Well, not anymore, because I dusted them. But there is a layer of scum in your shower that I don't even want to deal with. But I will because that's my job. Your kitchen smelled rotten. There were plates and glasses literally stuck to surfaces. I had to soak them off! There's even a layer of dust on your furniture. I could write my name on the top of your couch."

Thomas breathed in morose contemplation. "I see." He took a sip of brandy. "That bad?"

"Epic bad, dude."

"Please stop calling me dude."

"Nope."

"It's so pedestrian."

"That's great." She rolled her eyes. "Change the subject. I don't care. But I will tell you this. I may not always be here to dust and sweep and cook shitty eggs. So, you better be thankful while I am here." Holly finished her brandy and walked her slushy mind to the kitchen to deposit her glass. Then to the staircase and up to her bedroom.

Had she actually just said all of that? Out loud? She didn't care. The simple pleasure of her alcohol buzz kept her from concern. She stripped off her clothes and flopped under her blankets. Tomorrow was sweeping day.

Chapter 5

The First Movement

Week one wasn't so bad. It sucked. But Holly had done worse things. At least she wasn't stuck behind a desk, lying to people about their insurance, or telling her boss that, yes, he was a perfect gentleman at the company picnic. Or dealing with the bitches that normally occupied any office ever.

She'd rather scrub toilettes than deal with them ever again. The ones who acted like they were the best fucking thing to ever happen in the history of anywhere. Small-minded big fish in a little sea. So petty and needlessly competitive.

Sweeping day got combined with vacuuming day, as it made more sense to vacuum everything at once. She took the crevice tool to every corner along the floor, up the walls, and where the walls met the ceiling. Then the window tracks. She shoved furniture around and vacuumed the area rugs, then rolled up the area rugs and vacuumed and mopped under them. May as well mop since she had everything moved. She'd finish the mopping and wiping after the sweeping and vacuuming.

At lunch, she noticed Thomas had left his plate by the sink. The English muffins eaten, but the eggs were untouched. Apparently, he could still see the whites. Holly scraped them into the garbage disposal. Such a waste of the decent efforts of a chicken. At least he'd eaten the English muffin. Holly made a baloney sandwich and brought it to him for lunch. He sneered at it.

"I can't bear baloney."

She rolled her eyes again. This was getting very old. "Fine, I'll eat it. What do you like?"

He thought a moment and paused his typing. "I'm quite fond of tuna salad."

"Well, I already know I'll fuck that up. Tell me how Evelyn made it."

He instructed her on exactly how much mayo and sweet relish. Minced onion, only a touch of salt, and a piece of lettuce with a thin slice of tomato. If he left an empty plate later, Holly would consider it a victory.

By the third day in the house, she figured out that by whipping the eggs to death with a whisk, she could finally blend the yellows and the whites so his Lordship couldn't see the difference. Exactly three twists of the pepper mill, two shakes of the onion powder and a small pinch of salt.

She let the cheese melt on the top and scooped the eggy perfection onto his plate. She presented them to him with his English muffin and a side of strawberry preserves. He didn't bother acknowledging her. She shrugged and went on with her chores.

That day was a continuation of vacuuming and sweeping with some mopping. When she came down to the kitchen to refill her water glass, she noticed the empty plate next to the sink. He'd eaten the eggs. She could have done a handspring.

That afternoon, Janet called her to check on her.

"Darling! You're still alive! I'm completely dying to know how you're getting on."

Holly grinned. "So far, no murders."

"What a relief. How's my brooding brother?"

Holly leaned her broom against the wall. "He's awful. Like truly fucking horrible."

"He's just not used to having anybody in his space."

"I know, but he keeps telling me how Evelyn did this and Evelyn did that. If I don't replicate it, he loses his mind."

"Aww, have some sympathy."

"It would be easier to have sympathy without the tantrums."

"I'm sure he'll come around."

Holly rubbed her eyes. "I know everything takes time. At least the weekend is coming soon, and I can get out for a bit. Want to go do something?"

"I was thinking of taking the children to the zoo on Saturday. You're welcome to join us."

"Yes! It'll be nice to be around some mature company."

Janet sprinkled laughter through the phone. "Oh, Holly, you're terrible! I'll see you then."

Thomas heard knocking on his study door. The intrusion broke his precious concentration, and he glared at the source of it. Holly. What on earth could she possibly want this time? Even though her interruptions were limited, any interruption was too many.

He said dryly, "I've heard it said that the enemy of all writers in disruption."

Her honey eyes kept a kind light in them. "I'm sorry, but I'm washing linens, and I felt like I should let you know before I strip your bed."

Horror gripped his chest. "Strip my— Absolutely not! You will stay out of my room entirely!"

She escalated by opening the door further and stepping into the door frame. "Thomas, when was the last time you cleaned your sheets?"

"That's none of your concern. Leave my bed alone."

"It is my concern." She said, cocking a brow.

It was an expression, he was coming to understand, that she made when she meant business. She continued, "It's the exact reason I'm here. To clean up months of neglect. Look, it isn't up for debate. I'm laundering your linens. I just wanted to let you know I'd be in your Temple of Solitude." She whisked from the doorway.

Panic bolted through him. She couldn't touch Evelyn's side. It was unconscionable. He leapt from his chair and sprinted after her.

"No, you will not touch the bed!" he shouted. But the quick-footed bint was already up the stairs. "Holly! I'm not playing around here. Stand down!" He reached the top of the stairs to see her disappear into his room. As he arrived, panting at the doorway, she had a hand on one of Evelyn's decorative pillows.

"STOP!" he bellowed.

Holly froze.

"Don't you *dare* touch those."

She released the pillow. Her voice was carefully gentle. "When was the last time this was cleaned?"

By her tone, he could tell she was feeling quite justified in pressing the matter. But she didn't know that the last person to handle the pillows, or even that side of the bed was Janet, the day Evelyn passed away.

"Please. I don't want Evelyn's side to be disturbed."

Holly's eyes fell, and she folded her hands. "Thomas, I apologize for upsetting you." She walked around to his side of the bed and threw the comforter aside. "But you are sleeping in a sweat stain. I'm begging you. Let me do my job and get this house healthy again. And I'm sorry, but that's going to include moving those pillows."

Thomas shuffled and stuffed his hands into his trouser pockets. He glanced at his side of the bed. There was a visible darkened spot where he slept. And as much as he resented her for it, he knew Holly was right. *My God, what have I become that I can't even wash my own bed sheets? Dammit, but she's right. There's still sickness here. Have I even grown so attached to my own filth? What would Evelyn say about the state of me? She'd say let the girl wash the bloody sheets, is what she'd say.*

"Alright," came his sheepish voice. "But I will be the one to undress the bed. This time and all times. And I will be the one to put it back together. Are we clear?"

A sweet smile developed on Holly's face. "Tell you what; I'll leave, you dismantle this, and I'll meet you in the laundry room. Okay?"

He nodded. She stepped over to him and lay a hand on his arm. The touch jarred him. He'd been so at odds with everything that the last thing he expected was tenderness. Anytime he encountered it, it always bounced against his resistant soul.

"I just want to help, Thomas. Please let me."

He nodded, and she left.

"And don't forget the pillowcases!" she called from the stairs.

He stared at Evelyn's side. "I'm sure you must be laughing at me," he said to the pillows, "for being overly sentimental. Or perhaps you're giving me one of your lovely eye-rolls." He strolled to the bedside and lifted a pillow. "Why is everything so hard?"

Friday arrived. Holly had been staggering the laundry as she cleaned the house. She washed the towels, blankets, sheets, her dark clothes, and his dark clothes. The argument about tearing up his bed and ruining Evelyn's side was distressing. But Holly understood that people did strange things when they were in pain. Still, it took every bit of understanding and compassion in her to deal with his outbursts, sometimes.

Then, there was a brief fight about the folding of the towels. He burst at her with one of his 'no, no, no's' and 'this is all wrong's'. "Evelyn folded them in thirds, not quarters."

She didn't even want to think about the lesson he gave on how to fold a fitted sheet properly. It was exhausting living up to how Evelyn did things.

Standing by the washer, she shoved clothes into it, thankful there were only the clothes of lighter colors left to do. He walked in just as she was loading boxers and socks with his lighter colored shirts.

"What on earth are you doing?" he demanded.

Holly couldn't hear him to begin with, as she had her earbuds in. He marched over to her and slapped his hand on the washing machine.

She jumped and pulled out an earbud.

"I said, what on earth are you doing?"

"Laundry," She spouted in wide-eyed shock.

"No, no, no. This is all wrong."

"Oh Jesus, fuck."

"Watch your language."

"What am I doing wrong now?"

"Evelyn only included whites in the whites load."

"Well, I'm not doing a whites load. I'm doing a *lights* load. Everything that has a lighter color."

He looked incensed. "You can't wash whites with lights."

"Watch me." She began to load more light-colored shirts in with the white socks and boxers when his hand grabbed her wrist in mid-toss.

Her anger flared. "Do. Not. Touch. Me."

He released her as his eyes widened in realization of his error. "Forgive me."

Holly wiped a stray strand of hair from her brow. "Listen, I've been doing laundry since I was a child. I've always done it this way with zero problems. If you want it done a different way, then do it yourself. Oh wait, that would make you a fully functional adult, and I wouldn't even have to be here!"

Thomas drew a sharp breath through his nose. The look of astonishment on his face made Holly's heart sink into her stomach. She shouldn't have snapped at him. But in fairness, he deserved it. He pivoted and left the laundry room.

She poked her head out of the doorway. "Thomas?"

He halted but kept his back to her.

"I know you're grieving. But you need to give me a little room, too. I won't always do things the way Evelyn did them. I can learn some things, but there are others that I'm just going to do my way, okay?"

He continued his route down the hall away from her and saying nothing. She jumped upon hearing the door to his study close abruptly. She continued throwing the last of the lights into the washer.

"Impossible," she muttered to herself. "I probably didn't apologize the way Evelyn would have either. God, he burns me up!"

At the end of the day, Holly walked through the house in one of her beloved maxi dresses, admiring her work. She'd had a nice, long shower, managed to get all the laundry folded and put away, and there was a roast beef in the oven. The windows were open to the evening air, and the house finally didn't smell of dirt and muck. Thomas emerged from his study.

"Persephone is born anew," he announced.

Holly smiled at him. "That's great! Congratulations!"

He bowed to her. "Remember, never eat a thing when in hell."

She giggled, "Well, since I've been eating here all week, I guess it's too late for me."

He nearly smiled. "Has it really been that bad?"

Holly brushed a lock from her face, wrapping it around her ear. He was staring. She hated when he stared. "I've done a shitload of work here. Have you not noticed? Even that funky smell is gone."

"Funky smell?"

"You were probably nose-blind to it. Come on, take a gander at your house." She beckoned him with a twirl of her hand.

He tentatively stepped towards her.

"You see? Not a speck of dust to be seen."

He observed the bookshelves along the living room wall and ran a finger along them. Walking around the couch, he looked down at the area rug.

"Has it always been that color?"

Holly snorted. "Underneath the dust bunnies, yes."

He surveyed the room as the evening light filtered in. "And the windows?"

"Gah! Really? Do you always seek the imperfections? Could you not enjoy what I *have* done? I worked really hard, ya know."

Thomas turned to her; his blue eyes almost regretful.

She said, "The windows are on the list for next week."

He nodded. “Forgive me, I’m not used to giving compliments.”

“Not used to? You never give them at all.”

Thomas shuffled. “It, uh, looks quite nice indeed. Well done.”

Holly smirked, supposing that was better than nothing.

Holly woke at 1:30 in the morning to a thud. Remembering Thomas’ crying fit from the first night, she figured he was going through another one. She’d been checking the trash for empty booze bottles, but there hadn’t been any. She thought perhaps that night was a one-time occurrence.

Pulling from her bed, she wrapped her robe around her body and tiptoed to the stairs. Silence. She gently stepped down the winding staircase until she could peer into the TV room. It was empty. She continued down the stairs, and then her stomach knotted.

He was splayed out along the hallway floor enroute to the kitchen.

“Oh, shit!” She hurried to check on him.

A glass sat on the buffet, but his hand was around an empty bottle of scotch.

“Jesus, did you drink this whole thing?”

He didn’t move.

“Thomas?” She nudged him, her mouth going dry.

He groaned.

“Oh, thank God.” She carefully pulled the scotch bottle from his hand and dropped it into the trash. “Come on,” she knelt, trying to roll him. “Get up.”

His eyes fluttered. “Evelyn?”

“Christ. You poor bastard.” Holly helped him heave up and stand. She held his arm around her shoulders. Navigating the stairs with his heavy, limping form was not an available choice. She lumbered with him to the couch in the living room and plopped him down.

He murmured something, but she couldn't make it out.

"Shhh, it's alright, Tom. You're going to have to sleep here tonight."

He murmured again. "She's so nice to me." came his slurred words.

"Who is?"

"H-holly. Why is she so nice? Don't deserve her."

Holly covered her mouth as her heart skipped a beat. So, he *did* appreciate her. She pulled off his shoes and set them neatly on the floor. Then she brought a blanket down from the back of the couch and covered him. She wanted to comfort him somehow. Her hand went for his trimmed, dark brown hair.

She hesitated, having never touched him before. Not like this. It was... intimate. She regarded his fine features. He was very handsome. With his face relaxed in sleep, he was nearly angelic. But Holly spent most of her time resenting him, not examining him.

Her hand descended softly and smoothed from his brow to the side of his face. He didn't stir but assumed the breathing pattern of deep sleep. She continued stroking his hair. *The poor, tortured thing.* Holly made sure he was well covered with the blanket and went back up to bed. Hopefully, he would think he'd taken himself to the couch, and they could avoid any embarrassment.

Thomas opened his eyes. A small act which caused him a great deal of pain. He didn't remember getting to the couch. Very slowly, he sat up. His brain throbbed in a heavy fog. His stomach wasn't too happy with him, either. He let his feet find the floor, and sat up, leaning his elbows on his knees, and held his head in his hands. His shoes, neatly placed by the couch, caught his eye.

"Oh, shit." If he'd dragged his own self to the couch, he wouldn't have removed his shoes. Holly must have found him at some point during the night. "Damn it," he swore again. The distinct odor of coffee floated to him. He couldn't decide if it smelled good or not. He stood, but that may have been a mistake. He wobbled. "Ugh." Thomas dragged his feet to the kitchen for a glass of ice water. He needed to abolish the layer of paste in his mouth.

On the stove was a small saucepan, and there was a note on the counter.

"Shit." He made himself some ice water and chugged it down. Taking courage, he glanced at the note.

"Good morning! Rough night? I made you some coffee, but I usually don't like coffee on harsh mornings. Wasn't sure about you, though. I also made some broth. That always helps my tummy. If you don't want it, just put it in the fridge and I'll use it for soup later. At the zoo with Janet and the kids. See you later. And don't feel bad. We've all been there. ~Holly."

He rubbed his face. "Damn it. She's making it really difficult to dislike her."

Holly returned later that afternoon, along with the storm that was Janet and her children. She struggled with holding onto the hand of the bouncing Jake while Janet worked on controlling the wriggling Samantha.

"Aren't they supposed to be tired after all that walking?" asked Holly.

Janet's eyes flew up. "One would think. They won't crash until the stimuli stop. They're at Uncle Thomas' house now. Ergo, brand new flux of nuclear bursts."

"Well, that's great. Listen, Janet, Thomas was in a, um, *state* this morning. Might not be a good thing to have bursting little swarmers all over him."

"Oh? What kind of state?"

"A post-bottle-of-scotch kind of state."

"A whole bottle?"

"I don't know. I only saw the empty. No clue how long he was working on it. But I can tell you that he was wacko-gonzoed when I found him in the middle of the night. He was on the floor. I pulled him over to the couch."

"Well, that was generous. I'd have left him there, in his shame."

"That's awful!" Holly giggled. "He's very proud of his sense of dignity. I don't want to shame him."

"As nice as that is, Holly, you're not his sister. It used to be my profession to embarrass him."

The two of them shared a laugh as Holly began to open the front door.

"Seriously, Janet. We need to be nice and calm."

Janet nodded. She lay a light hand on her daughter's face. "Sam, can you do Mommy a very big favor?"

"Yes!"

"Be very kind with Uncle Thomas. He isn't feeling well. So, you must treat him gently and take care of him. Can you do that?"

"Uncle Tom sad?"

"A little. Be my very good, sweet girl for him, okay?"

Samantha nodded enthusiastically. "I a nurse!"

"Very good, my love. And Jake, you too. I want you to use all the gentle touches, yes?"

Jake screwed up his face. Holly knew he loved getting into things and didn't enjoy being held back.

"Jake, I mean it," said Janet firmly. "You will lose your ice cream privileges. Understand?"

The boy's eyes widened. Certainly, that was a stabbing threat.

"Okay," little Jake said. They entered the house.

Chapter 6

Too Much Brandy

The four of them poured in as quietly as possible. Thomas was not seen immediately.

"He's probably in his study," offered Holly. "Can I get you some lemonade? We can go outside. Let the kids finish running it out?"

"We can try," said Janet.

Thomas opened the door to his study and knelt. "Where are my little elephants?" He beamed.

Samantha shoved and leapt from Janet's grasp. Jake was already halfway across the room. They pounced on Thomas. Janet and Holly cringed, even though he seemed receptive.

"You little rascals!" Thomas chuckled as they tackled him. "I've got you now!" He proceeded tickling them until they all fell over and, one of the children farted. "There you go! Off to the garden, now."

Janet was already at the sliding glass door, pulling it open for her brood to rush through.

Holly was stunned. "You look well," she said to him.

"I'm completely not well. But I won't let them know that." Thomas pushed up from his knees and walked laboriously towards his sister. His arms gently embraced her. "Did you have fun at the zoo?"

"We did."

He released her. "Could we have some tea? It's just passed time."

Janet smoothed his face with her palm affectionately. "Of course. I'll get it started. Holly, are there makings for sandwiches?"

Holly thought quickly. "I've got bread, turkey, mayo, and some lettuce and tomato left. Is that suitable for his Lordship?"

Janet's lovely musical laughter spread throughout the room. "His Lordship? Oh, I love that! It suits you, brother." She walked to the kitchen.

"As you say," Thomas relented, rubbing his head. "Uh, but no mayo. For the love of God. Mustard, please."

Holly observed him. "I think you need some aspirin," she told him. "I'll be right back." As she turned to leave, she noticed Thomas' fleeting glance upon her. Her stomach rolled. She fled to the staircase. As she climbed the winding steps, her skin flushed, and her heart beat with unusual quickness. His glance bothered her deeply. He seemed apologetic. But if she didn't know better, she would almost have thought he looked longingly at her.

At the medicine cabinet in Thomas' room, she saw perfumes, lady's deodorant, face cream, and some gardenia-scented cleanser. All of Evelyn's toiletries were still there, along with a plethora of orange medication bottles leftover from her chemo. He'd not thrown a thing out. She located the aspirin and shook loose a couple of tablets to bring to him. On the sink was a holder with two toothbrushes in it.

"Jesus." She sighed sympathetically and went back down to the living room.

Thomas was sitting on his couch with a tall glass of iced tea in front of him. She noticed that the blanket with which she'd covered him the night before was folded neatly and back in place along the back of the couch. She offered him the aspirin. He accepted the small, white tablets, choked them down with his iced tea, and patted the seat next to him, indicating for her to sit. She did so. He leaned his elbows onto his knees and clasped his hands together.

"I should thank you for taking care of me last night," he awkwardly said in a hushed tone.

Holly wasn't sure how to approach it. It didn't seem right to chastise him. She'd had many drunken stupors herself. There was no judgment in her heart.

"No worries, Tom. I don't leave fallen soldiers. I've been one myself, many, many times." She peered sideways at him.

He kept his eyes on the coffee table, obviously ashamed.

"Listen, Thomas. It really is okay. You don't have anything to be ashamed of. I've picked up tons of drunk friends, and they've done it for me. It's all good. Don't worry about it."

Thomas clenched. He seemed visibly disturbed at her attempt to be understanding. "It's not okay for me. I shouldn't be wallowing."

"Why not? For God's sakes, you lost your—" Holly stopped. The sharp look of pain on his face was too much for her. She placed her hand gently on his forearm. "It's understandable. To wallow. I get it. We all... get it."

"I'm ashamed. No one has ever seen it."

Holly smiled warmly at him. "Thomas, look at me."

He didn't.

"Thomas, I'd hate to raise my voice and get Janet's attention."

He looked at her. His lovely, sad, blue eyes nearly cut her in half.

Holly took a steadying breath. "It's okay. I don't think any less of you. In fact, I think I might like you more. I wasn't sure you even had any emotions."

He huffed a smile-less chuckle.

She kept her calm, pleasant face. "It's fine. I'm totally the last person to judge shit, okay? So, just relax about it, and don't worry."

He nodded. "Thank you. I appreciate your discretion."

Holly's eyes darted. "I uh... may have told Janet."

Thomas sighed in frustration, hunching forward and resting his head in his hands.

She stilled. "I'm sorry. I was trying to tell her why she needed to get the children to be calm. I told the kids you weren't feeling well. But that's all. I told her you drank too much last night, and that's all. Nothing else." She searched his face.

He squinted his eyes at her over his shoulder. "What else is there to tell, Holly?"

She sucked in her lips nervously. He didn't remember his murmurings. She made herself relax and act completely casual.

"Nothing else, of course."

"And the broth was lovely. Really did the trick. Thank you."

"You're welcome."

Janet arrived with the teapot and a plate of sandwiches. The tea seemed to restore Thomas somewhat. Janet went on and on, gushing about how clean the house was. The children finally began to wilt and collapse. Their failing energy disintegrated their willpower. Janet and Holly carried them to Janet's Lexus, where she planted a kiss on Holly's cheek.

"I think you're doing him a world of good." Janet said laying Samantha in her car seat and buckled her in. Holly set Jake in his car seat and buckled him. They closed the passenger doors.

"Why do you say that? I'm pretty sure he hates me. I'm like a mold. An intrusion."

"Yes. You are. And that's exactly what he needs. Someone to snap him out of his self-destruction. I'm so glad you're here!" She wrapped her arms around her friend. "Even though he was a bit edgy today, I could see a difference."

"Really?"

"He smiled. And not just for the children. He smiled even when we were just talking. I haven't seen that in so long. You're his tonic, Holly. Keep up what you're doing."

"He doesn't always like what I do. Or how I do it. Like I told you before. I can't compare to Evelyn."

Janet shook her head. "You don't have to be anything like Evelyn. You're perfect the way you are, you daffy bat! And you should never try to be her. Evelyn was Evelyn. Just be you, my darling. Trust me. You're brilliant. Anyway, he needs a change. And he needs someone who'll stand up to him. God knows I can't do it."

Holly's eyes flattened. "Janet. Am I the bitch? Why do I have to be the bitch?"

Janet giggled. "You are the exact right and best bitch."

"Great. I'm the damned bitch. Can't I be the nice guy for once?" She drooped.

Janet hugged her tightly. "You are the good guy. Oh, God, don't you see? You're naturally strong. We might call it being a bitch. But really, it isn't. You're being the strong friend to him that none of us have had the courage to be."

Holly remained unimpressed, expressing it with a flat smirk.

Janet hugged her once more and rounded the front of her car to get into the driver's side. "I'm telling you. I think you're waking him up."

"Fantastic. I just want to save up enough money to get out of here and not have to be his maid anymore."

Janet tossed her a lovely, knowing smile. "Oh, Holly. Can't you see that you're already so much more than that to him?" Janet dipped into her car and started it up.

Holly backed towards the house, wondering about her words. The Lexus slowly pulled out of the driveway.

More than that to him? What on earth did she mean?

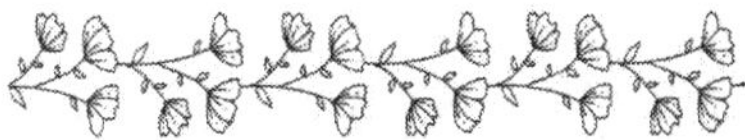

Holly kept her distance from Thomas during the rest of the weekend. She stayed in her room and read. Sunday afternoon was far too gorgeous, and she longed to go outside. Remembering how filthy the loungers were, she took a blanket down to lay over them and then reclined with some iced tea while reading her book.

Dinner was whatever they could scrounge on. Holly didn't want to cook on the weekends. She wanted two solid days completely free of tasks. But there were plenty of leftovers. The two of them grazed on whatever they found.

Some hours later, the sun was dipping low, making it more difficult to read. Thomas appeared at the sliding glass door. "What are you so engrossed in?"

"A book," she answered absently.

"What's it about?"

Holly sighed and glanced at him. "It's a murder-mystery-romance."

"And? What happens?"

She looked back at her book. "Well, there are three families. The head of each family is murdered at the same time on the same night. They're left scrambling, trying to figure out who did it and why. One family may kill the head of the other, but who did all three of them? And there are romances between the families. I'm in the fourth book in the series."

"Oh, it's a series?"

"Yes."

Thomas fidgeted. "Fancy a brandy with me?"

Holly sighed. "You know how you get irritated when I interrupt your writing?"

He studied his hand on the door. "Yes."

"That's how I feel about being interrupted when I read."

"But I've nothing to do."

Holly moved her bookmark and set the book on her lap. "Couldn't you watch TV or something?"

"Never much cared for it."

"How did you occupy yourself before I was here?"

Thomas' eyes went to the ground. "I've been writing since... Evelyn was lost. I've always had my characters and research. But now that's mostly done. Honestly, I'm not sure I've actually been alone yet."

She stared at him. "Even though no one else was here?"

"Well, I had Persephone. And Hades. Demeter. And the references from which I've been pulling my comparisons. I've been delving and lost in it. But since I'm done now. The house is empty." He looked at her. "Except for you."

An insufferable heat flushed her cheeks and chest.

"Now that you're here. I feel a need to... Well, connect. Is that so awful?"

Holly rubbed her eyes, irritated and compassionate at the same time. She placed the book on the dirty table at her side. "I guess it's getting too dark to read, anyway. Very well. Bring me a brandy."

Thomas lit up and disappeared back into the house. She laughed internally.

"If you're going to sit out here, you'll need something over the lounger." She pushed up and went to retrieve a blanket. When she returned, she bent to cover the lounger. As she stood, she nearly came nose to nose with him.

He stood there holding two very full glasses of brandy. They both froze with their eyes locked. She could feel his breath on her lips. His heavy eyes absorbed her briefly and she heard him take a thick inhale. Her abdomen clenched, holding in the flutters that burst forth.

"Here," he whispered, offering her a snifter.

"Thank you." She accepted it and went back to her lounger.

As he reclined, he said, "Do you know that until you started cleaning things, I don't think I ever noticed how bad things had become here. This lounger is filthy."

Holly smirked. "That's what I've been saying! It's pretty bad, Tom."

"Don't much care for being called 'Tom.' But at least it's better than dude."

Holly giggled. "His Lordship?"

Thomas smiled. Actually smiled. A full, ear to ear grin. It was magnificent and made his blue eyes sparkle. Holly looked away, trying not to gape.

They chatted mostly about Holly's old jobs. There were many. She wasn't well suited for office work.

A fact Thomas summed up perfectly when he said, "You aren't a rower of boats, Holly. You're the maker of waves. I can see that about you." His speech was slurring ever so slightly. They'd given up on refilling their brandies from the house, and Thomas had brought the bottle outside and set it next to his lounger.

"The maker of waves. Huh. I love that!" She chuckled.

Thomas' jovial smile appeared again. "You're a tsunami!"

Holly's stomach was clenching with joy, "I am! I'm a wrecker of shores!"

He calmed. "Well, you've certainly made waves in my life." He smiled again. The mirth faded into warmth. He was so relaxed. Almost like he was enjoying himself.

"Good waves?" asked Holly, watching his handsome face.

His placid grin remained. "Yes. I think so. I feel... better. Now that you're here." His glance wandered over her.

Something gripped Holly's stomach and didn't let go until he gazed back out over the dark yard. She sighed in relief when he stopped looking at her.

"I should get to bed," she said, suddenly getting up and teetering slightly.

Thomas rose as well. "Don't forget your book." He went to reach for it and lost his footing, falling upon her, and they tumbled back onto the lounger.

They landed laughing into each other's arms. No one had heard Thomas laugh in years. But Holly heard it. It was delightful. A wonderful rolling sound, not unlike his sister's tinkling laughter, but deeper. Must have been from their light heads and too much brandy.

When the laughter faded, nothing was left but a longing stare into each other's eyes. Holly's heart stilled. His lovely sparkling blues adopted a slight gravity and sank into her. She almost couldn't take the intensity. Thomas' arms still held her from when he caught her as they fell.

"Thomas..." she whispered in a breath.

He continued looking at her. His stare unnerved her and pulled her awareness into him. She trembled.

"What are you doing?"

His eyes ran along her face and back to her welcoming, light brown gaze.

"I'm not sure," he whispered back.

Something inside her relaxed. She'd not felt a man in her arms in a long time. A dormant longing woke. It was nice, even if it was Thomas Buckhorn. Her free arm took on a mind of its own and went to his ribs and side, sweeping along his back to his neck, fondling his nape. His own free arm was doing the same thing on her, stroking her face, neck, and shoulder until he was cupping the back of her head. His hand brought her towards him. Thomas' eyes wandered hers.

What the hell is happening? Is he going to...

His lips met hers slowly, then pressed insistently. Holly sharply inhaled through her nose as a wave of jitters tickled up from her stomach. His tongue parted her lips. Her entire body went rigid with protest, then limp with acceptance. Her own tongue responded instinctively along his. The warmth gliding in their shared mouths spread dizzying shivers through her. His gradual dancing kiss broke the venire of her barriers. Her body relaxed. She bent into him as he softly pushed his hips into hers.

Holly's instincts flared. Her body heated and triggered. She pulled him into her. He let his weight fall upon her, pressing his hips against hers until her legs parted. She could feel his erection forming through his trousers. He pushed it along her crotch as her hips welcomed him against her.

What is happening right now? It's Thomas. This is Thomas! Oh... God... Thomas.

Thomas pulled her closer to him so he could kiss her even more profoundly and hold her tighter. He struck the perfect balance between strength and tenderness. Holly's mind went blank. He moaned, pulling heat from her mouth directly into his. The beauty of his tongue's writhing skill emptied her brain completely. His tongue gently retracted. His lips held exquisite suction against hers until he released her. His dreamy blue eyes suddenly focused acutely on her face.

"Oh. Oh, God, Holly. What am I doing? Forgive me." He shoved away frantically and stood up from her. His palm pressed to his forehead. "I shouldn't have done that. I'm so sorry." The bulge in his pants jutted hard against his trousers. He quickly pivoted away, trying to hide it. "I hope you can forgive me. Jesus. Shit." He fled inside the house.

Holly was left, an erupting mess of erotic sparks on the lounger. *Damn it.*

Chapter 7

The Garden Minuet

The morning light streamed in cheerfully. Holly didn't feel too terrible but slept in later than planned. The brandy saw to that. By the time she made her way down for coffee, Thomas was already in his study. She thought it best to leave him be. He seemed very upset at himself last night. She, however, couldn't stop thinking about it. It was easily the best kiss she'd ever experienced.

Every time her mind drifted to his feverish lips and tongue, her stomach flipped and fluttered. The memory of his firmness against her groin caused an annoying pulse in her nether. Hopefully, this would wear off. It was mysterious, though, how a man with his chilly temperament could be capable of such talented passion.

She caught herself staring into space, reliving it. *Oh my God, snap out of it.* The task list for the week was what she should set her mind on. The windows needed to be cleaned, and the drapes laundered. Then, the deep cleaning of the bathrooms. There were still the stairs and hallways. After that, she'd start tackling the yard. Weeds were everywhere. And the rose bushes needed trimming. She wasn't sure how many days that would take. Meal planning and grocery shopping had to be done as well. They were nearly out of eggs and English muffins. *Oh! Breakfast!*

Holly slid off the buffet stool and went to his study door. She hesitated but found the courage to knock gently.

"Yes?" he answered.

She cracked the door. "Would you like breakfast? Or do you need any more coffee?"

He kept his eyes on his computer. "I would appreciate breakfast, and I've already had my coffee."

"Okay, I'll get on it in a couple of minutes."

"You're late this morning."

Her face drooped. He was back to his chilly self. "I wasn't aware I was punching a time clock."

"You're not. Just an observation. Please have breakfast no later than 9:30."

Annnd he's back. Old grumpy butt. Holly sighed. "I'll get it going." She closed his door.

Meal planning and grocery shopping were completed after breakfast. By the time she returned, he was ready for lunch. Holly stuffed bell peppers with chicken salad, trying to follow the same guidelines he'd given her for the tuna salad, even mincing up onion and tomato. She dropped it off in his office and took the empty plate from breakfast. At least he was eating her eggs now.

"I hope I got the chicken salad right," she tried to joke, but he didn't respond.

In fact, he didn't look at her at all. He bit into the bell pepper and nodded. No words, though. She closed his door again. *He's avoiding me. He's embarrassed. Well, he'll have to look at me during dinner. I won't serve that in his office.*

Holly pulled down the curtains and started them in the wash. After grabbing the glass cleaner and a roll of paper towels, she began wiping the interior of the windows. Then she did the exterior. She couldn't reach the exterior of the ones on the second level without a ladder, so she opened them, leaned out, and reached what she could.

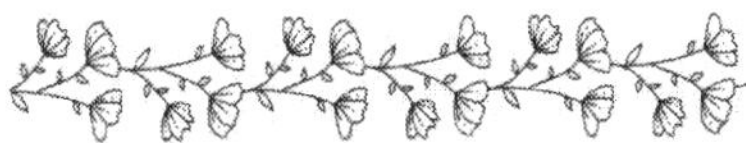

Thomas' phone rang with Janet's ringtone. He answered. "Hello, yes?"

"Thomas! I'm so glad you answered."

"I can let you go, and you can leave a voicemail."

"You wouldn't! Besides, you've trained me to be brief."

"That I have. So, do so and be brief. I'm working."

"I'm calling to see how you and Holly are getting on. I know I only saw you a couple of days ago, but I wanted to ask you privately. Is she doing well? Are you doing well?"

Thomas thought a moment. "What has she said?"

"I'm not going to tell you that, you sod! I want to know how *you're* doing."

He rubbed his nose and eyes. "It's well enough. She's finally got my eggs right."

"You're eggs? Whatever. What else?"

"The house looks better than it did."

"My love, a nuclear bomb could have made your house look better than it did."

Thomas straightened. "You too? Holly said something about burning down the place."

Janet's giggle fluttered out. "It was so bad. But I'm glad it's better."

Janet's effervescent tone always lightened his heart.

She went on. "Tell me, how do you like her? Have you had any good conversations? She's classically educated, you know. Music theory..."

Janet's voice faded out as Thomas' mind drifted to Holly's soft body under his. The sweet taste of her mouth when he sank his tongue into her. He thought of the wonderful parting of her hips when he pushed his hardening length against her pliant abdomen. How welcoming she was.

How she embodied the very scent of spring. He scrambled for something to say to his sister. "She... is prompt."

"Prompt?"

"Yes. Meals are always ready when I expect them."

"Is that all?"

"Well," an image of her lovely figure in a maxi dress appeared in his mind, "she wears these summer dresses in the evenings."

He could hear Janet's amusement. "She has an adorable figure."

Thomas' eyes bashfully flicked around his desk. "I can't say I've noticed that, Janet." He heard his sister snicker.

"Thomas, I know when you aren't telling me something. What have you done?"

His hand brushed through his hair, heavily. "Oh, God, Janet. I kissed her."

"You did? Brilliant! Then what happened?"

"Nothing. I fled."

"You fled? Oh, Thomas." He could hear Janet drooping in disappointment.

"Don't chastise me, Janet. I behaved like an animal. I shouldn't have taken advantage of her in our vulnerable state."

"What vulnerable state?"

Thomas sighed. "We'd had some brandy."

"So what? Brandy is the perfect catalyst for—well, never mind. So, you fled."

"I fled."

"And? The aftermath?"

Thomas fidgeted. "I'm avoiding her. I was a brut."

Silence on the other end of the call. Then she asked, "Did she respond favorably when you kissed her?"

Thomas' mind pictured her body bending to his. Her legs opening to receive his hips. Her hands caressing him.

"Thomas?"

He snapped from the image. "She was... No! No, Janet. This is inappropriate!"

"Thomas, if she accepted you, then you weren't a brut. And this might surprise you, but some women, like Holly, actually like assertive men."

Thomas was caught back. "What on earth are you saying, Janet?"

"You should go for her! You're a romantic! And she's intellectual."

Thomas groaned, rubbing his temples with one hand. "No, Janet. It isn't right. She works for me. She's been a family friend for years. Besides, I miss Evelyn. It hasn't even been a whole year yet. It feels out of place to simply throw myself at Holly merely because she's here."

Janet sighed. "No, of course not. But, if you like her, you shouldn't shut yourself down either."

Thomas pinched his brows with his thumb and forefinger. Janet could be so tiresome. How could he explain to his enthusiastic sister that feeling another woman's body was practically a violation in his heart. "Janet, I simply can't. You understand? I cannot—pursue—a, an, an anything! It's not possible! I miss Evelyn. It feels like cheating." He glanced at a picture of his wife on his desk.

The pause from the other side of the call hit his ears heavily.

"We all miss Evelyn, Thomas. But she's gone. And you can't wallow forever."

"I'll wallow for however long I like!"

"Fine, but don't deny yourself in the process. You're still alive, Thomas."

"No! I am not alive. I died with Evelyn that day! You weren't there. You didn't see—"

"Stop it! Damn it, Thomas. Stop it!" Janet breathed in heavily. "I'm sorry, my love. I didn't mean to yell. But you *are* still alive. And you *are* still a man. And you will go on having feelings, and there isn't anything wrong with that. Stop punishing yourself, I beg you."

Thomas gripped his chin. "I feel horrible."

"Well, don't. It's completely natural."

"Look, I appreciate what you're saying and what you're trying to do. Thank you for... whatever this was. A pep talk. I'm fine. Holly is cleaning things well, and I haven't noticed much of anything except that I'm paying a lady to keep my house now. A house that was perfectly fine before."

"It was not perfectly fine! Your house was a disaster! And you, my dear academic brother, are far better than that! Are you a gentleman, or aren't you?"

Thomas shifted in his chair. "I am indeed a gentleman."

"Then act like it! Tend to your home. Goodness sakes!"

Thomas smiled. "I assure you my home is now well-tended."

"Then, you should thank her."

"Who?"

"Holly! Don't forget to give her some praise."

"But I'm paying her to do it."

"Yes, you are. And it's also a good idea to praise a job well done. Don't you agree?"

"Ah. Yes. Of course. I shall do that."

"Good. And don't kiss her again unless you mean it. She's been single for a long time, and you'll only confuse her."

Thomas wilted slightly. "Yes. I—I understand. I told you already."

Janet sighed. "I love you. Behave yourself. But not too much!"

Thomas grinned slightly. "I love you too."

Dinner was ribeye steak with peas and baby carrots. Holly knocked and opened his office door. Thomas hadn't emerged from his study all day except to use the bathroom.

"Thomas, dinner is ready. Come on."

"I'll take it in here."

Holly bristled. "You won't take it in there. I'm not going to bring it to you in there. Now quit sulking and get out here."

"I'm not sulking."

Holly's eyes made their way to the ceiling. She threw the door open and marched into his room, crossing her arms.

"You're avoiding me."

"I'm working."

"Then why haven't you looked at me all day or said more than three words at a time?"

He took an audible deep breath. "Fine." He got up, walked past her through the living room, turned the corner, and went down the hall to the dining room.

Holly's eyes flared angrily. She grabbed his plate from lunch and nearly threw it at the kitchen countertop before joining him at the dining table. He sat staring at his steak.

"You didn't ask me how I like it cooked."

She seated herself. "You like it medium rare. I remember from some of the barbeques we've had."

He nodded absently and cut into it. It was a perfect medium rare. He almost looked disappointed that he couldn't complain about it. A little smile crept up Holly's mouth.

As they cleared the table, Holly deposited the dishes in the dishwasher. Thomas followed with the glasses. He set them on the counter and started slinking away. Holly gently grabbed his hand.

"Thomas. Please stop beating yourself up."

His eyes finally dragged up to meet hers. "I feel terrible about it."

"Why? You were actually smiling and even laughing. No one's heard that from you in years. We were having fun."

He huffed through his nose. "I shouldn't take advantage of you. I couldn't forgive myself if I did." He cast his eyes away.

Holly's head tilted to the side, speaking hesitantly. "Well... What if it wasn't... taking advantage?"

His wide eyes snapped to her face. Pity replaced the shock. "This can't happen, Holly. I behaved like an oaf, and I won't do it again."

"It wasn't that bad."

"You work for me. It's inappropriate."

"Because I work for you? Or because I'm not Evelyn?"

His eyes froze, and he slowly pulled his hand away. "No one will ever be Evelyn." Thomas went to the TV room for a scotch and the news.

Holly pulled her lips in regretfully. "Shouldn't have said that. Shouldn't have fucking said that." Shaking her head, she went to clean up the pans.

The more she thought about it, the more she understood that he was right. A drunken kiss between friends was one thing. If they slept together, who knew how awkward it would be afterwards? It could make things impossible. The last thing she wanted to do was ruin their friendship. Or whatever it was that they had. It didn't matter if she felt riled up and horny. Thomas was not the man to take that out on.

After spending two days scrubbing the scummy windows and the bathrooms, it was finally time, on Wednesday morning, to tackle the weeds. The weeds were a toil. Holly loathed yard work. She grabbed some garden tools from the shed and began poking and digging and pulling.

It was hot, and her sunglasses kept sliding off her nose from the sweat. When she put the tools away in the shed, she noticed a hat hanging on the wall.

After lunch it was more weeding. But this time, she wore the hat she'd found in the shed instead of her sunglasses. It was much easier not having her sunglasses slipping off.

That night's dinner was apple glazed pork chops with purple cauliflower and rice. Thomas dutifully took his seat and ate quietly. Holly felt like she was being punished, and the disappointment of it sat heavily on her shoulders.

They had been developing a more pleasant report. But his icy demeanor had taken back over since he'd kissed her, and he barely said a thing to her. At least he'd calmed down with the instructions of how Evelyn did everything.

The next morning, after breakfast, Thomas' frantic voice rang from the foyer as Holly was finishing the dishes.

"Holly! I need your help!"

She ran to him in a frenzy of concern. He turned to her and held his arms out from his sides.

"How do I look?"

"What?"

"I have a lecture at eleven. Am I presentable? Evelyn always used to help me, and I can't even tell anymore."

She sighed in relief and sent a chastising smirk at him. His tie needed straightening, so she went to his neck and adjusted it. His nervous breath gently flowed along her face. The heat from his body stirred her core, making her belly shiver. Holly couldn't explain it, but she desperately wanted to touch him again. She took the opportunity and smoothed his waistcoat, sweeping her hands down his warm chest when she was done, and stepped back. His face was a mixture of yearning and restraint. The muscles along his jaw convulsed with tension.

She folded her hands together and smiled sweetly at him. "You look fine."

"Am I coordinated? I've never been very good with colors."

"You're totally dressed in beiges. There's literally no way to screw up beige."

"And my tie. Is it straight?"

"I just straightened it." She approached him again and smoothed the cotton shirt down his arms, surprised by how well-formed they felt. "Thomas, you look perfect." Her eyes fluttered at him.

He stared at her. "You're sure?"

Holly pulled herself away from his proximity again and crossed her arms. "Why are you so worried?"

He fidgeted. "I don't know. It's a new class for the summer semester. Most of them resent their need to be there, and the other half are overachievers. I just want to look welcoming."

Holly laughed into the foyer. "Oh, Thomas! They won't care what you look like. But it's kind of sweet that you care about it."

He scowled. "Well, then. I'm off." And out the door he rushed.

Thomas started his car and pulled from the driveway. His spine was buzzing with a strange warm tingle. The sensation started the night he'd kissed her. It reappeared every time he saw her, now, much to his irritation.

As he drove on to the campus, old memories of Holly as a teenager floated up. She was always a pretty girl with a bouncy kind of vivaciousness. She and Janet were quite the mischievous pair. Always giggling and gossiping. He'd covered for them on several occasions when they'd missed curfew.

He tried to remember any conversations he'd had with her. Something about movies, and one about her playing piano at an upcoming recital. Mostly, Thomas had his nose stuck in books and didn't really notice her. *No, that's not right. I did notice her. It's just been ages.* Dozens of images of her either smiling or laughing flooded his mind. She always kept her honey hair trimmed either just past her shoulders or longer to the center of her back, like she had it now.

The night he'd kissed her, he stood at the screen door for nearly five minutes watching her read. Perhaps it was time to admit it. He was growing fond of her. He stole glances of her as often as he could. There was a gentleness in everything she did and in every way she moved. She glided.

Why didn't I make a move for her then? Because she was Janet's accomplice. That's why. Thomas smirked to himself.

An uncontrolled vision of her beneath him and breathing his name flew into his mind. Her welcoming arms around him and her dewy lips. He heard her moan as their tongues swirled. *Shit! Was that a red light? No. Whew! How does Janet say it? It was orange.*

He refocused on the road. Getting to his lecture unscathed needed to be more important than Holly. And her sweet smile... *No. I can't allow this.*

It was on Friday, when Holly knelt, digging up the roots of dandelions in the backyard, that she heard the sliding glass door on the patio open. Heavy footsteps plodded militantly on the patio stones, then stomped on the grass until they were before her.

"What the hell do you think you're doing wearing that?"

Holly squinted up at a red, pinched-faced Thomas. "Wearing what?"

"That is Evelyn's hat! Take it off immediately!"

Her hand went protectively to the straw darling that had kept her shaded during the week. She stared at him, measuring his panic against her willpower. "I will not. It's helping to block the sun. And I don't like wearing my sunglasses 'cause my nose sweats, and they slide down."

Thomas grew visibly agitated. "Remove it."

"Why? It's a hat! If Evelyn was here, she'd probably lend it to me."

"I won't have it! I simply will not, Holly. Take it off." His anger was clear. Thomas' body was so rigid he could have drilled straight to the center of the earth. Holly pushed herself up and squared with him. She'd about had enough of his outbursts. And none of them made any sense now that she knew how tender he could be. She'd reached the end of her tolerance for the yo-yo that was Thomas Buckhorn.

"I've worn this hat all week, and you're just now telling me that, for some reason in your head, that it's inappropriate?"

Thomas bristled and spoke in a low, measured voice. "I watched her garden for years in that hat."

Holly felt an arrow hit her chest. And by his pained expression, it must have been the same one that hit him. She imagined him seeing her out here in the hat. It must have looked like Evelyn was there. She heaved a calming breath, untied the ribbon, pulling it loose from her chin, and removed it.

"I wasn't trying to be disrespectful, Thomas," she said with soft irritation. She dared a glance straight into his eyes. "You're going to have to stop seeing her everywhere at some point. I'm not saying that to be cruel. I'm saying that because getting offended at every turn doesn't serve anybody. And it only hurts me, when I'm just here to help you." She handed over the straw woven hat.

His mouth hung open in tortured contortion as he took it reverently. Thomas turned abruptly and went back into the house.

"Fuck me!" she burst after he was gone. "That's it. I'm not pulling another fucking weed until I can have some decent shade." Holly dropped her clippers and went to the local garden shop for her own gardening hat.

A little later, when she went to clip the roses back, Thomas came hurling out of the house at her.

"No, no, no! What in the hell are you doing?"

"What the fuck now?" Holly yelled back, exasperated.

"You can't prune the roses now! It's way too late in the Spring! At this point, you must wait until after they bloom."

"Oh, thank God for that!" Holly flung the clippers at the ground so hard, they stuck in points first. She pushed up to stand. "Because I've spent the last half of this week pulling foot-long dandelion tubers from the yard. Anything I don't have to do is fucking welcomed!"

"Stop swearing! Why must you swear all the time? It's abrasive."

"My swearing? Seriously? You're fucking exhausting!" Holly placed her hands on her hips and dipped her head, taking a breath. "I am sick of you criticizing every goddamned thing I do. All I do is try to please you. Get your eggs right, don't play my music too loud, stay out of your way, and do my job. I've been nothing but be fucking nice because of what you've gone through. Well, buddy, I'm done with you being an asshole to me!"

Thomas blinked and caught his breath as if her outburst had winded him.

"I'm done hearing how inadequate and inappropriate I am! All you do is snipe at me, and I've tried so hard to be this—this calm, compassionate, understanding person. But you don't seem to give a shit! I'm done! The weeds are gone. I must have filled three lawn and leaf bags with them. My back hurts. It's Friday, and I'm fucking done." She bent, picked up her gardening tools, and stomped to the shed to put them away.

Thomas had disappeared back into the house by the time she re-emerged. Holly was only too happy to be rid of him.

Chapter 8

Evelyn's Piano

Holly had ignored the sheet-covered piano in the nook off from the kitchen until now. But it was there, teasing her just the same. She rubbed her left hand. The hand she'd broken right at the end of college when she'd been accepted to a mentorship by the Columbus Symphony. It was her life's dream and goal.

But she'd gotten into a car crash, which crushed her hand to bits. After three surgeries and a lot of time not fulfilling her dream of playing piano, Holly let the joy of music sink into a bleak pit.

Thankfully, her hand was fully functional again. But her heart wasn't. Hence the string of bleary office jobs. Her degree in music theory proved completely useless when she needed to find work.

The event broke her spirit completely, and she hadn't played much piano since. She had her Roland keyboard that she barely touched. It was in storage with the rest of her life, anyway.

The piano sat almost tauntingly, and the thought of playing it nagged her. Thomas was gone at a lecture. He'd probably yell at her for not playing the way Evelyn played. But he wasn't there, was he?

Holly stared at the instrument. She remembered how it had looked, having seen it before when Evelyn hosted a gathering one summer. A small version of a grand piano that some called a baby-grand. Dark, reddish, shining wood made its frame.

Almost beyond her control, Holly's body moved to it, and she pulled the sheet away. Her old, broken hand lifted the long wooden cover over the keys. Ivory pieces separated perfectly by black bars spread down in a beautiful lane before her.

"If you want me, you can have me," it said in her mind. *"I've been alone for so long."*

She felt the keys.

"Yes."

They were smooth and silky to her fingertips.

"Touch me."

She pressed. A rich tone rang from the wooden body. The note reverberated in the house. It begged her for a companion. She pushed another key. Its tone sang in the echo of its companion. Both perfectly in tune. Thomas must have kept it tuned in Evelyn's memory.

"More. Give me... more. Touch me. Play me. I'm so lonely."

Holly found her rump meeting the bench and her hands splayed along the ivory bars. She played a chord. The comforting beauty of the tones embraced her. She pressed another chord. The reverberating gorgeousness invited her to continue. Before she knew it, Beethoven was singing from her fingers. Then Schubert. Then her favorite, Chopin.

An hour passed. Then another as Holly's fingers danced along the keys, filling the house with her heart. She finished Chopin's Nocturn Op.9 No 2 and stilled. The deepest breath of the sweetest, most fulfilling air came into her lungs.

"You have the loveliest touch with Chopin."

A jolt rocked Holly's body, and she saw him standing by the kitchen buffet, staring at her.

"Truly. It's wondrous." He was complimenting her.

She almost couldn't tell it was Thomas. He stood leaning on the buffet with a hand on his chest. A look of fascination on his features.

"How long have you been there?" she asked, trying to pry her heart from the ceiling.

"Long enough to hear you."

Holly shoved from the bench fearfully. "I'm sorry. I should have asked you first. I know this was Evelyn's—"

"No. Please." He raised a stopping hand in the air. "Don't apologize. It was so..." He captured her eyes with his.

Holly lost her breath.

"It was so beautiful. I've never heard such a lovely touch on that instrument. Won't you keep playing?"

Holly's cheeks heated and reddened. "I— Wasn't this Evelyn's, though?"

His eyes tilted sorrowfully. "Evelyn was a magnificent player." He moved his glance to the walls with a heavy sigh of regret. "But she was technical. Perfect, but just so. You play with... love. Please, I beg you. Play something more."

Holly could have been blown over by a moth's wing. Finally, something he approved of. She moved back to the bench, thinking. What could she produce from her memory? Chopin was her favorite, so another from him seemed a good idea. Nocturne in C sharp minor No20 came to mind. She sat and placed her hands. The notes flew from her heart in quiet passion.

Thomas caught himself on the buffet, listening. Seemingly barely able to stand. The simple beauty of the music must have weakened his legs. When she'd finished, he was slumped over with his face in his hands. The room was intolerably still.

"Have I— Did I do something wrong?" she asked.

Thomas, red-eyed, looked sideways at her. "No." He stood, loosening his tie and pulling it from his neck. "That was so beautiful." He unfastened the buttons on his waistcoat and headed for his study.

Holly couldn't move as she watched him. The captivating emotions vibrating from him were incomprehensible. She couldn't stop observing the subtle movements of his body as he walked through the living room. He seemed lighter. When he reached the door to his study, he asked without turning around, "What are we having for dinner, Holly?"

She straightened and snapped from the trance of watching him move. "I have an, um... some chicken thighs. I thought maybe I could roast them with a compound butter and some fresh spinach with garlic? Some sauteed potatoes?"

"That sounds sublime. Let me know when it's ready." He closed his study door.

Holly stood, flummoxed by his demeanor, and performed some hand stretches to unwind her fingers from playing. Then she went to make the menu she'd just promised.

After dinner, Thomas asked her, "Do you play chess at all?"

Holly picked up their plates to take to the kitchen. "No. Well, I've tried, but I'm not very good at it."

Thomas followed her to the kitchen with the water glasses. "I used to play with Evelyn. She was quite good. Then Janet amused me with a game or two. I miss it." They set the dishes and glasses by the sink. "Would you be so kind?"

Holly turned to him. Something was off with him. He seemed... vulnerable. "You want me to play chess with you?"

He looked at the floor, then back to her. "Yes. Would you mind?"

"Of course not, Thomas. But you'll probably kick my ass." She smiled broadly. And to her surprise, Thomas smiled back at her. Teeth spread wide. It was magnificent.

"I can teach you. You'll be kicking my ass back in no time."

"Language!" she teased him.

He almost laughed, flashing his boyish blues at her. Thomas grabbed a bottle of scotch and a couple of glasses and led her to the chess table. They climbed the winding stairs to the opened space in front of his room. There was an old chess table sitting beside a window. Thomas helped her as best he could to understand the game. But her mind was distracted with how kind he was. Thomas was being gentle and helpful with teaching her. She'd never seen this softness from him before.

As the night wore on, laughter came more frequently from him. It was the most wonderful sound in her ears. When they became too tired to lift another pawn, they went to bed. Thomas stood in his doorway and watched her walk down the hall. She turned at her own door and saw him staring at her.

"Thank you. Tonight was fun," she said to his sorrowful, yearning face.

"It was. Thank you."

Holly went to enter her room, but his voice halted her.

"I hope that you will play the piano some more. Tomorrow?" He shuffled his feet against the doorjamb. "If you don't mind."

She said simply, "I'd love to play more. So long as I'm not disturbing his Lordship."

He chuckled. "I love to hear—" his face sombered. "You're playing is lovely, Holly. I should like to hear more of it." He quickly closed his door.

Holly backed into her room, closing her door, and regarded the space. Two walls of windows, some of which were open to allow the heavy, sweet-scented spring air to drift through. It was the dreamiest, most romantic time of year, and the smell of it always made her heart ache.

Thomas seemed to have made another turn-around to favoring her again. She couldn't quite put a finger on his temperament. But nothing made her puddle more than the dewy beauty of his kind voice.

Holly switched on the light beside her bed and pulled off her maxi dress. Her eyes were heavy from the scotch, and she could easily drift into a lovely sleep. But Thomas' eyes and glistening smile pounded forth in her mind like a beautiful rhythm.

She slid into her covers and turned off the light. Thomas' laughter and deep blue eyes formed in the darkness of her mind, and she felt that familiar beckoning in her loins. She rolled over, intending to ignore it. His kiss, hands, and the pressure of his hips between hers only brightened the feeling, and she realized she may have a yearning that needed quenching.

She slid her hand down to the softness between her thighs and circled, flicked, and rubbed as she remembered the heat of his kiss.

The next morning, Holly was in her small silky robe, waiting for coffee to pour into the pot. She leaned heavily on her elbow so the hem just barely covered the soft lobe of her bottom. Thomas came down and stood behind her.

"Holly." As usual, his abrupt voice, laden with disapproval, snapped her into the present and filled her with dread.

God, not this again. What on earth could she possibly be doing wrong at this moment? She was only making coffee and too tired for his bullshit.

"What?" she turned to him, wondering how she could have already ruined his day after being awake for only fifteen minutes.

"You must wear something more. I can't see you in such a state of—of—"

She groaned. "It's a robe, Thomas. I'm hardly indecent. Cut me a break, will you?" *How was he back? Grumpy butt. And after such a nice evening before, too.* Holly's body reflected her disappointment by dropping. She turned her back to him.

"It's terribly small. Don't you think? Hardly decent at all. Put some more clothes on. You do have more clothes. Wear some sweatpants or whatever."

She turned her head and gaped at him, wondering if this was some kind of act or defense mechanism. Whatever it was, she was already fed up and regretting that she'd fantasized about him while touching herself the night before. "Thomas, would it be too much to ask if you waited to yell at me until *after* my first cup of coffee?"

He stiffened. "Please go and dress yourself. I simply cannot observe you this way."

"Jesus, you're such a dick in the morning!" Holly poured fresh coffee into her mug, added sugar and milk, and went back to her room. She decided to finish her coffee in front of her laptop instead of going back downstairs.

Thomas' volleying behavior had worn her thin. He was a jerk, then he was charming, then back to the jerk again. She needed to either confront him about it or avoid him altogether. Since they weren't consistently personal, she opted for avoidance and stayed out of his way.

That week, there wasn't much to do. She'd finished all the deep cleaning and weeding. There were a few projects she'd spotted. Things neither Thomas nor Janet had mentioned. There was an old Hot Tub in the garden, and near the shed lay a shambles of a bench. Holly called a company to come sanitize and refurbish the hot tub, but it would still be over a week before they could make it out.

She had also observed small picket fences surrounding Evelyn's rose gardens. Some of the slats had fallen, and the nails were loose in places. The little barriers could definitely do with a fresh coat of paint. She started with those. By the end of the week, all the little fences were back in a state of sturdy, pristine grace. Bright white paint gleaming from their proud little pointed tops. In the evenings, she'd play piano before dinner. Thomas always complimented her playing, but Holly kept her distance. On the evenings when he seemed welcoming and congenial she remained aloof.

Reminding herself of the conversation they'd had on her first night there, she kept her distance. He was her boss, not her friend. In order to contain her sanity, she had to make the decision to be the consistent one.

The following week, she set her sights on the bench. It needed to be sanded and refinished. Holly drilled new screws and tightened the old ones. Then she attached a lattice on each side and one over the top like a little squared arch. She moved the whole thing into the center of one of Evelyn's rose gardens. A patch of yard surrounded by every one of Evelyn's favorite colors. A fresh coat of varnish and a few new cushions, and the bench was easily the best place in the yard to sit. Surrounded by blooms, one could nearly smell the difference in the colors of every rose. Red, orange, yellow and pink. It was delicious.

Thomas remained sequestered in his study. Holly was done acting friendly, deciding to embrace her role as a housekeeper. She saw him for dinner, and occasionally, he'd poke his head out while she played piano, but for the most part, they kept apart from one another.

By that Thursday, she enjoyed a glass of lemonade, sitting on the bench amongst the roses with a sense of pride. She called Janet. Janet had stopped by earlier in the week just to check on them. But Holly couldn't talk with her openly because Thomas was right there. They'd had tea with tuna salad sandwiches. But now, she was alone and could speak freely.

"He hates me, I know it." Holly spouted to Janet over the phone.

"Don't be daft, he doesn't hate you."

"Yes, he does."

"You must be looking at someone else, because I can plainly see that he's absolutely smitten."

Holly nearly spit out her lemonade. "Smitten? What the hell do you mean? I've gotten maybe two compliments from him in like, four weeks! I keep thinking he'll acknowledge me or my hard work, but he never does. I mean, talk about a thankless job! And I thought working in insurance was bad."

"Holly, listen to me. He's trying to ignore you because you disturb him."

"I'm sure I do! I've upset his entire serene existence. He's always irritated with me."

"No." Janet's tinkling laugh spread from her. "That's not it, silly! He's only acting angry because he's mad at *himself*, not you."

"Why on earth would he be mad at himself?"

"Because he likes you. He's completely falling for you."

Holly felt fragile enough to be knocked over by a dandelion seed. "Janet, that isn't funny," she said sternly.

"I'm not trying to be funny."

"Are we talking about the same person? You've got to be fucking kidding me."

"I'm not kidding! You're just in the line of fire of his self-defense mechanisms."

Holly worked on absorbing Janet's words. "Wait. Are you telling me that Thomas is being a dick because he... likes me? And not just 'is fond of,' but actually like-likes me?"

Janet's giggle perforated the phone again. "Yes! And you like him too. I can see it all over the both of you."

"Janet, that's ridiculous, and I don't want you to ever bring it up again."

She kept giggling. "Okay, fine. I won't. But I'm not wrong."

Thomas leaned back against his office chair with his eyes closed, listening to Holly play the piano. Every note from her hands tugged his inner base darkness, pulling it forward into the light. He hated her for it. He hated that she made him feel things. He longed. He ached. Thomas stood and went to his doorway to look at her. Her back was to him as she sat at the piano playing and burning his soul with every note.

Her fingers adored the ivories. Or perhaps it was the ivories that adored her fingers. Her touch upon them played out with the loveliest emotion. Schubert was her choice tonight. Holly's spirit erupted from her into the keys and flowed to the hammers that hit the strings. They sang for her, unafraid and bold into the world. She was lost in the melody, and Thomas was lost in her experience of it. He sighed deeply without realizing it.

Observing her slender form, he let his eyes wander and really take her in. There was a slight wave to her hair. Just enough to bounce as she moved with the playing of the song. His breath quickened and caught in his throat.

The rapture of the crescendo erupted from her hands and into the piano. A long-silent warmth made its way into his depths as her playing brought the slow ending to an agonizing stop. Blessedly, she only paused a few moments before beginning another piece. Chopin again. Halting at first, then delightfully flirty and fluent as it went on.

The fire in his core spread through him and quietly settled into a longing throb playing in his groin. It caught his attention when Thomas realized he was hard. Not just hard. Rock hard. Enough to knock down a tree. He quickly hid himself behind his doorway. But he couldn't stop indulging in the fantasy of her incredible fingertips as they floated along the keys. He pictured them floating along the white pieces delicately.

Then he pictured her fingertips playing along his hard length. They stroked him luxuriously.

Unable to shed the vision, he shuffled back and fell into his office chair, pulled open his trousers, and firmly grasped himself with tight, needy strokes. Her playing pronounced every beat of his heart in waves of chords as he gripped and fondled his girth, imagining her hands on him.

Then he saw her mouth. Her perfect lips wrapped around the tip of his cock. Hot vibrations shot from within, and he lost himself. Bursting warmth spread upon his hand as the smallest gasp escaped him, and he struggled to muffle his orgasm. His breaths came rapid and harsh as he lay back against his chair, wishing it had been her body upon him and not his own hand.

Thomas made a point of getting up early the next morning. He couldn't bear to look at her. He quickly hid in his office. Sometime after she'd presented his flawlessly scrambled eggs and English muffin with strawberry preserves, he noticed that the house was oddly quiet. He couldn't hear Holly shuffling about. He rose and used the excuse of taking his breakfast plate to the kitchen to search around. There was no sign of her. Finally, he peered out the sliding glass doors and saw her reading a book amongst the roses on a new garden bench that he'd never seen before.

His eyes stopped on her. The blooms beautifully framed her lovely figure and soft hair, which cascaded down in the sunlight along her bare shoulders. She was wearing one of those darling maxi dresses. The kind with no straps. Only a tight band of elastic bundling cupped her breasts, barely holding them up. She turned a page, and he couldn't find air.

She brushed a stray lock behind her ear, and he nearly fell to the side. Catching himself on the door, he kept his eyes on her.

Then his glance wandered along the patio and yard. Everything was clean, weeded, and pristine. The loungers practically sparkled in the sunlight. The little fences around the flower gardens glimmered with a fresh coat of paint. *When had she done that?* All of it was beautiful again.

Thomas looked away from the fenced gardens and back to the vision of Holly in the roses. The sight of her blew apart his chest, and he couldn't take it a second longer. He retreated to his study to work on editing his work. Unfortunately, he could still see her through his windows in the study. He found himself straying from his computer frequently to catch glimpses of her.

Finally, he gave up looking at his computer altogether and stared at her in the rose garden. The ample mounds of her breasts rose and fell in the rhythm of her breathing. His hands tingled with the desire to touch them. He imagined his thumbs sliding over her nipples. The warmth in his groin ached and nagged him again. He closed the curtains. *I'm torturing myself,* he thought. *I want her... This has to stop.*

Chapter 9

The Tortured Embrace

Holly made a simple spaghetti Bolognese for dinner. Tonight marked the fifth Thursday of her time there. As she cooked, the sudden sound of pages being turned confused her. Looking over her shoulder, she could barely believe that Thomas was out of his office. He sat in the living room, reading. This was new. She acted as if it was of no concern.

They ate quietly at the kitchen buffet when dinner was ready. He seemed oddly demure and quiet.

"How is Persephone?" she asked.

He chewed. "She's being edited. We writers think all we have to do is write. But honestly, we spend more time editing than writing. It's a chore."

Holly smiled. "Like music. You have to put all the right pieces in the right places."

He smiled back at her. "Yes. Something like that. Maybe even remove or add a note here and there."

Holly awoke to a thumping and a moan from downstairs. She sat up slowly. He must be having one of his rough nights again. She rose and wrapped her robe around her nakedness. She found him slumped over the kitchen buffet. A nearly empty bottle of scotch sat on the counter. Holly normally wouldn't intervene. She knew how he prized his privacy. And she didn't want to disturb the polished ideal he had of himself. As she watched him crying, her heart dragged against her chest until she couldn't take it anymore. She walked into the kitchen. He didn't notice her at first.

Holly decided to polish off the bottle on the counter since there were only a couple of sips left, then she tossed it in the trash. Seeming vaguely aware of her, he lifted his bleary eyes.

"H-holly..." he groaned.

She went to him.

He lifted a beckoning arm to her. "Help me to bed, please," he slurred.

She hooked his arm around her, and they cumbersomely made their way up the stairs. Thomas never let her in his room except when she did her thorough cleaning and to get his towels and laundry.

He dragged and staggered all the way to his bed. She tried to release him, but he wouldn't let her go. He flung his blankets back and pulled her down with him. Holly couldn't believe her eyes watching him knock Evelyn's pristine side apart so he could scoot over. Decorative pillows spilled over the side, and he shoved himself under the tucked covers.

"Here. Now there's room."

Holly oofed as he tugged her into place. "Thomas, I don't think this is a good idea."

"Course, it's good," he slurred. His stubborn embrace keeping her in place. "Don't leave me. You're not allowed to leave me." He clung to her, holding her in tightly, and wept into her shoulder.

Holly worked on rolling over so she could wrap him in her arms. He lay his head against her bosom and sobbed until he stilled.

Careful not to unsettle him, she worked on adjusting herself to get comfortable, snuggling against him. He smelled of scotch and the lingering hint of a pine-based aftershave. She wondered what would happen when he awoke next to her in the morning. She figured he'd either ignore it or go into hysterics.

After considering she'd rather avoid disaster, she tried releasing him and pushing away so she could get back to her room. His grip compressed. She wasn't going anywhere. Soon, she was sleeping away, cozied into his embrace.

She woke to him yelling at her to get up.

"What on earth do you think you're doing?" he blasted. "Get up! Get out of there!"

Holly clenched her eyes. "Hysterics it is." She rolled towards the harsh sound of his voice.

He was standing by the bedside. As she rolled, her robe opened and a plump, white breast with a perfect, tight, pink nipple lolled out.

Thomas erupted. "Get up! And for God's sake, cover yourself!" He turned away, holding his forehead in distress.

"You asked me to sleep here!"

He kept his back to her as she scooted out of the bed. "That's preposterous! Why in the hell would I do such a thing?"

"I don't know, Thomas!" She stood and secured her robe. "I found you in a stupor in the kitchen last night and helped you to bed. You wouldn't let go of me."

He shook. "Rubbish."

"You fucking pulled me into your bed and held on to me, you ass! I tried to leave, but you wouldn't let me!"

"I don't remember that!" He whirled around. His eyes quickly swept down and back up her figure.

She fumed, "What possible reason could I have to make something like that up?"

Then his glance fell to the bed. "You've ruined Evelyn's side!"

"You did that!" She brushed her bed-ruffled hair back in frustration. "You pushed it all apart and then cried in my arms until you fell asleep."

Thomas stomped to Evelyn's side of the bed and began fixing it. "This has gone far enough. I want you gone."

Holly froze. The electricity buzzing from Thomas nearly shocked her. "Gone?"

"Gone. Get out!"

"Of the room or of your house?"

"Both! Pack your things and get the hell out of my life!"

Holly's hands tightened into fists, and she stomped from his room. In her own room, she yanked on a pair of jeans and a tank top. Then she hunted for a suitcase, but she didn't have one. Janet had taken them all with her after dropping her off over a month before. Locating her cell phone, she prepared to call Janet when Thomas knocked on her door.

"Holly?" came his low, sad, regretful voice through the door. "I'm a terrible mess. I'm so sorry." He sighed lamentfully. "Shit."

She threw her phone onto the bed and regarded the door through slitted eyes.

"I am an ass. Please forgive me."

"You need to quit yelling at me and assuming the worst. I'm not here to hurt you, Thomas."

There was a pause. "I know."

"You're always yelling at how displeased with me you are. The garden hat, the laundry, the fucking eggs! Everything! I'm fed up with it! And last night was all you, dude. Not me! I kept trying to get back to my bed, and you wouldn't let me. You gotta quit thinking I'm sabotaging you. Because believe me, the last thing I want to do is sleep with you!" She heard a thud. Possibly, his head landing despairingly against her door.

Holly went to the door and opened it gently to see his withered, apologetic face. With a heavy breath, she leveled him and said, "Thomas, I think we need to talk about these heavy nights of yours."

He appeared surprised. His chest heaved with humiliation. "You've seen it before?"

She nodded. "About four or five times. I wake up and hear you sobbing. I didn't want to embarrass you, so I haven't said anything. But every time, I go and sit on the stairs until you've cried yourself out."

"You sit with me?" His head tilted.

"I'm sorry. I'm sure you think it's some violation against your dignity, but I just couldn't leave you alone. I know you're in pain, and I feel horrible for you."

His mouth hung open, and he hesitantly nodded in acknowledgement. "Then you've truly seen me at my worst. It's been a problem ever since..." He held himself up on the doorjamb and leaned his head against his arm. "It's the only way I can mourn properly."

"Drunken crying?"

"I don't cry, you see. I didn't even cry at her funeral." He rubbed his face. "Drinking is how I can release all of this awful weight inside me."

Holly softened. She reached a hand out to offer him a comforting touch but retracted it. "I understand. We've all been there. Drinking to let our sadness out. But you can't go on like this. Especially when you involve me in it."

He nodded. "There hasn't been anybody but me in that bed since she's been gone. I know it's not your fault. But when I woke up next to you, I nearly had a heart attack." His eyes found hers. "I can't understand what would have made me do that—pull you into bed with me. I can't make sense of it, even with my addled mind."

"Well, maybe, just maybe, you needed to be held."

"It's indecent."

"It's human."

He regarded the floor. "You really held me while I cried?"

She nodded.

"I'm so ashamed of myself." He rubbed along his eyes with his hands.

"Would telling you not to be embarrassed change anything?"

Thomas shook his head. "So as long as you're not angry with me."

"No. At least, not anymore. I was feeling very flattered, actually. Until you yelled at me."

"Oh God. I feel completely awful that I raised my voice at you. You've been nothing but kind to me, and I behaved like a buffoon. You don't deserve it. And I don't deserve you." He tried to look at her but couldn't.

"The house is wonderful. The garden is beautiful. You even painted those little fences around the roses and the uh... The other flowers."

"Peonies."

His eyes found her face. "Yes. You've truly worked wonders here."

Holly took a moment to absorb his compliments. He'd even said *the roses* and not *Evelyn's roses.* Anyway, it was so nice to finally be appreciated. "You know what I think?" she asked.

"What do you think?"

"I think you need to get out of this house."

He shoved away from the doorway and shook his head. "No. Absolutely not."

"There's a little place I know of. They have good beer, and darts, and pool tables. Oh, and a shuffleboard table. It's never too loud or too crowded. I think we need to get out."

"I couldn't."

"You need to. Come on, it's Friday. It'll be good for you. God knows I could use a night out."

His sheepish eyes glanced at her. "Very well. But I promise you I'm not a very good time."

She grinned. "Well, I am! And if you really hate it, we can leave."

Thomas relented and nodded. A hint of levity lightened his face.

Holly braved a gentle touch on his arm, and her eyes looked right into his. "Would you like some broth?"

A weak smile spread across his mouth. "Why are you so nice to me?"

"You need someone to be nice to you. You're suffering. And I'm actually a nice person. Even when I have to push back sometimes."

"I deserve it when you push back." He studied her meekly. "I'm a hard man to deal with most of the time."

"Exceedingly." She chuckled.

His mouth gave a hint of his sparkling smile. "Yes, Holly. Some broth would be just the thing to set me right. Thank you."

After breakfast, Holly undertook her daily chores. She began with a light dusting of the furniture, a load of towels in the washer, and then swept the floors. By lunchtime, she'd done everything and wondered how to pass the afternoon.

"Thomas, would you mind if I played the piano?"

His head raised from his computer and turned to the side. Apparently, this was a big decision for him. He usually didn't mind her playing in the evenings. But it was the afternoon. Maybe it'd be too much of an disruption.

"No. I wouldn't mind. I love hearing you play."

Holly tapped the wall gleefully and went to the keys.

Thomas could barely move when she started playing. His breath caught as he heard her begin a pensive nocturne. Beethoven? He tried to pin it down. Perhaps it was Schubert again? He found himself leaning back in his chair with his eyes closed.

The notes perfectly floated through the air with such loveliness, it nearly brought a tear to his eye. Chopin. It had to be Chopin. She played him the most beautifully. His heart instantly beat heavily and ached in his chest. His pants tightened.

What on earth is happening to me? Every time she played, it made him hard. The last couple of weeks had been torturous. The delicacy of her fingers along the piano keys could be felt inside his body. He wanted nothing more than to pull her away from the instrument and ravage her right there on the piano bench. His stiffening cock pushed against the zipper of his trousers. *I can't keep masturbating every time she plays that damned thing. I've got to get a grip! Calm down, Thomas.* He'd done it three times this week already. Even daring to leave his office door cracked while stroking himself to ecstasy. His body throbbed with every note. *Shit. How am I going to spend an entire evening with her if this keeps happening?*

He decided a shower would be the thing and left his office. He walked gingerly through the living room, desperate to keep the tent of his pants from being visible to her, and went up the stairs to his bathroom. *A nice cold shower. That's just the thing. Should help my head as well.* He turned the water on and stripped. The shower's initial chill cooled his hot skin, and his erection faded. This was all beginning to feel inappropriate.

I should have let her leave this morning.

Holly pulled into Zeke's. It wasn't upscale by any means. A real working man's place. Blue collar through and through. But it was clean, and the staff were cheerful. She headed straight to the bar and ordered a couple of lagers. Thomas stood stiffly behind her. Holly handed him a pint and clinked her glass against his.

"So, what'll it be? Pool? Darts?"

"I actually quite enjoy shuffleboard," he told her.

She led him to the back, where the shuffleboard table was. Thomas sprinkled a fresh layer of sand on the playing area and positioned himself on the end with the blue pucks. The night went on, and the beer loosened him. When their game ended, Holly brought shots of whiskey.

"I thought you said I needed to calm down the drinking." He smiled at her.

Holly still couldn't get used to the sight of it. He had the most dazzling smile. Her heart danced in her chest.

"Well, the drinking and sulking alone, yes. But we're having a night out together. That's different." She raised her glass. "Cheers. To getting our shit together."

He let out a small chuckle. "Speak for yourself, missy. I'm still a complete shamble."

"No, you're not." She drank down the shot. "You just can't keep house for shit."

Out came that wonderful laugh of his. He drank his shot down. Holly kept watching his face. Was she staring? Crap, she was staring! What was even worse was that he was staring directly back at her. The air between them condensed.

"I think you won," she said.

"I definitely did." His eyes sparkled at her.

She nearly lost control of her knees. "The game. You won the game."

"Yes. That's what I meant, of course."

She took his shot glass to set their empties on the table. Her fingertips brushed his knuckles, and he inhaled through his teeth. He quickly turned from her.

"Shall we play again?" he asked.

"Yes, but this time, I'm going to kick your ass!"

"Oh, I'd love to see your attempt!"

Holly guffawed at him. Thomas being so relaxed was practically the best thing she'd seen since she'd arrived at his house. He was brilliant. He was even fun! "You set it up. I'll go get us another round." She went to the bar. As she stood waiting for their drinks, a man approached her.

"Buy you a drink, sweetheart?"

She sized him up. Blonde hair, mostly well built, with a bit of a paunch. Brown eyes. He had the look of a fun fuck-n-leave. If she'd been there alone, she may have entertained the idea of him.

"No, thank you. I'm here with someone."

"That guy? You can't be serious. He doesn't look like he knows how to handle a woman like you."

Holly was instantly self-conscious. "He's more of a gentleman than your daddy was."

The man laughed and reached for her back and caressed it.

"Oh, you're a spicy one. I like that. Come on, let me get you a drink. Show you what a real man can do."

"I said, no thank you."

"If you're fond of your hand, I suggest removing it from her person," came Thomas' voice.

They turned to him. He stood rigidly fixed and predatorial like the slightest twitch from his opponent would cause him to leap at him.

The man squared Thomas. "Hey, man, I'm just trying to buy the lady a drink. No harm in that."

Thomas matched the man's posturing. Unyielding, he leaned in slightly to express his dominance. "She said no. Now, please. I don't want to make a scene."

"You think you can make a scene? Buddy, I'll have you laid toe-up before you can raise that limp wrist of yours."

Thomas' eye twitched. Faster than anyone could notice, he flicked the man's nose with his fingertip. The stunned expression on the guy's face gave into fury, and he prepared to punch. Thomas quickly grabbed his wrists and held him in place.

Holly's heart pounded in her ears.

"I'd rather not ruin this evening for the fine people around us. Let's relax and move on, shall we?"

The man's body slowly relented, and he dropped his arms.

"There's no need for a tussle," said Thomas.

"I could-a dropped your limp ass."

Thomas grinned. "I can assure you, there's nothing limp about any part of me right now. And all of it is sharper than your cranium."

"My what?"

Holly snorted. "He means you're dumb, jackass." She picked up the lagers and handed one to Thomas. "Come dance with me. Let's show this jerk how a real man treats a woman like me."

Thomas took a deep swig of his beer, offered his arm to her, and sneered at the man. There was a fire in him that Holly had never seen before. How he handled himself! She had no idea he was capable of that. They set down their glasses, and he grabbed her into his arms.

Holding her against him, he proceeded to expertly lead her on the dance floor. She'd seen him dance with Evelyn a couple of times. He had the most perfect posture and just the right tilt to his head. He seemed to glide. Holly figured Evelyn was a natural glider, too. But much to her astonishment, she noticed her own body gliding. The slightest movements of his hands and arms nudged her body, telling it where to go and what to do next. The control he exhibited over her turned her into putty.

"You were amazing with that guy," she told him.

"I wasn't about to let that little twat-stain bother you."

She giggled. "Twat-stain. I didn't know you had it in you. Do even know how to fight?"

He looked into her luminous brown eyes. "I used to box in college."

"You did?"

"I dare say there's quite a lot about me you don't know."

Holly's body melted as he pierced her with his clear baby blues. She tried not to let him see that she was breathing deeply. Her skin blazed, and a tingle ignited between her legs.

"Holly... You're blushing."

Damn it.

Thomas brought her hand to his lips. "It's alright. How would you say it? It's human." His lips brushed the backs of her fingers.

Holly nearly gushed in her jeans. The song they were dancing to ended, and a new one began. Come On Get Higher, by Matt Nathanson.

"Oh, I love this song! Can we dance again?" Any excuse to stay in his arms would have done, but thankfully, she really did love the song.

Thomas kept her in his embrace. His arm around her back strengthened against her, bringing her closer to his body. His hips picked up and gently snapped with the tempo. A hand slowly descended to her belt line, helping her move with him. Holly's hips responded.

They were practically grinding, and she could barely stand it. Yearning for him to pull up her shirt and touch her skin, she lay her head against his cheek. Her hand around his back tenderly fondled his shoulder blades.

A gentle stubble grazed her temple. Rough. Something was rough about him, and it twirled her belly into a knot. He may have come off as reserved and proper, but she sensed a storm in him. She recognized his strength. Part of her would have almost liked to have seen him take on that twat-stain at the bar.

Is this chemistry? I think we have chemistry. She worked to interpret the responses exploding from her. Something in his touch. The masculine firmness with which he held her made her want to take a bite out of his neck.

Her mind drifted to that beautiful kiss they'd shared a month ago. Thomas was capable of such depth and passion. Her heart wanted desperately to explore it. Their bodies gently swayed, rubbing slightly against one another. A mound formed against her. *Is that? Is he? Aroused?* Her smile expanded. *So, he is mortal.* There was hope for him yet. The thought that she could affect him in such a way satisfied her immensely.

When the song ended, they slowed to a stop. Thomas didn't let her go immediately. Holly felt him ever-so-slightly nose her hair and inhale. *He's smelling my hair.* She pivoted her head, resting her nose against his cheek. If she moved anymore, she knew she'd go straight for his mouth. Desire for another heart-exploding kiss from him obsessed her.

Finally, he slid his hand from around her waist. They released each other and let their eyes linger for a moment.

"Game of pool?" she asked, faking composure.

"Rack them. We'll see if I can add a third game to best you at."

"Oh, I don't think so, Lancelot! This is something I'm actually good at."

He selected a pool cue and said under his breath, "You're good at a number of things." He may not have intended for her to hear him. But she did. Fire rushed up her spine.

Watching Thomas' form stretched out over the green felt table, sternly holding the pool cue, had her in a fit. She never noticed the fine muscles of his arms and back before. His ass wasn't bad either. Sometimes, he'd go for a run after breakfast, and Holly had no idea that simple jogging could keep a man in such good shape. His fingers gripped the cue with steady determination. She wondered how they would feel along her skin.

Thomas couldn't stop his eyes from flowing to her sloping cleavage as she bent over the pool table. Her close-fitting tank top stretched around her form, showing every bobble of her breasts as she took her shot at the cue ball.

When she stood, there was a display of the daintiest bump on each mound as her nipples pushed against the fabric. He choked on his dry throat and quickly grabbed his beer. His mind wandered to watching her swallow a shot. Those perfect lips rimming the glass and downing the liquid. Her bottom lip stuck to the glass for a millisecond of torture.

Thomas wasn't sure where to put these odd feelings of desire. They were thundering over him almost faster than he could keep up or contain them. He wanted to bite her bottom lip, rip off that tight tank top, and shove her to the floor.

He shook his head briskly, needing to rid his mind of the vision.

Holly's ball rolled directly into its intended pocket and sank. She walked around the table, gliding her beautiful long fingers along the rim. The fingers that made such fantastic music. Fingers that he envisioned gripping his shaft and made him want to come as she played Chopin. Fingers he'd grazed with his lips only minutes earlier. He wasn't sure if it was the right thing to do. But he had to kiss them. His mind took over, imagining his cum spilling over her fingers around his cock.

Goddammit, Thomas! What's gotten into you! Can't very well shoot pool with two poles!

Thomas urgently reached for his beer, and their dance floated into mind. He'd learned from experience that dancing was a good way to test the waters. And judging by her blushing response, she enjoyed their proximity. It took all of his restraint not to pull her fingers into his mouth and suck each one of them. Arousal began swelling in his pants. He drank his beer, trying to calm his burgeoning stiffy.

His mind seized on dancing with her. He had her in his arms. Holding her form against him was excruciating. He almost cupped her rear end. Thank God he'd stopped himself at her waist. Hopefully, it seemed intentional. When they finished dancing, he'd almost kissed her. He was losing control of himself. He remembered his sister's words. *"Don't kiss her again unless you mean it."*

What scared him to his bones was that he would have meant it. But things had been so tense, and he'd been such an ass. He couldn't take advantage of a tender moment on the dance floor. But she had hinted a few weeks ago that the kiss they'd shared wasn't all that unwelcomed. Perhaps she... *No. Why would she want you after you've been such a brut?* And yet she'd been so kind. So pliant on the dance floor.

He hadn't only felt her body responding to him, but her ribs expanding for more air. Could she have been in a state of slight arousal, too? Her eyes were soft. Her eyes were always soft. Soft, welcoming, and kind. And there was her tempting cleavage. Every time she bent over across from him to take her shot at the futile balls on the table, those pretty mounds bounced, and his brain along with them.

Holly bent over in front of him, presenting her heart-shaped behind, to take her next shot. The fabric of her tank top stretched along her waist and tucked into the denim that hugged her plump rear. Thomas found himself staring, breathless. A silver belt resembling daisies swathed through the belt loops. He pictured his fingers tugging the belt loops and bringing her backside hard against his hips.

"Woo-hoo!" she jumped excitedly, pivoting to him. "You may have got me at chess and shuffleboard, but I am wiping this pool table with your ass!"

He saluted with his beer glass. "Well done." *Am I sweating?*

Holly joined him and sipped her beer. "You doing okay? Having fun?"

Thomas couldn't look at her, unable to bear the sight of her pretty face staring up at him. He would come completely undone. He was sure of it. He stiffly held his beer.

"I have to say, I really am enjoying myself. This was a good idea."

"I'm so glad." She drank her beer. "It's still my turn, but I want another shot." She swaggered to the bar. He watched her swaying rump, unable to take his eyes from her, and when she swung around and caught him, Thomas fidgeted, trying to hide his hard stares.

Oh, Gods, he thought, *I've never felt this height of lust before. Even Evelyn was just a lovely thing until she was mine. But Holly... I'm going to lose my mind. This is new.*

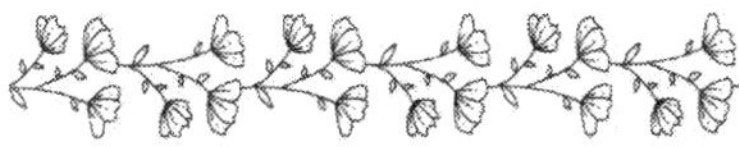

Holly ordered two more whiskeys and felt the heat of Thomas's gaze from the back of her head. She turned to see Thomas' shadowed eyes on her. A thrill rippled through her chest. Her nipples solidified. *Damn it. Should have worn a looser shirt!* While she brought the shots of whisky back to their spot, she held them high and subtly pressed her forearms against her breasts, desperate to get her nipples to relax.

His tense expression greeted her. Was he becoming agitated from being around all the people? Maybe it was time to get him home.

"You look a little uncomfortable. We can go after this game if you want," she said.

"I told you, I'm fine. I'm having a splendid time." He seemed to force a smile.

"You say that. But you don't look like it. I think we may have hit your limit."

Thomas tinked his shot glass against hers. "You are startingly more observant than I give you credit for."

It was nearly eleven, and even though she could have stayed until the bar closed, she knew it was time to go. Thomas' balance between mirth and seriousness had swung in an unfavorable direction. That couldn't be a good thing. They finished their pool game, and Holly went to pay the tab.

"No, please. Allow me," he said, pulling out his wallet.

"It's okay. I don't mind."

He regarded her flatly. "This is the first time I've been out socially in almost three years. I owe you. Please. It's the least I can do."

She nodded and took her card back from the bartender, who then ran his card for the tab.

"Make sure you tip her well."

He looked incensed. "Twenty percent, I believe. Is it not?"

"At least."

"I've got it." He tried keeping his stiff demeanor, but there was a pleasant curl to his mouth.

They were both silent on the drive home. Holly wasn't sure what to say. She couldn't stop thinking about how strong his arms looked. How tight his legs looked in his pants. The firm hold he had on her on the dance floor and how he controlled her movements. The way he stood up to that jackass. She opened her mouth to take in more air as her breaths deepened.

Rain started falling in little splats on the windshield, and she hit the wipers as it fell heavier. The sound was a welcomed distraction. A storm was beginning.

She knew he'd been stealing glimpses of her all night. Holly could feel every time his eyes were on her. It was like a gentle weight. Each time, her breasts swelled, hardening her nipples to poking nubs that she couldn't hide.

They silently entered the house, and both went for the stairs.

At the top, she asked him, "Are you going to watch the news tonight?" She wasn't sure why she asked him that. It was far too late for the evening news. She wanted a plan. Something else to do. Anything to keep spending time with him.

"It's late for that." He turned to face her, and her belly clenched. "Holly. I have to tell you," he hesitated, seemingly lost in her eyes, "I really had fun tonight. And you were so good with me. I'm not very good with crowds, you see. They've always made me a bit nervous. But you were... You were completely perfect. Thank you."

Holly reached out and took his hand. "Thank you for getting me out. I had fun with you, too." A compulsion she didn't question drew her closer to him. She leaned in and planted the most delicate kiss on his cheek. Perhaps a bit too close to his lips. She expected him to stiffen and protest. But he didn't. He was receptive. She heard his sharp inhale when her lips touched his skin.

He turned his face to her as she pulled away and brushed her lips with his. She stalled, letting their lips linger together. He slowly formed a perfect suction on her mouth, brought his hands around each side of her head, and tenderly parted her lips with his tongue. Holly's body went volcanic.

She let her arms sweep around him, feeling along his back and fondling the taut muscles through his shirt. His mouth moved along hers in a symphony of perfection. His tongue glided and swooped along hers. Tender fingers stroked along her cheek, jaw, and down her neck, leaving tingling trails on her skin. She whimpered.

He slowly pulled away and brought her eyes into his luminous blues as both of them sought to find their breath.

"I swear, if you apologize for kissing me again, I'm going to lose my mind," she said.

He stared at her in wide-eyed astonishment. "Oh, God, Holly. I can't seem to stop myself." He pulled her into him again, sending his magical tongue back into her mouth with a fervor that jellied her very bones.

He lifted her chin, angling her for a deeper kiss, smoothly gripping her body to his and holding her up as her legs wanted to give out underneath her. His hands slid around her, feverishly pulling her closer. She felt his caress sliding down her backside and gripping her rear. Her clit throbbed in response to every dive of his tongue and movement of his touch. She thought her nipples would rip open her shirt. Her own hands daringly swiped hungrily down his hips to feel the firm rounding of his ass.

She felt her own shirt being tugged up, and hands found their way under it onto her prickling bare skin. The tickling of his strong fingers along her back caused a flutter in her lungs, making her head spin. A desirous touch made its way to her lace-covered, mounding breast. His thumb circled her nipple through the fabric of her bra as his hand clutched the soft flesh. Holly gushed.

Thomas held her to him desperately, slowing his kiss, but the intensity remained. He brought his hand out from under her shirt and caressed her face, gently pulling from her mouth. His eyes, heavy with desire, stared into her.

Through heavy breaths, he said, "I wasn't uncomfortable because of the crowd tonight."

"Why then?"

His fingertips continued their glide along her features. "Because of you. I was beginning to lose control. Wasn't sure if I could keep hiding how badly I wanted to do this." His mouth pressed wantonly into hers again, stealing the air from her lungs.

Has he been dreaming of me the whole time I was dreaming of him? Were his mood shifts just a self-defense mechanism like Janet said?

"God, Holly," he whispered huskily. "Should we stop?"

"Why?" Her eyes sent thick longing to him.

"Because if we don't stop now, I'm going to take you. I want you so badly."

Holly's whirling heart burst, sending needy vibrations through her. No words came to her mind or mouth. She released his body and took his hand. One step at a time, she forced her limbs to work and pulled him behind her to her bedroom.

Chapter 10
The Rhythm of Rain

Thomas stood in her doorway and watched her walk through the dark room. She turned on the small lamp at the little writing desk and opened a window to let the humid, fresh, rain-scented air blow in. Lightning flashed with thunder quickly behind it. She turned around and approached him. There was no hiding the tent in his trousers this time.

He kept his eyes on hers as she came closer. He was hypnotized. She reached down and pulled up the bottom of her tank top, lifting it over her honey locks, which spilled freely over her shoulders. He stared at her plump, lace-covered breasts. Next, she worked her jeans and slid them from her hips.

His fantasy was standing before him. He reached for his belt, every pump of his heart begging him to free his cock from the cotton restraint surrounding it. Thomas pulled open his trousers, knowing he was moments from actually having her beautiful fingers upon him. He nearly came just thinking about it. He walked from his fallen pants and moved closer to her.

Gently taking her hand, he placed her lovely fingers on the rod in his boxers. Its tip nudged through the opening of the shorts, practically pointing itself at her. Her perfect, long fingers found the aching shaft of him and stroked delicately down its length, bringing the fullness of his erection through the slit in his shorts.

Her fingers glided along it. His eyes rolled back. The pleasure of her finally touching him built in his loins and pushed up through his lungs. He released a deep groan of satisfaction. At last, her beautiful fingers were touching him.

He remembered he also had hands and brought them to her breasts, rimming the lace along the top of her bra. He stepped closer so he could reach the clasp behind her back and free her chest from the garment. Holly's hand ceased its marvelous dance on his hardness to let her bra fall. His eyes were immediately entranced by the most flawless pair of full, tantalizing breasts and the sweetest pert nipples.

He hesitantly brushed her bare skin, taking a breast in each hand. The silky, plump flesh yielded to his touch. Holly reached for his sides as if she was about to teeter. Her breath came heavier now. Her response encouraged him. She wanted him. How long had she wanted him? Why did she want him? What was happening? How was this beautiful, kind, vibrant woman wanting him to make love to her? *You're overthinking, Thomas. For God's sake, just enjoy her! Seize your Venus!* He continued working his magic on her lips until she moaned.

Holly's fingers worked the buttons of his shirt, and he let it drop. Then she pushed the elastic of his shorts down slowly, dragging her thumbs along the ridges of his hips and down his thighs until the shorts fell to his ankles. His heart couldn't be calmed. His mouth opened with a gasp when she sat back on her bed, wrapped her hands around his rear end, and brought his erection to her mouth.

He'd dreamed of this. Now, he watched as the real Holly's beautiful lips rounded the bulging crown of his hardness. Her warm, wet, impossibly soft suction brought him in, and he almost lost control. The firm, smooth texture on the roof of her mouth slid along his tip. Another groan drifted from him. He gripped her smooth shoulders as she sucked on him. Her back teeth gently grazed his tip. His pulse hammered into his erection as she glided, squeezing her lips along him. Every tight pull from her mouth and stroke of her velvet tongue was sweet agony. The urge to explode down her throat consumed him.

He knew she had no idea of the fantasies he'd played out in his head about her. How long he'd desired her hands and mouth on him. She had no idea that he'd come by his own self-gratification while listening to her playing the piano and dreaming of this moment. The reality of it was overloading him, and the need to come in her was costing him his sanity.

"You should stop," he barely rasped.

Holly pulled from his engorged erection. She scooted to the center of the bed, and he fell onto her. The wonder of her supple form underneath him brought him to the brink of madness. The way she spread and opened to him. His cock rested and glided against the heat of her crotch, meeting a satin barrier.

"Those will have to go soon," he huskily whispered into her ear.

She kissed along his chin until their lips touched. He needed to calm down, but her pulling kiss was making it impossible. He attempted to slow his breathing. If he entered her now, he'd blow immediately. Her fingertips skated along his skin, raising little bumps of pleasure everywhere she touched him. Thomas pressed his mouth against hers, wrapping her tongue with his as his hands fell upon the creamy mounds on her chest. Her nipples hardened between his fingers. He rolled them, pinching and encouraging pleasurable sighs from her throat.

He had to taste them and pulled from her lips to take a nipple into his mouth, pushing her downy breast against his face. His tongue tickled the solid nub, and she arched her back, displaying her lovely neck. He grazed the other pink bulb with his teeth, and she groaned. He sucked her breast into his mouth as her sighs and arching body began pulling a beast from him. *Slow down, Thomas. Slowly. Gently. Gods, above, I have to pace this.*

Thomas pulled the satin at her hips. She quickly took over, shoving it down and kicking it off her ankles. He pushed himself down her belly, nipping the tender skin, causing little gasps from her as he descended to the heat radiating from between her thighs. The most wonderful little pearl greeted him, protruding daintily through delicate, peach-fuzzed folds. *She must shave. Gods, it's delicious.* His fingers lightly brushed her clit, and he watched it respond to his touch as its color darkened. Blushing for him. *Beautiful.*

Running his fingers along the soft, welcoming folds around her opening, he watched his finger glide around the orchid of her body. He spread her silky fluid along her labia and clit until everything glistened. Holly's moans encouraged further exploration. He slowly pushed two of his fingers inside, fascinated as they disappeared into her. She grabbed his shoulders, gasping.

Penetrating her downy vagina was a privilege Thomas hadn't anticipated this night. But there he was, between her legs, fondling every delicate, luxurious fold of her most sacred place. He found a swollen nest of folds with his fingers inside her and rubbed it, knowing what it would do to her. Her hips lifted with the most marvelous, heated groan rising out of her chest.

The need to taste her overtook him, and he hungrily lowered his tongue to her slit, lapping her moisture. Musky and sweet, the enticing scent of her surrounded his nostrils. He licked the welcoming flesh. It yielded easily to his strong mouth as he enjoyed every tender offering of her with his tongue. Wet, warm, tight folds compressed his fingers as he explored her inside.

Holly tasted like nourishing mineral water and tangy honey. He sucked her moisture up greedily and stroked his tongue to her swollen clitoris. When he sucked it hard, the lovely little thing firmed in his mouth. She writhed around his face. Small squeals floated from her. Hearing her erupt was the most beautiful music of all. He wondered what she sounded like when she came.

Her fingers gripped his hair as she rhythmically pushed against his mouth. His body began to rage. He needed to be inside her. His pounding ache must be quenched.

"You're gonna make me come," she whimpered hotly.

More pleasing words could not have been spoken. As much as he desperately wanted to hear the music of her climax, he knew he'd rather feel her around his cock, pulsing and grinding when she came. He withdrew.

The perfect way he kissed her mouth was even more perfect on her clit. Holly's body consumed itself in fire and blistering euphoria. An orgasm teased in the background.

"You're gonna make me come," she breathed, barely clinging to reality.

He pulled away from her and crawled up her body. *Oh, God. This is it. He's gonna be inside me.* Thomas leaned into her form. She looked into his beautiful face. His brows clenched, full of intensity and longing. He stroked her hair and kissed her brows. The softness of his angelic lips along her forehead was conflicting with the raging hard erection prodding against her vagina. Holly brought a hand up to smooth his face, realizing he was trying to regroup.

"It's okay," she whispered, kissing his sweet lips. "You're not taking advantage."

A slight, affectionate smile spread across his mouth. He kissed her. "I want to know that we'll be alright... after."

Holly's body forced her to inhale. When had she last taken a breath? She continued enjoying the wonderful fragrance of rain and his pine cologne as she stroked his face. Her fingers feathered through his dark brown hair.

"I think we'll be okay. I've wanted you since the night you first kissed me," she admitted.

He blessed her with another heart-exploding touch from his lips against hers.

"It was the piano," he confessed. "Something about your touch. I can't explain it. Maybe even before then, but I'll be damned if I'll admit it." He grinned as she giggled.

"Are you nervous? You're hesitating."

"Shit, Holly. I could drill a hole in stone with this thing." He pushed against her, confirming his point.

She nearly came from the pressure of it and groaned.

"If I'm being honest. I'm trying to breathe for a moment. I've been fighting my explosion since you started undressing. I'm afraid I won't last. I couldn't bear disappointing you." He kissed along the ridges of her lips. "I'm capable of pulling out, but God… I won't want to. But I can, if need be."

"You haven't even gotten in," she teased, nipping his lips. "I'm ok, you know. In *that* area. You won't have to pull out." Holly kissed him again and continued strolling her fingers through his hair.

"That's good since I haven't any condoms in this house. No reason for them. And I completely didn't expect this to happen." His hips slid along her, shooting quivers of desire through her loins.

She widened her legs, drawing her swollen clit along his cock. She plunged her tongue into his mouth for his fabulous kiss. It was in the way he moved his jaw. Opening and nearly closing. Pulling every movement from her own mouth, he worked her tongue, triggering butterflies in her stomach.

She wrapped her arms around him and pushed on the firm muscles of his buttocks, encouraging him. The thought of him filling her with his ample hardness broke her mind. She longed for him to be inside her.

He whispered against her lips, "I've wanted you in ways you cannot imagine. And now I'm finally going to have you. I can't wait to hear you come."

Holly disintegrated.

Lightning flashed, and thunder rolled around them as the rain continued pummeling outside.

His hand descended, took his shaft, and guided it into her. His arms swept around her as he pushed in. Holly's hips met him hungrily. Her opening constricted him tightly, nearly preventing his full entry. She tried calming the strength of her inner muscles to allow the bulging head of his cock to part her and plunge into sweet agonizing wonder inside of her. She felt every shape of him lunging deeply in until he filled her completely.

Satisfaction pulled a sigh from her. "Oh, Thomas."

Thomas kept his eyes steady on hers, kissing her occasionally while finding a rhythm as gentle and insistent as the thunder in the background. She dug her heels into the mattress, surging with the swells and dips of his movements. Lightning flashed. The storm was intensifying.

"Jesus, Holly." His chest heaved as he smoothly dove inside her. "You feel like pure silk," he groaned, sinking his hips into her and meeting her lips for another kiss.

Electricity pulsed through her. Holly's mind whirled. *It's Thomas... How is this Thomas?* The pace of his kiss and thrusts increased, escalating the pleasing friction of his hard girth.

Pine-scented cologne consumed her as if they were making love in a forest. Holly ground against him, triggering an eruption she hadn't experienced in so long. She was close. And by the sound of his heavy breaths, so was he.

Her sounds sharpened in his ear. Thomas slowed his movements to the most unbearably slow undulation. Deeply grinding, he controlled her ascent to excruciating pleasure as he created her orgasm one sublime plunge at a time. Wave after wave mounted from the friction of his swollen crown pushing inside, receding, pushing...

"Oh, my God! Thomas!" Squealing, she dug her nails into his back. Her body blew apart in mounting spasms until the universe exploded around her.

Thomas sped, churning into her seizing muscles until his gasps pitched, and he called out. The sound of him climaxing was beautiful. Everything about Thomas was beautiful. The graceful way he made her come. His relentless hips, his erection exploding and filling her. His strong hands dug into her skin as he rushed her in his delirium. How he slammed into her ferociously as he finished.

His mouth pressed against hers as they caught their breaths and relaxed. Thomas caressed her face, staring into her eyes. Lightning flashed again, but the thunder was slower to rumble. The storm was moving away.

"You're so... so beautiful, Holly."

She grinned like a ravaged idiot at him. "I can't believe this."

"I can." He caressed the side of her face. "You are my Persephone. Doomed to serve me and fated to make me love you."

Holly kissed him. *Was that what happened? It was.* She'd been laboring away in his house. A place laden with death. Surely, he was Hades. Moody Lord and Master of darkness and sorrow. Until she came, cleaned it all up, and charmed him.

She decided to ignore the fact that he just said he loved her. Surely, that was his loose post-orgasmic brain rattling around. Better to not make a fuss. Holly only wanted to indulge in this blanket of complete satisfaction and relaxation. She could feel his cock shrinking and reached for the box of tissues near her bedside. She brought them over.

"Here," she offered.

"Thank you." He took a few and pulled out of her. She shoved some tissues against herself, catching the results of his explosion. Thomas rolled away to the side of her. After he cleaned himself, he ran a tender hand along her belly and breasts.

Holly finished cleaning herself and stretched, enjoying his luxurious caresses. Her skin, being extra sensitive now, rippled with sweet tickles at the slightest touch from him.

"Can I sleep next to you tonight?" he asked hesitantly.

"I'd like that. But you have to promise not to freak out in the morning."

His mouth curved upward. "It won't make sense at first, waking up holding your exquisite nakedness. But I'm not drunk. And if I forget one second of tonight, I'll never forgive myself." He pushed up and kissed her again. His face swept down to her chest, and he sucked her breasts again. "I can't seem to get enough of these wonderful things," he teased.

Holly giggled. "Take as much as you want."

Chapter 11

Deceptive Cadence

The unfamiliar smells accosted him first. Thomas' eyes flew open. A woman's head of soft, honey waves lay in front of him. His arm was around her naked body as she lay curved against him. He pressed gently into the skin of her belly. Soft, warm, and sweet smelling. Holly.

He rose up on an elbow and daintily kissed her ear and down her shoulder. Images of her clamped eyes as she came entered his mind. The groans she made that ended in sharp squeals as her climax took her. The way she clenched around his hardness and those beautiful breasts bouncing in the lightning flashes.

His nether stirred. His cock began pressing into her backside.

It had been at least two years since he'd made love. Evelyn couldn't endure it during the final year of her illness. And honestly, it was the last thing on his mind while he tended her. The awful feeling of just having slept with a woman who wasn't his wife rampaged through him in sickening waves. The unpleasant prickling along his skin distracted him from what should have been a lovely moment.

Very carefully and slowly, he pulled away from her body. She stirred but didn't wake. He shifted out of the bed as deftly as a cat. Once on his feet, the cool air in the room met his bare skin and was still heavily scented with rain.

Thomas quietly padded around the bed, picked up his discarded clothes, and left Holly's room for his own. He tossed his clothes in the hamper and dressed himself in clean pajama pants and a t-shirt.

A mixture of fulfillment and anxiety tumbled through him, turning the inside of his chest into a puree. The glow from making love to Holly still thrilled him. Every time a flash of her passed through his mind, his heart gave an extra hard thump, prompting a smile.

But there was the damned shock of it. She was safely distant, and suddenly, he was consumed by her. And what of her feelings? Would she be alright? Would their dynamic change? He'd come to rely on her for the stability in his home. A stability Evelyn used to provide.

Evelyn. His eyes inadvertently strayed to her side of his bed. The pristine decorative pillows lay as an almost perfect memory of his devotion to her. He couldn't look at them, fighting a tremor of sorrow. He sought the view out his window instead, thinking of how bright and lovely the day looked outside.

His old English Tudor was a home again. Holly was a tonic for life. As much as his heart nagged him with shadows of Evelyn and how he'd just made love to another woman, he felt released. The bonds of his past loosened and seemed to fall away in the brilliant light of Holly's presence.

Thomas needed to distract himself and let his turbulent mind settle. He decided to brew some coffee and have a look at his manuscript. If last night was a fluke of passion, he would accept it as a beautiful gift. But in his truest self, he hoped it was the beginning of something. And he dearly wanted to do nothing but plunge back into Holly again. Though at the moment, he knew that no words could describe the boiling of his heart.

Holly awoke. She had fallen asleep with Thomas wrapped around her. The morning air was heavy with the fragrant remains of rain and wet tree bark. Her lungs filled with the splendid aroma, and she stretched with a sigh. Thomas wasn't next to her. She hoped to wake up with him behind her, hard and ready to make love again. But she was alone. She rolled over and stared at the dent his head left in the pillow next to her. The pine scent of his aftershave lingered there. *Oh, God... What if he regrets it? That would be just like him. Boil over with passion and then flip out. Just great.*

She pushed up from the bed as her mind grappled with his hot and cold nature and grabbed her robe, pulling it around her body. If he didn't like the sight of her in the little robe, then he could just get stuffed. Holly hoped that wasn't the case. With all her heart, she hoped she was wrong. Maybe he'd simply gotten up and wanted coffee. She was probably overthinking. However, she had to admit that it was a sudden coupling. She decided to be as open-minded as possible and girded herself for his response to her. Whatever it may be.

She went down to the kitchen, where a pot of coffee waited. She poured herself a cup and added milk and sugar. The tapping of keys on a computer keyboard could be heard from his office. At least she'd located him. As if he'd be anywhere else. She leaned heavily against the counter. Her mind spilled over with memories of his wonderful kiss and superb cock inside her, bringing her to delirium. A flick of warmth pulsed in her clit. If she couldn't have him again, it would break her heart. Halfway through her coffee, she decided to find out and pushed from the counter to pad towards his office.

Holly leaned against the doorjamb. "Good morning," she greeted pleasantly but as neutrally as possible.

He kept his gaze forward.

"Good morning." His tone was congenial but hardly affectionate.

Shit.

"Listen, uh," she took a much-needed deep breath, "if you think last night was a mistake, I'll understand. I don't want things to get weird between us."

He stopped typing and looked out his window, saying nothing back.

She tapped her coffee mug with her fingertips. "Alright, then. Got it. I'm gonna go take a shower." She turned and made her way to the bathroom, rejection stinging her with every step to the winding stairs. How was it possible? They weren't drunk. He was so clear and determined. *"It was the piano,"* he'd told her. He'd wanted her for a while; he'd made that clear enough.

Maybe he was scolding himself for giving in. Upon reaching the bathroom, she turned on the water and set her coffee mug next to the sink. Then it occurred to her. He hadn't been with anybody since the last time he was with Evelyn. Was he in shock or feeling guilty? He probably needed time to process it. Maybe he was struggling with the fact that he was still a human man with needs and desires. Holly wondered if he really wanted her or if she simply happened to be the nearest available female. *It figures.*

His words floated through her head. *"You're my Persephone. Doomed to serve me and fated to make me love you."*

"Well, whatever. At least it was a good lay." In fact, it was a fantastic lay. No, it was more than that. It was an incredible experience in seduction and lovemaking. The most intense, erotic desire and satisfaction she'd ever experienced. He was... mind-blowingly good. Holly smacked herself on the cheeks. "Snap out of it, dear. Time to come back to earth." She heaved a sigh. "Fuck. I don't want to come back."

Pulling off her robe, she stepped into the large, square, stone-tiled shower. She washed her hair, sinking with the worst tugging sensation in the pit of her stomach. She liked Thomas. Really, really, really liked him. Every tortured, lovely, brooding, passionate ounce of him. And every level of whatever this dejection was sucked. She rinsed her hair, resisting the urge to cry. Her chest caved in and fluttered uncontrollably, and some tears came anyway.

A dark form approached the frosted glass of the shower door. She stilled, watching it, and hugged her arms around her body. The door opened slowly. Thomas stood before her. His eyes did a sweep down the length of her wet, naked body. She hoped he couldn't tell the shower water from her tears. He sighed, and his expression softened, taking the sight of her in with an affectionate smile.

"Last night was not a mistake," he said simply.

Holly's ribcage filled with a sudden rush of air. She finally realized he wasn't wearing any clothes. He stepped into the shower and closed the door behind him. In an instant, he had her in his arms, pressing his amazing kiss into her mouth. She melted against him, sobbing. Every fiber of her exploding in thankful relief. She didn't realize how afraid she was that he'd reject her until her body trembled uncontrollably in his embrace. Her arms wrapped around him.

"I was afraid you were having second thoughts," she managed between breaths.

"No second thoughts," he said quietly. "This isn't a mistake. This is life returning." He dipped his talented tongue between her lips again. When he pulled from her mouth, his eyes sought hers again. They were full of hope. "I couldn't say anything earlier. I don't understand why. Couldn't find the words, I suppose. There's so much happening inside me."

"I know the feeling." Gentle laughter erupted from her.

"If this feels half as strange to you as it does to me, then you don't know what to do next, either." He lay sweet kisses along her wet face. "Do you want to know what happened when I woke up naked, holding you in my arms this morning?"

She nodded.

"I stared at you. I looked at every curve of your pretty face." He tenderly caressed her face with the backs of his hands. "I kissed your ear and along your shoulder and arm." His hands stroked lightly down her shoulders and arms. "I smelled your hair, and I could smell us and the rain from the storm, and I was overwhelmed by all of it." He placed his hands on her back. "The memory of making love to you, with you, only a few hours before. It was all so enormous, Holly. I couldn't take it." He brushed his fingers along her back as he spoke.

"Did it scare you?" she asked.

"A little. I wanted to have some quiet time alone. So, I got up, made some coffee, and thought about things in the kitchen."

"But no regrets?"

"No. Not a shred. But I had to reconcile these new feelings with my old ones. And when you came into my office, I can't describe what froze me. I think I was worried that I'd upset you, and I couldn't deal with your emotions as well as mine." He lay a sweet kiss on her lips. "But I'll be damned if I hurt you, Holly Reynolds. Just know that it may be a bit rocky from time to time while I adjust to this."

Holly ran her hands along his firm buttocks. "And this is something you'd like to adjust to, also?" She gave his bum a squeeze, indicating her desire.

His smile spread. "Oh, yes."

Her own grin took over. "Wake me up. Make love to me again."

Confusion passed behind his eyes.

"The next time you wake up overwhelmed and don't know what to do. Wake me up. Make love to me. Let me help soothe your mind."

"Noted." He pulled her fingers to his burgeoning erection.

She began stroking it. "I want you," she blurted.

He smoothed down her wet hair. "Then have me." He kissed her again and pushed her against the tiles at the back of the shower. Pulling up her leg around his hip, he sent his newly formed steel hardness into her. He clasped her rump, supporting her as he slid inside.

Their arduous gasps echoed in the room. He cautioned her, "I should warn you, though," he spoke in between breaths, "I fall fast, and I fall hard. And I never look back. Once I want something, I'll seize it with everything I've got." Dropping his chin, he looked hopefully into her eyes. "It may overwhelm you."

She could barely register his words as the pleasure of him filled her and pulsed in her body.

"I can take it," she managed. Her lips tugged at his, nipping and sucking until she had his tongue dancing along hers again.

Holly pulled a maxi dress over her head. After their blissful shower together, Thomas had gone to his room to dress. Her body was still humming joyfully from him, and she already couldn't wait to feel him again. He was intoxicating. Now, she had to figure out what to do with the day. Thomas would no doubt be in his study, editing. Her stomach rumbled. Breakfast. Or brunch, by now. She went down to the kitchen and pulled out the bag of English muffins and the eggs.

Heavy caressing hands smoothed around her body. He had approached her from behind to embrace her. His touch sailed down her belly, fondling the crease of her legs. She leaned back into his arms, resting her head against his clavicle.

"How about something different for breakfast?" he suggested, smooching her temple.

"Like what?"

"I don't know. Surprise me."

"And his Lordship won't disapprove?"

He sighed heavily. "His Lordship requests that her Ladyship make whatever she wants to make." He nibbled her ear. "And he will eat it."

Holly giggled. "Alright. How about me on a plate?"

"That sounds perfect." Thomas kissed her cheek, pulled away from her, and smacked her bum before heading to his study. She yipped and turned to watch him walk through the living room. There was something vastly different about him. He was... swaggering. Nearly floating. Quite a change from his usual heavy, disapproving steps. She wondered if she had sexed all the stuffy Englishman out of him. Although that would make her sad. She was starting to adore how proper he was. She even developed a mild fondness for how cranky he could be.

When breakfast was ready, Holly entered his study with a plate of French toast topped with melted butter, and blueberries sprinkled around with a little cup of syrup on the side. She brought it in and set it on the one clear spot there was on his desk. He never stopped reading and typing, barely eking out a "thank you" as she left. She finally understood that he wasn't being rude. He was just that engrossed in his work.

"Wait," he called. "Come here."

She did so, tummy fluttering. He ran his hands along her haunches and kissed her belly. "Thank you." He looked up at her. She bent down to kiss him.

"You're welcome." She kissed him once more. "That's the first time you've thanked me for breakfast."

His mouth lifted in a smile, a hint of recognition in his eyes. "I'm a work in progress, Holly. Adjustments must be made."

She grinned and left him to his work. She ate her own French toast and cleaned up the kitchen. Most weekends, she'd sit and read. But she was restless today and needed something to do.

Perhaps it was the excitement of a new blooming love that had her jittery. She went up to her room, where her laptop sat on the little writing desk by the window. The ruffled bed caught her eye. A vision with flashes of lightning illuminating Thomas' face as he moved slowly above her, moaning in his heat, played in her mind. His talented tongue... She salivated.

She should make the bed. That's something to do. The faint scent of them lingered on the sheets. A hint of his pine cologne and her flowery perfume mixed with the earthy fragrance of evaporated sweat. She made the bed in a daze.

Absently, she went to sit in front of her laptop. After checking her email, she idly scrolled through news headlines when an ad popped up for the local symphony orchestra. The Dayton Performing Arts Alliance. They were starting their outdoor summer concert series.

She clicked on it and looked at their playlist. Mozart, Vivaldi, Beethoven. The usual suspects that could be expected for a summer concert series. A sentence at the bottom caught her eye. *"Play with us! Some openings available! Click here."*

Something inside her snapped and jolted her. It had been so long since she'd considered playing for an orchestra. The articulation of her damaged hand had been returning nicely over the last couple of weeks. But was she "symphony ready?" She found herself clicking the link and reading about the openings. Finding a gig as a pianist was difficult because there was only ever one spot in any orchestra available.

Sometimes, there could be two if they had a duet or swapped out. There was always theater, ballet, and opera to play for. If nothing else, she could submit herself for consideration and maybe get a few nights filling in here and there. That might be a nice start.

Returning to her old dream hadn't seriously crossed her mind in over ten years. But something inside her was awakening. An old longing suddenly stirred up fantasies of performing again. *What am I thinking? I'm not back to concert form! What on earth makes me believe I could possibly apply for this? It's been so many years.* Before she knew it, she was hunting down cats playing piano on YouTube.

The sun was telling her it was the afternoon now. Holly looked at the time. 3:30. She closed her laptop and went down to Thomas' study. Tapping her knuckles gently on the doorframe, she asked him, "Would you mind if I played for a while?"

"Holly, you don't have to ask my permission. Just please go forth. You know I love listening to you. Oh, and here." He held up his empty plate from brunch. "Can't remember the last time I had French toast. It was delightful, thank you."

"Delightful? I got a 'delightful'!" She took his plate and turned to leave.

"Wait. Come here."

She did so as her stomach filled with butterflies.

He pulled her down to kiss him. "You must come and kiss me frequently. My lips get dry when you're away. Can't bear dry lips."

She curtsied. "If his Lordship commands it."

"He does." He pulled her down again for another smooch.

She floated to the kitchen, deposited his plate, and sat in front of the piano. Nothing came to mind. She'd played her own personal memorized repertoire so many times now. The longing for something new tugged her restless mind. Most pianists kept song books in their bench, so she stood and opened the bench, the inside of which revealed a treasure trove of sheet music and books.

She rifled through them. All the classics were there, and some contemporary arrangements. She selected one that said, "*25 of the Best Sonatas and Nocturnes.*" She set it on the music stand and opened to the first song. Mozart. It's always Mozart. She read the piece first, attempting to blow the dust off of her brain cells. She recognized it, positioned her fingers, straightened her back and sank into the keys.

Thomas listened to the notes ringing out with uncertainty. Not Holly's usual confident style. After her first run-through, she played it again, this time with that passionate lilt he'd come to love. He allowed the notes to flow into him as he read through and made corrections to his manuscript. The song was cheerful with changing tempos. *Must be a sonata.* A familiar part of the melody jogged his mind. *Mozart?* The next song was Beethoven. The next was Liszt. Then Schubert.

How did he know exactly what song she would play next? *Wait, is that Evelyn's music book?* He pushed up from his desk and stood in his study's doorway. Holly sat playing with a spiral-bound book in front of her. Yes. He'd gotten it for Evelyn for Christmas shortly after they were married. The image of Evelyn sitting and playing flickered in and out of Holly's presence at the piano. His heart thundered through his body, and his forehead broke out in a sweat. On weakened legs, he caught himself against the doorjamb.

Holly heard him thud against the doorway. She stopped abruptly and turned to find him in the midst of an anxiety attack. She rushed over to him.

"Thomas! What's wrong?"

His heart was breaking in his chest, but he'd be damned if he let Holly feel bad. "I'm sorry. I don't know what happened. I'm alright."

Her arms were around him, helping him stand.

"I told you your playing affected me." He made a feeble attempt at a smile for her.

But Holly's scrutinous eyes fixed on him as if she knew better.

"It wasn't that good. I haven't played that song in ye— Oh, God! It's Evelyn's songbook. Shit! I'm so sorry! I should have asked!"

The look of horror on her face crushed him. This couldn't go on. He couldn't continue like this. "No, no. Please don't feel bad. It's music." He ran a hand across his brow. "I can't expect to go through my life not hearing it. Or banish it from my life because it was something she played. That's ridiculous. It was around for hundreds of years before she was. It's unrealistic. You go on and play whatever you want from that piano bench. I need to learn to deal with this once and for all." He held Holly's sweet, concerned face. "It's time I moved on."

The loveliest smile spread across her perfect lips, and her fingers wrapped around his wrists. "Do you really mean it?"

"God, Holly, if we're sleeping together, I'd better. Don't you think?"

She giggled. To his ears, it was the sweetest little tumbling noise. The wonderful softness of her mouth met his. "I'm glad."

"Perhaps you could... play them out of order. Just until I get used to hearing them again."

"I can do that." She kissed him once more and resumed her posture at the piano. Thomas returned to his computer and listened to her relearning other pieces. What were the odds that he'd fall for two piano players in a row? Of course, for Evelyn, it was more a hobby, like knitting. But for Holly, it was a passion. When she played, one could tell it was the reason she'd been put on this earth.

After Holly made her way through "*25 of the Best Sonatas and Nocturnes*," the sun was hanging lower in the sky. She needed to give her fingers a stretch and a rest. It was getting close to dinnertime. She went to Thomas' study. He was shutting down his computer. *Shutting down his computer? That thing never goes off!* What was he up to?

Holly asked him, "Would you like me to cook? Or shall we order something?"

He walked to her and slid his arms around her waist, cupping her rump. "I was thinking we'd go out." He stopped her breath with a beautiful kiss and pulled her against his body. Her arms found their way around him. A bulge poked her abdomen. He pushed his firm excitement into her.

"What's this?" she teased.

"Do I really have to explain it to you?"

She released a giggle. "No, I know what it is. Why is it?"

"I told you that your playing affects me. This has been happening to me for weeks."

"Goodness." She kissed his lips. "No wonder you were ready to pounce on me last night."

"And this morning. And... now."

She stroked his cheek, raising her eyebrow. "Even after you had a flashback?"

"Shhh... I'm fine. Adjustments must be made. And you are before me—in all your beautiful melody. I must have you."

"Oh, your Lordship," she cooed.

His eyes adopted a seriousness that silenced her. In a deep, husky voice he whispered, "My Lady." He bent her back, clasping her firmly and bracing her against the power in his need. Holly's bones dissolved. He held her and guided her to the couch in the living room. He quickly pulled open his trousers and sat down.

Holly stood before him and lifted her dress, feeling the hem caress her thighs. She wore nothing underneath. Holly set a knee on either side of his hips, straddling him. Thomas pulled her abruptly to the tip of his cock. The thrilling enthusiasm of his desire blew her body into an instant rolling fire.

"This is the first time I've been able to have you right after you've played. I've been satisfying myself with a dream of you. I'm no longer about to wait or take my time." He gripped her hips, pulling her down onto him.

She let her opening part, welcoming his length into her. Gently at first, then he plummeted hastily into her.

His grip on her haunches tightened as he bucked and pulled her against him enthusiastically, thrusting with breathy moans. She met every buck of his hips. Holly pulled down the top of her dress, allowing him to suck her breasts feverishly. His body pushed into her with a boldness she didn't think he possessed. His animalistic fire burned through her, consuming her completely to ashes.

Holly lowered her mouth to his for the hot blessing of his kiss. Something in the tone of his voice when he sighed and moaned prompted her vibrations. The sensation of him was more than enough. She rubbed her clit against his abdomen with every thrust, spreading tremors through her. But it was his vulnerable yet powerful groaning that really tipped her over the edge.

She churned in spasms, flung her head back, and cried in pure rapture. She rode him hard, squealing and smacking against him mercilessly until he grunted and seized, releasing and finally collapsed back against the couch.

Holly wilted over him, twitching. Whatever beast had lay dormant in this man was more than welcomed. She was literally dizzy and unable to remember her name.

Thomas' gentle hands guided her mouth to his for the tenderest kiss. "Your lips are cold," he whispered.

"Are they?"

"They were cold last night after you came, too."

"Were they?"

"Oh, dear. Two-word sentences. I'm afraid I've ruined you."

"So ruined." She sent her tongue into his mouth for another kiss. "I'm ravaged utterly," she sighed. "I never would have guessed you could be so ... aggressive."

"I told you, Holly. There is a great deal about me that you don't know."

"I didn't realize Chopin made you an animal."

"It wasn't the Chopin. It was how you play Chopin. What was that last one?"

"Impromptu No. 1 in A flat major."

"Oh, God, I love it when you talk dirty!" He launched and bit her neck. She squealed, laughing.

Holly chose the most torturous dress she could find. It was a shiny, skintight, strapless mini-dress of sapphire blue. The color brought out the strawberry highlights in her hair and the gold flecks in her eyes. Thomas said he wanted to take her out for a proper date at a nice restaurant. She added a slight curl to the tips of her hair with her curling iron and did her makeup in light shades of earthy pinks. She dabbed lilac perfume around her body and donned her favorite heels. Grabbing her small, black handbag, she went to meet him at the front door.

She could feel him watching her legs descend until the rest of her came around the curving stairs. He wasn't breathing when she saw him. Holly was all smiles at his astonished face. The sight of him standing perfectly erect in a black suit was devastating. His hands were shoved casually in his trouser pockets, but his arms remained composed and stiff. She nearly lost her footing, trying to take in how handsome he was, looking dangerously like James Bond. He even had a touch of product glistening in his hair.

His eyes followed her every movement and caused that familiar swelling in her breasts. She suddenly became uncomfortably self-aware.

"Dear God, Holly. I think that dress is illegal in five countries." He gawked.

Her eyes rounded. "You don't like it? It's too much, isn't it?"

"I think there's hardly enough of it."

"You disapprove."

"I'm afraid I like it a bit too much. The ideas it's giving me could get me arrested."

"I can change."

"No. You're extraordinary. I'll just have to try extra hard to be on my best behavior."

"But this dress is designed specifically so you won't be on your best behavior." She stared brightly at him, batting her eyes.

He huffed. "You're a torment, woman. Come here." He blasted her with an astonishingly deep, toe-curling kiss while his hands glided along every curve of her. "You feel as good as you look. I can barely tell where the satin ends and your skin begins."

Holly's chest swelled as she tried to calm herself from his delightful assault. "I almost don't want to go to dinner, now." She laughed.

"Tsk, tsk. I have reservations. Come now, straighten yourself and get your perfect buns into the car before I have another go at you."

The restaurant was easily the poshest she'd ever been to. Dimly lit chandeliers, linen-covered tables, and servers in vests with bow ties. Thomas resumed his stiff demeanor as they were led to their table. He kept a hand gently on her lower back. The host went to pull out Holly's chair, but Thomas stopped him.

"I'll do that, thank you."

"As you like, sir." The host went and pulled out Thomas' chair. Thomas waited for Holly to sit and aided in scooting her in. He kissed her cheek and sat in his own seat. The host handed them small, leather-bound menus. "Anything to drink for you?"

"Can I have a glass of your port wine?" Holly asked.

"Yes, ma'am. For the Gentleman?"

"A martini, please."

"If you say shaken, not stirred, I will die right here." Holly giggled.

His brilliant smile flashed at her. "Dirty vodka."

"Yes, sir. I'll have those brought out for you. Darlene will be your server tonight. She'll be coming around with water and to discuss the menu shortly." The man whisked away.

"Never had anyone compare me to James Bond before," Thomas mused.

"I'm legit losing my mind." Holly grinned.

She could tell the flattery tickled him as he chuckled, holding a smile together. They opened their menus. Holly couldn't stop looking over her menu at him. Perfect sitting posture. Stiff neck and all. The level of gentleman that he was couldn't be properly defined in her mind. He opened every door, held her hand respectfully when he helped her from the car and offered his arm to her as they walked together. He was positively dashing. She'd never been treated like a real lady before. It was thrilling.

Thomas said, "If they have the duck breast tonight, I highly recommend it. Ah, yes, there it is."

"I've never had duck breast before."

"It's superb."

"Have you been here a lot?"

"It was Evelyn's and my favorite place. We used to come here every couple of months. She used to get the seared..." He caught Holly's furrowed brows and pouted lips.

She asked plainly, "Please tell me you aren't trying to insert me into your memories of Evelyn, Thomas."

He looked like a wall had fallen on him. "Oh, God. You've lain me quite bare, haven't you? I didn't even think of that. It was the first place that came to mind when I thought of taking you out. It's been a long time since I've been here. I missed it." His eyes darted away and down. "Now I feel foolish."

Holly remembered him telling her there may be rocky patches. She decided that must include some old habits. She reached across the table and took his hand. "It's a lovely restaurant," she comforted. "I'm glad you chose it. Gives me some insight into the things you really enjoy." She gave his hand a squeeze. "Next time, let's try someplace new. Maybe we'll discover our own favorite place?"

Thomas nodded and attempted a smile. Their drinks arrived.

The duck breast was indeed superb. A carafe of wine with dinner had them laughing and cheerful again. When they got home, Holly pulled Thomas by his tie to the back patio. "I have a surprise for you."

"Does it involve my tie? Because I have a couple of suggestions."

She snorted. "You, sir, are a dog!" She opened the sliding door and pulled him to where the hot tub sat. She uncovered it and turned it on. The lights brightened, and the water began churning.

"Look what you've done!" he marveled.

"Well, I didn't do it. I had a company come out."

He stared at it in wonder. "This thing hasn't run in almost two years. I never did have it checked after it stopped working properly."

"There was a clogged water jet and a broken heating coil. But other than that, it was just dirty."

Thomas gently let his hand glide along the bubbling surface of the water. "I got this for Evelyn right after her diagnosis." His words were wistful and choked. “The doctors said it would be good for her circulation.”

Holly slumped. Of course, it was for Evelyn. What wasn’t? She rubbed her arm, wondering if she’d ever be out of Evelyn’s shadow. Her presence was in and around everything in this house. His bed, the kitchen, the folding of the towels, the piano, the roses in the garden... everywhere. Even the damned restaurant he thought to take her to. Holly’s eyes wandered downward as she fought feelings of inadequacy. She would never compare to Evelyn. Making love to Thomas hadn’t changed anything. Her heart was singing, but his was still locked up in the memory of his wife.

Gentle, warm hands smoothed her arms. She looked up at him.

“Why are you pouting?” he asked softly.

“I’m not—”

“You are pouting, Holly. I know every single one of your expressions. God knows I stare at you constantly.”

Her sorrowful eyes took in his sweet, adoring face. “I don’t know how to put it into words. I don’t want to hurt your feelings.”

“I’ve brought up Evelyn again. That’s it, isn’t it?”

A stinging tear fell from one of her eyes when she clenched them shut and nodded. His fingertips stroked her face.

“You will never be Evelyn,” he said plainly.

“No. I won’t. And I’m constantly fighting her presence.”

“I know how that can feel.”

Holly gazed at his gentle smile. Now, she felt even worse. Of course, he knew all too well about his beloved Evelyn’s hanging, heavy apparition. Thomas pushed her chin up with his finger. “But Holly, there’s something more that you don’t realize.”

“What?” she sniffed.

“She could never be you.”

“What does that even mean? If she was here, she wouldn’t have to compete with me.”

“No. You’re right,” he said calmly, barely speaking above a whisper. His heavy lids remained downcast as he took her hands and watched his fingers stroke hers. “But my heart competes for you. I was clinging to the past until I was dead, too. Don’t you see?” He brought a hand up to cradle her face, stroking her cheek with his thumb. "You've brought all the vibrancy of life back to this place. Wherever I look now, I see your efforts." He swallowed.

"Holly's made the kitchen white again. Holly's got all the old, hanging dust gone. Holly's got the grass trimmed. Holly's got the picket fences and lounge chairs sparkling. Holly's got the hot tub working. Holly brings me tea and music. Holly has made this a home again." His enthusiastic eyes glowed at her. "It's all you, now. You are everywhere I look."

It was such a breathtaking thing to say. Her bottom lip trembled. His thumb stroked the tremor on her pouting mouth.

"And you've brought life back to me. I was in a spiral to hell until you came here and rescued me from the clutches of Charon himself."

"Who's Karen?"

"Charon is the boatman who ferries souls to the underworld. I'd given up. I probably would have drunk myself to death inside of the next year."

"No more late-night crying?"

"No more late-night crying." He caressed down to her shoulders.

Holly wiped her eyes. "Sorry. I'm sorry I'm being such a dope."

"You're not a dope, Holly. You're trying to figure this out just like I am, and—I know it's difficult for us both."

She nodded.

He ran his fingers through her hair. "Perhaps I should have better tried to control my lust. Taken a bit more time. I think this whole thing has taken us both by storm."

Holly's slender arms wrapped around him, and he returned her embrace, kissing the top of her head. "Just promise me something," she prompted.

"My word to Zeus."

She pulled away to better take in his strong, handsome features in the glowing lights of the hot tub. "Do not try to control your lust."

"Ha!" His wonderful laughter burst forth, and he bent his head to kiss her lips. "There's something you missed tonight. I've been waiting to see if you'd catch it."

"Shit. What is it?"

Thomas held up his left hand.

"Oh, Thomas!" she gasped. "You've taken off your wedding band."

"Time for new beginnings." He sent his articulate tongue into her mouth. Her body erupted. The warm acceptance of his embrace and the sensation of his hand holding the back of her head awoke her center with happy electricity. If he'd taken off his ring, it meant he was truly ready for something new. He was finally moving on.

"Does that mean you're on the market?"

He smiled. "No, I'm afraid not. You see, I've already met someone." His eyes leveled her.

"Oh, no." She feigned disappointment.

"It's true. It's still very new, but—she plays my heart as beautifully as she plays Chopin."

Holly melted into him with another kiss. "That's too bad. I was just looking for a sullen, perfect gentleman who writes about Greek myths and gets hard when he hears Chopin."

"That is astonishingly specific, young lady." His eyes glowed.

"What can I say, Thomas? I know what I want."

He pulled her into him again and brushed his lips along her jaw, setting off the butterflies in her stomach. "You really think I'm sullen?"

She snorted. A sparkle caught her eye. "Oh, look! Thomas! Fireflies!" The yard came alive with little yellow fairy-glows zooming around. She watched them flickering in wonder.

Thomas continued nibbling along her neck and shoulders. She felt the zipper on the back of her dress being dragged downward.

His husky whisper was hot against her ear. "As much as I love seeing you in this dress, I think I'd much rather see you without it."

"Will you get in the hot tub with me?"

"Can I have you on my cock?"

"Thomas!" She pulled away, grinning, staring aghast at the mirth in his eyes.

"What? It's a legitimate question," he defended with a devilish hint in his smile.

Her amusement creased her cheeks. "That's surprisingly crass for you."

"Oh, I beg your pardon. Would you prefer something more poetic?"

She threw her arms around his neck. "What have you got?" She spread her fingers through his hair at the back of his head.

Thomas held her and cleared his throat. His fingertips caressed the place where he'd already undone the zipper at the back of her dress and could touch her skin. Laying more kisses along her face, he spoke in a low, dewy tone. "Persephone, Persephone. Bring my springtime back to me. In darkness dwelling under graves, bring my love's eternal waves. A show of lightning bathe me in. For mine is yours, my heart to win. No moon nor flower nor budding fair can compete with honey hair." He ended with the softest kiss on her lips.

She was neither blinking nor breathing.

He finished with, "Or with the lovely gold flecks in your eyes."

"What's that from?" She sighed, hesitating to assume the obvious.

"I wrote it this morning. I'm thinking of putting it in my book."

"You wrote that?"

He came close to her ear. "For you, Persephone. You've brought the spring with you." He brushed his lips delicately across hers. "Do you like it?"

"I'm overwhelmed."

"Can I have you on my cock now?"

Holly burst with laughter. "I'd ride you all the way to Hades right now."

Chapter 12

A Dream of Summer

Holly woke in bed to the sensation of Thomas spooning her and undulating. His strong erection slid between the lower lobes of her rear end and nudged against her opening. She inhaled deeply, enjoying the sensation of his hard bulb pressing into her.

His arms held her; hands fondled her breasts, and his face nuzzled her neck. Sweet, hot breath flowed down her from his exhales. A graze of teeth along her shoulder ending in a nibbling kiss. One of his fingers made its way down and stroked her to wet arousal. Her sighs heated. He spread her and entered her from behind, holding her hip against his him.

The force of his erection filled her with delightful tremors. Her head curved back against his shoulder as she pushed back in response to his thrusts inside her. Pleasant waves increased and soared through her body. The gentle fire of him surrounded her. He took her wrist and gently placed her hand to her own warmth until she was rubbing her clitoris.

His arms were free to hold her more effectively as he thrust in harder. A rumble sounded in his chest. He held her firmly, still biting softly along her shoulder and neck. Holly increased the speed and pressure of her finger's circles on her clit and reached down further to touch his smooth shaft entering her wet opening. He groaned hotly in her ear. The sound of it sent shivers through her. She rubbed her palm against herself and sent her fingers along their joining and the phenomenal gliding of his cock.

When the shudders began for her, he was already coming. She was only a step behind him. His teeth on her neck bit down, sending her through the roof. They both gasped, meeting one another in blessed ecstasy. As their breaths slowed, they undulated slowly. Holly's body applauded.

After reaching for some tissues, she rolled over and kissed him.

"Oh, Holly, you were right. That's the perfect way to handle being overwhelmed when I wake."

"Mmmm. That was a proper good morning." She smiled.

"I love it," he said, still breathing heavily in recovery and nuzzling her with his nose. "It's a most brilliant way to start the day." He smooched her lips.

"I need to get the coffee going. And your breakfast. Wouldn't want you editing on an empty stomach." She began scooting away, but he held her and brought her back to the warmth of his bedspace.

"No. No editing. It's Sunday. Just us today. I think we could both use a day off from our routines. Maybe we can see a movie and have lunch. Something new."

Holly's grin brightened her already glowing eyes. "I'd love that," she said, meeting his lips. "But I still want coffee."

"Yes. There must be coffee. But only after I'm done coming down from that exquisite orgasm. Let me hold you a few minutes more." His arms smoothed around her rear, pulling her further into the cozy nest of his chest. She snuggled into him. The fragrance of pine, chlorine, and sex brought the events of the night before to the front of her mind. After she'd rode him in the hot tub, they languished, fondling each other and kissing until they were pruned. The hot tub was no longer Evelyn's. And neither was Thomas. He was hers now. Holly released a contented sigh.

They had coffee and a shower together, bathing each other's bodies. The intimacy building between them was like a delicious nocturne. Flirting, building, entrancing.

Holly checked movie times, and a few hours later, they were curled up together in the back of the movie theater, watching a matinee from heartthrob Marcus Hemming and up-and-coming star Lexi Ember. It was a heart-wrenching tale called *Blue Boy*. Holly lost herself in tears at the end. Thomas kept his arm around her. Then they went to a bistro for lunch, and Holly suggested a game of shuffleboard at Zeke's.

"No," said Thomas. "I prefer to be outside today. There's a nice park down the way. Let's have a stroll."

"A stroll..." Holly's eyes glistened at him. "I like it. Let's do that. Lead the way, your Lordship."

They arrived at a sprawling park around a pond. The lush emerald grass, newly mowed, greeted them with the fresh smell of intense green wonder. Birdsong was heavy in the air. Thomas held her hand as they strolled along a little path through trees, shrubs, and blooming flowers. His hand was warm and firm and so large it nearly swallowed up her delicate fingers. It felt nice. Holding hands. She couldn't think of a simpler pleasure.

They made their way back to his car. He opened the door for her and she plopped into the passenger seat. Holly looked at her phone. She had a missed call from Janet.

"Janet called me." Holly began to call her back when Thomas covered her phone with his palm.

"Please, don't say anything about us yet." His eyes pleaded with her. "I'm not ready to deal with her fountain of gush and 'I told you so's.'"

"What 'I told you so's'?"

He nearly flushed. "Um... we had a conversation some weeks ago about you. Well, it was right after you arrived. The first night when I lost my head and kissed you."

"Oh. I see." Holly couldn't hide her amusement.

"She pried it out of me, the wretched schemer. I can never lie to her. She can always tell when I am. I'm honest to a fault, anyway."

"You told her that you kissed me?"

He hesitated with a breath. "I did. I'm sorry, Holly. I couldn't stop myself. It was as though she already knew."

"But it's been five weeks since then. I'm sure—"

"Trust me, she's already onto us. She was onto us before we were."

"Ugh! That's true. She told me you were crazy about me a week ago. She said she could see it all over the both of us. She's way too shrewd for her own good."

Thomas nodded. "I know this may not mean anything to you or make a great deal of sense. But I've done nothing but lament my wife's passing."

"Yes, I'm aware."

"So, I'd like some time to figure out how to explain my, my um—"

"Me. Your relationship with me."

"My sudden fall. I want some time to think of how to explain things properly, and I'd prefer things to make sense."

Concern pulled at Holly's face. "You sound like you need more time to think about us and this."

"Yes. But please dial down your insecurity. I don't need time to think about you or us. I need time to think of the right words to explain it. You've made more sense than anything else has in the last year. But I've spent a lot of time ensconced in my own misery. I've built it all up, you see."

"You mean your dour, mopey, sour-puss personae?" Holly was smiling now.

Thomas responded to the sweet chiding in her eyes. "As you say. Yes."

"Janet's happy dance will only last a minute, and it'll be over. You know that."

"God, I hate it though. Could you just do me the favor of keeping it down for now? I'm only asking for a bit of adjustment time. I can't very well go bounding in all smiles and kisses. They haven't seen our process. You understand, don't you?"

She smirked at him. "I can do that. Christ, I don't even know how I'd tell her, either. I think it's best to wait. When we figure out what to say, we can say it together. Would that be okay?"

His relief was palpable. "Yes. That would be okay. You're so good with me, Holly."

She smiled pleasantly at him and leaned over to smooch the corner of his mouth. Then she called Janet back as Thomas pulled out of the park's parking lot. The lovely voice of her best friend hit her ears.

"Holly!"

"Janet!"

"How are you, love?"

"We're great."

"We?"

"Y-yes," Holly stammered. "You always ask how we're getting on. And things are good."

"Splendid! I'm so glad to hear it. Listen, I wondered if you and Thomas would come over next Sunday for a barbeque."

"Oh, that'd be fun. I know I'll be there. And next time I see Thomas, I'll ask him." Holly winked at him.

"Good. Eleven-ish. We've got the pool all set. So, bring your swimsuits. And bring potato salad. Ask him how Evelyn made it. He loved her potato salad."

Holly cringed. "I'll do that."

"Besides that, how have things been between you two? You haven't texted much."

"There isn't much to tell. I've started playing piano again."

"He let you play Evelyn's piano?"

"He didn't have a lot of choice," Holly said, taking in Thomas' sideways glance. "He was at a lecture, and I couldn't resist it anymore. And you know me, I lost track of time, and he came home and caught me."

"Did he have a conniption?"

"Actually, no. He seemed to like it."

Thomas grabbed her thigh and rubbed up to her hip. Holly sucked in a breath.

"So," she cleared her throat. "I have permission from his Lordship to play it now."

Janet's laughter tinkled out. "Oh, that's fantastic! He'll never admit it, but he has a thing for women who play the piano."

Thomas strode his fingers into her crotch and pressed. Holly stifled a gasp.

"You don't say."

"Well, anyway, I'm so glad you're back at it. NO! Jake! Put that down! I have to go. Love you. See you next Sunday." She hung up.

Holly placed her phone back in her purse. "Thomas, if you want me to hide this, it doesn't help if you start turning me on when I'm talking to her."

He chuckled impishly. "Just thinking of you playing piano turns me on. Anyway, what do you need to ask me?"

"Well, she wants us over for a barbeque on Sunday."

"Us?"

"Yes."

"That sounds rather coupley. She's on to us."

"She's so on to us. But we do live together."

"True."

"And she wants me to make potato salad. She said I should ask you how Evelyn made it."

"She did make good potato salad. But I fancy trying it your way."

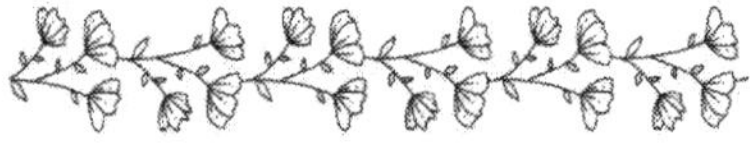

When they arrived home, Thomas pulled out a bottle of sherry. "Game of chess, my lady?" Holly blushed. Something about him calling her 'my lady' sent shivers all through her.

"Sounds good. Let me get out of these jeans."

"Would you like some help?"

"I'm sure I can manage." Holly kissed him. As she made her way up to her room, she was wrapping her head around the complete 180 that he'd done. He'd gone from being one of the most intolerable asshats she'd ever had the displeasure of dealing with; to the most loving, warm, seductive, pleasant, beautiful... And this must have been within him the whole time. Just bottled up in a jar of sadness and despair.

How had she never seen how good he was before? Maybe she had. She replayed memories of him dancing with Evelyn. Laughing with her. Being tender with her. Holding her hand. It was always there. In his natural state, he was like a clam; tight, closed off. He seemed to need a good woman to shuck him. Holly giggled. She changed into a maxi dress and met him at the chess table.

"Would you like to play some music? Something from the collection on your phone?" he asked.

"Really?"

"Yes. What do you listen to when you aren't contemplating the classics?"

"I'll be right back." She retrieved her cell phone and pulled up her favorite channel.

Matt Nathanson's "Come on Get Higher" began playing. Thomas set up the chessboard, and his eyes twitched to the side.

"I remember this song. Why do I remember this song?"

Holly regarded him with a sweet smile. "It's a song we danced to when I took you out to the bar."

Thomas' blue eyes fogged over. "Ah, yes. The first time I held you." He rose, pulled Holly into his arms, and commenced dancing with her. "I almost kissed you then."

Her eyes flew to his with a smile in them. "On the dance floor?"

"Yes. It was unbelievably hard not to."

"I'm glad you didn't stop yourself when we got home."

"I was beyond saving by then. And I won't tell you what I was thinking watching you bend over that pool table."

"Something else you acted on when we got home?"

"I haven't bent you over anything yet. But now you've got me thinking." He kissed her and tenderly took her bottom lip between his teeth, pulling it lusciously and sending a tingle down her spine.

They spent moments of lovely time staring into each other's eyes. Their bodies, pulled by their own attractive gravity, closed any space between them. All Thomas did was slightly lower his head, and Holly's mouth was there on his in an instant. She sought his muscular tongue. He gripped her body joyously. The lightning in their touch sizzled around them. When the song ended, Thomas released her.

"I will think of you every time I hear that song now."

She giggled. "I've ruined it for you."

"No more than you've ruined Chopin for me."

Holly's head flew back with a hearty laugh. "Are we going to play chess or what?"

Thomas' eyes spent one more moment smoothing his hands along her back and rump. He sighed. "Yes. Let's."

A couple of games later, after Thomas had wiped the board with her both times, she stretched.

She said, "Well, I think I've had enough of losing for one night. I'm feeling snacky. I'm going to find something to munch on." She rose, kissed his temple, and went down to the kitchen.

She found some baloney and made a sandwich. Thomas joined her.

"Nothing for me?"

"You don't like baloney."

"No. But I adore how you are so fulfilled by simple things, like baloney."

She smiled through her chewing. "I can make you some tuna salad."

He grinned at her. "No. Don't want to trouble you. It's our day off. I believe there's a bit of salami left?"

"In the meat drawer."

Thomas made a sandwich. Holly sliced up a cucumber, and they dipped it in blue cheese dressing while they ate their sandwiches. Thomas could hardly keep his eyes from her. Every chance he got, he was glancing at her with his sweet smile and longing eyes. Holly's cheeks were in a fit of a never-ending flush.

"Maybe some hot tub after we eat?" she asked.

Thomas stuffed the rest of his sandwich in his mouth. "Actually, I was dreaming that you would play for me."

"Dreaming? But I always play. I thought we were supposed to do something different today."

"I said, more than that, Holly."

She stared at him.

"I asked you to play for *me.* Just for me. Your favorites. The things that stir you up. I want to hear them."

"I've been playing them."

"But play them *for me.*" His hand grazed her breast and smoothed down her side, reminding her of how he burned her up with his particular style of passion.

Holly's loins lit with warmth as she understood. He wanted to hear her play from the place that he stirred inside her. Like a serenade. She pondered, bringing the feeling of him into her music. Her eyes glossed over with thoughts of his powerful, intense kisses. His fingers. His tongue. The sublime friction of his cock inside her. She sighed heavily without realizing it.

"That's it," he said. "You're thinking of me. How I touch you. How I make you feel."

"Yes," she said in a thick exhale.

He brushed her nipples with his thumbs, bringing them to tight points. He leaned into her neck and kissed her there, grazing his teeth along her flesh. A commanding whisper rumbled from his throat, "Play for me."

Holly liquified into a trance, rose, and descended upon the keyboard of the dark, cherry wood piano. Her posture erected. Her wrists lifted. Her fingers fell upon the ivories with Chopin's Nocturne in D flat major Op. 24 No. 2.

The song began with longing. A sweetness. Anticipation built. Tension increased. Thomas approached her quietly and knelt. He pulled her dress up over her knees and lay on the floor. He began stroking up her legs, teasing her with his fingers. He caressed the calf muscle of her right leg as it moved her foot along the suspension pedal. Holly's breaths deepened. His fingers wound around her knee. She clenched her eyes as the skin on her leg prickled up from the electricity of his touch and sent a zing to her belly. The music softened and crescendoed, then softened again. Thomas continued his stroking along her leg as the song ended.

"Play another," he commanded huskily.

Holly knew exactly what was next. Chopin again, her favorite always. This time, Op 9 in B major, No. 3.

Thomas pushed up from under the piano and stood behind her. He took her honey locks into his hands, pulling them from her shoulders and letting them fall in a cascade along her back. Then he caressed her bare shoulders and smoothed down over her chest. He delicately tucked his fingers under the elastic at the top of her dress and drew it down over her breasts. Cupping her delicate flesh, he swirled her nipples in his fingertips.

Holly's concentration wavered with her swelling inhales and the moisture seeping from between her legs. Her clitoris began throbbing with the rhythm of her increasing heart rate, and warmth spread to every corner of her body.

Thomas brushed her hair to one side of her neck, smoothing delicate palms along either side of her throat and down her shoulders. Her playing's intensity increased as he drew down her back with his fingertips.

The climax of the song was fast and disruptive. Thomas responded by gently but firmly biting the crux of her neck and shoulders. He brought his hands under her arms to luxuriate along her breasts again.

Holly could barely see through her own quickening flush. Arousal welled through her body, and her lungs heaved to bring air into the tremors that shook her being with excitement.

He palmed her breasts enthusiastically as she pounded out the crescendo. His hands smoothed over the dress and down between her thighs, massaging the flesh between her legs. Holly went dizzy.

When the resolution approached, she heaved a breath to calm herself. He responded aptly, removing his teeth from her skin and deftly pressing his fingers into her center. His fondling touch released the charge in her clit, and she nearly came.

Sensing her tension, he pulled away and returned his hands to her breasts as he continued lightly nibbling and kissing her neck. The song slowed to an end.

Holly's skin burned, and the pulse in her nether was begging for more attention. "Do you want another?" she asked, realizing she was panting. The dizzying desire of her body wanting nothing but the fullness of his hard rod inside her.

"I want you."

Holly spun on the bench to face him. He pulled her up against him, his swollen cock hard against her in his trousers. She sighed, feeling weak and powerful at the same time. He wrapped her desirous lips in a kiss that split her with want.

Her hands flew to the buttons on his shirt, undoing them and wrenching it from his body. She pushed off her dress as Thomas rid himself of his trousers and pulled her with him down to the floor.

Thomas lay beneath her with menacing, steamy eyes. She could tell he was already fucking her in his mind.

She slid tantalizingly against his erection. "Why does Chopin make you so hard?" she asked as she kissed his swollen tip with her divine, wet opening.

"I told you." He breathed heavily, holding her hips and dragging her satin moisture along his erection. "It isn't Chopin. It's you. He's your favorite, isn't he?"

"He is."

"It shows in how you treat his music. So full of passion. Oh, God Holly. Let me in."

She spread her thighs further and held his erection with her hand to guide him in. He pressed into her, and his hips lifted up. Holly arched back with a loud gasp as he filled her.

She braced on his abdomen and bucked against his hips. Thomas groaned, pulling her dulcet haunches against him. His swollen knob a tight fit inside her as she gasped and galloped on him. Their impassioned flesh collided as they clutched each other with needy hands.

She melted downward, in heaving gasps along his beautiful chest, kissing every bit of flesh she could until she reached his lips. His tongue slid so deeply into her mouth that it nearly tickled her mind. He braced and rose enthusiastically into her. She charged against him in ecstatic rhythm. His teeth grazed her breasts hungrily; nails raked her sides. Her body lunged on his slamming desire, gasping and pushing with his grunting bursts.

"I love when you're an animal, Thomas," she moaned.

"You've awoken me, Persephone."

"I love it when you're gentle, too. God, I love everything you do." Her hips swooped and ground into him, and she squealed in the joy of it.

He rumbled in exaltation, clutched her hips, and shot upwards into her as she crashed down onto him. He grabbed her hair, bringing her to his face. "Fuck me, Holly," he growled.

"You want it faster?"

His eyes rolled back. "Yes."

Holly shoved in delirious tempo until her body mounted aching waves. She focused on a beautiful pounding feeling until it tickled enough to burst. “I’m gonna come,” she cried.

Chapter 13
Dolcissimo

He was gone again when Holly woke in her bed. It was Monday. Her chores came unwanted into her mind. Shopping and meal planning, then house maintenance. But their dynamic had changed. The conflicting ideas of working for him, cleaning his house, doing his laundry, and making his meals again as she used to, along with the passionate love that was forming between them, were things she needed to balance. Were they just living together now? Or was she still his "employee?" This needed to be addressed at some point. And soon.

She had to remember that Thomas was cold and withdrawn when he worked. She needed to be okay with leaving him be. That's what he needed. The weekend of passionate touches, knee-bending kissing, and fantastic lovemaking was the best thing she'd experienced in... ever. And the source of it was a fish-cold writer who needed to be left alone when he needed to be left alone. Holly worked to reconcile this and manage her expectations for the day.

Now that they were at the start of a new week, she hoped they could strike a balance between employer and lover. *Shit. Is this what being a housewife is like?* Holly pushed from the bed and wrapped her robe around herself. She went down for coffee. As she sat at the buffet, scrolling through Facebook, tender, intent arms enveloped her body.

"Good morning," he said, with a loving kiss on her cheek.

"Good morning." She happily accepted his embrace.

"I wondered if I could have French toast again? But with strawberry preserves, and the same amount of butter. It was perfect the way you did it the last time."

His touch undid her mind, and she worked on responding verbally to him. "The amount of butter or the French toast?"

"Both." His mouth trailed down her neck with dainty presses of his lips. He whispered hotly, "Do it exactly the same. But with strawberry preserves." He needily cupped her breasts.

Holly's eyes fluttered. "Yes, your Lordship."

This was not a cold fish writer, and it surprised her in the most wonderful way.

He chuckled and nuzzled near her ear, smooching her temple. He went to the coffeepot with a contented smile. "Look at me; you've got me all swoony. And before my second cup of coffee."

"And you don't mind me being down here with my little robe?" She raised a playful brow at him.

Thomas poured his coffee, still smiling. "Oh, Holly. The reason I made such a fuss about your little robe being so little was because you were too scantily clad for my sensibilities at the time. I couldn't stop wanting to open it, and—well, you were entirely too sexy. I was helpless and in a fit of lust, fighting naughty, devious thoughts." He smirked at her, sipping from his mug.

Holly snickered. "That was before I started playing piano. Are you going to admit you were attracted to me before the music?" She teasingly pulled the hem of her robe to the crook of her thigh and hip.

Thomas watched. He brought his second cup of coffee to his mouth again and drank pensively. He moved across the kitchen and cupped her cheek, saying, "I'm quite sure music entered this house the moment you did."

She felt her body levitate and sway. Holly reached for him to smash her lips into his. "That is literally the nicest, sweetest thing I've ever heard."

He returned her kiss. "You will never know the level of torture you brought upon me. Constantly. Your stunning body bending over everything, cleaning it. Your sweet face. Even when I was cross with you, I'm sure all I wanted to do was grab your shoulders and kiss you. And then your piano playing... Haven't I explained this already?"

She sat with her mouth hanging open. "Not in this specific way, no. And you were always locked up in your office. How were you even seeing me bending over and cleaning?"

"I didn't look at first. But after a while, I couldn't resist looking at you. I may have stolen glances as I went to the restroom. I may have stolen glances whenever I could." He leaned over the buffet next to her and gazed at her pleadingly. "I am still a man."

She cackled. "You finally admit it! A mere mortal, after all!" Her laughter filled the space. "And if you'll remember, you were kind of a dickhead at the beginning. You yelled at me all the time."

Thomas looked down. "Weren't we talking about your small robe in the kitchen?"

"We were."

"You have lovely legs, Holly."

She grinned, letting him get away with avoiding the accusation because she adored how he was coming to understand himself. And every word from him kept elation shooting through her as she sipped her coffee.

"You have a beautiful rump and... outstanding tits." He sighed. "You know what you have. Why am I going on? Oh yes! Because this little robe of yours made me insane."

Her eyes slowly moved up to his. Her fingertips glided along his sternum.

"You don't have to hold back now," she tempted. "You don't have to hold back anymore. Touch me if you want."

Thomas stepped closer and slid her robe aside, exposing one of her sloping breasts.

"Oh, dear," he said. "You're quite exposed."

She smirked. "Oh no! Your Lordship, whatever shall we do?"

Thomas looked into her playful brown eyes. "Well, we must make it even." He pushed the other side of her robe, exposing her other breast.

"There. My dear, you are quite indecent." He stared at her perky nipples. "This is terrible. It will be quite the scandal at court," he teased.

"No! We can't have that." She shoved her chest towards him playfully. "Quickly, you must hide them! Cover them with your mouth! It's the only way!"

Thomas' eyes were wholly focused on her nipples. "I think you're right." He dove, smashing her breasts into his face as he sucked and licked. Holly's jubilant laughter rang out.

Thomas parted from her beautiful, erect nipples and became solemn again. He brought her chin up to look into her eyes. Bright, intense blues leveled her. "I love to play with you. And I need to tell you this thing." His hands became insistent on her; eyes deepened in seriousness as he clasped her waist. "I hadn't been aroused in a couple of years. And I was still sunk in my mourning. How could I look upon another woman and want her?" He searched her compassionate eyes. "It was impossible. I wasn't angry with you for your darling little robe. I was angry with myself for lusting after you."

Holly felt absorbed by his cloudy blue stare. "Janet actually said that to me a couple of weeks ago. That you were being gruff out of guilt. I didn't believe her. I didn't believe you liked me at all." With a smooch on the corner of his lips, she pulled away and sipped her coffee.

He was left with an ironic smirk. "Isn't it something how we work so hard to deceive ourselves?" He brought his own mug up for a drink. "Janet."

Holly passed a sighing laugh. "She sees through everything."

Thomas nodded. "I both wonder at her and resent her."

"And yet, she was right. You are still a man."

"In the end. Yes. One has to admit it."

"A man who was lusting."

He shifted. "I was. You can't know how ashamed I was. Like I was disrespecting Evelyn's memory."

Holly's eyes softened, realizing that this process must have been difficult for him. "I admire your devotion." She watched him.

He flashed her a look that told her he was listening and appreciative.

She said, "I love that you were rationalizing how attracted to me you were. I love that you were looking at me. I love that you wanted me." She leaned over and kissed him again. "I love that you opened up to me and want me now."

He shifted again and set his coffee mug on the buffet. "The first night we made love, something very strange and wondrous happened," he said.

"What's that?"

"Evelyn didn't cross my mind once. All I saw, all I thought of, and all I wanted... was you."

Holly's spine tightened. Jittering applause fluttered through her being. She strolled along his chest with her fingertips.

He said, "And you're right about something else."

Holly couldn't speak.

"I do want you now." Thomas slipped a hand around her head and pulled her lips to his.

Holly pulled away. "I have coffee breath."

"So do I." He sent his sublime tongue into her mouth. He gripped the hair at the back of her head, not giving her room to move anywhere but closer to him. He pulled her from the chair and clutched her to his body. Holly found his bulge and stroked it with her lovely fingers until it was hard and arcing.

She broke their kiss to say, "And here, I thought you'd be cold to me today and back to work."

"I could never be cold to you. Not anymore." He pressed his needful kiss into her. "Remember my request. My lips get dry, and I'll need frequent kisses throughout the day." His eyes flitted to the buffet counter. "I'm going to fulfill another fantasy, Holly." He slowly turned her away from him and bent her over the buffet counter.

Elated and filled with anticipation, Holly reached along the counter, steadying herself. Thomas lifted her little robe. She pushed her rear out for him in anticipation of his delicious, hard cock. He slid his thick need into her. She gripped the counter, letting him fill her.

Thomas reached around her hip and stroked her budding clit as he pleasured her with desirous, wanton thrusts. She lifted a knee up onto a stool to further open herself and allow his deeper penetration. Her own hand took over his touch on her clit in growing circles of pleasure. He held her belly, jubilantly thrusting into her until she came, gushing like a fountain in a piazza. Dousing them both with her excitement and nearly pushing him out. It only spurred him. He grabbed her hair in a bundle with his fist and pulled her head back as he shoved into her with aroused groaning until he climaxed.

Holly was a puddle of gasping bliss. Thomas slumped against her.

"Now, it's a good morning," he said into her ear. "Let's have a shower. Then you owe me some French toast." He pulled her around to kiss her deeply, and Holly was liquid against him, still gasping.

"Not to ruin the moment, but paper towels first. Then shower. You're going to help me clean up after us before we bathe."

He looked incensed. "But I have a girl who does that."

Holly gasped and thwapped him playfully with her hand. He laughed all the way to the paper towels.

Holly floated through her day. She left him to his work and occupied herself with meal planning and grocery shopping. Then, she did some light cleaning and a load of dark clothes. She washed the sheets from her bed, which she almost hated to do because she loved all the smells from them.

But she knew they'd be re-scented soon enough. At lunch, she brought him a grilled cheese sandwich and kissed him. He 'hmmed' in response and continued working. That evening, he emerged from his office to watch the news with a scotch while she fried up fish and chips.

After dinner, they cleaned up the dishes together. Thomas never helped with cleaning the dishes before. It was wonderfully normal.

Holly curled up on the couch to read, and he went back to his study. As the hour became late, she knocked on his door. "Come to bed?"

"Mmm. Yes. I should. No piano tonight?"

"I suppose I could squeak something out."

"Do. Squeak away. It'll give me a chance to find a good place to stop here. Besides, I haven't had an erection in at least thirteen hours."

"Thomas!" she spouted and giggled.

"What? Don't you want to make love before we sleep?"

Holly entered his office and approached the back of his chair. She stood behind him, bent over his shoulder, and ran her hands along his chest, down to his abdomen, as she lay kisses along the side of his face. "Every chance I get to have you, I'll take. You're exquisite, your Lordship."

He leaned his head against the back of his chair. "You, see? It's working already."

Holly found a growing mound between his legs.

"So, I don't need to even play the piano?"

"I'm pretty sure all you have to do is breathe the same air as me, and I'll react thusly. But I'd still enjoy hearing you play. If it's not too much trouble, my lady?"

Holly let out a twittering giggle and kissed his head. "As you wish."

After firsts, there are seconds, and so on, until one loses count and daily life turns into routine. Holly expected they'd cool down after the passionate weekend they'd spend together. That their enthusiasm as raging lovers would fizzle into the doldrums of the workweek.

She was mistaken. When Thomas warned her that he could be overwhelming, he wasn't kidding. He wanted her every day, sometimes twice. And especially if she played a Chopin nocturne.

He was slow and passionate some nights and a ravaging animal on others. Holly was sure she'd be bow-legged by the end of the month. She'd never encountered such an enthusiastic, desirous lover before. Not that she minded. Every time she visited him in his study to kiss him, his pine cologne scent would fill her lungs, and she'd throb for him. It was triggering a response in her body, like Pavlov's dogs. If they could sustain this, that would be quite a feat indeed. Holly knew that things were always hot during beginnings.

She could genuinely understand why Evelyn left her home country of England and traveled all the way to America to marry him. Holly was certain she'd follow him anywhere. He was far too delicious. She was practically butter in his hands and melted at his every word and touch.

A renewed confidence bolstered her, and the idea of playing piano professionally nagged her more and more. Perhaps it was how encouraging and affirming Thomas was about her playing. He'd lit a long, dormant flame in her. Inspiration. His support, and not to mention how he rewarded her, had her thinking that perhaps she could have a decent chance at her dream again. Her brain tumbled with "what-ifs" and "maybe-I-coulds."

At the end of the week, during dinner, she asked Thomas about it. "I've got everything here under control pretty well, wouldn't you say?"

"You do," he agreed, sipping some cabernet and stuffing a bite of salmon into his mouth.

"So, um. I feel like maybe looking for a job."

He stopped. "A job? But you have a job. You work for me."

"Yes, and as much as I love the perks and sleeping with my boss, I'm getting a little bored during the days."

His eyebrows raised. "You are? I shall have to increase my efforts to make a mess."

She smiled. "You didn't think I'd just settle in and be your housekeeper forever, did you?"

"A man can dream. And remember, at first, I didn't want you here at all. Now, the thought of you not being here makes me want to panic." He stared down at his plate. "I don't want you to leave, Holly."

"Oh, I'm not leaving. I'd only be gone during the day."

"But what about all of my kisses? My poor chapped lips. Have mercy." He pushed out his bottom lip in an adorable pout.

She snickered.

He granted her a sweet, flirtatious smile. "And anyway, you'd hate another office job."

"I'm not thinking of another office job." Holly sipped her wine. There were two topics biting the edges of her mind. She took a deep breath and spoke hesitantly. "Don't you think this is more of a, well, an um..." Holly stumbled, trying to figure out how to explain what was in her head. "It's weird. I mean— We're together, right? Should you still be paying me? Isn't this what normal people do? Live together, cook and clean, and make love?"

"Do you mean to ask if you are my girlfriend?" He sipped his wine.

"I guess, maybe I am asking that. It changes our dynamics, doesn't it? Am I your housekeeper-lover? Or your girlfriend who does the normal things like taking care of the house she lives in?"

"Do you want me to take a knee and give you a promise ring?"

Holly's brows flattened. "Thomas, this is not the time for jokes."

He chuckled. "I'm sorry. To be honest, I hadn't thought about definitions. I have been... simply enjoying it."

Holly took a long sip from her wine glass. It had only been eight days since they'd first made love. Why did it seem like longer?

"I was thinking of applying for the symphony again. Maybe some other opportunities."

He set down his fork, finished the brussel sprout in his mouth, and sipped his wine again. He sat with his fingertips fidgeting against his thumbs. "So, it wouldn't be a daily thing?"

"No. It might surprise you, but piano jobs are hard to find. And they usually happen in the evenings and weekends. But if I can pick up something steady, there will be rehearsals, and those do happen daily."

He bristled. "You want to know what I really think?"

"I do."

"Would my feelings or opinions of it alter your decision?"

"Maybe."

Thomas sent her a knowing eyebrow scrunch.

"Doubtful," she admitted.

"I see." He swigged the rest of his wine and took his time refilling his glass from the bottle on the table. He was visibly disturbed by the thought. "I don't fancy the idea of you not being around for my every beck and call. I hate the idea of you being gone in the evenings. Especially weekends. The truth is that I don't like the thought of being without you at all. And I especially detest the idea of being in this house alone." His fingers agitatedly tapped the table.

"I'd rather keep you in a cage like a bird so I can look at you whenever I want." He sipped his wine again. "But I also know that you are not a bird. Any performance that could have you as a part of it would be very fortunate indeed. So as long as you always come home to our bed when you're done."

Holly's chest warmed and swelled. *Home to our bed.* That may have been the only thing she heard.

"I'll still play for you. Just for you," she offered.

His eyes met hers adoringly. "I will miss you. And when you're here, I will love you just as I do now."

Her heart dropped into her belly and fluttered as if it was caught in a net. "Thomas, those are very strong words."

"And I mean every one of them."

She tried playing it off with a laugh. "You can't really mean that you're in love with me already."

"It's not a new thing, Holly. Only a new admission." He flashed his devastating blue eyes at her.

Her lungs finally heaved for air when her body caught up to her brain.

"I've shocked you."

She could only barely nod her head.

"Come with me." He stood and offered her his hand.

She took it and let him lead her through the house to the living room and the back sliding glass door. He opened it and pulled her to the patio. The fireflies danced and glittered everywhere in the heavy air of dusk. He pulled her body to him and began to sway as if there were music playing somewhere.

He leaned his jaw against her temple and kissed her hairline. He said into her ear as he swayed with her in slow purpose, "Persephone. Your absence could be my demise. You've pulled me from death. Given me all the sweetest parts of you. Maintained your kindness when I was a brut. Aroused me with the music of your fingers and heart. And turned my home from a hell of death to a dream of summer. How could I possibly keep from loving you?" He stared into her eyes.

Holly could barely breathe from how he captured her.

"And I know a secret."

"What's that?" Holly asked, entranced.

"You love me too."

Her eyes froze on his handsome, angular face. Dark hair and heavy brows framing those gorgeous, light eyes that seemed to get bluer every time she looked into them. The taut strength with which he held her reaffirmed his masculine fire. The heavy, humid summer air surrounded them with the scent of blooming roses and peonies. Crickets chimed rhythmically. Holly realized he was dancing with her to the gentle trill of the cricket symphony.

"Have I misjudged?" he asked, suddenly appearing concerned.

She found herself shaking her head. "No." Then her mouth moved, and as if magnetically attracted, her lips pressed into his. She slid her tongue into his mouth, and he met her with his perfect suction.

The wonderful movements of his jaw made her want to send her tongue in as far as she could reach. His expert oral talent disintegrated her. She finally pulled away from him, dizzy and tingling everywhere.

"I do love you, Thomas. You're not the only one who's afraid."

"Oh, Holly. I've never felt braver." He drenched her with another magnificent kiss. Thomas' arms slid around her, and he picked her up. She chirped in surprise, and he carried her to the grass beneath the fireflies and knelt with her, laying her down gently in the soft green of the lawn. He lay upon her, smoothly working down her hips and pulling up her dress.

Holly undid his belt and pants. They quickly rid themselves of their cloth barriers. He was back upon her, his hips between hers and kissing her fiercely.

Holly's hands explored his tight, wondrous muscles as he bit and nipped down her neck until he pulled on her breasts with his mouth. He slid his hardening girth along her welcoming opening as she widened her legs and wrapped her calves around his thighs. He dragged along her until he could enter her effortlessly. They gasped together when he entered. She rose into him as he pushed in, nibbling her lips.

"God, Holly. How could I not love you?" He thrust in, and she cried out with his swift movements. Every shudder from her seemed to spur him. He ground slowly. Holly's entire being vibrated from his caressing hands and hard penetration. She wandered her fingers around every bit of skin she could reach along his form.

The sensation of his warmth, his softness, and tender undulations caused her body to bloom. She moved and met him, thrusting with him, sighing, and meeting his lips between gasping joy. Dewy grass prickled along her naked body while the smell of heavy summer growth surrounded her and combined with his pine cologne. She was Persephone. Exploding with life and bursting with love for him as they ground into the earth.

"I do love you, Thomas," she said as her voice gave out from the pleasure of his friction inside her and against her.

He carried her churning spasms without changing his tempo, listening to her come. She finally relaxed, limp, and spent under him, unable to sustain the madness of her shaking body. She was in darkness. Swirling, beautiful darkness. He didn't falter in his continued thrusts.

"The sounds you make when you come are the sweetest music of all," he said.

She couldn't respond, laying limp and mindless. He pulled up her legs and held them in the crooks of his arms. Bracing himself, he quickened against her. A new set of tremors fired in her body as he pulled her up to an angle that hit her sublimely. She could only moan as he shoved quick bursts of pleasure through her.

His own music formed in high-pitched sighs. Then his sound lowered right before he came. Holly's tension blew her apart again. Deep waves rocked through her. Her arms writhed along the grass. Her body wriggled as he held her firmly, pushing through his own explosion.

"Oh, God." He gasped and grunted softly.

Holly groaned, wrapped in ecstasy and the heavy scent of summer grass.

As Thomas released and spasmed, his mind blanked. He felt his cum leave him in exquisite muscular spasms. Stars formed behind his closed eyes. When darkness recaptured him, he opened his eyes. Holly lay bare under him. As much a part of him as his own legs. Breasts softly lolling over her heaving ribs. A panting mess of delirium sprouting from him. Beautiful. He shoved into her once more to recapture a moment of that hot squeeze she provided around his cock. She responded, constricting around him. He groaned.

Why did an orgasm have to end it? He pushed once more. Again, she tightened around him. Her sublime squeeze spurred him. He began another small thrusting rhythm in her. His semi-limp rod sparked to life inside her tight suction. He was soon engorged and thrusting hard again with gentle undulations. He lifted her haunch, angling her for deeper pleasure.

Holly's body clenched again; breath ragged with groans. He watched her stomach muscles tense and release with their movements.

Will you come again? God, I hope so. Give that to me. The spasms. I want them again. Fuck, you're sublime.

Her eyes clamped shut as she gripped the grass. "God, Thomas... what are you doing to me?" she moaned.

"I'm showing you how much I love you," flowed out of him. Her hips churned needily on him, writhing and trying to breathe through her squeals.

Her warmth surrounded him in squeezing spasms along his shaft. Pure pleasure. He had her in a zone of undulation and clenching. It was magnificent. A pulsing rush of new exuberance strengthened in his shaft.

"Yes," he sighed out loud and resumed a thrusting tempo to help her come again. He held her hips up, positioning her in an angle that, by her sounds, would have her screaming again soon.

Dropping one of her legs, he held the length of her other leg along his chest to achieve the angle perfectly. The agonizing begging of his body re-emerged.

Holly exploded in cries of delirium. Her hot, tight muscles clenched spasmodically along him. An animal burst forth, and he gripped and pounded into her cravenly until he found the edge of his own sanity and it broke. His body split. Pulses erupted in waves that released him into her. He shook with bliss a second time, thrusting and grunting like a boar and losing his mind.

The world was silent. He was drained of essence. He slowed, released her leg, and fell upon her soft body, trying not to smother her with his spent form. His lungs begged for air, and his mouth begged for her kiss.

He found her mouth with his lips while his hands explored her skin. She was so delicate and tender beneath him. And even more delicate now that she was a breathy mass of bliss. Her honey hair splayed in messy tendrils around her in the greenery of the earth, and her eyes rolled around as she tried to recover from the pleasure he'd just given her. He'd never seen anything more beautiful. His lips found hers. They were cold. He loved knowing that her lips cooled from the rush of her breath when she came. He kissed her hard, heating her mouth with his tongue, and exhaled.

Holly wrapped his heaving body in her arms as he kissed her in sloppy euphoria. He was limp with pleasure upon her. They lay in panting joy. Holly's mind was a blissful blank. She knew only that she could sink into the earth. A puddle of ecstasy beneath him. She could take him with her below the grass and sink together into the green.

Chapter 14

The Crescendo of Janet

Thomas and Holly drove to Janet's house. His hand wandered over to Holly's lap, snuck his fingers under the hem of her short summer dress, and grazed along her thigh.

"Thomas, please don't turn me on before we get to your sister's house. I'd die of embarrassment. Especially if you want me to keep this newfound obsession of ours down. You can't get me all riled up."

"I know. But I love touching you."

Holly took his hand firmly in hers. "How's that?"

"Your fingers make me think of your piano playing, which makes me hard. And of how you touch my cock."

"Oh, good grief!" she giggled. "What am I going to do with you?"

"I'm hopeless. It's true." He brought her hand to his lips and kissed it. "I'll behave."

Thomas remembered to drop Holly's hand right before Janet opened her front door.

"My darlings!" she beamed, holding out her arms and hugging Holly around the bowl of potato salad in her arms. She kissed Holly's cheek, then smothered her brother with a hug and smooched all over his face. The galloping of little feet came flying to the foyer.

"Uncle Thomas! Auntie Holly!" Jake and Samantha squealed, leaping at Thomas as he entered.

Thomas squatted, catching their wriggling forms. "How are my little elephants?"

"Uncle Thomas, will you come swimming with us?" asked Jake.

"I certainly will, old boy."

Janet pulled the bowl of potato salad from Holly's grasp so her children could tackle Holly next. "I'll take that for you." She turned and headed for the kitchen.

"Ana Hollee! Ana Hollee!" Samantha was bouncing joyfully with her arms outstretched to be picked up. Holly lifted her into her arms.

"Oof! You're getting heavy, sweetheart."

"I big girl."

"Yes, you are! And getting so pretty!" Holly smooched around Samantha's angelic little cheeks. "And you know what else?"

Samantha's wide eyes became wider.

"I bet you taste pretty good, too."

"No, Ana Hollee!"

"In fact, you're quite... delicious! Nom-nom-nom!" Holly smooch-nibbled into Samantha's little neck and ear.

The girl squealed and squirmed, giggling sharply. Holly put her down so she could go running through the house deliriously. "How about you, Jake? Are you delicious?"

The six-year-old smiled confidently, scrunching his face, and crossed his arms. "Nope!" he declared and tried to turn to leave.

"I'll bet you're squishy!" Holly snatched him up and hugged him, leaning him left and right, smooching into his cheeks as he snorted, trying not to laugh.

"Aunt Holly. I'm too big to be squishy," he protested, pushing on her.

"Jake, I have a secret for you."

"What?" He stilled.

"All boys are squishy." She hugged him again and smooched his cheek, squeezing a cackle out of him before releasing him.

He looked up at his uncle, who was standing with a misty tint to his face as he watched Holly. "I'll bet you aren't squishy, huh, Uncle Thomas?"

Thomas straightened his face and bent down to Jake with all seriousness. "Jake, I can assure you that I am incredibly squishy."

"Gross!" Jake went running through the house to the back patio door.

Thomas righted himself. Holly slid her arm around his back.

"You're squishy, eh?"

He leaned towards her. "When it comes to you, I am completely squishy." He met her lips with a lingering kiss. They suddenly remembered they were in Janet's house and stiffened, fearfully looking to see if anybody caught their intimacy. It seemed clear.

As they arrived at Janet's expansive kitchen, which overlooked the family room and a casual dining area, Holly set her bag down. She'd packed a canvas bag with swimsuits, her purse, and a bottle of wine. Janet was spooning a mouthful of Holly's potato salad into her mouth.

"Holly, this is really good! But it isn't Evelyn's potato salad."

Holly fought blushing. "I didn't make Evelyn's potato salad. I made *my* potato salad."

"And his Lordship didn't disapprove?" Janet raised an eyebrow at Thomas, who avoided looking at her as he strolled to the back patio to greet Wesley.

Wesley was helping his daughter with her water wings by the pool.

"Time for new things, Janet," Thomas commented with his usual cold, casual voice and slipped through the sliding screen door.

Janet's eyes glinted as she watched her brother's lighthearted step and casual avoidance of her. Her eyes shot to Holly, who froze.

"What?" Holly blurted.

"Uh-huh." Janet produced one of her Cheshire cat grins and took the potato salad to the refrigerator. Holly smacked her forehead. She could hear Wesley's weather report.

"Hey, Thomas! High of ninety-six today! Could be a heavy scorcher with sixty-five percent humidity. Perfect for swimming, wouldn't ya say?"

"Indeed," Thomas responded. "Jake, I see you. If you push me into the pool before I've got my shorts on, I promise you'll regret it."

Holly saw Jake veer from Thomas and jump into the water. She heard a beer cap shoosh open behind her. Janet handed her a cold bottle.

"I know you love these. We can open your wine later." It was one of Holly's favorite lagers.

"I do love these." She took a swig. "Is there anything I can help you with?"

"Nope. Go put your swimsuit on and play with the kids. They've been wild all day from excitement that you were coming over. Anyway, I want Thomas to help me. I've put some beach towels for you in the guest bedroom upstairs. You can change up there." She swished away to the screen door. "Thomas! Come help me with the crudité platter!"

Holly swore under her breath as she picked up her canvas bag and pivoted to go to the staircase. Janet was isolating Thomas. Which meant she was going to pry everything out of him before he was ready. Not that they had any reason to hide it. But they'd barely figured out what was happening for themselves. It was too soon to have a talk with Janet. But that was Janet's way. Once she suspected something, she'd pick and pry at it like a scab until it was loosened and freed.

After Holly changed and made her way to the backyard, passing by the kitchen, she caught Thomas's eye-bulging, worried glance. She grabbed her abandoned beer, pursed her lips, and tried not to snort. Wesley and the kids were already playing in some new water sprinkler thing that floated in the center of the pool. She went out and jumped in with them.

Thomas was tasked with slicing vegetables. He'd done the cucumbers, peppers, broccoli and cauliflower. He was down to the carrots and began hoping he just may get out of this unscathed. Janet brought a bowl of ranch dressing and placed it in the center of the round tray of meticulously sliced vegetables. She slid an index finger along the spot where his wedding band used to be. His spine chilled. *Dammit. Maybe I should have worn the thing today. Anything to avoid that bloody look she's giving me.* He ignored her suspicious glance.

"So, how serious is it?" Janet asked.

"Bloody hell."

"Is it true love?"

"Can't keep anything to myself."

"If you really wanted to hide it, you'd have kept your ring on." She patted his arm affectionately. "You never take your ring off. Never. And..." She trailed off to build suspense.

"And what?"

"And I saw you kissing her in my foyer."

"Blast it. You see everything!"

"Developed by a lifetime of spying on you. And I have small children. I've learned to see everything." She turned away from him with a knowing smirk and leaned against the counter.

The edges of Thomas' mouth pinched up.

"So, is it love, or are you just shagging?"

Thomas ceased slicing carrot sticks, sighed, and said, "You're the one who sees everything. What do you think?"

She examined him with an enormous grin. Popping a cucumber spear in her mouth, she said, chewing, "You're sunk, chum."

"And why do you say that?" He raised an eyebrow, trying not to smile too wide.

"Because you've been smiling since you got here. Because as soon as I brought it up, you got scrappy. And I'm pretty sure I heard a chuckle. I haven't heard you really laugh in years. And also, Holly can't stop blushing. She always does that when she's trying to keep a secret."

Thomas sighed again and stared at Holly swimming with Wesley and the children outside. "She's incredible, Janet. Incredible."

"I know. That's why she's my best friend. Bit of a train wreck since her accident, but she tries hard and bounces back. I've always admired how resilient she is. And she's never let me down. She was there for me in my most difficult time." Janet stared wistfully at her friend outside. "You'll never find a truer spirit."

"She bounced me back."

"I'll bet she did. Several times!"

Thomas couldn't stop a guffaw from escaping him. "Oh, God, Janet. You're right." He glanced back out at Holly. "I am sunk." He resumed slicing carrots.

"I'm happy for you, darling." She slipped an arm around his waist and squeezed him.

"You know something, Janet? I'm happy, too."

"Good! I knew if anybody could bring you back to life, it was Holly."

He stopped slicing again and sent her a flat, suspicious glare. "Janet, please tell me you didn't suggest putting her in my house just to set us up. You weren't playing matchmaker, were you?"

She pulled her arm back and leaned against the counter again. "I'm rather smart, Tommy. But even I didn't think this would happen. I was of the mind that what you two needed most was regular interaction with another person. Especially you, living like a mushroom. And for some daft reason, I thought you'd get on. Call it intuition. She's strong enough to stand up to you, and you were sinking. Besides, you already knew her. You have to admit, it was kind of brilliant."

She stared at the floor and sighed. "I'd been trying to pull you out of your pit, but you stopped listening to me." She reached out and grabbed his forearm. "You needed new hands to grasp you. You needed to be snapped out of your spiral by a stronger voice than mine. Or at least a different voice." Janet looked away and thought for a moment. "I guess I thought she could do that. Either that, or you'd both have psychotic episodes."

The two of them laughed.

"There it is. That laugh I've missed." She exchanged loving, bright smiles with him.

Thomas straightened himself. "Janet, I'm not prepared to fully talk about it yet." He looked back out through the window at Holly helping Samantha paddle around the pool. "But I will tell you this. Your intuition was spot on. I did need her." He sent a bashful look to his sister.

Janet beamed. "Mind the carrots. You always cut them crooked."

"I do not!" Thomas finished slicing up the carrots and placed them on the tray next to the rest of the vegetables he'd precisely crafted.

Janet continued. "I'll confess to this; I did see sparks. And heard them in your voices when you talked about each other on the phone. I never made a big scheming plan. But as soon as I thought there could be something there, I encouraged the hell out of it!"

Thomas put his arms around his sister, embracing her tightly. He spoke against the top of her head. "Holly and I are still figuring this out. So, please. Don't make a fuss."

"I won't fuss," she said against his shoulder.

"You always fuss."

"I don't!"

"Janet..."

"Ugh, fine!"

"We need time. I need you to be gentle and to allow us to work this out."

"Alright."

"Especially me. This is, well, Christ, Janet, you know I haven't done this sort of thing since I was twenty years old. It's been, what? Almost sixteen years? A long time and a lot of life since then. I'm still processing this. So, please, be nice to me. And to Holly. She's been such an ace. Can you behave?"

Janet deflated. "Of course, I can, my love."

"Swear it."

"I swear."

"Good." He kissed the top of her head. "I love you. Can I go swim now?"

"I release you."

He kissed the top of her head a second time and went to change into his swimming trunks.

After swimming, Holly changed back into her day clothes and returned to the kitchen to help Wesley with hot dogs and potato salad while Thomas helped his sister get the children dried and dressed.

After lunch, Janet put Samantha down for her afternoon nap. Jake was setting up a video game to play with his uncle and father. Holly helped Janet clear leftovers. Janet pulled out a freshly baked blueberry and goat cheese tart from the oven.

Thomas guided Holly into the sunroom.

Panicked, Holly whispered harshly, "What are you doing? Janet could see us."

He chuckled. "She's already confronted me."

Holly rolled her eyes. "I figured she was going to trap you. I'm sorry. Should I have intervened?"

"No." he said dourly. "There was nothing you could have done. And it was better that I addressed her on my own."

Holly's sweet smile spread along her rose-colored lips. "What did you tell her?"

"I told her you are incredible."

Holly's cheeks heated. "Oh, is that all?" Her eyes fell bashfully away.

"Even though I'm a writer and quite capable of waxing poetic on occasion. Sometimes even I am lost for words."

Holly's eyes flashed to his on a quick inhale. "Oh, Thomas."

He brought her hand up and brushed her fingers against his lips. "I can hardly be expected to go a whole hour without a kiss, Holly. And it's been at almost three." He gently smiled and slowly began his wonderful lip movements against her mouth. Holly's arms smoothed around him. He pulled away slightly at the sound of his nephew's demanding voice.

"Uncle Thomas! The game is ready!"

Then Wesley's voice. "Yes, Thomas. Give Holly a rest and come play with us!"

"Oh, fuck. Him too?" Holly gasped, dropping her forehead against Thomas' chest. She could feel him silently chuckling.

Thomas smiled. "We aren't very good at being covert."

She picked her head up and looked into his eyes. "We suck at covert." She tilted her head, inviting one more fantastic kiss. It was difficult to find the willpower to pull away from him.

"When can we leave?" he asked with a dangerous slant in his eyebrows.

"After you're done playing with your nephew and when Janet's finished interrogating me. Cuz, I know that's next."

He grinned. "I'm sorry. If I could keep my hands off of you, maybe we could have escaped her."

"Oh, no." Holly let him go and headed to the kitchen. "There's no escaping Janet." She continued to the kitchen and her fated conversation.

Thomas went to sit between Jake and Wesley on the large sofa in the family room, picking up a game controller.

Janet flashed a sharp smile at Holly. "I've covered the rest of the potato salad, and it's in the fridge. There isn't much left. Everybody seemed to love it. Especially Thomas."

"Yes. I've been getting better at cooking. He doesn't protest so much anymore."

Janet flashed her another one of her knowing smiles and grabbed a corkscrew from a drawer. She uncorked the wine Holly brought and poured it into large wine glasses.

"Come sit with me on the patio?" Janet went to the sliding screen door and pressed a button on the wall. A shade rolled out over the patio to protect them from the sun.

Holly loved Janet, but she felt herself tensing. She'd have to talk about Thomas, and the anticipation rolled her stomach. She'd barely talked with herself about him. They'd gone from one blissful experience to another. There hadn't been much time for thoughts. How was she going to explain anything to her best friend when she could barely explain it to herself?

Adding to it was the fact that she was seeing Janet's brother. If things went badly between them at some point, it was a much bigger deal than if it was some stranger. Holly took a heavy sip of wine and followed Janet out to the patio table.

Janet sat quietly, sipping her wine as well. After a few moments, she asked playfully, "So, are you going to start, or shall I?"

"Start what, Janet?" Holly batted her eyes.

"Not you, too! It was enough pulling it out of Thomas."

"I'm sure he didn't struggle. He's no match for you."

Janet's wind-chime laughter trickled from her. "It's true! Sometimes I feel bad about it. But I'm too fond of being right."

Holly smirked.

Janet got right to the point. "So, you want to explain what's going on between you and my brother?"

"Not really. But I see it's my turn to be interrogated."

"I like getting the whole story. You know that."

Holly attempted to be sly, even though she knew it would fail. "And what if I told you nothing was going on?"

"Then I'd say that nothing had his tongue halfway down your throat a few minutes ago in my sunroom, and you better start talking!" Janet's grin could have lit up Broadway.

Holly couldn't help herself. She beamed, laughing, holding her knuckles against her mouth. "We weren't exactly ready to talk about it," Holly said after catching her breath. "It's still really new. And you know that beginnings are full of... not a lot of thinking."

"But a lot of breaking furniture!"

"Janet!"

"Oh, come on, Holly! I know you two are sleeping together. It's all over the both of you."

"Christ." Holly leaned her head in her hand, attempting to sideways sip her wine.

Janet let a moment pass, sipping her own glass. "He loves you, you know."

A torrent of red filled Holly's cheeks. "I know. He's already said it."

"Wow! That was fast."

"Wait, did you think you were going to spoil it for me? Tell me he loved me before he could?"

Janet's head rolled back with a chuckle. "No, course not!" Then she stared at the table. "I mean, no, not really. But I can see it! I suppose it would have been a little teensy spoiler. I thought I could encourage you, but I see my love-sick brother has beaten me to it."

Holly's mind couldn't help it. She had to know. "Was it faster than when he said it to Evelyn?" she blurted.

Janet fidgeted. "I don't know that. They were in England the first time he told her. I didn't even find out he had a girlfriend until months after. But I do know that he has a laser focus once he's chosen a woman."

"Yikes! That sounds so primitive. 'Chosen a woman.'"

"Mind you, I've watched him go through obsessions since he was twelve. He got every single one of them, too. There's something about him. Girls have always swooned at him."

"American girls can't resist an accent."

"Yes, but that hardly mattered when he was in England. And he never went for very many over the years. He's been quite selective. Always searching for that forever love. In fact, I can't think of any time he ended a relationship. They always left him."

"You mean to tell me that he's never broken up with someone?"

"Never."

"Ghastly."

"He's a devoted, heart-sick Romeo. If you take my meaning."

"Oh..."

"Mmm." Janet's eyes stayed on Holly while she sipped her wine as if giving her some secret message.

Holly drank down the rest of her wine and refilled her glass, also topping off Janet's. Holly's throat tightened. "Is this the part where you warn me about breaking your brother's heart?"

Janet sighed in gentle mirth. "No. I'd never threaten you, my darling. You know that. Just... be careful with him. I understand if things change for you. And I understand that things don't always work out. I just want you to be very, very careful with him. Especially now. He's so fragile at the moment."

"God, and his last love, left him by dying on him. It's so sad."

"He's in a particularly tender place right now."

"Shit, Janet. Maybe I shouldn't have—"

"No! I'm not trying to frighten you." Janet patted the table persistently. "I encouraged this, remember? I'm completely buzzing for you and Thomas." She glanced out at her yard. "I only wanted to give you a hint about what you're in for here. He's devoted to a fault. He won't leave. Not unless you ask him to."

Holly joined her staring out at the swing set and playhouse in the backyard, which was scattered with toys. So, this could be a forever love for Thomas. This could be *the it* if she wanted it. And maybe someday she and Thomas could also have a yard strewn with toys.

But realizing that he'd hoped all of them were that forever love made her wonder if she was just the next one in line. And that made her feel miserably insignificant.

She worked on keeping the nausea down. It was only a beginning for Holly. Forever wasn't even a shadow of a thought right now. Thomas had said they were only enjoying things. He wouldn't even say the word "girlfriend" yet. *Christ, it's only been ten days!* Surely Janet was being over dramatic?

"I'm just starting to get used to him. I don't want to think about all this heavy shit right now," Holly said, grabbing the wine bottle again.

"And you don't have to. I'm not trying to ruin that lovely space of beginnings that you're in." Janet's face brightened.

Holly frowned. Nope, she was not about to let Janet get away with this. She kept her tone practical. "Aren't you, though? Trying to ruin things? Scare me a little? You're making me think about the rest of my life with a man that I've barely really knew until recently, Janet."

Holly rubbed her face. "I'm sorry. I know he's your brother, and we practically all grew up together. But that's just it! He's always been just 'your brother' to me. I've never had thought one otherwise about him until now. And you're telling me he's uber-selective, and I need to start thinking about forever and shit! It's freaking me out! Can't this just be new and innocent? I mean, he hasn't even used the "girlfriend" word yet. And now you're telling me that I have to think about what colors I want for my fucking wedding! Give me a break!"

Janet's shocked look fell to the table. "I'm sorry. You're right. I'm meddling." Her glance went back to Holly. "Maybe I think it's really cool that you and I could legally be sisters one day."

Holly's heart swelled, and her hands unclenched. She shook her head to the side and back. "I don't need to marry your brother or even have some document to tell me that you're my sister, Janet."

Janet's eyes beamed. One corner of her mouth pinched up. "Nothing would make me happier, though."

Holly and Janet shared a loving moment in the summer sun. Holly snapped out of it. "Jesus, how are we talking about fucking marriage? Can't I just enjoy where I am right now?" She wanted to say, 'enjoy your brother', but that would have sounded wrong.

Janet perked up. "I'm sorry! You're right. I got a bit heavy there, didn't I? But I guess what I'm trying to say is this: I love the both of you so much. I'm not saying you're headed for the altar per sé, but I am saying that he won't be the one to take it slow. If you want to take your time, then you'll have to be the one to set the pace. I didn't mean to scare you."

Holly softened. "Janet, he already told me he falls hard and fast and that it can be overwhelming."

Her friend arched a brow. "And are you overwhelmed?"

The wicked smile that fled up Holly's lips couldn't be stopped.

Janet cackled. "Okay, okay. I don't want to know!"

The pair went into a fit of laughter.

Holly changed the subject. "I'm thinking of applying for a symphony again."

Janet's face glowed. "Really? Ohh! Tell me about that!"

Chapter 15

Second Movement

As soon as they made it through the door of the two-story Tudor, Thomas was on her. His hands pressed along her body, lips kissing every place along her face and neck.

"You were amazing today with my sister," he panted, guiding her towards the TV room. "We didn't make love this morning, and I'm positively bursting. I've wanted nothing but to be inside you all day." He pulled at her clothes and pushed her against the wall at the archway.

Holly tensed as Janet's words tumbled in her mind. "Thomas..."

"And you're so good with the children." His mouth continued its heavy movement along her jaw and neck.

"Thomas."

His touch, which would normally burn her alive, was doused with her new-felt concern about them.

He's obsessive.

His tongue played against hers in her mouth.

He falls too fast. Faster than he can think, maybe.

Desirous hands pulled at her dress and brought her leg up against his hip.

He thinks every love is the forever love. What makes me so special? I'm just... next. That's all.

His hand made its way up her thigh to the soft, moistening panty between her legs.

I don't want to be just next. I want to be significant. I want to mean something. I want to be new.

She wanted to resist him, but he felt so good fondling her tender spaces, pulling down her panties, his delicious tongue, perfect lips, and jaw movements against her mouth. His touch erased her willpower as he stroked along her body. Holly arched into him instinctively, yearning for the flame of him.

Yet she was terrified of things not working out, difficulties surfacing, and hearts breaking. She felt muddied and dark, and thick with worry.

"Seeing you in that bathing suit. You're lucky we weren't alone." He kissed her hungrily until her knees trembled. Her panties fell upon her ankles, and his strong finger rimmed her opening. Even though her skin was pulling her towards him, she stiffened.

He pulled back. "Holly, is something wrong?" He immediately removed his hand from her crotch and held her hips.

She grimaced. The absolute last thing she wanted was to upset him. "I have questions." She eked out.

"Shit. Janet." He released her. "Goddamned Janet." He pushed off and turned slowly away from her, shaking his head and entering the kitchen. "Always mucking about in my affairs." He produced a bottle of single malt from a cupboard and hunted for two glasses.

Holly kicked off her panties and followed him. She set her panties on a bar stool and watched him.

"What did she say to you?" he asked.

Holly fumbled. "We should pour that first."

"Fuck." He actually swore with the F-word. Which meant he was intensely bothered. She'd never heard him say 'Fuck' before. Unless he was asking her to fuck him. Which was... Holly drifted until she noticed the glass he offered her.

Thomas leaned against the kitchen buffet on the opposite side of her. "Please, tell me things aren't ruined."

His worried eyes melted her, and she struggled to ignore the throbbing nag between her legs. They loved each other. She knew it. Start from there. Holly's sweet smile spread. This could end well, but she had to say some things. It was a matter of saying them in the right way and being gentle.

"Things aren't ruined. Pull your heart off the ceiling."

Thomas sighed with immense relief. His shoulders relaxed.

Holly said, "I love you. It jacks me up how much I love you already. Especially since I could barely stand you just a couple of weeks ago." She smiled at him again.

He chuckled. "That's one good thing. I'm afraid to hear the rest."

"Janet told me a few things, yes."

Thomas peevishly blew air out his nose. "Like what? I'm hopeless? I'm obsessive? My heart is an eternally beating and broken thing? That I never leave, but they do?" He sipped from his glass. "It's what she always does."

Holly stilled. That was practically word-for-word what Janet had told her. "That is essentially what she said, yes. What do you mean she always does it?"

"She always either threatens them or tries to convince them of my sainthood. Every goddamned time I want someone, she does it. Every girlfriend in high school. One in college when I did my first year here before transferring to Cambridge." He brushed his hand over his hair. "God, it was such a relief when I returned to England and could actually date without her meddling."

Holly's head spun. There was no way she could accept that Janet would ever be insincere with her. "I'm a *them?* Oh, come on! How does she threaten them?"

"She did the same thing with Evelyn, too, you know." His finger tapped his glass. "She told Evelyn that I'd never look back and she'd better never break my heart. She told her that I've never left any of the girls that I've ever loved. Told her that I was devoted and sick with love. Constantly searching for the forever love." He buckled his lips.

Holly went very still, hanging on his every word.

"I suppose that was her way of encouraging Evelyn to stay." He sighed. "Which, of course, wasn't true. I do actually date around before I select a woman. And I have ended more than one relationship." Thomas paused with a tentative glance at Holly, then took a swig from his glass. He leaned against the buffet.

"It has been a long time since I've searched for love. I mean, obviously. I was married for nearly ten years, after all." He leaned towards Holly and captured her eyes with his longing stare. "Except this time, the perfect woman came to me. Landed right in my lap, as it were. And I'd very much like her to keep her."

She couldn't help the flutters jiggling through her body. Or the tingles that spread through her being as he gazed at her with those deep blue eyes.

He continued, "Some of the splits I've had in my life were rather friendly. Amicable."

Holly nearly whispered, "She told me every girl you were ever with since the sixth grade left you. That you were the most devoted Romeo of them all."

Thomas snuffed and sipped his whiskey. "It's the same story she told Evelyn. And it's very sweet of her, but it isn't true. Janet is very clever. One of the best. But she's far too protective of me. Bless her. For a little sister, she's always taken on an almost motherly role with me." He sighed.

"And anyway, I haven't shared every detail of everything that had happened in my life with her. I love my sister. But sometimes, there are things I prefer to keep to myself. It's my way of keeping separate from her, I suppose. She's terribly nosy. Always has been. Sometimes, I want to keep things private. So, no. I don't tell her everything. And she certainly doesn't know everything about my escapades as she likes to think. And she doesn't know everything about Evelyn. But you will, now."

Holly shrank into herself but tried to appear relaxed. The sun began its descent, and the light through all the windows along the back wall intensified to a brilliance that only happened right before sunset. The place was bathed in golden light.

Thomas tensed and brought a hand to his face with a release of breath. "I had the normal experiences of any boy. But Janet saw how in love I was with Evelyn. And when I told her she was thinking of going home, Janet was desperate for Evelyn to stay with me. Not just to keep my heart whole but to keep me here, in America. I don't think Janet could have endured my leaving again. And I would have. I'd have gone gallivanting after Evelyn, right back to England, sword in hand." He sipped his whiskey reflectively.

"But Evelyn was getting homesick. It had been a couple of years since she'd come here with me. We'd only taken maybe three trips back to see her family. Then my father died. Everything here was a mess. You remember."

Holly nodded. She recalled the Buckhorn family in complete meltdown. She was on call for Janet and helped every moment she could with whatever was asked of her. Empathy formed and flowed from her to Thomas.

"After my father's funeral, Evelyn said she wanted to go home. So... I proposed. I thought, if I could keep her here, maybe everything would be alright. Sorting things out here and being present for my mother negated my idea of living in England."

Holly covered her gaping mouth with her hand.

"I couldn't lose Evelyn. I was already lost with my father gone. I'm sure you recall how close I was to my father?"

Holly nodded again.

"Yes. Well, I couldn't leave my mother either. Her grief was so..." He made a fist in the air. "So enormous. I couldn't abandon her. But I couldn't very well lose two people that I loved. So, I proposed to Evelyn, and we married the following spring."

Holly drank heavily from her glass. "Yes, I was at the wedding."

He seemed surprised. "Were you?"

"Was life with her everything you hoped it would be?"

Thomas stared at the floor for a long moment. "She was perfection." He tried to hold back a huff in his chest. "She had her ways. She programmed me. She programmed all of us to love her. She was bliss." He rubbed his forehead and drank from his glass. "She was practically life itself." His head fell. "Forgive me for romanticizing, but I think it best to be honest right now."

Holly hoisted herself onto a stool, entranced by his description of his late wife. Small pangs of jealousy stabbed her, but his grief and love-filled reminiscence captivated her. She found herself not minding listening to his descriptions. This didn't feel comparative. More like a confession of his past. And, of course, everyone has a past. How a man could be so entrenched within another person was beautiful to her. This exemplified the depth of love of which he was capable.

"I'm so sorry, Thomas. She sounds amazing."

He reached for the bottle and replenished their glasses. "She was."

Holly watched him and whispered, "This must be why you have your hard nights."

He set the bottle down and rubbed his eyes. "Yes."

Holly wasn't sure what to do. Should she reach out to him? Touch him? Or... was he about to grieve again?

Thomas sipped his whiskey. His lovely eyes, capable of such rich love, landed on Holly. "Then you came along and—oh, for God's sake, you're brilliant! You're my greatest comfort." He tried looking at her, but his vulnerability in the moment overwhelmed him, and he pulled his gaze away. "I haven't felt normal in a long time." While his eyes searched the walls for comfort, he reached for her. Holly held his arms across the buffet, relieved that he reached out at all.

He said, "I forgot what normal even meant. But the simple act of bringing me English muffins and how hard you tried to scramble the damned eggs just right." He let out a soft, reminiscent chuckle. "I may have started falling in love with you then. I may never know exactly when I fell for you because I don't think I'm very good at knowing myself."

He released her arms and brushed his face with his fingertips. "But I can tell you this. If my sister gave you the 'everybody leaves him, but he's a saint who never leaves them' line of bullshit, she really wants us to be together." His eyes lifted and captured hers. "I love that she did that. It's her way of trying to glue us together. As odd as it seems." He stretched across the buffet again for Holly's hand. She clasped his hand as his gaze continued to penetrate her. "And now, I love *you*. I want you. And I'm sorry I brought up Evelyn again. I want—"

Holly lifted up and pulled across the buffet until her lips were on his mouth, hushing him.

"Enough," she said. "Enough. No more talking, now. I've heard enough. I hear that you loved your wife. You had a wonderful life together. I also hear that you love me. And I hear that you know I love you. I hear that your sister wants us to be together. I know that we should be together. And that's enough right now. Stop drowning yourself in words."

Thomas' brows lightened in sweet acknowledgment. "I do love you, Holly. I'm sorry I can't be an easier person. I'm sorry this can't be easier. Life is incredibly messy." He searched her eyes. Holly sent her loving acceptance into him.

He said, "I'm just grateful that you are so accepting of my—my chaos."

Holly hopped off of the stool and walked around the buffet to hold him close. "I accept *you,* Thomas. You aren't that chaotic. Shit, you're one of the most regimented people I've ever met. But you're grieving, and grief is messy. You were upset, and I upended everything that was comfortable for you."

Thomas pivoted to hold her properly. "That's exactly what I needed." He brushed his lips against hers.

She stared up at him with her bright, honey-brown eyes confidently and began a procession of nipping kisses along his lips. Thomas caressed her body tenderly. His skillful tongue found its way into her mouth. When she released him, she asked, "Would you like me to play some Chopin?"

He sighed. "No. Just take me upstairs to our bed. I feel melancholy and desirous. And all I want to do is drown myself in your body. Let me make love to you. That would make me feel better."

A warm shiver spread between her hips. "Okay." She took his hand and began leading him to their bedroom, knowing he would be tender and passionate tonight. She couldn't wait to indulge in his slow rhythm.

Thomas pulled her into him one more time at the bottom of the twisting staircase. He coated her with love and kissed her so tenderly she forgot her own name.

"Thank you," he whispered to her.

"For what?"

"For listening. For being your open, forgiving, loving self."

Holly's eyes filled with compassion. Her cheeks flushed. She gently brushed his lovely, serious face. "You make it so easy to love you. I never would have believed it before. But I'm ridiculously glad you let me in."

He smiled. "And here I thought it was you who made this so easy." He kissed her slowly, smoothly. When he released her, he led her up the stairs.

Holly gazed blankly at her laptop. She was going to do it today. Apply as replacement piano for the Dayton Performing Arts Alliance. The website glared harshly back at her. Her left hand twinged. She breathed in deep and blew out slowly through puckered lips.

"Okay." She filled out the form. She hit send. She closed her computer. It was done. If they wanted her to audition, she'd know by the end of the week. She wandered down to Thomas' office. He was reading his manuscript and typing.

"Can I help you with something?" he asked without looking at her.

"I thought maybe I'd read one of your books."

He paused his editing. His office chair squeaked as he turned it to face her.

"I'm sure they aren't for you."

She crossed her arms and raised an eyebrow. "Oh, no? Why not? Am I not cranial enough for the work of the great Thomas Buckhorn?"

He guffawed. "Not at all. I just can't imagine you being interested in the subject matter."

"Try me."

His brows lifted. "Alright, how about *The Trials and Tyrannies of Zeus?* Or *The Lessons of Warrior Nature and the Wisdom of Athena.* Perhaps *The Blaming of Medusa*? She was raped by Poseidon, you know. And punished for it by being turned into the hideous gorgon by her matron Goddess, Athena. For the crime of being a victim."

Holly's head slanted. "Tell me more about Medusa."

He looked thoughtfully at her. "Things beyond our control can alter the trajectory of our lives. I do a comparative study in the psychology of PTSD, blaming the victim, and how someone who has been abused can become a monster. But it isn't their fault. They don't understand. They react."

"I'd like to read that one."

His face twisted in suspicion. "Holly, have you been abused?" He caught himself. "Forgive me. It's none of my business."

She smiled timidly. "No. But I was taken advantage of in college. He was a football player. And I was the one who was called a slut. Janet helped me through it." She regarded her feet.

Thomas knit his brows in disgust and support. He tilted his head tenderly and hopped up to select the book from a stack on a bookshelf. "Here it is."

Holly took it, and Thomas brushed her arm affectionately.

"I'm so sorry that happened to you. Men can be... such vile excuses for pigs sometimes."

"Yes. They can." She took the book and kissed him. "But I'm alright. It wasn't violent. It was... drunken non-consent. That's all."

"Non-consent is the same drunk or sober."

"I know. It's not okay. But I am. That's what matters."

Thomas' mouth slinked up in a tender smile. "Janet was right about you. You do bounce back."

Holly smiled. "I just don't believe in letting the bastards get you down."

Thomas gently kissed her. As she turned to leave, he asked, "Can we have tea today?"

She thought. "We're out of tuna. But I can make um... shit."

"What?"

"We're down to baloney."

"Yuck."

"I can fry it? It's a little different that way."

Thomas sneered. "Can't bear boloney."

Holly perked up. "I have cucumbers. Aren't cucumber sandwiches a thing in the UK? I've no idea what's involved, but—"

"Cucumber slices with cream cheese mixed with lemon juice, salt, pepper, and chives," he recited.

Holly blinked at him. "I don't have chives. Would minced onion suffice?"

Thomas turned away from her and went back to his computer. "We can try it."

Holly grinned. It amused her to see her stuffy Thomas back. She bounded to him and took his jaw to kiss him.

"Cream cheese, salt, pepper, and onion."

"And lemon juice." He smooched her back. "It needs acid."

"And lemon juice." She kissed him sweetly. He pulled her hand to his crotch. She whipped her head up. "Your Lordship! I am but a humble scullery maid. This isn't appropriate!"

"But scullery maids have such soft hands." He pulled her mouth back to his lips.

She fondled along his mound until he finally let her go.

"You'd better get back to the kitchen, wench, or I won't get any work done today."

She giggled. "You started it!"

"You kissed me first."

"By order of his Lordship."

"Hmm... Got me there. I don't like my lips getting dry."

"Or your penis."

"Oh, yes. That, too. I think we should have some Chopin tonight. I'm dealing with Hades in my editing today, and I'm feeling a pinch aggressive."

"I see." She kissed him one more time and turned to leave his office. "I'll play some Chopin, but I want you on the patio tonight. It's beautiful out there."

"It is." He looked out his window. "Agreed. Chopin after dinner. And I think I may take you upon that little bench out there. Wherever did you get that? I've never seen it before."

"I found it by the shed. I cleaned it up and attached the lattice."

"Yes, I think I remember. It was here when we moved in. You did all that? And the lattice arch?"

"Yep." She backed away to the door of his office. "I'm quite handy."

"It's wondrous." He watched her happily beaming at him from the doorway. "I will take you there tonight. We'll christen it."

Her chest swelled. She curtsied and withdrew.

That night, after Chopin, there in the rose garden, on the bench Holly had refurbished, he sat with her straddling him. Her knees on either side of his thighs. Their mouths entwined, devouring each other until he sunk his face into her bosoms. She held onto the back of the bench to push with hard leverage on him.

His sighs filled her ears, and she let her head roll back as she relished the feeling of him inside her. His hands curved along her skin with heavy, appreciative strokes. They whispered words of love in the hot breath of every grunting gasp amongst Evelyn's roses.

Chapter 16

The Key Change

Holly typed in her password and waited for her email to display. She'd been checking for a response from the Dayton Symphony almost three times a day. Her shoulders sagged, expecting to see nothing again.

But there it was.

An email from an admin account. RE: Your recent application. Her heart stopped. *Shit. Crap. Fuck. Shit.* Holly jump started her heart with a strong inhale and clicked it.

> *Ms. Reynolds,*
> *We are impressed with your responses to our application and are happy to invite you to audition next Thursday. Please arrive with a selection of music which you think best exemplifies your talent and spirit as a pianist. You are slotted for the 2p audition time. Please be prompt. Additional details and the address are below. If you have any questions or are ready to confirm your audition, please respond to this email appropriately. We look forward to seeing you.*

Holly's heart galloped in her chest. Her breaths escalated to keep up.

"Oh, my God. They want me? Oh shit! What will I play? Fuck! Am I ready? Why did I do this? I'm not ready. I'm not ready for this. It's been ten years since I've been on a stage!" Her hands shook almost uncontrollably. *Now I have to respond. Oh, God, why did I apply? SHUT UP, HOLLY! This is what you've always wanted!*

The rolling energy in her gut spiraled up her sternum, and she howled with victory.

Thomas was serenely tapping and editing when he heard a shriek from the bedroom above him. He sat up in alarm.

"What? Holly? What's happened?" He heard Holly's feet beating against the upstairs floor to the stairs, down them, and she arrived at his office door, panting.

"They want me!"

"Who wants you?"

"The Dayton Performing Arts Alliance!"

He paled. "For—Piano?"

"Yes! They want me to audition on Thursday! Oh my God! Thomas! I'm so excited!" She jumped and bounced exuberantly.

He wanted to be happy. He did. But he couldn't share her mirth. His heart sank. This could take her away from him, and he dreaded nothing more than that. His eyes flew open with joy for her, anyway. He stood and welcomed her leaping body with hugs and kisses.

"Aren't you happy for me? I might finally get to play professionally! It's what I've always wanted!"

"Of course, I'm happy for you."

"Do you think I'll get it? Oh, God, I hope I get it! It's only supportive for a couple of months. Their pianist is retiring. I could have a real job and a stable income. A real gig!" She kissed him all around his face. "I can start repairing my credit!"

"H-how frequently do they play?"

"I don't know. I need to go look. I haven't even accepted the audition yet. I was so excited; I flew right down here." She bounded from his office, and he heard her trotting back upstairs.

Thomas sighed.

"Eventually," he said to himself. "Persephone must return to Demeter. She leaves Hades and brings spring to the rest of the world." He took another deep breath and stared out at the beautifully blooming rose garden and peonies. The bench they'd made love on only a few nights before sat gleaming in the sun. *You're not losing her. She's a fully-fledged woman who needs her own life. It doesn't mean that she's leaving. She's just... damn it.*

Thomas worked on bringing his attention back to his manuscript. *She won't love you any less just because she has a job. In fact, she may love you more. Gods, but I don't want to be alone in this house. I need to talk to Janet.*

He found himself absently punching up Janet on his phone, then closing off the screen and set the phone back down. Maybe he needed to wait until after the audition. See if she actually got the position first. Then he'd call Janet. Why was he panicking? Because he'd be alone when she was gone. In this house.

Again.

Holly walked onto the stage where a perfectly glossed, ebony grand piano sat smugly. The lights were bright on her, and she couldn't make out much in the seating area. She could kind of see five, maybe six, figures occupying seats.

"Ms. Reynolds," said a female-sounding voice from the shadows of the theater. "What will you be playing for us today?"

Holly nervously cleared her throat and thought of Thomas. He'd offered to be there with her, but she told him she wanted to do this on her own. She had finally found the courage to embrace the full circle of her life, and she wanted to be alone in it. Before she left for the audition, he embraced her, nearly crushing her and splitting her mind with his kiss.

He had said to her, "I love you, Holly. You're going to blow them all away. Now, go and change your life."

Holly stood staring at the piano.

"Ms. Reynolds?"

"Yes. Hello. Thank you for your kind attention today. I'll be performing part of Schubert's Shwanengesang, Standchen D957/4."

The piece was a slow, pensive melody. Holly knew that most hopefuls would play complicated pieces with crowded notes to impress the judges on their technical prowess. But this song was quiet, passionate, and simple. It required a delicate, loving touch. Something only skill and heart could show. She prayed she'd made the right selection.

"Go ahead whenever you're ready," said the woman's voice from the shadows.

Holly approached the enormous ebony instrument. It regarded her with casual disdain. It was not her piano, and it had a far worse attitude than Evelyn's. At least Evelyn's piano wanted to be played by her.

This one seemed to mock her as if it was saying, *"Oh, so you think you're good enough to play me? Ha! Only the best, unbroken hands may touch my keys!"*

Holly arrived at the bench and sat. She whispered to the beast, "Look, I'm very good. I promise you. As soon as you feel my fingers, you'll be coming in no time."

"What was that?" from the gallery.

"Nothing." Holly inhaled. "Just a prayer." She placed her fingers on the mocking grand instrument. She whispered again, "I'll have you purring for me." She straightened her back, lifted her chin, held her wrists delicately over the ivories, and took a full, relaxing breath. *You're mine.*

She pressed her first notes. Her fingers lingering on the keys to add a longing tone that pulled at the heart. She brushed when appropriate and pushed deeply when needed. Her fingers tickled and floated effortlessly along. The piano bent to her will. It sighed under her touch, and she felt it soften to her.

"You're right. I'm yours," it said to her.

She fluttered along with the music, thinking of Thomas' desirous touch on her shoulders. She imagined his heavy glide down her chest as she played. The dragging nibbles of his teeth along her neck boosted her when she needed emphasis. She imagined that her breasts were exposed and Thomas' arousing, needy fingers rolled her nipples. The fire of it consumed her as she played the notes that inhabited the room, filling it with longing and desire. She felt his hand slinking between her legs and let the exhilaration of it consume her fingers on the keys.

This song was a chase. A chase between two lovers; the lower octave and the higher octave. One echoing the other. They were out of sync at first. Then gradually, they come together until they consume each other in a crescendo. A moment of separation and pensive resolve occurs. But then they work together in the resolution.

When she was finished, she was practically out of breath. She sat with her eyes closed, listening to the last wavering notes leave the instrument like a sigh. The room beyond her was silent. Someone cleared their throat from the seats.

"That was... quite moving, Ms. Reynolds. Thank you. We'll be in touch next week."

Holly rose from the bench. "Thank you, all." She bowed and walked off the stage. From the darkness behind the curtains, she heard,

"Add Schubert to my list of arousing artists that you play."

She jumped. "Thomas?"

He walked from the shadows. "I'm sorry. I couldn't resist. I wanted to be here for you." He swept her up in his arms and kissed her. "That was so beautiful. You were right. You belong here."

"I just hope they see that."

"How can they not? They'd be foolish to deny you. I know I can't." He smoothed a stray piece of her hair with his fingertips. "I need to apologize to you."

"Why? What horrible thing could you have possibly done?"

He righted her and pulled away slightly, keeping a firm hold on her hands. His yearning glance fled downward as if he were ashamed of something.

"Thomas? I can't imagine it's that bad." She tilted her head and took his face in her hands to gaze into his glistening blue eyes.

"I didn't want you to succeed." The words tumbled from him remorsefully. "I wanted them to hate you so I could keep you locked in my golden cage and look at you whenever I wanted. I was afraid of missing you and being alone again. In that house." He raised a hand and brushed it along her cheek. "I was so wrong. You do belong here. People should have the pleasure of hearing you. I was being selfish. I'm sorry."

Holly's form curved towards him charmingly. "They only get the piano. You get the piano and all the rest of me."

Thomas softly let his lips curl in gratitude. "You really are brilliant. I don't suppose her Ladyship would indulge me by having lunch with me?"

Holly flushed. "That sounds nice, but there's something I want to tell you first."

"Yes?"

Holly pushed closer to him and nibbled his jaw up to his ear. She whispered, "I was thinking of you touching me while I was playing." Her mouth wrapped his earlobe, and she whispered again, "I imagined you squeezing my nipples, pulling them, and fondling my breasts. I felt your hand on my cunt. Pressing and pulsing on me." She gently bit his jaw, dragged her teeth along it with sucking motions of her mouth, and released. The effect she had on him pleased her. Thomas was butter.

He exhaled tensely. "I think we should just go home."

"We can order Chinese."

"After I have you in the foyer." He held her tightly with need. "Then the hall. Then the stairs." His mouth pulled at hers, and she wilted against him.

"Don't forget over the buffet."

"You're a delightfully wicked thing, Holly."

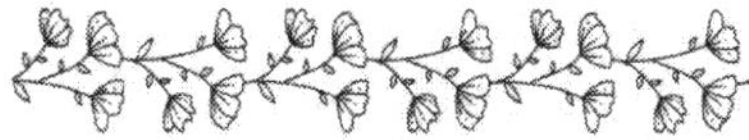

Holly's phone rang with a number she didn't recognize. She answered.

"Holly Reynolds?"

"Yes, this is me."

"This is Harriette Adams with the Dayton Performing Arts Alliance. We'd like to extend the offer for you to try out for mentorship with our master pianist, Henry Watson. He loved your performance."

Holly's guts fell to the floor, and she went cold. "Henry Watson was i-in the audience?"

"Of course he was. He wants to pick his replacement himself. Under our advisement, naturally. We were all very impressed with your performance. We've narrowed it down to three finalists, which Mr. Watson will look at individually and then *he* will make the final choice. Would you consider it?"

Holly's body was frail enough to be knocked over by a rose petal.

"Ms. Reynolds?"

"Yes! I'm here. I um. I'm sorry. Just a little moved. I'd love to accept. Oh, my goodness! Yes!"

"Very good. Mr. Watson would like to meet with you on Monday morning. You'll have two hours to play together. You'll meet him every other day for two weeks until he decides if you're right for his tutelage amongst the candidates."

Holly's nerves vibrated with electricity. "That's fantastic! I'm so honored. Yes. Where and what time?"

"The auditorium of your audition, and we'll have two pianos set for you. You'll be the first of the day at nine o'clock."

"I'll be there promptly."

"I'm sure you will. Congratulations, Ms. Reynolds."

Holly's feet felt hollow as she made her way to the auditorium. Henry Watson was an Ohio legend. Over the years, she'd watched videos of him on YouTube. And when she let her own bitterness go enough from her past to attend a concert, she always adored his performances. He seemed jovial and exuberant, but she had no idea what he was like in person.

A gentleman of his late seventies, he had wild, unkempt white hair that reminded her of Albert Einstein, a large beak of a nose, and a sharp jaw leading to an even sharper chin. On many of his personal concerts, he'd wear a white tailed-tuxedo and even played barefoot. He seemed a whimsical fellow, but Holly knew that the stage personae and the real person were often quite different.

As she approached the stairs at stage right, she heard a loud, welcoming voice.

"You must be Holly Reynolds. Welcome, my dear!"

Holly saw him standing on the stage next to one of the two formidable full grand pianos. He was barefoot.

"Hello, Mr. Watson!" she greeted from the aisle and waved.

Once she got on the stage, he walked to her with his arms outstretched and took her hand in both of his own. "Such a pleasure," he said. "Hope you don't mind," he indicated his bony bare feet. "I find that I'm more grounded this way. Feel free to remove your own shoes if you like."

Holly's nerves rattled out a tight giggle. "I do usually play in my bare feet at home."

"Splendid!" He kept one of her hands and led her to the piano on stage left. "You'll be here, my dear." The two pianos faced one another with their bowing frames interlocked but not touching.

Holly kicked off her shoes and seated herself, trying to keep her stomach intact even through his darling attempts to put her at ease. He took his place behind his own keys and stared at her for a moment. Her stomach clenched, sending up some bile, which she swallowed down quickly.

He sprang into action playing without announcement of the song. He playfully pounded out the first few notes of Beethoven's 9th.

Holly pitched her head to the side and answered him with successional notes. He took it a few bars further, which she answered.

A broad smile crossed his mouth. "Wonderful! I'm just kidding, though. Let's try this." He began a simple waltzing bass line.

She recognized it immediately. Tchaikovsky's Waltz of the Flowers from the Nutcracker Suite. Her fingers moved without a need for thought, and the notes for the treble sprang from her. Watson continued, and she followed him nearly flawlessly.

She hadn't played this piece in ages. It surprised her that she could call it to mind so rapidly. It must have been his prompting presence evoking the muscle memory from her hands. As she went through the piece, the quaking nervousness left her and her focus took over. There was nothing in the world that she wanted more in this moment than to please him. She had no interest in impressing him, knowing he'd seen it all. She just wanted to make him happy.

"Ha!" he cried when they'd finished the piece. "Next!" He dove straight into a Mozart arrangement. "Just try and follow me!" he spouted gleefully.

Holly recognized Sonata in D, KV 448. Her fingers flew along the keys with his until she began to detect subtle changes from his notes. *This must be the four-hands arrangement!* She had seen videos of it but had never had the chance to play it with anyone else. Listening to how much fuller the piece was with them both playing sent her soul into flight.

Mr. Watson stopped after they came to a natural pause. "What fun! You're a delight to play with, my dear." He was every bit as spirited and exciting as she hoped he'd be.

Holly's enormous grin hurt her cheeks. "Thank you, sir!"

His face straightened, and he stood. Holly began standing, and he flapped a hand at her. "No, no, you stay. I just wanted to warm you up a bit, you see. Break the ice, if you will. Now, I shall listen to you play." He went to the back of the stage, grabbed a folding chair, brought it just behind her right shoulder, and plopped himself down. "Go on. Anything you like."

It had to be Chopin.

Three weeks later, another call came. Holly was reading on the couch in the living room.

"Ms. Reynolds?" A joyful, raspy voice greeted her. It was Henry Watson himself.

"Yes, Mr. Watson?" She felt the oxygen leave the room.

"I wanted to extend my heartfelt congratulations and welcome you to the Dayton Performing Arts Alliance. You are my selection."

Holly bolted up. The book she was reading fell to the floor. "Oh, thank you, sir! I'm overwhelmed!"

"I wanted to tell you myself. You have the loveliest touch on the keys. I've only heard its equal once before."

Holly struggled to breathe. "May I ask who that was, sir?"

He chuckled softly. "My own."

She gulped. "That's... high praise, sir."

"Yes. And I especially liked that you took off your shoes. You were the only one to do so. I think we must be our truest selves when we play, don't you?"

Holly guffawed awkwardly. "Yes. Technicality is one thing, but the heart is where music truly lives. We have to be at home with our art."

There was a millisecond of silence where Holly's chest clenched. *Too deep?*

"I couldn't agree more, my dear."

Whew.

He continued, "I want you up and ready for our first formal rehearsal on Tuesday. 9 am. We play until 12:30, break for lunch, and play again from two to five or so. We'll practice with the symphony some days and not on others. Some days, we'll have to go quite a bit later."

"I understand."

"At this time, we're preparing for the Hallow's Eve series, which starts its performances on the first weekend of October. You and I will have some duets and switch off when I think you're ready."

"That sounds really good. Thank you, sir."

"Fantastic! See you Tuesday, my dear." He hung up.

Holly clicked off her phone and jellied. Her rump fell back onto the couch. She sat in numb shock for a few moments. "Tah—Thomas!"

"Hmmm?"

"Thomas!" She heard his chair squeak.

He appeared at the doorway to his study, and she shot her excited face at him. Her eyes told him everything he needed to know.

"You got it."

"I fucking got it."

He descended upon her and swept her into his arms as he sat next to her on the couch. "I knew you would," he said into her hair.

Holly's body convulsed with joy as he held her.

"We should call Janet. She'll be thrilled," he said.

She nodded against his shoulder but she didn't let go of him. She took a deep breath of his comforting pine aftershave. "Are you sure you're okay with this?"

He pulled from her to look her in the eyes. "Holly. I'm hardly in charge of you. You made that quite clear on your first day here." He relaxed and sat beside her, still holding her hands. His eyes fluttered down. "I will miss you. I'm—I'm anxious about being alone." His eyes lifted beautifully up to her. "As irony would have it, I used to be anxious about having anyone in my space at all. I wanted nothing else but to be alone. Now, I can't bear the thought of being here without you." He brought her hand up and kissed it. "But it's for a good cause. I shall endure." He worked on a smile.

Holly's eyes glowed. His lovely blue orbs pierced her with earnestness.

"And besides that, I'm too proud of you to grouse about myself. And I meant what I said. So long as you come home to me and sleep in our bed,

I'm happy. Kiss me, ride my cock, and continue making your splendid French toast."

Holly spat with laughter, falling against his chest.

"I love you, Thomas. I mean it. I love you."

He clasped her harder. "You're too much for me to think I could keep you all to myself. I don't like it, but it will be my honor to share you with the world." Thomas ran his fingers through her hair. "My Persephone."

Chapter 17

Ostinato

A couple of weeks later, high on classical music and the mentorship of a great master, Holly came home, and Thomas was not in his office. She dropped her bag on the couch and tossed her keys on the buffet.

"Thomas?" She climbed the twisting stairs to see if he was taking a nap in their room. As she went towards the hall to their bedroom, she noticed the door to Evelyn's room was cracked. He'd mostly avoided the master suite, having brought the majority of his clothes into Holly's room.

She could sense it immediately. His sadness. The air was heavier somehow. Something had happened. She gently pushed the door open further. He was slumped over, sitting on Evelyn's side of the bed with his elbows on his knees and his hands grasping disheveled hair. He looked like he'd been hyperventilating.

She ran to his side and prompted, "Thomas?"

He sighed heavily. After a moment, he gaped at her. His red face with glossy vein-riddled eyes confronted her. The sight of him rocked her.

"I missed it, Holly."

"What? What did you miss?"

"Evelyn's... The anniversary of when she... When she passed. I missed it."

Holly spread a comforting arm along his shoulders but was met with rejection. He tensed and shrank from her.

"No, please. Please don't touch me."

She stopped and backed off. "I'm so sorry. When was it?"

His voice squeaked out in ragged grief. "Last week. I can't even believe it. How could I have missed it?"

"Maybe you're just," she looked at him helplessly. "Maybe you were too distracted with happiness? You know, not so wrapped up in—"

"I shouldn't have fucking missed it!" he bellowed.

Holly jolted.

"I'm sorry. I shouldn't have yelled. I'm just beside myself." He rocked forward and back in quick agitation. "I was so caught up with finishing the book. The deadline. My agent. I had to get it to my editor, and you've been busy with rehearsals. Every day was a blur of editing and checking my work. Then smothering you as soon as you got home. I lost track of everything!" He clutched his dark brown hair between tense, white fingers. "And now, all I can do is see her dying over and over again in my head." He cried in agony. "Oh, God."

"Oh, Thomas. I'm so, so sorry. Please tell me what I can do." She went to embrace him, but he pushed her arms away.

He heaved a few breaths and said quietly, "I need to be alone."

"Okay." Holly turned to leave.

"Holly?"

"Yes?"

"No piano tonight. I can't take it."

Holly needed to practice, but she wasn't about to debate him in this state. It was best to leave him be. She could go to the auditorium early tomorrow. Holly left and closed the door so he'd have his privacy.

What to do? She went to change into one of her maxi dresses and then back down the stairs to find her phone. She grabbed a wine glass and the last of the cabernet and went out to the patio. Continuing to the bench in the garden, she sat down heavily and pressed Janet's name on her phone, sipping the wine.

"Hello!" rang Janet's cheerful voice. "Haven't heard from you in a couple of weeks. How are things? How's the symphony?"

"It's amazing. I love it. But I'm calling because I think something catastrophic just happened, and I may need your help."

"Uh-oh. Sounds serious."

"Do you know what happened last week? Something that changed everybody's lives a year ago?"

There was silence as Janet thought. Then a gasp. "Oh, my God! Evelyn's death. It was a year ago last... damn it. Last Wednesday! How could I have missed it?"

"Guess who else missed it?"

"He didn't."

"Yep. He's up in their room right now in pieces."

"Shit."

"Shit."

"You're right; I should come over."

"No, no. Don't. I think it'll overwhelm him. Maybe in a day or two. Let him mourn. He closes everything off when he mourns. God knows it took me almost two months to get through his exterior."

Janet sighed. "How did you get to know him so well, so quickly?"

Holly flushed. "Being around someone constantly does help you learn their patterns."

"We must have all been happy for the first time and unworried. I'd like to blame you and thank you for distracting us all with the joy of normalcy, but I feel that would burden you somehow."

Holly exhaled through her nose. "It's a compliment and not one at the same time."

"What about you? Are you okay? Not worried about competing with Evelyn's shadow again, are you?"

Holly recognized the tension locking up her neck and shoulders. "I am a little. I'm concerned we're going to take a big back-step. I don't know if he'll come out of that room and be fine. Or if he's going to start wallowing all over again."

"I wish I could tell you, sweetheart. I don't know either. I hope he doesn't, um..."

"Doesn't what?"

"I hope he doesn't sink back to where he was before."

"You mean before I came along?"

"Yes."

Horror crept up Holly's spine. If he slid that far, it could undo all of their progress. It could undo them. What if he didn't want to kiss her or hold her anymore? Or make love. Holly couldn't exist in that reality after all their romance. She couldn't fathom the withdrawal of it. She'd rather be alone again than deal with his rejection.

She asked Janet very slowly, "Do you think it could be that bad? Like... Do you think he won't want me anymore?" Her eyes stung with fearful, threatening tears.

"Oh, I'm sure it won't be that bad. You two have been completely happy for the better part of four months! No reason to think this could threaten that. Not with how I've seen him look at you and how he talks about you. I'm sure this will pass, and you'll be back to having your hands all over each other again in no time."

Holly choked out a giggle, wiping her eyes of the tears that poured from her. "I hope so."

"Oh, my darling. Don't cry. Hey! Why don't I bring tea tomorrow? I can do a little sibling intervention."

Holly sniffed. "I'd love that."

That night, Holly made dinner. She thought something light would be best. Linguine with Alfredo sauce and shrimp. She went to knock on the door of the master suite. "Thomas? Dinner's ready."

Shuffling sounded from the other side. The door opened. He looked wretched. Hair tousled, eyes drawn and red. He only glanced at her briefly as his chest heaved. Like seeing her broke his heart all over again.

Holly wasn't sure what to make of it or what to do. She stood, utterly lost.

"Won't you come down?" she asked gently.

Thomas opened the door and shuffled past her. He rounded her to the staircase and went down. She followed. He went to the dining room and sat where she'd set a plate down for him.

She sat next to him. He smelled as if he'd already been drinking. Twirling his fork in the noodles, he watched the creamy sauce squeeze from the bundle of pasta. He pulled up the fork laden with only a smear of sauce, dipped it into his mouth, and dropped the fork onto his plate. He chewed absently until he forced himself to swallow.

"Forgive me. I haven't any appetite." He rose and went to the kitchen. She heard him rummaging through the liquor bottles.

"Nope, we are not stooping." Holly stood and flew after him.

Thomas held a bottle of scotch and an on-the-rocks glass. He was just getting ice when she stood before him with fiery defiance. Holly breathed into her heart and the flames in her veins, desperately trying to be calm and careful with him.

"Thomas, no. This is not the way. Don't not eat and then plug down a bottle of scotch on top of whatever else you've already drank. You promised no more late-night tears."

He hesitated but wouldn't look at her.

"Please. Let me help you," she begged. "Let me be here for you."

Thomas shoved his glass against the ice maker in the refrigerator door until it was full. "Holly. With all respect. Fuck off." And he went to the stairs.

Holly was nearly too stunned to move. That had to be the most out of character thing she'd ever witnessed from him. Her brain spun. *Oh no, he didn't!*

"What the fuck, Thomas? I know you're in pain, but Jesus! We've come too far for you to sink like this and push me away! I will not let you do this to yourself or to us."

He continued to the stairs. "What part of fuck off didn't you understand? The fuck? Or the off? I told you I wanted to be left alone."

"Nothing you can possibly drink is going to help you, Thomas. It won't erase the last year or even the last ten years! It won't bring—"

He spun towards her and pointed at her with the hand that held the scotch bottle. "Don't you dare say it! I'm warning you."

She cringed, eyes bulging. He exhaled forcefully through his nose and turned to go up the stairs.

"Fine!" she yelled after him. "Drink yourself to death for all I care!" She heard his door slam. Holly went to shove dinner back into the pot because she'd lost her appetite, too. After that, she hunted for her cell phone to text Janet.

Holly: He just told me to fuck off
Janet: He WHAT?

Holly's phone rang. She answered Janet's call without even saying hello. "Just what I said. He told me to fuck off." She went outside so Thomas couldn't hear her.

"I don't believe you."

"He said, 'with respect, fuck off.'"

"I can't imagine him saying that to you. Or anybody!"

"I know! It's so out of character."

"Tell me what led up to it."

"We were having dinner, although he didn't eat anything. And Janet, I could smell booze on him."

"Oh, no."

Holly began furiously pacing around the patio. "So, he didn't eat, then got up and grabbed a bottle of scotch. I was begging him not to keep drinking and to let me help him, and he told me to fuck off."

"That barmy little bastard! I know what he's up to."

"What? Cuz I'm at a loss here."

"He's pushing you away. Do you know what he said to me a while ago?"

"What?"

"He said that sometimes being with you made him feel like he was cheating on—you know."

Holly's knees buckled, and she fell on her bum onto a lounger. "You're fucking kidding me. God dammit! When did he say that?"

"It was early on. But I ignored it because he launched right into how much he loved you. How you lit up his world and brought spring back to Hades or something."

Holly fought the sentimental flutter in her belly. "Persephone."

"That's what that reminded me of, yes!"

"Janet," Holly sighed heavily as a tremor jittered through her, "you know what I'm afraid of?"

"Tell me."

"I'm afraid I was a—" she barely found the strength to eke it out, "a rebound."

Janet thought quietly. "I don't want to acknowledge that, Holly. I don't want to consider that or even think it."

"Neither do I." Holly's voice strangled inward.

"Don't cry, sweetie. Maybe he just needs a night."

"Maybe. Maybe he needs to drink it out of his system."

Janet groaned. "That cannot be his solution every time, though."

"I agree."

"Listen, steer clear for now, and I'll come for tea tomorrow."

"Yeah."

"Okay. I love you. Try not to get stuck in your head too much, ok?"

"I'll try. Love you too."

Thomas sat on Evelyn's side of the bed, sipping scotch. All day, he'd replayed through memories. The day they met, her smile was bright in the misty English sunlight. Her perfect skin and dark hair, her loving chocolate brown eyes, rose-petal-shaped lips, and blushing cheeks came alive in his mind. Only one side had a dimple. It was the most darling little thing.

He watched her carrying books across the Cambridge campus, trying not to look at him while still casting sweet glances his way. Her eyes continually flashed over as he helplessly stared. It took him nearly three weeks to work up the nerve to talk to her.

They went for lunch. He committed himself to keeping her smiling so he could always see that little dimple pinch in on one side. She was studying horticulture and botany. She loved everything that grew from the dirt and every little worm and creature that moved under the soil. It was so dear how she'd try saving every hapless roly-poly and stray beetle. When it rained, she'd go out to rescue the worms from drowning or getting stuck on the concrete.

Over the next few weeks and months, he'd recite poetry and tell her the wonders of the Grecian pantheon as she listened wide-eyed while running her fingers along his chest and jaw. When his father became ill with seizures, it was just after they'd graduated. He had intended to stay in England with Evelyn. But Janet was drowning with all the family stress and begged him to come help her. She'd recently married Wesley and had a miscarriage. She could hardly cope with keeping herself sane, much less keep their mother from falling apart while their father was suffering and slipping away daily from the strain of his disorder.

Thomas was able to convince Evelyn to come with him to America. He promised it would be temporary. But a year went by. Then two. Then his father died. After the funeral, Evelyn told him she believed they'd done what they'd come to do and wanted to go home. Thomas went immediately and bought a ring.

He brought her to the botanical gardens and took a knee. The radiance in her tearful face was one of his favorite things to think of. She slipped on the ring and kissed him. They made love for days before they finally came up for air and told their families.

Then there was the wedding. Evelyn chose a simple gown with lace along the arms and a bare back. He knew there was never a goddess in the history of any pantheon that was as gorgeous as she was that day.

His mind continued through time. The day they bought the house. How she meticulously planned out and planted her gardens. Mostly orange roses, her favorite. Especially the large floppy ones with pink tips. He could never remember what they were called. But he adored how she delighted in them. He took a job lecturing and teaching a class at one of the local colleges while he wrote his historical books and supported Evelyn's gardening habit. Then there was the piano... Thomas stopped breathing.

Holly.

He'd been horrible to her. Some faint recollection of telling her to fuck off swam in his drunken brain. But that couldn't have been him. He'd never say that to her. He glanced at the clock. It was nearly two in the morning. Then his dreary eyes fell upon the framed picture of him and Evelyn on their wedding day. Her glorious smile beaming out as sunlight highlighted her hair and wedding dress, making her glow. He reached for it and held it. That's when the tears finally poured from him. They'd been leaking from him through the day and night, but now the torrent released, and he grieved in bellows.

He woke curled up among the decorative pillows on Evelyn's side of the bed, clutching their wedding picture. It was late in the morning, and the house was silent. He detected the fragrance of coffee. Unwilling to rise, he rolled over, avoiding the cheerful sunlight of late August.

He remembered waking up the day after Evelyn died, and her body had been removed. Janet changed the bedding. She even sprayed some of Evelyn's perfume on the pillows. Thomas had slept in the guest bedroom that night to escape the smell of cancer and death. He remembered waking in shock and disbelief.

Wesley stayed home with the children while Janet helped him. Their mother came and made soup. Having lost her own spouse, she understood the complete darkness and confusion of it.

When evening came the day after Evelyn died, Janet went home, and their mother tucked her son into his bed and stayed in the guest bedroom. She stayed for days, but he couldn't remember how many.

Thomas remembered very little of the first days after Evelyn passed. He could recall his mother checking on him, bringing him fluids and soup. At one point, she forced him to bathe. He never cried. Just lay in a blanketed cloud of shock and denial. Like someone told him the sun would never rise again.

Then there was the funeral. He stood between his mother and Janet, staring at a large, glossy, brown coffin covered in orange roses with pink tips. He didn't utter a word to anybody for weeks. The first time he spoke was when Janet brought tea. Little Samantha, just two years old at the time, was not about to have silence from her uncle. Her sweet face and enormous blue eyes started bringing him back. Her tiny, unafraid probing fingers petting his face as if she knew he needed pets and loves. Thomas remembered taking her tiny digits, curling them over his finger, and smooching the back of her little hand.

"Sad," she said.

"Yes. But I'm better now that you're here." He recalled Janet beaming and giving him his favorite tuna salad sandwiches. The next day, he went back to work. He hadn't taken a break since... Holly!

He bolted up. She must be at work. And the dear thing left him coffee and most likely broth. The brightest spot in his world since he'd descended into Hades' realm. *My Persephone.*

One last memory surfaced. One he'd ignored until now. Evelyn lay in her bed, pale and thin. Thomas helped sit her up to drink some tea. When she lay back down, she rested a hand on his arm.

"Thomas, I want you to move on."

He set her cup on the side table and said nothing back.

"I know this isn't an easy thing to think about. But I know you'll lose yourself in grieving once I'm gone."

"Evelyn, I don't—"

"Hush, love. I need to say this."

His head drooped.

"After you've got yourself back on your feet. I want you to find love again."

Thomas felt his chest caving in. "Please, I can't—" he choked. "I can't think of that now. Please don't make me."

Evelyn's graceful smile never twitched. Her warm eyes enveloped him with love when he finally looked at her.

She said, "You've so much to give. It'd be such a waste of a solid good man were you to stay alone. Please don't deprive yourself of love."

Thomas could do nothing but gaze hopelessly at his wife, trying to not let her words be real.

"I just felt that—that I should say you have my permission. Not that nature doesn't take its course. But I know you. You'll die alone if I don't release you."

He cupped her face affectionately and said, "Let's not dwell on that today."

The vision faded as his eyes refocused on the photo of Evelyn in her wedding dress. Thomas kissed the picture. "Evelyn, I love you always. But I think I'm ready to get on with my life. You were right. Nature does take its course. And thank you." He set the picture back on the nightstand and stood. He was surprisingly dizzy. The hangover was thick and heavy in his body. He smoothed himself down as best as he could and left the room without straightening Evelyn's side of the bed.

As he landed in the foyer and turned for the kitchen, he was surprised to see Janet sitting at the buffet, calmly sipping coffee and scrolling through her phone.

"Janet?"

"He lives." She smiled at him compassionately.

"What are you doing here?" He shambled to the coffeepot and poured himself a cup.

"I'm here to make sure you eat and drink something today before you expire from dehydration."

"I am thirsty." He took a glass from the cupboard, filled it with ice and water, and chugged it. He repeated the process of filling the glass with water two more times. "Good Lord, I really was parched."

"You should be. You haven't come out of your room for two days."

"I what?" he was horrified. "That can't be true! I only just fell asleep a few hours ago after I... Shit. I told Holly to fuck off." He clutched his forehead and a chunk of hair, groaning. "How mad at me is she?"

"Thomas," Janet said, gently setting down her phone. "That was two nights ago."

His jaw fell. "Tuh... two? That can't be."

"I want you to drink all the water you can and have a cup of coffee."

"Is there broth? Holly always makes me broth after a hard night."

"Ahhh. That must be what that congealed substance was that I found on the stove. She must have made it for you yesterday. I'll fix you some fresh." His sister smiled sweetly and set about putting a pot of broth together. "Chicken or beef?"

"I like the beef broth. That's what Holly always made." He felt a distinct, odd stillness in the house. "Janet? What happened? Is it botched?"

She kept her back to him. "Hydration, caffeine, and nourishment first. Then we'll talk."

He crumpled onto a stool at the buffet. "Why do I get the feeling this is really bad?"

"Because it is, Thomas."

Chapter 18

The Final Movement

Holly's heart felt like a shoe stuck in the mud as she got out of bed. Waking up without Thomas next to her was a hollow, sorrowful event. She searched for him, but he wasn't anywhere to be found. Probably still in Evelyn's room. She made coffee and a pot of broth for him. After her own coffee and a bowl of oatmeal, she took a shower and went to the auditorium.

Mr. Watson noticed her distraction and chastised her several times. The day passed with difficulty, but it would be worse when she got home. She looked in the trashcan in the kitchen. There were two empty bottles of liquor in there.

"Fucking God! Has he been drinking all day? Jesus, is even still alive?" She sped up the stairs and knocked on the door.

"No," was all she heard.

At least he hadn't died of alcohol poisoning yet. She opened the door a crack and peeked in.

"Thomas?"

"No."

She peered in farther and saw a bottle sitting on the floor and a glass on the nightstand. He was a balled-up heap on Evelyn's side of the bed, clutching a framed picture. "Sweetheart? Have you eaten anything?"

"No."

"Do you want to come sit with me? Maybe it'll be good to get out of this room?"

Thomas rose and set the picture next to him on the bed. "I have to piss," he stated in slurred words and got up to stagger to the bathroom.

Holly pulled her arms up, nervously chewing a nail. This broken fragment of the beautiful man she loved was almost more than she could bear. Her brows clenched in disbelief and despair, wondering what to do. Janet said she'd come over in about an hour for tea. That would be helpful. Maybe the two of them could wrangle him.

The toilet flushed. Thomas opened the door to the ensuite and stared at her darkly. Holly felt a chill. There was a shadow around him. He stood stiffly with his hands in fists. He was Hades, the God of death once again.

He spoke with difficulty. His mouth struggling to form the words through his haze. "It has become clear to me... that... I haven't completed my grieving process. And I'm afraid I can't—I can't be around you any longer."

Her body froze. "You're drunk, Thomas."

"I can't be with you H-Holly. Thank you for all you've done. It's time you left."

Her blood turned caustic. "You don't mean that."

"I do. I'm s-sorry."

"Thomas, I want you to consider this very carefully. I don't think you're in a condition to—"

"I've thought about it all day. I want you gone. I can't do this. I—I can't do this."

"If I walk out of that door, I will not come back."

"I need you gone now. I can't sustain this." He hobbled back to the bed and sat like an anchor at the bottom of the sea.

"But—but what about all that about how you couldn't help but love me? Do you not... love me anymore?"

"How can I love you while I still feel like I'm cheating on my wife? I can't do this to Evelyn."

"Evelyn's dead!"

He boiled over and stood very quickly, marching awkwardly towards her. She backed up fearfully as his firm fingertips met her sternum, and he pushed her through the bedroom doorway with the force of his furious energy.

"Get—out. Get out of my house! Get out this instant! I can't stand the sight of you! I need to be alone!" He slammed the door in her face.

Holly stood for one breathless instant until tremors overtook her body. Tears mounded and fell silently from her eyes. Without another word, she numbly walked to her room, lips trembling. She called Janet to bring the suitcases. Janet protested. Holly begged her to just fucking do it. It didn't matter if Thomas was spouting drunk ridiculousness. He had literally pushed her out. She was done with his dark moments. He made a promise that this wouldn't happen again, and he broke it. And how dare he lay his fingers on her like that! She wasn't about to live in fear of his drunken temper tantrums.

She gathered every bit of furious strength and began pulling her clothes out of the closet and drawers. Finally, her heart cracked, and she collapsed onto the floor in a heap of sobs.

Janet sat next to Thomas on the couch, watching him leaning further and further over his lap, burying his face in his hands, and wilting in disbelief as she conveyed to him the story Holly told her.

"Oh, God," he moaned in horror. "Please tell me I'm dreaming."

"I'm so sorry, Tommy." Janet lay a comforting hand on his back, rubbing it affectionately. "Holly thinks that she set you off like that by telling you to move on because Evelyn was dead."

He heaved a shaking inhale and stared into the air at nothing but his life falling apart—again. "No. I mean... I don't remember it. But she wasn't wrong, was she?"

"No. But it was harsh. She's always had a bit of a sharp tongue on her."

"She wasn't being harsh. She was being honest." His hands ran over his head with another exasperated groan. "So, she's gone?" His voice trembled. "Packed up and everything?"

Janet's heart broke for the pathetic shape of her brother in front of her. A grieving husk again. But this time, because of his own foolishness. "Yes, my love."

He sat up. "I'll call her. I'll apologize. Shit. Do you think she'd come back to me?"

Janet rolled her lips inward. "I don't know. In all the years I've known her, I've never seen it happen. Once she's out, she's out."

"Perhaps she'd make an exception. It's only been a day. Oh, Christ! Why do I have to be such a drunken arsehole? Damn it!"

"You can try calling, but she's proper cheesed off at you. And honestly, I don't think it was so much what you said."

"How do you mean?" Thomas rubbed his hand over his forehead.

Janet took a breath. The last thing she wanted was to harm anyone. The idea that she finally had to confront her brother about his drinking fits wrapped her guts in a tangled, fidgeting ball.

"You physically pushed her out of your room."

Abject horror covered his face.

"You scared her. That and she's..." Janet swallowed, trying to bring up a shred of courage. "She's tired of your drinking fits." She watched her brother slump over his knees even lower. Her heart nearly disintegrated. "She's seen it so many times, Thomas. Last night, she told me all about it. And I'm concerned because it's been happening all this time, and none of us would have even known it weren't for Holly. For the love of—you're halfway to drinking yourself to death."

"I—pushed her? With my hand?"

Janet nodded.

"Dear Christ, I am a brut." He collapsed over his own lap again. "Disgusting and undeserving of her. And I broke a promise. I promised her no more nights like that." A mournful breath took him.

Janet sent a comforting hand along his back in a slow circle. "You know I won't ever lie to you."

"I know," he whimpered. "One of your more redeeming qualities."

"You can't go on getting pissed every time something upsets you."

"I'm such a goddamned fool!" Thomas launched off the couch. "How could I be such a goddamned fool? I had all the aces! All of them! And I just set them on fire like some damned, fucking idiot!"

Janet could tell he'd had enough. Time to switch to her solution-oriented brain. "How's your head?"

"I could use an aspirin—or five. Perhaps some plyers to pull this arrow out of my chest."

Janet's brows knit sympathetically. "I'll get you some aspirin. Just breathe. Drink water. Don't call her yet. Wait for me. I may have an idea."

"I hope it's one of your better ones. I can't lose her, Janet." His bleary, red, swollen eyes stared at her with a desperation that galvanized her love for him and for Holly.

"I know, darling. Let me think." Janet went up to the bathroom for aspirin. Her mind raced as it search for ways to salvage this. There had to be one. Maybe if Holly agreed to go out on a date or something? Certainly! They could start small again. Build back up.

Holly understood drunken craziness. She'd been there herself. And she'd been there for Janet's nights of delirium as well. Holly was one of the most loving, forgiving people Janet knew. She'd appeal to Holly's sense of compassion and empathy. That usually worked.

Holly lounged by the pool while Jake and Samantha ran through the yard, shooting each other with water pistols. Wesley floated on a raft in the water. It was a Saturday. One day since she'd been tossed out by

Thomas' meltdown. Janet had gone to tend to him. As far as Holly was concerned, he was no longer her problem.

For now, she wanted to enjoy the last few remaining days of August before the chill of September turned all the greens to browns. Her phone rang with Janet's ringtone. She reached under the lounger and answered the call.

"How is he?" she asked.

"I'm terrible." It was Thomas.

Holly sat up. "Nope." She hung up. A whole fifteen seconds passed before it rang again. She sighed. "Janet, if this isn't you, I swear to God—"

"It's me, it's me."

Holly bolted up from the lounger and quickly went into the house for privacy. "That was not fucking okay!"

"I'm sorry. It was worth a try."

"I don't want to talk to him."

"Holly, he's wrecked."

"He's always wrecked!"

"Yeah, but this time, he's wrecked for *you*. He doesn't remember anything he said to you. He was completely blacked out."

"That's not my fucking shitting problem now, is it?"

"Now I know you're upset. You're doubling your profanities."

"You're goddamned fucking lucky they're only coming in pairs right now!" She began pacing furiously around the family room. Her pacing took her past the sunroom towards the kitchen, and she could see through the screen door to the pool. Wesley was lounging on a floater.

"Holly, I've seen you have blackout tantrums too."

"I know, but it's not a normal thing for me, is it? It's a very rare occurrence. And I didn't shove you! And we weren't fucking, were we, Janet?"

Holly heard Janet muffle the phone and say, "She's really angry. I've never heard her so furious." There were some tones from Thomas, but Holly couldn't make them out. Janet uncovered the phone. "I think you're this angry because you really love him, and this really hurts."

Holly let out an exasperated huff. "Thanks for that, Captain Obvious!" She increased the speed of her pacing. "Tell his Lordship that

I am not speaking to him. He can drown in his issues until Hades freezes over."

"I'm not telling him that!"

"Fine. But I mean it. I don't want to hear his fucking voice."

"Holly. You didn't stop loving him in twenty-four hours. Now calm down, and please talk to him."

Holly gripped the bridge of her nose.

"At least let him apologize so you won't be mad that he didn't."

Holly's head lolled back, and she stared at the ceiling. *Damn her.* "Fine. Put him on."

"Holly?" She could hear the hangover in his voice. He probably wouldn't be right again until after the weekend.

"What did you have, three bottles?"

"I think so. I'm so sorry, Holly."

"You scared me."

"I know, I know. Janet told me. I can't begin to express my—"

"No more crying nights. You promised!"

Regret coated his halting words. "I did. Just... missing the anniversary caught me off guard. But I was an angel till then. You must admit that."

Holly's chest warmed. She slouched. "You were."

"I don't expect you to bring back all your things because I know I hurt you, and you're angry with me. You've every right to be. I screwed up. I ruined it. I don't know how I'm going to live with myself."

"How about the same way you did before I got there? Find something else to write about. Find another Persephone."

There was a brief silence. "There's only one Persephone."

The yearning love in his voice made her stomach do an annoying little flip-flutter. *Nope, I am not letting him get me that easily.*

"Thomas, I'm not coming back to that house. I will not."

"How about dinner? At a restaurant? Not the house."

"Then what? Then what, Thomas? We date again. Say I even relent and move back in with you. Then, next August, you fall apart all over again. And shit, we haven't even gone through your wedding anniversary. I am completely done competing with Evelyn. And I'm not trying to be a hard-ass. I've been nothing but compassionate about your situation. But I simply will not go through this over and over again with you."

"In my defense, it's only happened the one time. I could be completely cured by next time."

Holly let out an audible sigh. "That house has yours and Evelyn's room. The room where she passed away. Her stuff is still in the bathroom. Her jewelry boxes, and her clothes; even her toothbrush and face cream! They are all still there."

"Yes. Perhaps it's time for me to deal with all that."

"Her dishes, her pots, her furniture, her fucking roses, and her goddamned piano!"

"So now you hate me, the house, and everything in it?"

Holly stilled. "I do, now."

"What do you want me to do? Sell it? You can't expect me to sell it. I love this house."

"If we start dating again, will you be happy with me in my own apartment?"

She could hear him thinking. "No. I'd want you here."

Holly made a fist. "I am *not* going *back* to that house, Thomas."

"Holly, please. Be reasonable," he pleaded.

"Look. You hired me to clean it all up. I've done that. I've fulfilled our contract. Now it's up to you."

"Up to me to what?"

"To move on. Really move on."

"I may need more time."

Holly fired up with irritation again. "You know what? Maybe you were right. Maybe we did move too fast. Maybe you should have controlled your lust."

"Oh, come now! Surely you don't mean that. And you were bursting at the seams, too, if you'll remember."

"You need therapy, Thomas."

That silenced him.

Holly felt his angst, and it shattered her heart. She nearly unraveled. Calming herself, she said remorsefully, "Get some grief counseling. Part with some of Evelyn's things. It's been a year now. It's time. Then call me."

"I—I have to think about it."

"Alright, Thomas. You think." She ended the call. Holly's body lost all strength, and she caught herself on the staircase, collapsing down. Tears burst from the pain tearing her chest apart.

"Aunt Holly! Come play water squirters!" came Jake's enthusiastic voice.

"Squoot! Squoot!" shouted Samantha.

The two of them had opened the screen door and were staring hopefully at her. Holly forced herself to smile and look at them.

Wesley was right behind them. "I'm sorry, Holly. I got them." He grabbed his son's shoulder. "Come on, monsters! Daddy will play squirters with you." He shuffled them out and closed the sliding glass door. God bless Wesley. Janet really had found herself a gem of a man. He'd been nothing but kind and considerate since Holly came to stay. He always made sure the kids didn't jump on her too much.

She hauled herself up and nearly tumbled up the stairs to the room she was staying in. Falling onto the bed, she released herself. Tears shook her until she balled up in agony. With all of her willpower, she fought thoughts of Thomas' wondrous, knee-quaking kisses. His sparkling smile and loving, intense eyes and tender hands. Hands that touched her as if she were made of pure gold. His beautiful moans and the way he cried out just a little when he climaxed. Her body shuddered with sobs.

Chapter 19

Cadenza

Thomas sat on the bench Holly had made within a circle of Evelyn's roses, holding a cup of tea. The crisp of autumn was near. He could feel it in the air. All the joy of spring and summer was ending. And with his Persephone gone, it all seemed oddly appropriate.

Life without Holly had been a larger adjustment than he'd anticipated. Cooking for himself proved to be a nuisance. When the laundry bin filled, he hated doing the washing. Dust was piling up again on his bookcases. And specks of dirt and dust bunnies gathered along the floors and rugs. He decided to try to do one chore a day. At least he could attempt to prove to himself that he was, as Holly had put it one day, "a fully-formed adult."

Working on his book was almost the hardest part about losing her. He didn't realize how accustomed to her sounds he'd become. The house was unnaturally still. And every time he paused from his work, there were no kisses. The silence from no piano playing in the evenings had him feeling gray and dried out.

Sometimes, he'd even sleep in the bed in the guest room. It was the only place with remnants of Holly's smell. He'd settle into the blankets and nuzzle her pillow, breathing her scent until he slept.

Thomas sipped his tea again and stared out at a patch of grass where he had made love to her under a sparkling canape of fireflies. Every inch of him was numb from missing her. But if Holly wanted him to prove himself ready to love again, then that is what he must do.

What to do? Where to start?

When he was finished with his tea, he dropped the cup off in the kitchen and made straight for the linen closet. He knew the first thing he wanted to do. He took a flat sheet from the closet, went to the nook off the living room, and stared at the piano. After closing the lids over the strings and keys, he shook the sheet loose. With a sweeping motion, he covered the instrument.

"I'm sorry," he said to it. "I can't bear to look at you. It's not your fault."

With that, he located his phone and called his sister.

"Darling!" came her affection chime.

"Janet. I'm ready."

Thomas was already resisting a panic attack when Janet arrived. He opened the door, and she entered with her arms outstretched.

"Give us a hug," she said.

Thomas embraced her and squeezed.

She placed her palms firmly on his shoulders and said, "We'll get through this. It's going to be alright."

He attempted a smile. "Easier said than done, old girl."

"I know. But it's true." She entered his home and placed her purse on the kitchen buffet. She slowly twirled, taking in the state of the house. "Wow. Look at this place. You're actually keeping it up."

He grinned sheepishly. "More or less."

Janet approached him and placed a hand on his cheek. "I'm very proud of you."

Thomas crumpled, and his face turned a bright red as he held in frustrated tears.

"It's alright to cry, my love. Might do you some good."

He huffed as his eyes reddened. "Oh God, Janet. I'm so scared." He sniffed a gob of snot as she brought him in for another hug.

She tried soothing his back with slow strokes of her hand. "It's okay. It's okay to be scared. I've got you, chum."

His shoulders shuddered with a couple sobs. Thomas wasn't used to crying sober, so he worked to stuff his emotions back down. He raised his head, smoothing his hair and wiping his face. "I've uh, got some uh—boxes upstairs." He turned and Janet followed him to his master bedroom.

A small stack of boxes sat by the door.

Janet thoughtfully gripped her chin. "Do you think this will be enough?"

Thomas shook his head. "I don't know."

"Well, let's get started, shall we?" She patted him heartily on the back.

Thomas opened the closet and stared at Evelyn's clothes. "I don't think I got enough boxes."

Janet humphed. "Well, I know how to handle hanging clothes without boxes. Where are your trash bags?

"No! I won't simply toss them in a bag."

"Don't worry. I have ways. It will be very respectful."

He looked away and fiddled with the bottom of his shirt. "The bags are in the pantry."

"Why don't you get started with her toiletries?" Janet left to retrieve trash bags.

Thomas stared into the closet. A maroon dress with an open back that Evelyn always wore with her favorite gold necklace. A black dress that was so tight her rump was practically illegal in it. Skirts and slacks of every color hung on clipped hangers. He was staring at a silken white blouse with little red rose buds dotting it when Janet reentered the room. He lifted the blouse from the hanger bar while Janet watched him.

"She used to wear this with a black skirt. I remember it. Sometimes with the solitaire ruby I got her. Sometimes with her grandmother's gold locket." He replaced the blouse in the closet and pulled out the sleeve of another one. A lacy fitted chemise with fluted sleeves. "I bought her this one for our trip to Florida."

Janet set the trash bags on the bed and stood next to him. "My love, we'll never get through them all if you have to tell the story of each one."

Thomas looked bleary-eyed at her. "Even if it helps me to let go?"

Janet's face softened. "Alright. Tell their story and then hand them to me." She turned and pulled a bag out.

Thomas took the lacy blouse out. "Our trip to Florida. It rained half the time. But we had such fun." He handed it to Janet, who placed it in the bag and threaded the hook of the hanger through the bottom of the bag.

She held it up by the hook and showed him. "You see? It's like a garment bag."

"Yes. Very clever." He turned back to the closet. "This one was from her mother on her birthday..."

Four garbage-garment bags later, Evelyn's side of the closet was empty.

"Well, that's that," he announced sullenly.

"Break?"

He rubbed his eyes and the few tears that had leaked. "Yes."

Janet took his hand and let him out of the room. "Best to change the scene, I think."

Thomas stood at the sink in the bathroom, staring at Evelyn's face cream. He unscrewed the lid. He shouldn't have done it, but he did. Inside, left in the cream, were swipes from her own fingertips. Then, the scent of it wafted to his nostrils.

He let out an anguished "Oh!"

Janet was by his side in a flash. Her hand covered his, and she pried the jar from his fingers. "Why don't I do this room? You go on and box the shoes."

Thomas released his other hand's grip on the counter and shuffled to the bedroom. He boxed up Evelyn's shoes and sweaters while Janet packed Evelyn's toiletries and delicates. They went through Evelyn's books, notebooks, and nick-nacks and put together a special box of her precious items, heirlooms, and memorabilia to send to her family.

The pair of them stood at the dresser, and Thomas opened Evelyn's jewelry box. He fumbled through gold and silver necklaces, rings and earrings. He pulled out her grandmother's gold locket.

"This ought to go back to her mother." He lay it reverently on the top of the dresser. After further rummaging, he pulled out a couple of other items. "These should go to her sister." Then he closed the jewelry box and handed it to Janet. "I think you and Samantha should have the rest."

"Oh, Tommy, are you sure? There's nothing in there you want?"

He shook his head. "No. What would I do with any of it? It's better being used by you and that little terror-pixie as soon as she quits breaking everything."

Janet's wind-chime laughter rang out. "She is a little terror-pixie!" She took the box and ran her hand along his arm. "You did very well today."

He cast his forlorn glance down. "I—I feel like I'm losing her all over again." His eyes reddened and filled with moisture.

Janet immediately set down the jewelry box and clutched him. He let his head fall onto her shoulder and gently wept.

Thomas opened the front door for Janet as she was leaving.

She pulled a business card from her pocket. "Remember when Wesley's co-worker lost her husband?"

"No."

"Well, she went to see this wonderful therapist." She presented the card.

Thomas hesitated, then took it.

"Give it a try. Can't hurt."

Thomas nodded.

"I'll come again Saturday next. We'll go through the garage and the rest. Alright?" She kissed his cheek. He gave her a last squeeze, then closed the door behind her. After Janet had gone and the boxes that contained Evelyn's memories with her, Thomas shuffled to his kitchen. A hulking white form on the other side of the kitchen caught his attention. The piano sat silently under its sheet.

"If I could pack you in a box and ship you off, I would," he told it and reached for a bottle of scotch.

He woke on the floor with the sun pouring in through the living room windows. His head ached, and he cursed the bright light. He rolled over slowly, and his painful eyes stared through the open windows at the patio and yard. *Broth would be nice. After several glasses of water.* He raised up in slow motion. The empty bottle caught his eye. And the glass, laying on its side, which had rolled under a chair. *What the fuck is wrong with me? I can't go on like this.*

Thomas gathered the glass and bottle and placed them on the nearby coffee table. Laboriously, he hoisted himself to stand and made his way to the kitchen for water. After drinking three glasses, he began searching his cupboards for beef bouillon. He also grabbed a small pot, filled it partway with water, and set it on the stove.

"Now, how did she..." He examined the beef bouillon jar. "How much of this do I put in?" He squinted at the words on the label, but his eyes hurt, and the tiny print didn't make sense to him. "Oh, blast it! If I can't make bloody, goddamned broth!" He furiously opened the jar, grabbed a spoon, and shoveled its contents into the pot. He threw the jar across the kitchen. It flew down the hall towards the TV room and dented the wall. Then it fell and cracked to pieces on the floor, setting the remainder of its contents oozing out. "Fuck!"

Thomas held a bottle of wine and a bag of presents as he waited for Janet to open the door. The house and yard glowed with multi-colored lights. Wesley delighted in being the brightest house on the block for the holidays. A display of successionally flashing reindeer pulling Santa in his slay blinked happily in the yard.

He stared at a large wreath of pine and holly. His stomach sank. The door opened, and Janet's usual jolly demeanor overwhelmed him. When she'd invited him to Christmas dinner, he almost said no. But he knew that he needed to get out of his house. Especially this time of year.

After hugging his sister, he squatted to receive the enthusiastic arms of his nephew and niece.

"Uncle Thomas, are these for us?" asked Jake, peeking into the bag Thomas had rested on the floor.

"They are indeed, old boy. But you must promise not to open them until I say so."

"Prezzies!" squealed Samantha and went to plunge her hand into the bag. Jake gently grabbed her arm. "No, Sammy! Uncle says wait."

The little girl flung her head back with a melodramatic groan. Then, her face brightened again. "Unka Thomas, look! My new dess!" She spun in an awkward whirl of pink satin.

Thomas hoisted himself back to his feet. "My, my, Samantha. You look gorgeous, darling."

"Here ya go, Tom." Wesley, donning a large red velvet Santa hat, held out a glass. "Dirty vodka," he said cheerily.

Thomas accepted the martini.

"I'll put these under the tree." Wesley trotted off with the bag of gifts.

Thomas took a step further in the foyer.

"Ah-ah. Shoes, please. And give me your coat as well," said Janet.

Thomas set his glass down on a nearby credenza and followed his sister's instructions.

"May I come in now?"

"Of course! I've got some little snackies, some chocolates, and a bit of brandied eggnog too."

"Splendid." Thomas entered the open family room and kitchen area, letting his eyes sweep around. Decorations of ribbon-bound pine boughs with accents of holly leaves and berries interwoven with fairy lights were everywhere. Janet's enormous Christmas tree twinkled by the fireplace. Heavily laden with ornaments, it slowly rotated around.

Wesley made his way to the sliding back door and observed the snow beginning to fall. "There it is. You see, babe? I was right again."

"You're very rarely wrong, love."

"Should get at least four inches." He turned to his son, "Snowman weather, eh, Jakey?"

"Yes! And snowball fights!"

Janet called from the kitchen, "But no black eyes this year, please." She approached Thomas and clinked her own drink against his. "You look better. Therapy going well?"

"It is, thank you." His eyes met Janet's momentarily.

She was studying him. It was unnerving.

"And the book?"

"At my editor's, I'm happy to say."

"Brilliant. And the lectures?"

He could tell by Janet's astute gaze that she was trying to work something out in her head. "We're off for the holiday now, but I've picked up a few more for spring semester."

"That'll be nice." She sipped her drink, and her cheeks pinched a bit. "We had Holly over last night for Christmas Eve."

His chest jolted. "Oh?"

"She's looking very well. The orchestra has a week left in their Christmas performances. I thought it would be fun to go."

"Do enjoy yourself. Has old Mr. Watson finally retired?"

"I thought we could all go together, and no, he hasn't."

"Well, I wish he'd get on with it. He's been teasing retirement for what, six months now?"

"It takes a long time to train a replacement for your life's work, and I really do think you should join us."

"No, Janet," he nearly barked. He sheepishly glanced at her. "I have other things going on."

She continued peering at him, and he was unable to shake the feeling that he'd done something wrong.

"What? Gods, I hate it when you look at me that way."

She smirked. "You look guilty."

Thomas rolled his eyes.

"Yes. You're hiding something, I can tell."

"Oh please, Janet."

"Don't you 'please Janet' me! I'm an expert in you, ya know."

Thomas slouched with an annoyed sideways glance. "Alright, fine. There's no use in trying to keep it from you. I am—seeing someone."

Her eyes blew open wide. "Are you insane? What about Holly?"

"Dear Christ, you know she doesn't want me."

"You idiot, of course she does!"

Thomas released an exasperated breath. "I'm not ready."

Janet cocked her eyes. "Not ready? Not ready for the love of your life, but ready enough for some other tart!"

"Helen is hardly a tart."

"Oh, it's Helen, is it?"

"Yes. She's a mathematician. Teaches at one of the universities I give lectures at."

Janet shook her head in disbelief. "What is the matter with you?"

"Nothing! You've been telling me to move on! And when I finally do, now you're upset?"

"Move on, yes. With Holly, you daft shit!"

"Goddammit, Janet!" he yelled inside a whisper, careful not to upset the children. "Will you *please* stop meddling in my life?"

His sister stilled.

Thomas gathered himself, pinching his brows with his fingers. "I'm sorry I roared. I'm doing the best I can. I needed something else."

Janet tilted her head, relenting but still studying him. "Something else?"

"Yes. Someone not... Someone that has nothing to do with anything. Who doesn't remind me of anything. Understand?"

She slowly shook her head. "No. I don't."

Thomas took a few steps, suddenly becoming animated, gesturing with his hands. "Look, I was on campus. A beautiful woman started talking to me. We went out for drinks, and now we're shagging. There. Make sense now?"

Janet spoke in a sweet, low voice. "What happened to your romantic, dreamy self?"

Thomas huffed. "My balls were drying out."

"Oh, for God's sake, Thomas!"

He stepped towards her, grinning, and nearly released a chuckle. "Do you know what an utter delight it is getting you all riled up?" He said, wrapping his arms around her.

"You're an absolute prick."

"I know. But I'm your absolute prick.

Janet hugged him back, giggling.

"Helen is lovely, you'll see. Maybe I'll bring her round after New Year's."

"One more thing." She released him. "How's the drinking?"

Thomas raised his glass. "This is the first liquor I've had in weeks. I enjoy some wine or a brandy now and then. But I don't buy the really hard stuff anymore."

"Just the one relapse, then?"

He nodded. The oven beeped.

"Oh! That's my roast."

When Thomas returned home from Janet's, the house was as dark and cold as a crypt. There were two occasions when Holly's absence struck him the hardest. When he came home to a silent house, and when he woke up every morning alone.

He clicked on the hall light and removed his shoes. His phone chimed. After taking off his jacket and hanging it on the coat stand next to the winding staircase, he pulled his phone from the pocket.

> **Helen:** Merry Christmas! Want to come over? I need my Brit fix.

Thomas sighed heavily. He wasn't in the mood for Helen. Maybe he'll feel differently tomorrow.

> **Thomas:** Perhaps tomorrow? I'm knackered.
> **Helen:** Fine. But be prepared to get worn out!

He smirked despite a slightly unpleasant shiver that ran through him. Helen was fine enough. If nothing else, she served a purpose, and that was to keep him from getting too lonely and receding back into his alcoholic doldrums. She was a nice distraction that, so far, seemed content with being a friendly shag now and then.

He walked toward the kitchen to put tea on. The white shadow in the nook caught his eye. It seemed as discontent to be without Holly's touch as he was. Soon, he had the kettle filled and set it upon a hot burner. He searched for the right tea for evening. He selected one with mint and dropped a couple bags into the teapot.

While he waited for the water to boil, he continued staring at the piano. His brain bubbled with thoughts of what to do with it. Finally, he said out loud, "You're more Holly's now than you ever were Evelyn's. Since neither of us can have either of them, the least I can do is set you free."

He poured tea into a mug and went to change into his pajama bottoms and a sweatshirt, wishing he had something stronger to soothe the dried-out crevices of his soul.

Chapter 20

Winter Breve

Holly's hand shook slightly with elation as she put her key into her apartment door. She'd just finished with the first rehearsal since the January break had concluded, and Mr. Watson had announced his retirement. Letting go of his position in the symphony was understandably difficult for him. But he told them that at the urgence of his wife, he was officially handing the reins to Holly.

She was able to rent a small studio apartment near the performing arts center. At least it smelled better than the last building she'd rented from. Setting down her bag, she went to the utility kitchen for a glass of wine. Taking a pause between practicing with the orchestra and coming home to practice refreshed her.

She resurrected her Roland keyboard, as it was impossible to get a piano into her apartment, and she could keep the volume down, or play with earbuds. She could hardly afford a real piano, anyway. The touch was different, though. Even though it had eighty-eight weighted and touch-sensitive keys, the action still left something to be desired. Nothing compared to the silken feel or tone of a real piano.

Sometimes, she'd go to the local community college, and they'd let her use their piano to practice. She enjoyed the change of scenery. Plus, the string section of the orchestra would often have to stay later at the auditorium, which prohibited her from using the piano there.

She finished her glass of wine while changing into some sweatpants. She'd have about two hours, then she'd make dinner. Janet said she'd meet her for drinks later at a local pub.

Holly ordered a lager and sat at the bar at Zeke's. The place still reminded her of Thomas, but She'd been going there for years before him, and she wasn't about to let the memory of a perfect night ruin her love for this haven. Janet arrived a few moments later, greeting her with a warm hug. She ordered a gin and tonic.

"So," Janet began, "how's the symphony?"

"It's fantastic. Mr. Watson just officially announced his retirement today! I'm finally taking over as first piano at the Ostara series."

"Oh!" Janet made little mini claps with her hands. "How wonderful! I'm over the moon for you!"

"Yeah." Holly beamed. "But I'm gonna miss him. He's such a lovely man. I adore working with him. So much refinement and class. And he's taught me so much. It'll be a little scary without him there. Like taking off the training wheels."

"You're going to be brilliant!"

"I hope so."

Janet's drink arrived, and she sipped through its little red straw. Holly's eyes awkwardly wandered the bar as she worked on figuring out how to ask the question itching the back of her brain. Janet's astute mind picked it up instantly, and she flexed an eyebrow.

Holly's eyes flattened. "What?"

"Go on."

"Go on, what?"

"Ask about him. I know you want to."

Holly sighed. "How's Thomas?"

Janet pursed her lips. "He's doing better. Much better, actually."

"Well, that's good." Holly sipped from her glass.

"Yes. He's poured himself into his work, of course. I think the Persephone book is going to come out in the middle of spring."

"Seems appropriate."

"Mm-hmm." Janet sipped through the skinny red straw. "We finished going through Evelyn's things."

"The hell you say!"

"We did."

"I'm impressed."

Janet's smile retained a hint of sadness. "It's taken a long time, and been very difficult. I'm almost glad you haven't been there."

"Why's that?"

"Because I believe it was something he needed to do just with himself. And me. Since we were together during every step of the last three years of her life."

Holly nodded.

"He actually cried. A lot."

"Without drinking?" Holly slapped her chest with her hand almost trying to keep the pride and joy in.

"Without any alcohol of any kind. It wasn't the balling, pouring tears kind. Just the weepy kind."

Holly nodded, keeping her smile pinched so as not to give away how glad she was. "That's good. At least he's learning to hit his release valve a little."

"Yes, and you'll be very happy to know that he did find a therapist."

Holly nearly choked on her beer. "No fucking way."

"He did. We started going through Evelyn's things at the end of September. He had one more relapse with the booze-crying. And right before Halloween, he finally booked a therapist."

"The season of death and transition," Holly murmured.

"Too right! It spooked me a nip, too. The cycle of his life during these last two years seems completely in sync with nature. I've never seen anything like it. I mean, look at when you arrived and left. He spent the entirety of the fall and winter in mourning for his wife. Then, you showed up in the spring and resurrected him through the summer. He was alive again. Then you leave, and it all went to back to darkness. Exactly in time for fall and winter. Maybe you really are his Persephone."

"Janet, don't. If he wants to call me, he has my number."

Janet nervously made quick work of the rest of her gin and tonic. Holly's eyes darted all along her friend's face. She knew that tense pinch in her mouth and cheeks.

"What aren't you telling me?"

"Another? Please?" Janet prompted the bartender.

"Janet."

"What about you? Are you seeing anybody? Lots of dishies in the orchestra, no?"

"Now I have to know what you aren't telling me."

"Don't ask questions you may not want the answers to."

Holly quieted. "I'd like to know."

Janet got her second gin and tonic. She was stalling.

"Janet!"

"Bullocks! Alright! He's seeing someone."

"Oh." The news smacked Holly like a slammed door. But she couldn't protest it. He was free to do as he pleased. "Guess I really did open him up." Holly chugged her beer. "Well, I mean, that seems completely natural, doesn't it? He's single. Finally, dealing with his issues. I mean, it's normal. Totally normal. Hey!" She waved down the bartender. "Another lager and a shot of Jim Beam, please."

"Don't you start drinking too," Janet scolded.

"I'm not. You know I like bourbon."

"Yes, and I also know it's your comfort-booze."

"So?"

Janet put a soothing hand on Holly's arm. "If it's any consolation, none of us can stand her."

Holly made a feeble attempt to smile.

"The kids avoid her, and Samantha can't shut her gob about how she isn't her Ana Holly. I almost feel sorry for the girl. My three-year-old has her completely out-matched."

Holly cackled. "Another pianist?"

"No. He actually sold the piano."

"He... sold it?" A soap bubble could have knocked her over.

"He said he couldn't bear looking at it anymore. Reminded him too much of you."

Holly wavered in her chair.

"No, this one's a mathematician. She works at one of the universities he lectures for. They're too alike. God, she's dull."

"Thomas isn't dull."

"Not when he's with you."

Holly slumped.

"Sod it, I'm sorry Holly. This may or may not make you feel better, but I think she's just a—a placeholder. Like a bookmark."

"Yeah, that's great. A bookmark he's sleeping with." Holly choked on the thought. Imagining Thomas' body and impossibly beautiful skills being used on some other woman was nearly too much for her.

Janet stared into her drink. "Honestly, I don't know why he's with her. I've never seen him do this before. Normally, he only goes for a woman he's sure he can love. And I can tell he doesn't love her. They seem more like co-workers rather than a couple. It's certainly of character for him."

Holly couldn't help herself. "Janet, I know you think you've got him all dialed in, but even *he* dates girls just to date them sometimes. No love involved."

"You mean for casual... enjoyment?"

Holly nodded.

"And you know this because..."

"He told me. He said he doesn't tell you everything about his life. He's even initiated some of his break-ups. So, he's not necessarily the heart-sick Romeo you think he is."

"Rubbish!" Janet swiped the air with her hand. "Of course he is! When he's in love, he's completely heartsick. And that doesn't change the fact that his seeing this woman is absolutely out of character for him."

"Maybe he's trying something different. You said he's really picky."

Janet nodded, sipping on the red straw.

"Is she smoking hot?"

"Well, I wouldn't say 'smoking.' But, yes, she's very pretty."

"And since she's a mathematician, she's gotta be super cranial. So, there ya go! A hot, smart girl sounds exactly like his style."

Janet shook her head in bewilderment. "I can't believe you're justifying this. You, of all people! There are absolutely zero sparks between them. She's dull as an old spoon! And so unpleasant. We're actually looking for excuses *not* to hang out with them."

Holly let a giggle out.

"Besides, he's obviously still in love with you. He asks about you all the time."

Holly's eyes fell. "Well, that hardly matters if he's got a mathematician bookmark thing."

"I think you're still in love with him, as well."

A moment of silence passed between them.

Holly rubbed her temple. "I don't think I want to talk about this anymore. Anyway, I'm happy where I am. And if he wanted me back—" Holly's throat clinched, "he'd have called me by now." She squeaked.

Janet reached across the distance between their barstools and hugged her.

Thomas held a bundle of files and lecture notes as he walked down a hall in the community college on his way to a lecture. His mind recited lines about Perseus and Andromeda. *The quests he must go on to prove himself were fraught with dangers. No. Fraught with peril. Tasks were set upon him to... No. Seemingly impossible tasks were set upon him. And in our own lives, we may find ourselves facing down the demons like the gorgon Medusa. If any of you read my work on the tragedy of Medusa, you'll know she is quite literally a monster made of trauma.*

Perseus slaying her shows us that beautiful things can be created from slaying trauma. From Medusa's blood sprang the mighty Pegasus. Perseus reminds us that sometimes we begin a journey without always knowing how it will end or how we will solve the problems presented to us. We must think on our feet. We may not have Zeus to give us magical weapons, but we can rely on the weapons in our wit—no. Mind. Yes. We can rely on the weapons of our... His ears pricked to the sound of a piano's faint echoing chime, halting his thoughts.

He shook it off and regained his stream of memory recital. *Perseus comes upon the beautiful Andromeda when she is tied to a rock, ready to be sacrificed to the mighty Cetus. A whale-like creature sent to smite...*

The piano's enchanting tones began tingling along his spine. The touch upon the keys light and loving. Passion burst forth in crescendo, then decrescendo to a haunting transition. He stopped in the hall and listened. The sound of the player so familiar, he knew who it was in his bones. But it couldn't be...

Hesitantly, he stepped to the room from where it was coming. Thomas peered around the doorjamb. She sat with her immaculate posture; head ever-so-slightly tilted towards the instrument. Honey hair pulled up into a careless bun, exposing the gentle grace of her neck. He not only lost his breath, he forgot how to breathe completely. What on earth was she doing here?

No mortal woman could play so magically except for Persephone. Or was it Andromeda now? As she seemed tied to the heavy thing in front of her. *No,* he thought. *She doesn't need rescuing. But I wonder if she still wants a man. Perhaps one who isn't a hero per se, but retained the heart of one? Could I be such a man? Could I prove my worth to such a woman? I did it once.*

Her music sent its magic through him and carried his spirit from the ground, levitating him. The warm spread of desire found its dance between his hips. *Oh, no.* He was hard enough to drill a hole in stone. That hadn't happened since the last time they'd made love. Helen could arouse him, but not nearly to the heights of his Persephone.

Compared to the Magnum opus that was Holly, Helen was a polka. Why was he even diddling such a—Thomas tried correcting himself. Helen was a very nice girl. Extraordinarily intelligent. She kept him from getting too lonely and sinking again. But he'd been realizing that she wasn't fulfilling him. Seeing Holly again only confirmed that he was wasting his time on the math teacher.

"Mr. Buckhorn?" a young voice sounded next to him, making him jump. Panic shot through him, and he shoved his armful of folders and papers over his lap to cover his arousal. He winced from slapping himself too hard.

"Mr. Buckhorn, I'm struggling with your lesson on Zeus and the God Complex. I was wondering if you could help me a little?" The bright-eyed little blond in front of him was smiling hopefully. He remembered her. She always sat in the front and stared dreamily at him. He shuddered internally.

"Ehhh..." He backed away from the doorway.

"Julie."

"Julie. It, uh, it has to do with narcissism. The narcissist regards all beings around them as tools for their own desires. So do the Gods. Start there." He turned to head down the hallway. He had to get away from Holly's piano playing and calm the raging beast between his legs that wanted to roar forth and bend her against the piano bench. He was about to present Perseus to roughly sixty-five students and needed to be calm and collected. Not distracted and hungry.

"But, Mr. Buckhorn..."

"I'm so sorry, Julie, but I'm late for a lecture. Send me an e-mail, won't you?" he called, shuffling rapidly away and leaving the little blond disappointed.

He nearly ran straight to speaking hall. As he attempted to gather himself, he set up the PowerPoint display for his lecture, but his mind drifted to delicate, long fingers on piano keys.

He pulled notes from folders and heard Chopin in his mind. His loins stirred. *Stop it! Get ahold of yourself! Christ! Can't let these kids smell blood in the water. I've got to focus!* He arranged his speech cards on the podium and took a sip from a bottle of water. The soft swooping of her neck and the sweet flesh along her spine. Stray honey strands lay like lace against her skin. He imagined sweeping them aside and absorbing her tender flesh with his mouth. Desire filled his body.

"Professor Buckhorn? Are you ready? We're about to start."

Thomas stared wide-eyed at an administrator. His glance swept up to the theater-style seating. It was almost full. *That's more than sixty-five. When did they all get here? Oh, gods, please tell me I'm flaccid!*

The room lights dimmed, and the presenting stage lights brightened. He quickly hid behind the podium to cover his partial erection.

Thomas Buckhorn cleared his throat. "Good morning. I am Professor Buckhorn, and I'm here to bore you entirely in the matters of the ancient Greeks."

Slight laughter rumbled through the space.

"Who here knows who Perseus is?"

Hands raised, but all he saw were feminine hands on a keyboard.

Thomas' lecture may have been a well-intended train wreck, but he didn't give a shit. His scattered mind was in three places. The lecture, the woman he needed to let go of, and the woman he knew he loved more than heat loved fire.

Helen was passive and usually unemotional. But sometimes those types could be the worst to deal with under stress. He wasn't sure what he was in for. Thomas knew one thing for sure. He was done being a waste of a man, and he was certainly done wasting his time. He wanted real love again. Real heart-splitting, gut-wrenching, ball aching, beautiful love. He wanted Holly. Life had brought her to him once, and it seemed to have led him to her again. She was his goal.

As soon as he was done with his lecture, he texted Helen.

Thomas: Where are you?
Helen: Just finished my class.
Thomas: Meet me on the grounds by the "Hiddleston

Triumphant" statue.
Helen: See you soon! (with a heart emoji)

He rolled his eyes.

Thomas paced as he waited for her. Helen approached. She really was lovely. Dishwater blond and warm brown eyes. Her figure was shapely. Plump in the rear, but slender in the middle. Thomas ceased his pacing as she approached.

"Thomas? What's this about? I've been working out the equations, and I have my theories!" She beamed at him.

He looked away from her. The way she compared everything to math was tiresome. The bright twinkle in her eyes told him she probably thought he was going to suggest taking their relationship to the next level and make things more official. But his heart had seized on Holly, and he'd rather not dally with this distraction any longer. The best way to do this was to do it efficiently.

He took her hands in his hands seriously. "I'm quite sure you didn't plan for this."

Her smile faded. "What's wrong?"

"I've thought long and hard, and I can tell you with all certainty that I do not ever see this going anywhere." He watched the light leave her face. "The truth is, I'm in love with someone else. Someone I met long before you. I thought I was over her, but I'm not. I'm... sunk. She sunk me months ago. We ran into some problems, But I realize that I'm ready to face those problems."

Helen's brows scrunched so closely they were nearly one thing, but her voice remained calm. "So, being with me has no problems, and I'm the easy solution. But you've decided that my easy solution is less desirable than your harder solution? She's more complicated. There are issues. But you'd rather let me go to pursue a more difficult formula?"

Thomas blinked and stared at her. "Yes."

"How dare you! I'm the easy answer!" She erupted with clear pain in her voice.

Thomas grabbed her shoulders, steadying her. "You are the easy answer. But you aren't the correct answer."

Helen sniffed, rubbing a hand along her face. "You're right. I didn't plan for this." She pushed him away and took up pacing. "There was no foreshadowing. No X to solve. We always made perfect sense!" She stopped pacing and squared him with moistening eyes. "Why didn't you ever tell me about your ex?"

Thomas drew his fingertips along his brow. "I've found that drudging up that past can mire the present. I'm sorry, Helen. I thought that being completely unhitched from previous things would help."

Her chest heaved, and her voice wavered. "But you weren't exactly *unhitched*, were you?"

"No." His head dropped.

She sniffed, taking in a defiant breath, regaining her composure. "We're over, then?"

"Yes."

"Well. At least you were honest with me. Jackass." And she walked away.

That was that. Cold as herring. Which was the warmest she usually was, anyway. Thomas sighed, letting relief settle the tension of his rigid frame, and smiled slightly as he went to his car.

He'd take Janet up on her offer of going to the orchestra's Ostara series. She'd been nagging him about it. Thomas decided it was time to face his heart.

The orchestra would play another series in June. The Symphony in the Park series that they did every year. The space from March to June would give him a good stretch of time to test his resolve. No liquor. No hard nights. No other distracting woman. A chance to really be alone with himself. When he went to see Holly playing in June, he would make his move.

One more chance. He had to try.

Chapter 21

The Rise of Spring

The Ostara concert series went flawlessly, and Holly was received with great applause. Mr. Watson brought her a large bouquet of red roses to officially welcome her as lead piano.

Backstage, as she gathered her bag and sweater, Mr. Watson approached her and took both her hands in his.

"You were splendid tonight, my dear," he said with his beaming wide grin. "I'm truly confident I made the correct choice in you."

Holly's chest clenched, and she could feel a sting behind her eyes. "I'm going to miss you. I hate thinking of being here without your presence," she squeaked.

"Oh, come now, this is the moment we all dream of. Taking on the reins."

He was right. Holly had wanted this from the time she was eighteen and just starting college. The foggy remembrance of her car accident and years of recovery, shitty jobs, and depression seemed distant and unimportant now.

Henry Watson brought her in for a bony embrace. "You take care of my orchestra, now. Okay?" He released her.

"I will, sir."

A shorter, plump woman with a gray pixie cut approached them. "Ah! Allow me to introduce to you my bride, Stella."

Holly shook her hand. "It's an honor, Mrs. Watson."

"Oh, no. The honor is all mine. I'll finally have him at home. Maybe I can get him to paint the house like we've talked about for the last thirty years." She giggled through her nose, taking his arm.

Mr. Watson raised a flat hand to the side of his mouth like he was telling a secret. "But, you see, I've waited to retire till I'm too old to paint the house. So now we'll *have* to hire someone, and I won't have to do it!" He chuckled gregariously.

His wife patted his arm in playful scorn.

"I should like to pop in from time to time. Just to watch. Maybe play a piece or two?" he said.

Holly's grin widened. "That would be really cool. I'm sure we'd all love it!"

Mr. Watson nodded and escorted his wife away. Holly watched him in his white tuxedo and bare feet make his way to a chair where Mrs. Watson helped him put on his shoes.

High on the energy of it all, Holly floated to her car. Some of the strings, most of the winds, and all of the percussionists, except the timpani, were going out to celebrate at a nearby upscale restaurant with an elaborate bar.

As the Champagne and other drinks flowed, Holly blushed furiously at the onslaught of compliments and attention from the group. Even though she'd been with them since the end of last August, she hadn't really spent time with them. There was a Christmas party. But she wasn't the toast of the tribe then.

One of the violinists came up to her. "You were breathtaking tonight," he told her.

"Oh! Breathtaking. Thank you, uh..."

"Daniel."

"Thank you, Daniel. So, how long have you been with the orchestra?"

He sipped something on the rocks and lifted a casual eyebrow. "I've been with them for almost six years. I may be heading to third chair soon."

Holly feigned interest. "Oooh, third chair. How exciting for you."

"It really is. And a great complement from the Maestro."

"Naturally."

He leaned into her airspace and seemed to inhale. "You smell amazing. What is that?"

Holly's eyes narrowed. "Daniel, what are the rules for fraternizing with fellow orchestra members?"

"I'm not aware of any."

"Is that so?"

"This might surprise you, but this bunch," he indicated their fellow musicians, "most of them have slept together."

"Scandalous."

He chuckled. "It is. But we always manage to put our emotions into our music. There was only one big fight that I can remember."

She brightened and flapped her eyelashes at him as she sucked down her wine. "Do tell!"

"Well, a couple of years ago, one of the flutists was caught with her mouth around our lead Cello. The man, not the instrument." He let go of a chuckle that sounded like a car trying to start.

Her lip curled in disapproval of the sound.

He continued, "Nobody would have cared, mind you, but the Cello was married to our second-seat violin at the time."

"Oh dear. So, what happened?"

"They fought for a while. Things got pretty heated. Until one day, Maestro takes the three of them, shoves them into a storage closet, and tells them not to come out until they decided who got to stay and who left." His car tried to start again in a shambles of laughter.

Holly winced and took a deep swig from her wine glasses. "And then what?"

"The second chair violin left. She had taken an offer in Cincinnati, anyway."

"Well, I haven't delved much into the relationships going on, but I'm pretty sure none of the cellos are with a flutist now, right?"

"Oh no, they fell apart. I think he's fuh—um, with one of the French horns now."

"Charming. Guess he likes the girls with strong lips."

The car engine broke into a full laugh. Daniel swigged from his glass. "You're funny. So, how about you? Rumor has it you're not attached."

"Mmm..." Holly shook her head, navigating this transaction in her head. Sure, she could probably lay him pretty easily. She could tell his mind was halfway down her dress already. Or she could avoid the orchestra drama and just go home. She was really, really horny. But why stoop to this questionable specimen of a man? It would only involve her in the rumor mill. Even if it was easy and might be more fun than going home alone, he was awful. Good looking. But awful.

"I am attached. To my piano."

"Oh, you're one of those, huh? Marm type?"

She was incensed. "Marm? Oh no, dear, I just like a man who can last longer than a minuet." She put down her empty glass and left his shocked expression, staring into space.

"Hey," he called. "What have you heard?"

On her way out, she said goodbye to the few people she knew and shook hands with several others.

As Holly entered her dark apartment, she wondered if maybe she should have accepted the offer of Daniel, violinist, who might make third chair next year. Nahhh. She'd rather touch herself than let that nincompoop have bragging rights that he'd bedded the new lead piano. *Man! Screw that guy. Yuck!*

If she was being honest with herself, it was proving impossible to find a man who could even compare to Thomas. He'd spoiled her. But not only that. Janet was right. Holly was still in love with him. She wondered how he found it so easy to sleep with the mathematician. So many questions.

No. Do not torture yourself. It won't do any good.

As she stripped and slid into her bed, she thought back to how she'd felt when Thomas touched her and grabbed her vibrator. God, how she missed him. She thought of his deep kiss with its perfect suction while rubbing her clit with the vibrating wand. His hot breath and tender but strong, caressing hands. His tongue pressing and circling her nub. Holly came in hollow cries of happiness that burst from her orgasmic body but not from her heart. She was empty without her loving, passionate, fiery Hades.

The symphony always took a small rest between programs, then started up vigorously for the next round of concerts. Symphony in the park would be underway before Holly knew it and she increased her rehearsal time since now she no longer had the comfort or feedback of Henry Watson.

One afternoon, she received a text from Janet asking her to go for drinks the following Friday. They met at Zeke's again. Holly always arrived first, ordering a lager and Janet's gin and tonic. She wondered if it was going to be a night for comfort-bourbon. She hadn't been drunk in a while, and honestly, the idea sounded very appealing. Janet arrived as Holly sipped her beer.

"I love it when my drink arrives before I do! It's why I'm chronically late." The two hugged.

"How are the babies?" asked Holly.

"They're splendid! Jake is getting ready to graduate from the first grade. Can you believe it?"

"No. Time goes by so quickly."

"Especially when you gauge it by how tall your son is getting. And you will come to his graduation, won't you?"

Holly harrumphed. "Isn't a ceremony a bit highfalutin for grade school?"

"Yes. But everything is a ceremony now."

"Will Thomas be there?"

"That shouldn't matter, Holly."

"But it does."

"I don't know. He keeps asking me if you will be there."

Holly groaned.

Janet continued, "And then Samantha will be starting preschool in the fall. My little chubs, turning into a proper lady."

"Ghastly. I'm going to miss her being a baby."

"Me too." Janet sipped her drink sentimentally, then perked up. "I saw your Ostara event. You were amazing!"

Holly blushed. "Aww, gee, shucks."

Janet snorted. "And, uh, I wasn't the only one who saw it."

Holly's tummy tensed and flipped. "Why are you teasing me, Janet?" She sighed. "Did he bring the mathematician?"

"No." Janet's cheeks were bunching up. "They... are no longer a thing." Her impish smile nearly split her head.

Holly's breath caught. "Oh, fuck."

"What? I thought you'd be happy."

"Janet, don't you realize what last month was?"

"Apparently not."

"His and Evelyn's wedding anniversary. They would have been married fourteen years."

"Yes, and it passed without event."

"No, it didn't! He broke up with the mathematician! You see? I told you he just can't get past a date that involves Evelyn. No one will ever *be* Evelyn."

"That's not why he ended it with her. He ended it with her because she wasn't you." Janet checked Holly for a reaction, which Holly tried not to give.

Holly motioned to the bartender. "Shot of Jim Beam, please?"

Janet continued. "I think losing you messed him up more than he's willing to admit."

"You mean losing Evelyn."

"Oh, will you leave off! I mean, losing you."

"I don't get it."

"I swear your Evelyn filter is stronger than his was. He wants to get healthy again, you know. In his mind. For *you*. That's why he started seeing the grief counselor."

"No. He's seeing the counselor to deal with his grief. About Evelyn."

"While that was true, first, and she's done him a world of good, especially while he was going through the house and parting with all of her things. But, from what he's told me, he's gone past Evelyn and has mostly been talking about you."

Holly shook her head and accepted her bourbon from the bartender. "Nope. That's ridiculous! He had twelve perfect years with Evelyn. Why on earth would he be grieving me after only four months together?"

Janet leveled her with a serious but hopeful face. "Because he had you. Because you're still alive. Because you're in the world and not with him. He misses you."

Holly threw back her bourbon. "Then why hasn't he contacted me, Janet? I haven't heard from him since... shit... since I left his house. That was last August! Eight months ago. Nearly twice as long as we even spent together." Holly drank down some of her lager.

"Oh! Speaking of, he put his Tudor on the market."

Holly's entire being imploded. She visibly rocked from the shock of the news. "No—way."

"Yes." Janet's eyes flared.

"Evelyn's house? With Evelyn's roses?"

Janet nodded at her.

Holly paled. "I don't believe you."

"It's going to be officially listed in May."

Holly sank back against her chair from the sudden heaviness in her body. "Hey! Another shot, please!"

"It makes you nervous, doesn't it?" Janet's devilish smile spread up her face. "I'll take another gin and tonic, too, please!"

Nervous didn't cover it. Nervous was the feeling one gets watching a spider crawl across the ceiling above you. This was much deeper. If Thomas was selling his beloved Tudor, he was releasing Evelyn from every place but his heart. Something in Holly wanted to chatter that he should have done this when they were together. When they still had momentum and passion. But now... Now everything had gone cold like last night's leftover pizza.

He'd let go of Evelyn's things, sobered up, found a therapist, found a girlfriend, let the girlfriend go, and was now selling his house. What was he up to?

Holly realized she hadn't said anything in a while and caught Janet's placid yet amused gaze. She said, "Why on earth would that make me nervous?"

"Because it means he's actually moving on. And it means he's done everything you've asked of him before you'd consider getting back together."

Holly avoided further slumping by leaning her elbows on the bar.

Janet sucked up the last of her first gin and tonic. "So, are you seeing anybody?"

"One of the violinists came on to me."

"And?"

"He was a dick."

Janet's wonderful laughter flew from her. "So, you're not seeing anyone?"

"Don't you fucking scout for him! I'm not telling you a goddamned thing!"

Janet's laughter continued jingling. "It's alright. I already know you aren't."

"How's that?"

"Because you'd have told me by now. Especially since we're talking about Thomas."

"Does he think all these gestures, seeing a therapist, selling the house, and sending you to mediate, are gonna bring me back? Because I don't do backs, you know that."

Their new drinks arrived.

"I know you don't. But there's a first time for everything."

"Great." Holly rolled her eyes and drank her shot. "Are you going to ask me out for him, too? Or is he gonna find his testicles and ask me himself?"

"I am but a humble gossip, my darling. Thomas will make his move when Thomas is ready."

Holly smirked. "His Lordship."

Janet giggled.

"Just so you know, I'm very happy with my life, and I don't need any complications right now. So, you can take that bit of gossip directly to him from me."

"Mm-hm. Is that why you're trying to get drunk? Because you're so happy?" Janet's smile never left her face. One of Janet's skills was insulting you while complimenting you at the same time.

"No. I haven't been drunk in months. I'm due. I can order a ride home."

"Yes, you can."

Holly finished her beer and ordered another round. She noticed a man across the bar smiling at her. "God, this fucking guy." She bumped Janet with her arm, indicating for her to look over at a man who was tipping his glass to them. "His mustache makes me want to feed it a snack. Hey, buddy!" she yelled at him. "My mom already told me you were terrible. Okay?" The man's shocked face quickly turned from them as he pivoted his chair in the other direction.

"Jesus, Holly!" Janet laughed hysterically. "How can a woman of your refinement and classical education, who plays for the symphony, be so damned crass?"

Holly giggled. "You think I'm refined? That's adorable! I'm well-rounded. There's a difference."

As May began, a package arrived. Holly recognized the handwriting. It was Janet's. *Why on earth would she mail me something? She knows we can just get together.* Holly entered her little apartment and set her bag on the dining table. She took the package to her kitchenette to find a knife and cut the tape. The large rectangle felt like a book.

She cut it open and pulled out the contents. It was a book. *Hades & Persephone. Grief Transformed by Love. By Thomas Buckhorn.* Holly clasped her mouth. There was also an envelope on which was written, in his penmanship, simply, *"Holly."* She could hear his voice say her name, and her knees weakened. She grabbed the countertop to steady herself. Setting the book down, she went to pour herself a glass of wine.

After several sips, deep breaths, and a little pacing, she found the courage to open the envelope. There was a letter which read:

> *"My dear Holly,*
> *I promise I'm not stalking you and I didn't coax your address from Janet. I asked her to mail this for me. I know this isn't your usual reading fare. But you did seem to enjoy the one about Medusa. Anyway, I wanted you to have it. You inspired so much in it.*
> *I'd written most of it before you arrived. But all the edits and additions were made because of you. I realized I wasn't writing a book about Greek myths. I was writing about death, grief, rebirth and love. That realization added a depth to my writing that I never knew was possible. It has changed everything; my lectures and my current writing. And me.*
> *I've been trying to keep up with the house, but the garden went to shit. At least I'm no longer living like a troll under a bridge. Besides, I'm sure you will have heard by now from my sister that I'm selling the house. I wanted to thank you for helping me the way you did. And even though it's springtime once again, it doesn't feel like a proper spring without you. Nothing has felt proper without you. And I miss your French toast.*
> *~His Lordship, Thomas."*

Holly's vision blurred. The tears took her over, and she quickly set the letter down so she wouldn't cry on it. After smothering her face in a paper towel and blowing her nose, she opened the book. If the letter was a dagger to her heart, the dedication was the twist of the blade.

"For my own Persephone."

She grabbed another paper towel. He did still love her.

Over the next few days, Holly spent every free moment reading it. It started dark, moody, and brooding. Then it lightened, blossomed, and became an ovation to redemption and beauty.

He wrote of how one shouldn't be afraid to be either surrounded by one's own deathly gloom or by death itself. But to take power over it, as Lord Hades did. To rule it. That it was only from this darkest of places that one could truly heal. And from there, all transformation can begin, and all life can spring.

He used Greek myth as an allegory for his ideas. Losing a spouse and mourning. Being surrounded by death. Then being pulled from those dark, clenching jaws to light and life and a blooming of new love. Hades was a brooding mongrel. He needed his opposite to correct him. To correct the balance of the underworld. For after all, that is why Persephone was sent to him.

And Thomas hadn't even gotten to Persephone yet. When he spoke of her, she was nothing but effervescent innocence and loveliness. He spoke of her magic as a music. A music that played through the hearts of all who encountered her. He described how she charmed the dark creatures of the underworld. And how at first, she mourned being away from the surface and from her mother, the earth Goddess Demeter. He wrote that she wilted in despair and fought her circumstances.

Other examples of mourning followed with the sadness of Demeter and all of those whose loved ones were with Hades in the underworld. But Persephone carried their pain with love and ruled with grace, countering and tempering her husband. And when she returned to the surface. The entire world rejoiced and was fruitful again.

The tome evicted many tears from Holly's eyes. She read every word in Thomas' voice in her head. She heard his growth and the recognition of his own journey back to life. She had only set him on the path to recovery, but he was determined to finish it. For when Persephone returned to the surface for six months, Hades had to continue on ruling without her.

Thomas spoke of the addiction of sorrow. Holly wondered if he was alluding to his drinking fits. By the end, Hades realized he couldn't let his kingdom fall to ruin. So, on he went until Persephone returned to him.

The end of the book read: *"Grief is a never-ending cycle. But so, indeed is love. Though we may suffer loss. There is always another spring. And there is always the return of the Queen of the underworld."* Holly was about to close the book when she saw there was an afterward. Her breath caught. It was the poem he wrote for her. But in its completion.

Persephone, Persephone
Bring my springtime back to me.
In darkness dwelling under graves,
bring my love's eternal waves.

A shower of lightning bathe me in.
For mine is yours, my heart to win.
No moon nor flower nor budding fair
can compete with honey hair.

Tho all creatures in burrows hide.
I stand with triumphant arms a-wide.
Their autumn is my greatest dream.
As your smile returns its joyous beam.

And when you leave and back to earth,
my tombs darken, drunken mirth.
I shall sit on throne most cold
until your warmth returns my gold.

For I, the most impoverished lost
forget your love at twice the cost.
And mourning falls in morning gray,
wishing my own soul away.

Persephone, Persephone
Bring my springtime back to me.
Love me till the shadows fall.
and I, for thee, will give it all.

A tear fell upon the words.

Chapter 22
Reprise

In May, the orchestra was ready. They'd practiced long hours, seeking perfection. The summer of "Classics in the Park" was one of their most lucrative events, and the Maestro was obsessed with their success. They were to dress all in bright summer colors to offset the stuffiness usually associated with classical music.

The women were to wear floral dresses or colorful blouses, if they preferred, with trousers. The men were given the same direction. Floral shirts, but all accompanying trousers were to be white. And the bow ties were to be white. It was meant to give a clean but playful look. Holly found a white dress with a pattern of wildflower bouquets.

She was to do not one but two solos. The program was divided into three sections. The first contained two Mozarts, one Schubert, and her first solo, Debussy. This was arranged to lead into the finale of section one, which brought in the rest of the orchestra.

The entire second section was excerpts from Vivaldi's The Four Seasons. Apparently, this was a tradition. And she didn't mind, even though it was mostly strings. The Maestro found places for her to join, and it would also give her moments to stretch her fingers.

The third section was two waltzes by Straus and another Mozart and, at last, her beloved Chopin. Her final solo would again lead into their grand finale, The Ode to Joy.

Holly shook out her arms and did some stretches while chatting with some of the other musicians as they waited to take their places. She was learning to embrace the jitters that accompanied showtime. The only comparable rush was making love to Thomas.

They were asked to take their places. Holly pushed him out of her mind and went to the stage.

At 10pm the concert was finished. Holly walked in a dreamlike state after taking her bows and applauding the Maestro. As she made her way from the stage, the cooler air surrounded her, relieving her from the hot lights of the performance area. High from playing for a crowd, and soaking in the applause, she floated to her large bag, stuffing sheet music into it.

The evening was flawless. The performance, without incident and her heart was full of music. She and her fellow performers congratulated each other, hugging, shaking hands and slapping each other on the back. There was jubilance in every heart.

One of the flutists called to her, “Holly! Are you coming to The Station?” It was the pub they loved to frequent the most.

“Yes! I’ll be there!” She waved, strolling to the parking lot. In her large bag, she dug through sheet music for her keys. The night air was humid and clung to her bare skin. The fireflies would be initiating their fairy dance soon, and the heavy fragrance of blossoms and greenery permeated every breath. She adored this time of year.

She walked under the otherworldly orange luminance of the parking lot lights. Her hand wrapped around her keys, and she pulled them from the bag. Her car sat serenely awaiting her. She hit the fob to unlock it and heard a man's voice.

"It's terribly difficult to walk after hearing you play Chopin," came Thomas' deep, tender tones.

Holly's heart thumped and crashed. Her lungs filled with air as if it were her first breath. She forced herself to turn and look at him as she exhaled. He stood only a few feet away with a hand in his pocket. Eyes glimmering, a slight smile on his face. His brow was full of hope. She forced her body to face him. Beyond her control, a corner of her mouth peaked upwards. Then the other corner defied her and sloped up until she was smiling.

Her body seemed to lighten as he took a step towards her. Then another. Soon, he was directly in front of her. Almost within kissing distance. He kept his soft, blue stare on her honey browns. Her muscles weakened.

"I've missed you," he stated in a low register.

Holly still couldn't eke out a syllable. His overwhelming presence shocked her into the questionable solidity of a Jell-O mold. She was still levitating from having performed, and now her mind pounded her with memories of his passionate kiss and the strength of his arms. She trembled. Then she thought of reading his book and that beautiful poem. Her entire system began shorting out.

Finally, she pushed out, "You—enjoyed the performance?"

He reached for her hand, gently taking it and bringing her fingers to his mouth. "I didn't even mind the crowd. All I saw was you. You were magnificent." He brushed her fingers against his lips, laying soft kisses on them. "And with an entire orchestra supporting you. I don't think I've ever seen you more splendid or more beautiful."

At the very moment she was sure his blue stare would bore a hole through her head, she dropped her bag and flung her arms around him.

Their lips crashed together. Thomas created that beautiful, perfect suction. Holly whimpered from his strong tongue, dancing along hers again. His arms wrapped around her, holding her so tightly he almost brought her inside his chest. She would have loved it if he had.

When they finally came up for air, he begged huskily, "Come back to me, Holly. I'm a desperate mess without you."

"Yes... No. Wait."

His brows rose in amusement. "Gather yourself."

"I can't." She pushed away from him. "I can never think clearly when you kiss me, or hold me, or touch me." Her eyes flashed back at his wonderful lips. "Or look at me. Damn you. No. I'm mad at you."

His eyes tilted in a mixture of darkness and amusement. "You *were* mad at me."

"No. I'm *still* mad at you."

Thomas' arms fled from his sides in exasperation, his hands held palms up, beseechingly. "I have performed all of the tasks you set upon me. What else must I do to satisfy you? I've sorted Evelyn's things. I'm seeing a therapist. I've left Helen—"

"Helen?"

"The math teacher. I know Janet told you. And I'm selling my bloody house! What more can I do to prove to you that I want you? That I'm worthy?"

Holly folded her arms and glared at him. "I'm mad at you for doing all of that."

"What in Hades does that mean? Speak plainly, woman!"

"It infuriates me that you've done it all!"

"Why?"

"Because there's nothing left!"

"Yes."

"Which means I have no more excuses."

"That's the bloody point!"

"You have no more resistance?"

"None!"

"No Evelyn?"

Thomas sighed audibly and stepped closer to her with determination. He cupped her face, forcing her to look at him. "Dammit, Holly, there will always be Eveyln. You're going to have to sort that. I can't wave a wand and undo her. And even if I could, I wouldn't. I could no more erase her from my heart than I could you. And I'd rather like to keep you."

A flush bloomed up Holly's cheeks.

"Holly, the only thing I can do is try harder. Please accept me. Please come back. Let me prove it all to you. I've worked so hard to heal. But the last bruise I have is the one you left. And I can't seem to mend it without you." He silently caressed her lower lip with his thumb. "Nothing's right without these lips."

Holly wavered on her feet and leapt at him again. He caught her in another knee-melting kiss. He bent her back slightly, supporting the back of her head.

When he righted them, he said, "Don't make me carry you over my shoulder to my cave because I will."

"You wouldn't dare." One of her skeptical, threatening brows arched. "You're not a Neanderthal. You're a gentleman. And I'm not sure I want you back, anyway."

"That does it." Thomas lowered and heaved her up over his shoulder as she squealed. Orchestra members were still shuffling into the parking lot.

One of them shouted cheerfully, "So that's how you do it. Hey, need a hand there, buddy?" It was Daniel, the violinist who might be third chair next year.

Both Holly and, to her surprise, Thomas yelled, "Fuck off!"

Thomas began carrying Holly to his car. "Who is that twat?"

"Just a twat. Oh! My bag!"

Thomas turned back around, bent slowly under Holly's weight on his shoulder, grabbed her bag with a grunt, and rose. He continued carrying her to his car.

"Is this really necessary, Thomas?"

"Yes. I've gone through the mazes of the underworld and have risen. Now, I'm claiming my prize."

Holly released a series of giggles. The entire thing was impossibly out of character for him. She couldn't even fathom what was happening.

"You could have just asked me. We could go for a drink."

"You were hesitating. And I can't drag you. It'd ruin that pretty dress."

Holly snickered. He arrived at his car and set her down, pressing his body into hers against the door, and sent his magical tongue into her mouth once more.

"I have a confession," he said. "I don't have a cave because I'm staying with Janet. And I'll be damned if I take you there so she can gloat all over us. Can we go to your cave?"

"Oh, Thomas," she lamented. "You're sweet English Tudor."

"We can talk about that later. I just want to make sure you won't run if I release you."

Holly slid her arms around him and nibbled his chin. "I won't run. You're the only place I want to be."

He dipped his head down to kiss her once more. "Good." He opened the door for her, and she sat inside. He threw her bag in the back seat and jogged to the driver's side. "Tell me where to go."

Too many responses came to her mind. She settled on simply giving him directions to her apartment.

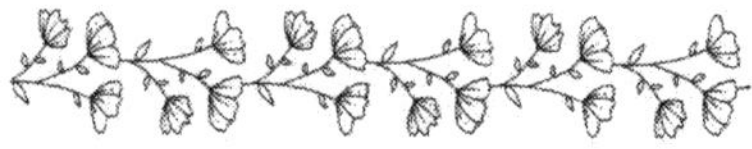

"So... you wanna tell me about things and stuff?" Holly asked as they drove through Dayton to her apartment.

He smiled. "My things and stuff?"

"Yep. It's been almost nine months since I've seen you. Janet's been a terrific gossip, but I want to hear it from you."

He watched the road pensively. "I'm reluctant to just spill everything, Holly."

"Fine. Spill some of it. How is your therapy going?"

He stopped at a red light. "It's good. I must admit, it has been nice to have someone to talk to who isn't my sister or a four-year-old."

"What about Jake?"

"Jake is a seven-year-old male. And not very interested in conversation at the moment. He's all about his games and collecting rocks. I think he'll make a fine geologist someday."

"Are you feeling better? More... whole? At ease?"

He took in a cleansing breath. "I am. I still miss Evelyn. But she's seeming farther away from me now. Like a beautiful dream. One that I'm learning to be content with having in the past."

"That is progress. I'm proud of you."

"Thank you. But Holly, there is one big problem."

"What's that?"

"I found another dream. One not so distant." He sent her a playful sideways glance.

A knowing smile tickled her suddenly warm cheeks.

"I tried moving on from it. But it didn't work."

"With the mathematician?"

He rolled his eyes, and his head followed.

"Janet couldn't stand her."

"As well, I know," he said as the light turned green.

Holly watched the streetlights passing. "I pried it out of her. She wasn't going to tell me. She didn't want to discourage me. She knew I was brokenhearted, and she wanted me to keep thinking you were going to be right back."

"So you were in pain, too?"

"Would it make you happy to hear that I was?"

"It would not. But it would be a relief. Not that you were unhappy. But a relief to know that you missed me. That some part of you ached for me as much as I ached for you. I know it sounds strange. But it would be a—a confirmation that you still wanted me. That you hadn't completely shut me out."

"I couldn't shut you out, Thomas. I was a wreck. Didn't Janet tell you?"

His hand firmed on the steering wheel. "She told me some things. She kept me apprised of your progress with the symphony. She told me you cried sometimes. She told me you weren't seeing anybody. But I didn't know if you'd—been with anybody."

She watched the lights illuminating his face in sweeping passes of light. "Thomas, I haven't let another man touch me since you have. None of them were you. I haven't even looked at another man."

Thomas swallowed hard. "I suddenly feel much worse." He rubbed his face.

"Why? Because you actually went out and met someone? There's nothing wrong with that. Did it bother me? Yes! But I had no claim over you. You were free to do whatever you wanted. And honestly, I'm glad you found the mathematician. At least you tried something new. And at least—at least you weren't bottling yourself up like you used to. You needed to move on. And you did. And that's—healthy. Besides, being with her somehow led you back to me."

Thomas' chest heaved up and bellowed back down. "I never loved her. If anything, she galvanized my feelings for you. Perhaps that was what I was testing."

Holly played with her seatbelt. "That's the only thing that makes it okay."

"She wasn't you."

"You mean she wasn't—"

"No. I know what you're going to say, and no. She wasn't *you*, Holly."

Holly felt a flutter in her core that propagated through her belly and limbs. She took a heaping breath of his pine scented cologne, which had been filling the car as they drove. God, how she missed the smell of him and his delicious bare skin. Anticipation for reaching her apartment mounted.

Hearing that he really did love her for her was what she needed to hear the most. She wasn't a replacement. He loved her for herself. Holly realized that she'd never fully trusted that. Maybe that's why she ran so quickly?

"I think..." Holly sighed, trying to figure out the right words for what was tumbling through her mind. "I think that I need to let Evelyn go, too." She stared down at her lap. "I've used her as an excuse for so long. I'm sorry, Thomas. I need to stop using her against you."

Thomas stilled; visually affected by her words. He drew his fingers down the corners of his mouth. "Thank you, Holly." He seemed to take a moment to steady himself. "I can't tell you what that means to me."

Holly let the moment have the gravity it needed. Her hand strayed up to the side of his face and stroked it delicately. "I guess I always thought I was just a stand-in for her. I knew you loved me. But I still wondered if it was because I was convenient. Because I was in the house. Because you were lonely. Because you needed an obsession. Not because I was—"

"Holly," he interrupted. He grabbed her hand and brought it to his lips for a kiss. "I love you because you are Holly." He held her fingers against his mouth for a moment, then brought their held hands down to his lap. "You're nothing like Evelyn. A fact I'm pretty sure I reminded you of frequently when you first arrived." One side of his mouth creased up in a sweet smirk, making her very bones go soft.

She met his smile with her own and said affectionately, "You did. You reminded me of it with everything I did."

His smile faded. "Do you want to know what I want?" he asked.

"What?"

Thomas straightened his posture. "I want happiness. Joy. Companionship. Sex. A family. And I want time." He breathed a moment. "All the damned things that life, or God, or the blasted universe, or whatever you call it, took away from me. That's what I want! I want what's owed me. I want a life. As every man does. A goddamned good, goddamned full life!"

Holly released his hand and smoothed his hair at the nape of his neck. His tortured face broke something inside her. "You nearly had it," she softly offered. "And it was taken. I'm so sorry, Thomas." Holly realized for the first time the grand scope of what he'd lost. It wasn't just his precious, perfect Evelyn. Thomas lost his future. And in the shock of having his plans erased, he couldn't move forward. So, he drank.

"Thomas," she hesitantly said, "I'm so sorry for—" saying 'for your loss' seemed cliché and vapid, so she settled on, "No one can ever replace what you lost."

His hand swept behind his head, pulling her fingers back to his lips. "No. Not replace." He turned his blue eyes briefly to bless her with a loving glance. "But I can start again."

Chapter 23

Chorus

"It isn't much," she warned, unlocking the door. "I thought taking a smaller apartment would help me save for a house."

"Does it have a bed?"

Holly's center erupted in explosive tingles at his question. The thought of making love to him was nearly enough to make her come right there. Her body zinged with anticipation.

"Sort of. I have a futon."

His hot breath hit her ear as he whispered, "As long as it's big enough to lay you under me."

That did it. Her clit bounced to life. Holly pushed her door open, nearly tripping over her own feet as they went inside. She recaptured her grace, still unwilling to let Thomas know he affected her so severely. After all, she was supposed to be angry with him. Or had she spoiled that facade already? She probably couldn't even manage being mildly aloof right now.

When they entered, Holly set her bag on the dining table and settled for trying to appear nonchalant. Thomas followed, closing the door behind him, and pressed against her backside. His arms swept around her, clasping her abdomen, spreading warmth through her, and desirous hands brushed up to her breasts. He certainly wasn't trying to act cool. He wanted her. No question.

Luxuriating in his caress, she lingered a moment, then found the strength to pull away and attempted to compose herself.

"You're awfully ready," she teased, taking a few steps away and turning to face him.

He closed the distance between them and said, "I'm more than ready." His strong lips caressed her mouth.

Holly struggled with keeping her brain in her skull. She pulled away again. "Would you like some wine?" She was already panting a little. "I think I even have some bourbon."

Thomas caught her up in his arms and nibbled along her neck and shoulder. "Holly, you know the state that listening to you play Chopin puts me in."

"I remember." Her efforts to resist him were failing. The foolish idea of acting like she didn't want him faded. "But we've had a car ride since then. And it's been over an hour since you heard me play Chopin."

A glint hit his eyes. "Yes, and every minute since then has been a torment. Give yourself to me. I know you're only trying to look strong. And I know you are strong. I admire that quality in you." He stroked her face gently. "You're stalling."

Holly froze. She was stalling.

"What are you afraid of?"

"I—" She wasn't even sure. "It's been a long time, Thomas. Last time, we had so much constant contact and build up. This is so different."

His glance fell down, and he let his forehead fall against hers. "Are we forcing it?" he asked.

"Maybe."

"I see." Thomas' heart thumped as he lifted her chin up, tilting her head slightly to slowly meet his lips. His mouth met her lips softly at first, then he increased the pressure of his kiss. He scooped her body to him.

"There has been something that's been bothering me," she confessed.

"Is that so?" His brow rose in curiosity.

Her eyes fell. "I'm almost embarrassed."

Thomas nudged her chin again. "Tell me."

Holly studied his pleading face. "I—oh, damn it. It has to do with what your sister told me."

He inhaled and released his shoulders to a slump.

She sighed. "I'm not going to lie to you. I felt like I was next in line. Just the next fixation. Even after all of your sweet, ovations of love, and all of our time together."

"What do you need, Holly?" His voice pulled her face back to his. Thomas' eyes radiated determination.

"I need to know that something about me is new. That something about this," she placed a hand on his chest, "is new. That I'm not just... next."

The pleading welling of her beautiful honey-brown eyes nearly melted his center. He bolstered himself with a determined, hard breath and gripped her. He was not about to lose this battle. He knew exactly what was new about her. It had unnerved him from the first time she'd played piano and unraveled him the first time they'd danced.

"There *is* something new," he said. "Something I haven't shared with you before." He prepared himself for vulnerability and admission with an excited pounding of his heart. "I—oh shit." His eyes fell away. This was going to be more difficult than he'd anticipated.

"Fuck, what?"

He cleared his throat. *I can do this.* He returned his resolute eyes to her. "I've—Gods, this is going to sound awful. I know it already."

Holly gripped his arms. "Jesus, Thomas, spit it out!"

"Fine. I've never lusted after someone so desperately before." Thomas was immediately unsure if her blank stare was one of happy shock or repulsed confusion. He decided to release her and pull back a step with a hand sweeping along his forehead.

"Listen, when I courted Evelyn, it was done by the numbers. Flirts, dates, parties. The first kiss. More dates, more kisses. It was four months before we made love. I was smitten by her as if by a fine piece of art. I was enrapt with the wonder of it and wished to have it."

"Oh." Holly fiddled with her hands as if trying to listen for the compliment.

Thomas made a quick, nervous circle while he talked. "But with you it was all upside-down. I resented you. Then I was in love with you. There was hardly an in-between. I, myself, was completely befuddled."

He faced her. "When we went to the bar that first time, I thought I'd lose my mind from looking at you." He worked on capturing her eyes again. "You're so alive, Holly. So fearless. So full of every moment and bursting with energy."

He took a step closer to her. "Of course, I remember you and Janet socializing when we were younger. I thought you were lively, pretty, and fun, even back then. But you were my sister's friend, and I was caught up in my studies. I wasn't looking at you in that way. The Gods know I could have fallen for you back then had I only paid attention."

Holly's eyes swelled.

He continued. "By the time I allowed myself to notice you, it was..." he struggled. "Well, it was as if all those years piled into that one perfect moment of finding you playing piano for the first time. Your passion burst something open in me. All of your loveliness and personality landed upon me all at once, and it knocked me for six!"

He stepped closer, taking her hands. "And when we went out and were laughing... I had never been so relaxed in a crowd before. Truly, not even Evelyn could get me to relax in a crowd. I knew I didn't want to date you. I didn't want to take my time. I wanted to make love to you immediately. Skip the formalities and dive straight into you." His eyes adopted a devilish pleasure. "And that's exactly what I did."

Thomas let go of one of her hands to tenderly lay his fingertips along her face, landing under her chin. "I've never not wanted to wait before. Not with Evelyn. Not with anyone. Perhaps I thought delayed gratification was more appropriate. Or that it would impress them if I waited. Or maybe it would be better, sweeter if I did." His eyes became heavy on hers. "But Gods help me, I couldn't wait with you. Nothing could have been sweeter than making love to you as soon as possible."

Holly's eyes were entranced. The gold flecks in them sparkled.

"I've never wanted anyone so badly as I wanted you. Not anyone, Holly. Do you understand what I'm saying?"

She barely nodded. His fingers holding her chin traced along her delicate face with the lightest touch he could manage. He brushed a hand behind her head, bringing her gently towards his mouth. Nearly salivating, Thomas spread her lips with his tongue and opened her mouth with his desire. He felt her body bend into him and wilt. He brought her tighter into his embrace.

He released the suction on their kiss. Holly's dreamy, fluttering eyes barely focused on him. He had her. He knew it. "I want you, Holly. Please. Don't deny me."

She heaved a lungful of air. The vulnerable curve in her brows bent his soul. He'd do anything to have her. They shared a long moment, assessing the love and desire inside each other's eyes. Holly's sweet lips pressed into his, and his body melted.

"Can we be soft?" she asked. "I'm not sure I want the animal right away."

His chest released all the tension held in it with a large exhale, and his shoulders relaxed. Thomas took her jaw in his hand and lay kisses along her brow. "I wasn't planning on rutting. Trust me." He pierced her honey eyes with his longing need. "I want you slow. I want you moving under me and pushing your wonderful hips against mine in a grind so deep that we combine into the same being."

Holly's eyes rolled.

Holly moistened. No one could seduce her like Thomas Buckhorn. Her mind flashed to his frazzled, pale face after he heard her play for the first time. She'd thought he was upset with her, or that she'd triggered some memory of Evelyn. But no, he was smitten.

Thomas cupped her jaw and blessed her with a toe-curling, gradual kiss. She barely had the time needed to process what he'd just confessed. He wanted her more than he'd ever wanted anyone before her.

It was a revelation greater than knowing he loved her simply for her. He was saying she was the one. His one. And as much as he and Evelyn were perfect together. All the truths were there in his stories of her. She was art. Perfection. Something to be cared for and admired. And when she passed it was like taking an ax to a sculpture.

Holly understood, now. It wasn't that no one could be as perfect as Evelyn. It was a tragedy of the unpredictable and cruel nature of life. But Thomas was telling her that there was another side to life. Where tragedy gave way to second chances for even greater depth and beauty. If only you have the strength to keep going long enough to find it.

Her left hand twinged. An injury that had taken her dream had given her time to figure out something even more beautiful. And the greatest gift was Thomas.

If Evelyn was fated to pass tragically, she couldn't have had a better partner than the devoted, love-sick Thomas.

Holly finally understood what he was saying. The rocking depth of his love for her as his mouth searched hers and he pulled at her body shook her soul.

It was so automatic; she didn't even realize her fingers were unbuttoning his shirt. When she felt the skin of his bare chest, a waltz began in her heart.

Thomas let the shirt fall. He kissed her again. His tongue made a prayer in her mouth while his hands slowly drew her dress up along her body. She liquified under his touch. The warmth between her legs pulsed.

Thomas dragged the dress up to her breasts and lingered again, massaging them through the material. Holly sighed from her gut, delighting in the arousal only he could inspire in her. She struggled to remember how to unbutton and unzip his trousers. She pushed them down his hips, and they fell. Her hand found his beautiful, bowed shaft, and she stroked it through his shorts.

He tugged the dress up. She'd have to raise her arms to let him pull it off of her.

"Promise me, when I pull this off, you'll put your hands back on me," he whispered desperately.

"Yes."

He pulled the dress over her head, and she went right back to stroking him. Thomas' head lolled with a groan.

"I love your hands on me," he said through thickening breaths.

Holly watched his eyes roll back with a wide smile. His responses to her were always so gratifying. He undid the clasp of her bra while kissing her again. They kicked off their shoes, and he bent and pulled off his socks as she tugged away her bra. His arms were around her again, backing her towards the futon. She quickly grabbed the release so the futon lay fully out from bent to flat.

Thomas overcame her, pushing her back until they were in the center of the large cushion. He lay upon her body, tongue penetrating her mouth softly, pulling whimpers from her as his erection firmly pressed against her through his shorts.

"Damn barriers," he exhaled and tugged her panties.

They worked to relieve themselves of the last of their clothes and paused.

Thomas lay between her legs and heaven, breathing heavily. "Holly, I've been in agony. You've no idea. I'm almost afraid to have you. It'll be over too fast."

She grinned, reveling in the heat of his exhales. "The first time. It's the first time, again."

"Your body was bathed in lightning flashes," he said reminiscently.

"Every thunder clash echoed your sighs," she responded.

"God, I wish there was a storm now."

"Go down on me."

He dove into her bosoms, caressing her breasts and sucking her nipples as she writhed and gasped beneath him. Holly's mind was zeroing out as it did when he began to make love to her. Her thighs were already around his hips, clasping him to her, encouraging him.

She moaned, "Oh, Thomas. Touch me everywhere."

His hands immediately strayed down her ribs, along her belly, and fondled gently into the warmth between her legs. She groaned happily as he descended along her torso, licking and kissing until he met her soft vulva with his mouth. Her moisture flowed as he enthusiastically licked her and feathered her clit with his tongue.

"Oh, Jesus!" she cried. He lingered a moment. The pressure and texture of his tongue released vibrant tingles through her. She squealed and grabbed his head, trying to pull him up before she exploded too soon. There was too much stimulation between them for foreplay. They were too needy.

"Unhh, Thomas, take me already!" Holly pulled him up and welcomed him back into her arms as he kissed her mouth hard enough to stop her heart.

His swollen crown spread her wet opening as the shaft followed, parting her and sliding in deep. The pair of them moaned in joy.

"Gods, Holly. No one makes me as hard as you do." He thrust in exuberantly.

She cried out in satisfaction, gripping his hips with her legs and welcoming the strength of his body. The pressure of his body sliding against hers and his arms nearly crushing her sped delirium.

Her pelvis rose to meet each delicious thrust as he shoved ecstatically. Too caught up in the phenomenon of their churning bodies to even kiss, they joined in gasping and lurching until the spasms came, blowing them into space.

Thomas gripped her, pushing his cock into her welcoming hotness. The sensation consumed him. Wet, tight, fire. He thought of nothing else. She was pulsing velvet around him. Her body met his rhythm. Holly was a soft, beautiful creature under him. Nothing on earth compared to her supple movements. The velvet slid up and back along his cock, spurring his pleasure. Her nails scraped his back.

The moment he heard Holly's squealing voice, his pulses threatened. He let out a mighty huff, trying to keep his spasms back. Nothing was more exquisite than her muscles crushing his length inside her when she lost control. His mind drained as his delirious throbbing claimed him, and his cum left his body.

He held her, thrusting euphorically until he collapsed. He wanted her skin against his lips again and buried his face into her neck, kissing and smelling her sweet, flowery perfume as they finished pulsing and twitching.

He kissed her softly. Her lips were cold. He was lost, enjoying the delightful sensation of her fingers brushing along his skin as his orgasm faded, leaving tingling relief in its wake. He brushed her hair with his fingers, studying the gold flecks in her honey eyes.

"I was such a fool," he barely whispered.

She looked like she might cry. "These last few months have been so empty without you," she whispered back.

"I never stopped loving you, Holly."

He lowered his mouth to hers and delved into her again. She accepted him. Her satin tongue slid along his as her hips glided against his body. He wanted her to absorb him. Take him in and consume him in her bliss.

Holly's mind was blank as they lay in a heap of mindless satisfaction. When they caught their breath, Thomas supported himself on his elbows, stroking Holly's hair away from her face and whispering that he'd never stopped loving her. A sweet shiver shot through her as he blessed her with warm, beautiful kisses. The open relief of their vulnerability and bare emotions nearly brought her the same joy as the orgasm she'd just had.

"I guess we were both wrong," he stated.

Holly stared up at him.

"We did need to rut."

She blew a laugh out and kissed him again. Giggling, she blurted, "Where have you been, you piece of shit? I was half sick hearing about how in love with me you still were, and not one phone call!"

He laughed and kissed around her lips. "Lost. So lost." Thomas pushed up and met her eyes with firm resolution. "My Persephone... I had to be ready. I had to earn you. And I was a little intimidated."

"By me?"

"By you. By how much pressure I'd built up because—you're everything."

Holly's mind spun away.

Thomas stroked her cheek. "Grief is a strange, relentless mistress, Holly. But she brought me to you. Not once, but twice."

Holly reached for the tissue box. He pulled from her, and they cleaned up.

He sat up against the wall in a sigh of fulfillment.

"I think I'll take that bourbon," he said. "Or I can get it."

"Oh, yes. That does sound good." Holly took their tissues to the trash and grabbed her bottle of bourbon and two glasses. She poured and handed one to him. "What do you mean grief brought you to me twice?" She sipped her drink.

Holly pulled a blanket from the arm of the futon and sat with her back on part of his chest. Laying the blanket over their laps, she cuddled into him. "Technically, you brought yourself to me the second time."

Thomas' hand vacantly strolled along her shoulder. "I wouldn't say that exactly."

"What do you mean?" She pivoted up to look into his eyes as his thumb played along her cheek.

"I may have been giving lectures at the community college in which you practice your piano."

A grin overtook her. "What?" She pushed up and shifted a leg over his lap to straddle him and look him in the eyes. "You're shitting me."

"I am not."

"I'll be damned." Holly sipped her bourbon and rested the glass on a side table so she could lay her wrists along his shoulders, letting her fingers fondle the hair at the back of his head.

"I used to stand by the door, listening to you."

"You didn't," she laughed. "What about your, um... how your, um..."

"What are you trying to say, Holly?" he teased.

"Well, you said my playing makes you hard. I'm surprised you let yourself be compromised."

His grin widened, displaying his teeth. "It was agony. And yes, I was so affected."

A roll of giggles fled her joyously. "I can't imagine you walking through campus with a stiffy!"

He cleared his throat. "It wasn't easy."

Her eyes widened. "Wait! Don't tell me you masturbated on campus!"

"Oh, Gods, no. That would have been wildly inappropriate." A corner of his mouth perked.

"You *did*, didn't you!" She shook his shoulders until a chuckle rattled loose from him.

"Alright, alright. Once. Only once."

Holly cackled. "I can't believe you! Only once? You swear?"

His broad, sparkling smile appeared. "My hand to Zeus. The other times, I hid it best I could under my folders and binders, but it was torturous, I assure you. The one day I finally gave in, it was either that or come in my trousers. Which would have been disastrous."

Her head rolled back with laughter.

"And you?" he asked. "You really were brokenhearted?"

She squinted at him. "Did you not believe that I was really in love with you, too?"

"Was?"

Holly huffed a sigh. "We are talking about the past."

"Of course."

"Why do you think I was so fucking angry at you?"

"I thought it was because of my behavior."

"It was! Because I loved you, and I thought you loved me, and you tossed me out!"

"I did love you!"

"Did?"

"Shit. You're right. That is frustrating."

Holly giggled. "You see? I was mad at your words, yes. But what hurt the most was how you pushed me away. Literally."

His eyes glistened with regret. "There is no apology in the world great enough for you to forgive me for that. And this is no excuse, but I literally didn't know what I was saying. I wasn't really even in my body at the time. I lost an entire day to a blackout."

Holly pressed her head against his forehead. His arms enfolded her.

She offered, "I've been blackout drunk before. Not my proudest moments, either. Part of me wonders if I should have just gone back to my room and stayed there until you sobered up. Then saw what happened."

"I really wish you had." He started tickling her rump and hips in delicate circles.

She raised her head and took his jaw in her hands. "But I was so done with it all by then. We'd had several of those kinds of nights. Well, maybe not arguments. But the drinking and crying and sadness. Once it escalated, I couldn't live that way, Thomas."

He paused, looking away from her shamefully. "I haven't gotten drunk, but one other time since. I rarely even buy liquor anymore."

"Afraid you'd chase away that mathematician?"

"Oh, don't! Do not." He gently chuckled. "Maybe I should have given her a dose. She had all the warmth of a slide-rule."

Holly barked a laugh. "Then why were you with her?"

Thomas leaned his head against hers, thinking. "I'm not sure. I think I was afraid that if I was left to my own devices, I'd slide again. And you were gone and mad at me. I wasn't ready to have you back, anyway. Still had all of Perseus' tasks to fulfill to win my Andromeda."

"So, I'm Andromeda now?"

"It's the next thing I'm working on. The similarities are there, are they not?"

"Don't know much about them."

"Perseus must succeed in a series of tasks to win the hand of Andromeda."

"Hmm. I suppose that's similar."

"Holly." The simple two syllables from his throat filled the room with love. "I don't want to be away from you again. I don't, and I can't. It would break me beyond repair."

"Thomas. I need to know that you will always be okay. Either with me or without me. I don't want to be responsible for your sanity."

His eyes fell. "No. You're right. I thought I was being poetic. I'm not trying to be codependent."

Holly's eyes rolled up. "You were being romantic."

"Yes, I was."

"And I totally ruined it." Her eyes returned to his.

He said warmly, "Yes, you did."

Her cheeks pinched up, blushing. "How can I remedy this?"

His hands came up, stroked the sides of her face, and brushed through her hair. "Tell me you'll not leave me again."

Holly's body lost all contact with reality. No cohesion registered. She disconnected from everything but his beautiful, soulful eyes. Eyes that had no borders. Blue depths that drew her in and pulled her senses into them. A pair of deep oceans inside which she completely lost all the edges of who she was.

A passage from his book came to her mind, and she said, "I'll be by your side in the darkness of Hell or the bright of spring. I'll never abandon the devotion I've sworn to you. Whether with you or away from you. I will always be yours."

Thomas stilled. A flattered spark of surprised recognition coated his face. "Said Persephone when she accepted her role as the Queen of the Underworld and realized that she truly loved Hades." His lower lip pushed up. "You quoted me."

"I loved your book. The poem at the end made me cry." She stared adoringly. "I missed you so much, Thomas." Holly exhaled peacefully, in full acknowledgment that Thomas had her heart.

He dipped his head slightly, and their mouths met. His strong arms wrapped around her, and he twisted over, laying her down as his tongue slid powerfully into her mouth. Holly's whole being sighed.

He was already between her legs. Delicious sliding began. His cock hardened. Her clitoris sent approving waves through her. She moved her hips to help him. His tip dipped in. He pushed. She felt every beautiful moment of his entry. Swollen tip, ridge, thick shaft filling her. They breathed and moaned together.

"Holly... God, I can't get used to it. It's so incredible."

"I can feel you," she whispered. "I can feel you all the way in my chest. Like you're making love to my heart."

He thrust in gentle need. "I am."

She rose into the wave of his body. They latched in a deep kiss within the frenzy of their beings embracing. Holly held him so she could rise and crash with him. He set the pace. The slow, undulating, bonding pace that united them. They were connected again. Euphoric.

Chapter 24

Persephone

The three-bedroom house built in the 1960s was perfect. Two stories with large windows everywhere, but God, Holly was tired of moving. This would be her fifth move in just over a year. She was grateful that Janet and Wesley came to help with all the boxes while the children were at Janet's mother's.

Janet pulled a silver sauté pan out of a box. "I'm glad you went with the stainless steel. I promise you're going to love them."

Holly began washing the pots in the sink. "I hope so. I'm nervous about burning things in them."

"Just watch your temperature. Hot, but not too hot." Janet took the box and walked out of the kitchen to add it to the mounting pile of cardboard by the front door.

Thomas' arms came from behind Holly, smoothing around her hips, and he planted sweet kisses along her cheek and jaw.

"Have I ever told you how adorable you are in a ponytail?"

She blushed. "I'll add it to the list of things that torture you."

He smacked her rump and left the kitchen as Janet returned. Her grin took over her face.

"I'm so glad you two are back together," she gushed.

"Me too," Holly sighed. "I was still surprised he actually sold his house. But I wasn't about to go back to it."

"Which is why he sold it."

"I feel a little guilty for being such an earthquake for him."

"Don't be! It's exactly what he needed."

Janet opened a box of new dishes. "Oh, I like these! I'm glad you went with the vine pattern."

"It was either that or the daisies, and I wanted something less aggressive." Holly paused from drying the pots and placed a hand on her hip. "I hope we did the right thing, Janet."

"What do you mean? It's a great pattern. And the vine relief; white on white. It's classic. You'll enjoy them for years."

"Not the dishes."

Janet's smiling eyes landed on Holly. "Do you mean buying a house together? Both of you selling all your old things to buy new things and committing to each other even though you've only been back together for a couple of months? That thing?"

Holly smirked, shaking her dish towel. "You're shit at instilling confidence. You know that?"

"Hey, I deserve the friend-of-the-year award for all we've gone through recently!"

Holly chuckled. "I don't disagree. Besides, my studio was choking us. Not that I don't love being in his presence, but shit it was tight in there with two people."

Janet tilted her head and brought a comforting hand to Holly's arm. "You did the right thing. Thomas is so mad about you it's made him goofy. And I know you can't think of being anywhere else but with him." Janet's knowing eyes washed Holly with acceptance.

Holly sighed and looked away. "I still have one concern."

"Which is?"

"We haven't gone through another anniversary of Evelyn's passing."

Janet shook her head and went back to pulling white vine-patterned dishes from the box. "I don't think you have anything to worry about."

"Why do you say that?"

Janet's Cheshire-cat smile betrayed her.

"Janet... What do you know?"

"I'm not saying a thing!"

Holly tossed her dish towel and strode towards her friend.

"Shit! Janet! Is he going to propose?" she whispered in a panic.

"I don't know anything! Honestly! And before you panic, no, he hasn't said anything. I just know my brother. It's on his mind."

"Fuck."

"Oh, don't act upset, Holly. I know you want him."

"I do. But there's wanting, and then there's having. There's a difference between dreaming and doing. I'm still getting used to all of this. It's a lot of transition! New job, new house, new things, new—well, new again relationship. I hope he gives me some time to get used to it all first."

Janet smoothed Holly's arm. "Thomas has always been in his own orbit and on his own schedule. If you're worried about it, then tell him."

"But I don't want to scare him off, either."

Janet snorted. "For heaven's sake! Make up your mind!"

The pair giggled. If Holly was honest with herself, she wouldn't mind a proposal. Her body responded to the thought of it with a happy flutter.

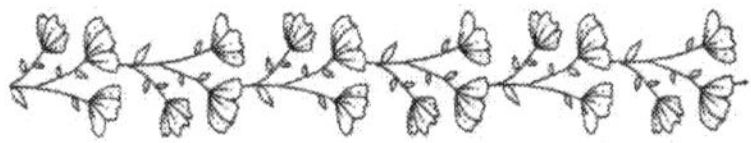

By the end of July, Holly and Thomas were settled and falling into a contented routine together. And mornings always included French toast.

The Symphony in the Park series was ending, and Thomas was hard at work in his new study on another book. "The Trials and Triumphs of Perseus."

The furniture and bookcases from his former study were the only things he'd kept from his old house. The familiar dark cherry-wood desk and shelves full of all of his most beloved companions brought him a comfort he refused to part with.

It wasn't Holly's idea for him to sell any of their things, except the bed that Evelyn died in. But her request for that to go spurred an idea that they should both start completely over with a clean slate. Perhaps the lingering ghosts held in the old furniture would vanish and haunt them no more. Holly brought him a cup of tea and a plate of cucumber sandwiches in his study.

"Ah-ah! Where's my kiss?" he asked.

Holly bent and kissed him. Her eyes held a hint of sorrow that was not missed by him.

"What's the matter? You've got that look."

"What look?"

"Pensive. Like you're chewing on something that I'm going to hear about later."

She smiled. "It'll be August next week."

"Yes."

"I'm worried I'll lose you again."

"Oh, Holly..." he put down the pen in his hand and beckoned her so he could slide his arm around her waist. "I'm not going anywhere."

"Even if it's only for a couple of days? You know, for Evelyn's anniversary?"

"Is that what's been nagging you?" He reached up and brushed her hair back. "Yes. Can't blame you for that. I've been thinking about it, and I believe I have a solution."

"What?"

"I'm still working it out. But part of it involves us going away. A vacation. Nothing too fancy. Just away somewhere for a few days."

A comforting sheet of relief covered her. "What a nice idea. I love that."

"Your orchestra will be breaking before the fall program during the last two weeks of August, correct?"

"Yes. We set forth again in September for Spooky Fest. I believe Maestro is looking at some Sleepy Hollow-themed pieces."

"That sounds marvelous. But before Ichabod Crane, there's Thomas Buckhorn. And he very much desires that we survive August unscathed."

"He's a smart man."

Thomas raised a brow. "I rather like to think so."

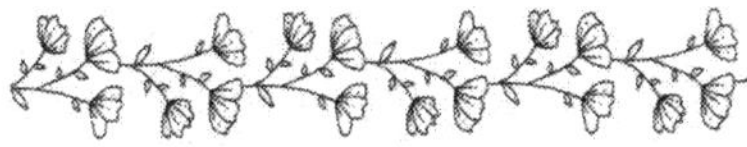

Two weeks later, Holly arrived home from rehearsal. She threw her keys on the hall table and kicked off her sandals. She went upstairs to change into a maxi dress. She liked to transition from work to home by way of altering her outfit. Then she'd get Thomas' tea ready. She always prepared tea for him if he wasn't lecturing that day. Then it was an hour or so of practicing on her keyboard before getting dinner together.

After changing, she started descending the staircase when a familiar, warm resonance floated up to her. An unmistakable sound that no electronic device, no matter how advanced, could make. No computer could truly duplicate the sound. It was a piano chord played on a real piano. Her heart pounded all the way up to her throat. Another chord sounded. She flew down the stairs.

There, in the living room, was the most beautiful thing she'd ever seen. A baby grand the color of soft, afternoon sun. Thomas stood with his hands on the keys.

"Am I doing it right?" he asked, not looking up. "I had lessons once when I was a boy. But it never quite took for me."

She took slow, disbelieving steps towards the instrument. "Oh... my..."

He playfully flung his glance to her. "What do you think? Will it do? I tried to get something to match that lovely honey sheen of your hair."

Her hands slapped over her awestruck mouth as her chest heaved with quick, happy breaths. Her eyes welled with joyful moisture. Thomas walked to her and wrapped his arms around her.

"I can't believe you spent the money on this," she gasped into his wonderful, pine-scented chest.

"Why? You needed a real one. You're a professional, after all. And I've been watching you pound that ridiculous little keyboard, and it makes me sad. When I thought about the resounding wonder that comes from a real piano, I think I wanted one almost as badly as you did."

Holly's eyes couldn't keep the tears away as she returned his embrace and smashed her mouth into his.

"I love it. It's perfect."

"Well, you haven't played it yet." He kissed her again and released her to touch the instrument.

Holly regarded it. It seemed to smile at her.

Hello there! Am I yours? It asked. *I've longed for a master.* It was excited to be played. *Touch me! I want to feel you. Let's play! I promise to sing for you*. It was hers.

She sat at the bench and placed her fingers upon the ivories, hoping the action was smooth and light. She began doing scales to feel the movement of the keys. It was like playing on a cloud. She pressed the first notes of a nocturne. A few bars in, she stopped and turned to Thomas.

"It's magic," she told him.

His dreamy, gentle smile sat happily on his lips. "We should open it up." He grabbed his cell phone and pressed a few places on it. "See what this baby can really do." The song they first danced to began to play. "Come On Get Higher" by Matt Nathanson.

Holly smiled even wider, matching her heart's stuttering and shivering, happy belly. "What are you doing?"

Thomas set his phone down on the coffee table and opened the large lid over the strings of the piano. As he raised it and secured the stand, Holly's eyes caught a dangling glitter.

She squinted, examining it. Taped to the underside of the lid was a string hanging down which tied to a diamond ring. Her brain struggled to make sense of it.

Thomas stood silently, watching her figure it out. She stood suddenly with a gasp, sending the bench scooting back as the shock and realization hit her. Her eyes seized on the twirling gold band and solitaire round-cut diamond. She detected movement from the corner of her eye and glanced over just in time to see Thomas taking a knee.

"Tah—Thomas." she barely whispered.

"Persephone. I refuse to live one more day in this realm without knowing you'll be mine forever. Will you have me?"

She was nearly sucked into his pleading eyes. Her face turned back towards the dangling treasure, and she reached to pull it from the lid. Untying the string from it, she turned it over in her hand. A smile, slow and full, crept along her cheeks.

"I already have you," she teased, delaying his satisfaction. She knew that made him insane.

Thomas stood, scooped her into his arms, and weakened her entire body with his breathtaking, perfect kiss.

"Marry me, Holly."

"We've only just readjusted to each other."

He sent his tongue sliding along hers, pulling any argument from her mind.

"Marry me, Holly." He said again.

Her wide eyes stared into him. "Okay."

"Something more definitive would be nice. Let's try this again." He plucked the ring from her hand, knelt down on one knee, and sent his blue gaze upon her, disarming her completely. Sweetening his beautiful face, he offered a hopeful smile.

"Holly Reynolds, will you do me the honor of becoming my wife?" He held the ring up to her.

Feeling sucked into his wondrous blue pools, she thought quickly of the journey behind them. Arguments, head-butting. Then love and passion. The wonderful conversations. And the way he could make her come as he took her with his singular passion. She knew she wanted nothing else but a lifetime full of him. This stuffy, proper, persnickety, beautiful, strong, splendid Thomas.

Holly's grin overtook her cheeks. "Yes, Thomas. I will marry you." She held her left hand out to him. He took it and pushed the ring onto her finger.

His glorious grin consumed his face. "That's better." He stood, swooped her into him, and filled her with love as his expert kiss went exuberantly into her mouth.

They held each other so tightly that they nearly became one thing. A kissing, smothering, loving embrace. All the dark shadows of Hades retreated, and the world bloomed.

"Holly," he said, stroking her hair. "You are my very breath. I only want to breathe you every day. And I am going to take you on this piano bench. You shall only think of me when you play. And I want to be in every note."

Holly's eyes were crossing with desire for him. "Thomas, you are the melody in everything I do. I feel you constantly. I want you every moment of every day. And when I play for the orchestra, I still think of your hands on me."

His brows raised. "Even when we were apart for that time?"

She inhaled. "Yes. Even then. I guess we need each other to make the music perfect."

He gently kissed her lips. "Isn't that what marriage is all about?"

Holly smiled, stroking his dark brown hair. "It's what I've always hoped for. The perfect song."

Thomas blinked at her. "I'm not perfect, Holly."

Love swelled in her chest. "I know. Neither am I. But I think that together our pieces fit into some kind of beautiful concerto."

Thomas' eyes swelled. "I love that." He smooched around her mouth. "You really will be my wife?"

She blushed and trembled joyfully. The thought of it was insane. When she first stepped her foot into his disgusting, sorrow-ridden house, she would have never believed that she was about to find her husband. Yet here they were. A diamond on her finger and the devil transformed into an angel.

"Are you sure you want to be my husband?"

He looked thoughtfully. "That's a good question. You can be quite peevish."

"What?" She let out a cackle. The nervousness in her needed release.

"It's true!" He chuckled and kissed around her cheeks. "But yes. I want nothing more than to be your husband, Holly Reynolds. Or, should I say, Holly Buckhorn."

Her stomach clenched. She stopped laughing. Her eyes widened as her lungs fought for air again. Janet once said she loved the idea that they would truly be sisters someday. Holly stared into his loving, amused eyes.

"I can't lie to you. This scares me," she said.

"It scares me too, Holly. But do you want to know what comforts me when I'm afraid?"

She nodded.

"Feeling your warmth. The thought of being without you is more horrible than any other thought." He took a deep breath. "I've already lost one love of my life. I'm not about to lose another one. I will fight for you until I can no longer stand."

His lovely face was so sincere, and every word from him fluttered her belly. She knew nothing else would ever be good enough. Thomas was the gold. He was the prize she'd always hoped to have one day.

She swallowed hard, trying to think of something equally meaningful to say back to him. "I'm so much better with you than I am with anyone else, even myself. I want this. I want you, Thomas." She ran a hand along his strong jaw. "You're my most beloved Lordship."

She marveled at him. He was entirely present. He was entirely hers. Their mouths connected through their own natural gravity and melded. She knew it completely. Their love. Their bond. Their passion and devotion.

She felt hope. Holly could taste it on his tongue. A future. The thing he'd lost was growing between them now. Future. Life. Family. She wanted to have all of that with him. As he caressed her, he pulled her to the piano bench. His loving touch lifted her dress as he lay her back onto it and he knelt between her knees. Hot breath and tongue played and gently kissed between her legs. Holly knew the security of every dream made real.

Chapter 25

Three Years Later

Holly sat in a chair in the living room, staring down at the small, cooing bundle in her arms. Her fingers played along tiny pillowy cheeks. Thomas set a mug down on the coffee table.

"Chamomile with honey," he said and leaned over the side of the chair, looking on in soft wonder at the little cherub in his wife's arms.

A small hand reached out. He let the miniature digits wrap around his finger.

"How is our little Persephone?" he asked.

"She's nearly out."

"Good. Goodnight, sweet Persephone. Return to your secret space of dreams." He came around the chair and tenderly kissed his daughter's brows. The baby mewled.

Holly smiled and rose from the chair. She kissed Persephone. "See you in two hours when you're hungry again."

Thomas released his daughter's hand and took Holly's jaw sweetly, bringing her lips in for his beautiful kiss. "Chopin?" he asked.

"You know it wakes her. The piano is too loud."

"But you aren't. Come, my beautiful wife. Put her to bed. Then come to me."

"I'll do you one better."

"Oh?"

"I'll come for you and with you. I'll come because of you."

"That *is* even better." Thomas held them in his arms, sending his blessed tongue into Holly's mouth. Holly's belly shivered and rolled at her husband's desirous, strong touch.

They had married in the springtime. The age of Persephone, as Thomas called it. Their daughter arrived two years later. Her name was a no-brainer for them. Thomas said if it was a boy, he wanted to call him Perseus. Holly hoped they would have a son next just so they could have a Percy. Thomas bristled and vowed to never call his son anything other than his full proper name.

Holly lay Persephone in her crib and padded to her own bedroom. Thomas was naked and waiting for her under the covers.

"Your breasts are amazing," he told her.

"They're full of baby fuel," she laughed.

Thomas smiled. "Pull your robe off. I want to look at you."

Holly shot him a reluctant glance. "You know, I feel weird about it now."

"My darling, that lovely pattern of stretch marks brought the life of our child into the world. They're beautiful."

"Meh."

"Holly, do not 'meh' me. You're gorgeous. Even more so now that you have the battle scars of creation. Now, take off your robe so I can kiss every line of them."

Holly giggled and dropped her robe. Her body wasn't as small or tight as it used to be. She had new, jiggly bits that she wasn't able to be rid of yet. Thomas scooted to the side of the bed and took her haunches in his hands, pulling her to his face, kissing every stretch mark. Then he pulled her into the bed. He rolled her over, caressing all the pooching parts of her.

"Nothing in the world is as beautiful as you," he said, kissing her and melting her brain.

"I don't feel as sexy as I used to," she admitted.

He furrowed his brows. "Well, that's unfortunate. I've never seen you sexier. Feel this." He brought her fingers to his cock. It was rock-hard.

"You see?" He kissed her. "You awaken every level of my lust. Admittedly, knowing I can make your body swell with my seed almost makes you even hotter to me. Must be a primal urge." he playfully bit into her neck. "I'll never stop wanting you."

Holly melted under his fervor and the intensity of his touch along her skin. His kiss inspiring moisture to flow from between her legs. She opened her thighs to him, and he glided his hard length along her pliant softness. The hard bulb of his head pushed inside. She groaned with every moment of his erection gliding inside of her. It was less intense since she'd been stretched from giving birth. But daily Kegels were helping. She still wasn't happy with not being able to clench him like she used to.

Her husband's contented sighs filled her ears as he held her, starting his magical rhythm.

"I'm so glad you still want me."

His perplexed voice spoke between heavy breaths. "Well, of course I do. How else are we going to give Persephone a sibling?"

She cackled. "Easy, killer! I need a break before we make another one."

"Naturally. But in the meantime," he paused for air, "I still want nothing more than you around my cock."

She grimaced. "I'm not as tight as I used to be."

Thomas stalled his movements, looked at her face, and blinked. "Holly, do you know how I used to think of how you felt around me?"

"How?"

"Like hot, wet velvet."

Her eyes widened. "Oohh, Thomas... That's," she sighed, "incredibly hot."

"So are you." He kissed her. "And do you know how you feel now?"

She sent a playful lift to her brows.

He resumed grinding deeply against her, adding a thrust to emphasize each word. "Like hot, (kiss) wet, (kiss) velvet." He plunged his tongue into her mouth and pushed his hardness into her, filling her with his satisfying girth and length.

Holly gasped. "Oh, Thomas..."

His perfect friction and beautiful kiss in her mouth sent lightning through her. She bucked her hips into his to grind and join the pleasure-filled rhythm they always made. Tingles spread inside her and intensified.

A deep breath filled her. "I love you, Thomas."

He gave her an extra hard thrust, making her gasp with delight. "God, Holly. You feel so good." He thrust again. "If I loved you anymore, I'd be God himself." His pace quickened. "You're amazing."

As he lunged within her, Holly lost her mind and held him desperately to her, meeting his hunger with her hips.

"Make me come, your Lordship," she whispered.

Thomas undulated into her and sent his fabulous tongue gliding along hers. His mouth echoing the need of his body.

"With pleasure, my Lady," he said under his breath.

Holly lost herself in their desire and sounds. All she could do was sigh and drown in the sweetness of him.

About the Author

Jayelle is an exciting new author who writes classy erotic romance in contemporary settings. The stories are character driven with layers and complexity. She favors spirited female leads with attitude and a trauma that needs healing. The men in her books are just as entertaining as the heroines, providing added personality and depth. Her stories draw you in and don't let go until the end. Jayelle lives in the foothills of Colorado with her husband and their dogs.

Thank You

As always I want to thank my wonderful, husband and supportive parents. My writing journey is made possible because of you.

I also want to thank my readers and especially those of you who take a moment to leave reviews. Your support is everything!

Other Books by Jayelle Dee

The *Breaking Fancy* Trilogy
Starstruck – Available Now
Midnight and Feathers – Available Now
Breaking Free – Available Now

The Pantheon: A series of standalones retelling beloved Greek myths.
A Summer With Persephone – Available Now
~ More to come ~

www.barnowlbooks.net on the web
JayelleDee.Author on Instagram
JayelleDeeAuthor on Facebook

Made in the USA
Columbia, SC
06 June 2024